TOKYO BLACK

A THOMAS CAINE THRILLER

ANDREW WARREN

ANDREW WARREN BOOKS

TOKYO BLACK

Andrew Warren

Copyright © 2016 by Andrew Warren. All rights reserved. This is a work of fiction. Any resemblance to actual persons living or dead, businesses, events or locales is purely coincidental. Reproduction in whole or part of this publication without express written consent is strictly prohibited.

Please visit:
AndrewWarrenbooks.com

Please Join my Readers Group!

You might get a chance to read the next Thomas Caine thriller for free! You'll also get access to special sales, contests, and new release info...

Please visit
AndrewWarrenbooks.com
for more details.
Thank you.

CHAPTER ONE

The pulsing neon lights of Shinjuku made the darkness of the alley seem even more black and desolate, like the cold, empty space between stars. A lone figure crept down the narrow passage. He stopped just before the edge of the shadows, peering out cautiously at the lights and commotion ahead. Like many streets in the East Mouth shopping district, this one was for pedestrians only. The throng of people passing before him was like a river of bodies. They pushed, jostled, and raged forward, a relentless force of nature in pursuit of the city's pleasures.

Tatsui Kentaro was dressed in a rumpled grey suit, the typical uniform of a Tokyo sarariman. Legions of these low-status, middle-income office workers filled the office buildings of Japan like drones in a beehive. Thick, black glasses pinched the bridge of his nose. Their lenses magnified his sunken brown eyes.

Tatsui brought a lit cigarette to his lips. He took a long, slow drag, then held it in front of him for a second, staring at the twin gold bands of the Mevius label. He shook his head, dropped the cigarette, and ground it beneath his heel. Running a hand through his salt-and-pepper hair, he looked left and right, checking the alley exit. No one in the massive crowd outside was paying any attention to him.

He laughed to himself. After twenty-five years of marriage, his wife was hardly concerned with his comings and goings anymore. The kids were grown adults now. Tatsui and his wife had reached the stage where infidelity was a tacit compromise, rather than a painful betrayal. Still, old habits die hard, and he couldn't help but be wary as he pushed his way into the throng before him.

Tatsui sniffed at the crisp night air. Grilled meats, garlic, fried noodles ... the enticing scents of yakitori reached out to him, comforting and seductive at the same time. For a moment, he considered stopping; it had been hours since he'd finished the small bento box lunch his wife had packed for him.

Instead, he stuck his hands in the pockets of his beige raincoat, hunched his shoulders, and pulled the coat tighter against the cold. He had other appetites to fulfill. And after hours of overtime in a cramped office, the illicit promises of Kabukicho's many temptations filled his gut with tingling excitement.

His anticipation grew as he passed the massive TV screen of Studio Alta. The giant display towered above the street, blasting the night sky with colorful images of anime and Japanese soap opera stars. The landmark provided a popular meeting spot for the area. As he ambled on, Tatsui watched couples embrace, teenagers laugh and roughhouse, and girls trade cell phone charms and gossip.

But for Tatsui, Studio Alta was something else ... a signpost. He was close now.

The pedestrian street crossed over Yasukuni-dori and led the sarariman to a large archway of flashing red lights. This was the gateway to Kabukicho, the most infamous neighborhood in Shinjuku and, indeed, all of Japan.

Here, the neon lights and signs continued to defy the darkness, but the services they advertised were of a different nature. The streets were lined with hostess clubs, massage parlors, pachinko halls... Tatsui lit another cigarette and resumed his journey into the night.

An attractive Japanese woman dressed as a maid stood at the corner near Bunka-Senta dori, passing out flyers. "Massagee, massagee?" she asked, her voice high-pitched and giggly.

Tatsui bowed and took a flyer, but he did not stop walking. His appetite led him elsewhere.

He continued past a group of what he assumed to be yakuza thugs camped outside a pachinko parlor. Clad in expensive suits, their wide-collared shirts exposed the ink of tattoos around their necks. They watched him with cold eyes and humorless smiles. Tatsui knew they would not harass him unless he owed them money, but they made him nervous nonetheless.

He hurried on, past the karaoke bars and the host club with the young, bleached blond men on the sign. Past the love hotels with their flashing pink hearts and teddy bears signs. Past the strip clubs, where the girls were Filipino, Chinese, even Russian, but almost never Japanese. Then past the old, rundown batting cages, where you could work out your tension swinging at balls or playing the old pornographic mahjong video game in the back room.

Finally, almost suddenly, Tatsui stopped. The crowd seemed to part around him as he smiled at a pink neon sign on the balcony of the building before him.

"*Shiro Kumo Tengoku*," it read. White Cloud Heaven. Images of beautiful Japanese women surrounded the kanji characters. Their naked bodies were strategically covered in sparkling white soapsuds. Tatsui gazed into their unseeing eyes and took a deep drag of his cigarette. He looked around again, making sure no one was paying any attention to his activities. He knew no one was, but he enjoyed the little intrigue, the imagined risk. It made the excitement of what was to come even sweeter.

Satisfied that he was just another anonymous pleasure-seeker in the night, Tatsui dropped his cigarette to the ground. Then he pushed through the front door and stepped into heaven.

Twenty minutes later, Tatsui lay on his back while a beautiful girl moved her hands across his body with slow, firm motions. She was naked, as was he. She said her name was Yuki, and she was a twenty-year-old college student. He knew none of this was true, of course. But he didn't care. Her body was warm and taut, her hair was thick and dark, and her face reminded him of an angel.

After he'd chosen her from a wall of pictures in the lobby below, she'd led him hand in hand to this warm but clinical room, where they had both stripped naked. After a warm bath in the Roman tub and a vigorous body scrub, they had moved to an air mattress on the floor. Then the evening's real entertainment had begun.

Tatsui smiled as Yuki ceased her massage, satisfied that he was aroused and ready for the next step. She dipped her hands into a bowl full of clear liquid gel. With soft, circular motions, she began to spread the warm, slippery substance across his body.

She gave Tatsui a sexy grin as she lowered herself onto him and began to slide her body up and down and across his own. The gel, known as Nuru, acted like a lubricant. It turned every movement of her body into a long, slow massage stroke.

Her small, perfect body glided down the length of his limbs as her pert breasts pressed into his flesh. Tatsui made a sound that was part moan, part joyous laughter. He was in heaven. The pleasure of the Nuru massage was like nectar, feeding him, making him feel alive. His body—old, tired, worn down, and battered—felt sleek and new.

Yuki giggled. He felt her intense heat as she clamped her legs around his and continued her gliding dance of pleasure. He was close now, and the girl was an expert. She intensified her movements, concentrating her warmth and friction on the focal point of his pleasure.

A loud crash echoed from the hall outside the room. Tatsui, lost in a sea of bliss, barely heard the noise. Yuki gasped and froze in place.

Jolted from his dreamlike trance, Tatsui propped himself up on the air mattress. He could hear muted shouting and footsteps coming from the other side of the door. He looked up at Yuki with alarm.

"What the hell is going on? Cops?"

Yuki shook her head. "Can't be. We pay the yakuza for protection. Hurry, get dressed!" She slid off him and threw on a pink silk robe.

Tatsui scrambled off the mattress and grabbed his clothes. Ignoring his underwear, he struggled to pull on his suit pants. His legs were sticky from the massage gel, and the fabric tangled around his ankles.

Tatsui looked up when he heard the sound of doors breaking, followed by a high-pitched scream. The noises were close now, and the commotion outside grew louder. He heard girls shrieking, men shouting, and customers complaining.

Yuki hid behind him as he finally buttoned his pants. The door flew open, showering wood splinters through the air. Yuki wailed as men in black suits poured into the room, their faces cold but determined.

One of the men grabbed the struggling Yuki and dragged her from the room. Tatsui realized with a start that they were all carrying guns.

Tatsui had never seen a firearm before, at least not in person. The police didn't carry them, and even yakuza gangsters rarely displayed them in public. Before, he had worried that police or federal agents were cracking down on the soaplands brothel. He had feared that he might be arrested and have to explain his activities to his wife. Now a cold, sickening fear filled his gut as he realized things were worse.

Much worse.

The two thugs who manhandled him from the room were dressed from head to toe in black. Black suits, black shirts, black shoes, black socks. One had left the top buttons of his shirt open, exposing hideous burn-like scars across his chest.

"Please, there's no need for this! I'll give you whatever you want, whatever I have," Tatsui babbled.

They ignored him as they dragged him to the lounge at the end of the hall. There, a group of naked clients and petrified girls huddled together. Yuki and two other girls lay on the floor, staring up at another black-suited man. His back was to Tatsui, but the terrified sarariman could tell he was huge. His broad shoulders looked like a wall of black granite.

"That's everyone," said one of the suits.

The monster nodded but did not turn around. He was showing a cell phone to the girls.

Yuki shook her head. "No, please, sir. We have not seen her. I swear! Please just leave us alone!"

"Do not lie to me, little one." His voice was like the echo of thunder in a canyon—powerful and booming, but strangely muted.

Yuki closed her eyes and turned away. Tatsui saw the tears streaming down her cheek, now smeared with makeup. Her interrogator raised his giant slab of a hand.

Before the big man struck Yuki, Tatsui spoke. His voice was a dry croak, and the sound of it surprised even himself.

"Please, sir. There is no need for violence. What is it you want?"

The big man lowered his hand and turned around to eye Tatsui. The other thugs immediately trained their guns on him, as if the sound of his voice had caused them to take notice of him for the first time. One clubbed him on the back of his neck with the butt of a rifle, and he collapsed on the floor.

The big man gave Tatsui's attacker a disdainful frown, but he did not offer the injured sarariman any assistance. He looked down impassively. It was the stare of a cold-blooded reptile ... motionless, unfeeling, waiting for prey to move that fraction of an inch too close.

Tatsui picked himself up and stood before the hulking, dark figure. The man's face was a nightmare of strange burns. Twisted scar tissue drew deep, jagged lines through his primitive features. In place of a left eye was a milky, unseeing orb.

Tatsui took a deep breath. "Please, just tell us what you want. If I can help you, I will. Then you can let us go."

The working girls ceased their panicked sobbing. The room grew silent, save for the dim noise of traffic outside.

The big man spoke. "What is your name?"

"Tatsui."

The awful, scarred face gave a small nod, an almost imperceptible tilting of the chin. Still, the motion was at least somewhat human. That comforted Tatsui somewhat. Perhaps there was a chance after all.

"I am called Bobu. I apologize for our rude behavior, but we are on a mission of grave importance. Please, do not be afraid."

Tatsui was dumbfounded by the sharp contrast between the man's smooth, calm words and his horrific face.

Bobu tilted his head, as if focusing the gaze of his injured eye on the man who cowered before him. "Forgive me. I know my scars can be frightening. But know this ... they are marks of purity. The heat and fire that made me this way also burned away the shame of my past. Do you understand?"

Tatsui nodded.

Bobu smiled. Tatsui watched the mangled, pink flesh twist and move; smiling was the most terrifying thing the man had done yet.

"We are looking for someone. It is important that we find her as soon as possible. She is lost." Bobu held out the phone to Tatsui.

It showed a picture of a girl in her early twenties. She was sexy and beautiful, like Yuki. But, unlike his masseuse, her beauty was not angelic and carefree. She looked cold, like a porcelain doll. Her dark eyes seemed worried. Haunted.

Color rushed back into the sarariman's features. His eyes lit up with hope. "Yes, yes! I have seen this girl!"

Bobu leaned in, his mutilated face inches away from Tatsui.

"Where?"

"Ah, wait, let me think."

Bobu's cold gaze never wavered as the flustered man racked his brain for details.

Tatsui looked up, a smile on his face. "Yes, I remember! It was in Roppongi, at Tiger Velvet! A hostess club. We were there after work, to celebrate closing a deal. Perhaps ... two weeks ago!"

"You are positive it was her?"

The older man nodded. "Yes, I remember her eyes. She looked unhappy to be there. I told her she should cheer up, and she spilled my sake in my lap! We complained to the manager, and he sent over a different girl."

Bobu stared at him for a few more seconds.

"It was her, I swear!" Tatsui added weakly.

Bobu spun around, and took a few steps away from the crowd. The other men kept their guns trained on Tatsui as the hulking man brought the cell phone to his ear. He spoke in hushed, short sentences. Then he slid the phone in his pocket and turned back to his men.

"Burn it down. No one lives."

Like a switch had been flipped, the room immediately filled with screams and shouts. Tatsui watched in horror as the men opened fire with automatic weapons. Yuki's lifeless face hit the ground. Blood mixed with the black tears of mascara that spattered her face.

He tore away from the men holding him and rushed over to Bobu. "Please, don't do this! We had a deal! Please sir, I have a wife. I have—"

Bobu pushed him away. It was just a light movement of his thick arm, no more than a shrug, but it sent Tatsui sprawling to the floor. In the midst of the massacre, Tatsui smelled gasoline fumes filling the room. A pair of the black-suited killers were dousing the curtains and furniture with cans of the flammable liquid.

Bobu slipped a large pistol from a shoulder holster under his jacket. He leveled the gun at Tatsui's face.

"Don't worry. You will not burn. You will not be purified. You are free."

He pulled the trigger. The gun roared, but Tatsui did not hear it. Or if he did, it was just an echo, a faint fragment of sound trapped in the mists at the edge of his consciousness.

For Tatsui, there was only the growing darkness. For a brief second, he could see the lights of Shinjuku ... brilliant flickering stars, a map of heavenly pleasures on earth. Then, one by one, the stars went out.

CHAPTER TWO

Mark Waters took a sip of his cocktail and looked over his shoulder at Soi 8, the street outside Lucky's Bar. Late afternoon was always his favorite time in Pattaya. The city seemed to take a deep breath, a relaxing pause before the relentless nightlife whipped the place into a frenzy.

Turning his attention back to the bar, he caught a glimpse of himself in one of the many mirrors hanging on the wall. Years of the intense Pattaya sun had turned his skin a deep tan and lightened his messy brown hair. He knew his prime was past—wrinkles creased his green eyes as he squinted at the image before him. But his navy linen blazer and khaki jeans still fit like a glove. His body was blessed with the lean physique of a natural athlete.

"Your turn, Mr. Waters!"

Janjai, the new bar girl, was grinning at him. Her lively brown eyes held a mischievous gleam, and her beautiful smile was genuine. She had not yet acquired that awful, generic pleasantness like the other bar girls.

Mark didn't blame them. After all, it was their job to entice male tourists into the bar any way they could. Still, after a few months on the scene, the girls learned all the tricks and lines. Their forced smiles, corny greetings, and flirtatious banter grated on his ears every night.

It only bothers you because you can see right through them, he thought. *It's not their fault you're an expert on living a lie.*

"You gonna go or not?" Janjai was staring at him, a friendly pout on her lips. Her crossed arms pressed the coffee-colored skin of her breasts up against the opening of her white tank top. Mark realized she was learning faster than he'd thought.

"Sorry, Jan. Let's see here.... I think you may have got me." Mark examined the Connect Four game that stood between them. The game was a three-dimensional version of Tic-Tac-Toe. The goal was to stack four plastic checkers in a vertical, horizontal, or diagonal row. Janjai's last move had cut off the diagonal line he was building.

He often spent his afternoons playing bar games at Lucky's. He figured it was better for Janjai to earn her money beating him at Connect Four than the other activities she might soon engage in. Most of the time, he let her win.

Today, however, Janjai's inevitable victory was due to her skill alone. With a sigh, he slipped a red checker into the grid. It fell into place, blocking the girl's vertical play, but it left her with an opening to make a horizontal row on her next move.

The Thai girl shrieked with delight as she dropped a black checker into the plastic grid. The piece completed her row of four and won the game. She clapped and laughed. "You lose, Mr. Waters! I too smart for you!"

Mark chuckled as he slipped two-hundred baht notes from his wallet and lay them on the counter. Janjai snapped them up with a child-like glee.

"Truer words were never spoken, Janjai. Now, how about you take pity on me and make me a drink?"

"Sure thing, Mr. Waters. Then we play again! You want another sabai sabai?"

"Sounds good to me."

Janjai prepared his drink, a refreshing combination of sugar, lemon, club soda, crushed basil, and local Thai whisky. As she worked, Mark stole a glance at his cell phone. It was a prepaid model from the electronics stand down the street. It showed no incoming calls. *This doesn't feel right*, he thought.

The trucks should have arrived at the docks forty minutes ago. Lau was supposed to check in as soon as they arrived and then again when the merchandise was loaded onboard the boat.

Mark always stayed far away from the docks when a delivery was scheduled to arrive. It was up to his partner, Lau Somchai, to keep him in the loop and confirm that everything was all right. That left two options. Either Lau was keeping him in the dark ... or everything was not all right.

Janjai set the drink down in front of him.

"Ready for next game, Mr. Waters?"

Mark gave her a warm smile and placed another two-hundred baht on the counter. "Give me a few minutes to recover from that last beating, okay? But consider this my reservation."

Janjai nodded and moved away, sensing his wish to be alone. As she wiped down the counter with a wet rag, Mark scanned the bar again. He kept an eye out for Lau or anyone who didn't belong.

His gaze settled on a young Thai man sitting near the railing that separated the open air bar from the street. He was wearing a white dress shirt open at the collar. His sleeves were rolled up, and sweat stained the fabric at the armpits.

He appeared intensely focused on a wrinkled newspaper he was flipping through, an issue of the *Pattaya Times*. He paid no attention to the steady throng of attractive women walking up and down the street outside, many dressed only in bikinis and sarongs.

Mark hadn't noticed him until now. The man had been in the bar for some time, but until this moment, Mark hadn't given him a second thought. He felt wrong somehow. Mark took a deep breath, shocked to realize just how much his skills had atrophied over the past few years.

Keeping a lock on the man from the corner of his eye, Mark angled back towards the bar and took another sip of his cocktail. He let the cold ice linger against his teeth, using the pain to sharpen him up. He allowed himself another unobtrusive glance in the man's direction.

He could just make out the large color photo on the front page of the rumpled newspaper—girls dancing in pink evening gowns. Something about it was familiar.

"Janjai?" he said without looking away, his voice low. "Does Lucifer's Bar still do the beauty pageant thing? You know, where the girls put on fancy dresses and do that fake pageant?"

Janjai leaned over the counter. "Sure. They raffle off the winner for the night. They do that on Wednesday, I think."

It was Saturday afternoon. That meant the man was fully absorbed by two-day-old news.

Mark drained his drink and slammed the glass down on the bar. "Time to make a deposit!" he announced. Janjai giggled but gave him a concerned look. He slipped several baht notes onto the counter. "In case I don't make it back for the game," he whispered. "You probably would have won anyway."

He purposely avoided looking at the Thai man as he made his way to the dingy men's room at the rear of the bar. He staggered and swayed as he walked, giving the impression that he was drunk. With a sigh, he shut himself in the tiny, dark room.

As soon as the door closed, he sprang into action. Tearing his cell phone from his pocket, he popped off the rear cover and disconnected the battery. He threw the battery in the trash and stomped the dead phone into pieces with the heel of his boot. Then he dumped the pieces into a dirty bucket of mop water that stood in a corner. He had no idea who could be tracking him. Based on the lone watcher he'd spotted, it was probably just the Thai Royal Police. But that was far from the only possibility, and the other options could be much more deadly.

Outside the door, he heard Janjai talking. "Please wait, sir. Someone in there!"

Mark uttered a silent curse as footsteps hurried towards the bathroom door. He grabbed a dirty towel that hung from a rack of cleaning supplies and wound it around his arm. Gritting his teeth, he smashed his padded elbow into the dirty glass of the bathroom window. The dusty pane shattered and exploded outwards.

The noise outside grew louder. Janjai was screaming, and someone—most likely the Thai man—was shouting.

Might be calling for backup, Mark thought, *which means if I don't get out now, I don't get out.* Loud thuds echoed through the bathroom as the door shook. Someone was trying to break through.

Mark took a deep breath and vaulted through the broken window into the alley behind the bar. Crouching, he looked up and down the thin strip of dirt. There was a commotion at the south end, the ocean side of town. Five armed men in civilian dress rushed around the corner, charging towards him. One dropped to his knees to take aim with a pistol. Mark launched into an all-out sprint as the weapon roared behind him. The bullets struck the dirt, sending a small cloud of dust into the air near his ankles.

Ducking around the corner of Lucky's Bar, he hurtled into the crowded street of Soi 8. He ran north, away from the beach. A motorized growl grew closer and closer as he ran. A three-wheeled tuk tuk followed close behind, weaving through the pedestrians and bicycles. The tiny vehicle bore the yellow and purple markings of the Thai Royal Police. Three uniformed officers rode onboard.

This is all wrong.

Mark increased his pace, sprinting towards a narrow alley that led towards Soi 7. *Since when do the Royal Police give a damn about some counterfeit jeans and designer purses?* He looked back. Unable to fit down the narrow passage, the tuk tuk had turned away. Mark figured it was probably headed down the boulevard that linked Soi 8 and Soi 7.

Panting, Mark burst out the other end of the alley and turned north again, heading up Soi 7. Behind him, he heard the tiny vehicle screech around the corner; the driver must have anticipated his route. A wailing siren now rose above the whine of the tiny motor.

Pedestrians and motor scooters swerved left and right, clearing the street for the police as they closed the gap. Mark gasped for breath, knowing it was only a matter of time before they caught up to him. Even at his peak, now several years behind him, he couldn't run like this forever.

A small truck pulled into the cross street ahead of him. The driver leaned on his horn, trying to clear the throng of pedestrians from the crosswalk ahead.

Mark dropped to the ground and slid under the truck. The rough pavement tore at his clothes and scraped his skin. Ignoring the pain, he rolled out from under the other side of the vehicle and leapt to his feet. He turned and continued his frenzied run.

Behind him, the tuk tuk driver slammed on the brakes, but he was too close and traveling too fast. The tiny vehicle fishtailed in the street, sending the crowd of partygoers clambering to the sidewalks. The passengers leapt from the unstable vehicle as it rolled onto its side and slammed into the truck.

Mark couldn't resist the slightest grin of satisfaction. He dodged to the left and ran into an outdoor beer garden. Finally, he had gained some distance on his pursuers. The sirens and shouting grew fainter as he lost himself in the crowd.

Mark stood in a shadowy corner of the Venus Club, a sleek, modern structure of glass and chrome, built to resemble a popular bar in Bangkok. The bar's interior was a sci-fi fantasy: each of the club's go-go dancers held a laser pointer, which they flashed around the room as they slithered and swayed atop their chrome pedestals.

The glass-enclosed bar was suspended above a parking garage in the wealthy, modern neighborhood of Amaya Hill. Several beautiful

Thai girls danced near the edge of the structure, grinding their bodies against the clear walls. They aimed their lasers at the pedestrians below, hoping to lure more young, rich partygoers into the club.

Ignoring the beams of light dancing over his body, Mark scanned the crowd from a second-level catwalk. The height gave him a bird's eye view of the girls and their customers, and the shadows helped hide his torn, dirty clothes. He had been able to avoid the police so far, but he knew they were still looking for him. He would have to keep a low profile until he could get out of the city.

Still early in the evening, the crowd was sparse. As he surveyed the room, he spotted the man he had been looking for. Lau Somchai.

He watched as the short, chubby man ambled into the club, laughing and gesturing expansively with his arms. He wore a loud Hawaiian shirt and expensive-looking slacks. The bar girls immediately marked him as "money" and began moving closer, teasing their laser beams across his body. The lights danced across his partner's face. Mark saw quick flashes of greasy, pockmarked skin and dark, beady eyes.

Lau peeled off baht notes from a shiny money clip and tossed them onto the bar with a flourish. The bartenders set up a round of drinks for Lau and the lingerie-clad girls that surrounded him. All the girls were beautiful, but Mark knew Lau's favorite was Kandi. Within minutes, the waif-like Thai-Filipino girl was at his side. She laughed and ran her hands across Lau's sweaty, bald head while whispering into his ear.

Lau threw down some more money, then took Kandi's hand as she led him up the metal stairs to the catwalk. Mark left his perch for one of the small glass rooms that surrounded the slender stage. *It's only a matter of time now*, he thought. Hopefully he'd paid Kandi more than Lau had.

Inside the room were dark velvet curtains, and Mark drew them closed. Outside, the loud beats of dance music overrode all other sound. The bass washed over his body like an ocean wave, penetrating him to the core, shaking his bowels and organs. Mark stood motionless in the corner next to the door, waiting in the darkness.

He didn't flinch when the door opened, even though he could neither hear nor see anyone approach. Two shadowy figures appeared: Kandi and Lau. *Should have paid more for the lap dance, you cheap bastard!*

Mark let Lau walk past him before emerging from his corner. He slid his body between the short, pudgy man and Kandi. Before either Lau or the dancer could react, Mark lifted his right foot and stomped down hard on the inside of Lau's knee. With a surprised grunt, Lau lurched forward and tripped. He landed face-first on the plush velvet couch that dominated the room.

"Take a seat, partner."

Mark kept his back neutral, not wanting to give Kandi an opportunity to betray him. He turned and saw that the petite brunette in purple lingerie hadn't even entered the room. Mark held up a wad of bills. "Thank you," he said. There was no warmth in his voice.

Kandi blinked as a barrage of green lasers flashed over their faces through the open door. She took one look at Mark's cold, hard eyes, grabbed the money, and hurried off. He swung back to face Lau.

He shut the door to the room, muting the music outside. Lau gasped and groaned as he pulled himself up to a seated position on the couch. Mark pulled aside a curtain, letting a crack of light into the room. When Lau saw his face, the look of confused anger melted away, replaced by an almost supernatural calm.

"Waters. I knew you come looking for me."

"I was worried about you, friend. Had a little run-in with the Royal Police this morning. Figured if they were after me, they might come looking for you." Mark gestured with his hands and looked around the room. "But, obviously you're not too concerned. Not enough to stop chasing underage tail, anyway."

Lau spat on the floor in front of Mark. "You still don't get it, stupid farrang! I not your friend. I was your partner. I with you to make money!"

Mark lurched forward and grabbed Lau by the lapels of his colorful shirt.

"We were making money, you stupid bastard! What the hell did you do?"

Lau glared at him. "We making peanuts. You wasting my time. You too scared to take the next step, so I take it for you!"

Mark slammed his fist into Lau's gut and dropped the coughing, sputtering man to the ground.

"Why are the Royal Police all over this? Why are they so worked up over a bunch of counterfeit purses and designer jeans?"

Lau wiped his mouth with his arm and glared up at Mark.

"Not jeans, asshole. Not this time. Something bigger. Your bribe too small now. You no longer protected."

Mark took a step towards Lau's prostrate body. He kept his voice low, but even with the thumping music outside, his words cut through the room like a blade of ice.

"Drugs?"

Lau laughed, a short, pained bark, and propped himself up to a sitting position on the floor.

"Not drugs. Guns."

Does it matter? Mark wondered. He knew both charges carried the death penalty.

"How did the police find them?"

Lau shrugged. "I tell them, of course. I change the shipment. I inform Chief Battang of the new arrangement. He get to make big arrest for gun smuggling. Now that you out of picture, he get bigger cut for future shipments."

Mark stared at the man in shock. "You told him? You burned an entire shipment of guns just to sell me out?"

"Could have burned two ... three, fuck it! Money well spent. You think too small. We have the contacts; we have boat. The police are in our pocket. We making pennies when we could have big score! Drugs, guns, women! This my operation now. Consider this your retirement!"

In the space of a heartbeat, between the pulses of laser light, Mark's anger burned into white-hot fury. His mouth twisted in a silent snarl.

Lau gasped in fear and tried to shield himself with his hands. Mark grabbed him by his shirt, hoisted him into the air, and threw him back against the wall with all his strength.

He pummeled Lau's pudgy face, first in a series of measured, one-two strikes. But soon the punches became more erratic. Each wild swing battered Lau's flesh with a dull thud.

"You have no idea!" Mark screamed. "No idea what you've done! You hear me, you piece of shit?"

Mark's fist rose to strike again, when he felt a sudden blunt impact on the back of his head. He dropped to the ground as more blows rained down on his body. Several Royal Police had stormed the room; in his rage, Mark had left his back to the door.

One of the officers helped Lau to his feet. The traitor could barely stand, but he pushed the officer away from him. He grabbed a white towel from a bottle of champagne in the corner to wipe the blood from his mangled face.

He knelt down in front of Mark.

"I know exactly what I did, farrang. I did what you afraid to do. You don't belong here anymore. You never did."

Lau stood back up and took a long, hard look at Mark, who was moaning and rolling on the floor. His leg shot out, kicking Mark in the face. The force of the blow rolled Mark onto his back. He stared up at the blurred faces of Lau and the policemen.

A lone thought went through Mark's mind before he slipped into unconsciousness. After he was arrested, the name "Mark Waters," along with his fingerprints, would be processed through Interpol's computers. The results would show up on the daily logs of every intelligence service in the Western world.

That was going to cause problems since his name was not, in fact, Mark Waters.

It was Thomas Caine.

CHAPTER THREE

Rebecca Freeling ran.

Raindrops bounced off her skin as she drove her body forward. Her long, lean legs moved back and forth with smooth, rhythmic precision. Her arms pumped in time to each step.

The early morning sky was cold and grey. Ominous rolling clouds were backlit by the first stirrings of sunlight. This was the meridian between day and night. Light and darkness. This was her favorite time. This was when she ran.

She shifted her weight as the road curved around a grassy hill. The soles of her running shoes gripped the wet pavement as she leaned into the turn. She was careful not to push too hard. Some runners had taken nasty spills on this part of the route, and the last thing she needed was a broken leg or twisted ankle. The thought of months in recovery, trapped, unable to run ... a shiver ran through her body. She dug in as she left the turn behind, picking up speed on the straightaway.

She struggled to clear her mind of stress and fear. No job. No compromises. Just the rain, and wind, and the smooth, percussive beat of her footsteps.

An electronic chirping interrupted her serenity.

Rebecca moved to the shoulder of the road and slowed to a stop. She stretched her arms up as high as she could, arching her back like a cat. The cell phone clipped to her waist continued its soft ringing. It would go on forever, she knew. There was no voicemail. When that phone rang, she was expected to pick it up, come hell or high water.

As her breathing returned to normal, she tapped the screen to answer.

"Go ahead."

The voice on the other end had the nasal, high-pitched whine of a teenager, though Ethan Maslin was in his twenties. Ethan was her information specialist, a hacker busted in an FBI sting operation. Now, to avoid a jail sentence, he put his talents to work for the CIA.

"How do I know it's you? Maybe you've been kidnapped and replaced by a robot duplicate."

Rebecca sighed. "It's too early for this, Ethan. I'm in the middle of a run."

"You know, you do work behind a desk, Rebecca. What's with all the exercise? Do you have field ops envy?"

"The better to kick your ass with, Ethan. Hanging up now—"

"Wait! Bernatto called. He's set a meeting. Kryptos, 9:00 a.m. on the dot."

She checked her phone's clock. Just enough time to finish her run and get ready. A short buzz indicated Ethan had already sent the invite.

"Thanks, Ethan. I'll be there. See you in a couple hours."

"Hey, Rebecca?"

"Yeah?"

"How's your time?"

She laughed. "Shitty, as always. Trust me, Ethan, it's not about the time."

She hung up and spared herself a minute to look around, soaking in the tranquility of the cool morning. The truth was Rebecca had run this route dozens of times ... and she had never once timed herself. For her, it really wasn't about the time.

It was about the escape.

She picked up her feet and resumed her pace. The morning mist grew thicker, surrounding her, and then she was gone, lost in a cold, grey cloud.

Two hours later, Rebecca had traded in her damp sweats and sneakers for a charcoal Helmut Lang suit. Her long, fiery red hair was slicked back into a thick ponytail, and she wore a navy blue raincoat, belted at her waist.

The sharp lines of her designer clothes made her feel like a shark —a smooth, deadly predator, relentlessly moving forward. Her black heels clicked on the walkway between her office and the New Headquarters Building. Up ahead, a courtyard separated the two buildings with a centerpiece known as Kryptos, a sculpture as enigmatic as its name suggested.

Rebecca strode up to the eight-foot-tall copper statue. The sheet of metal rose up from the ground in a curved S-shape. It stretched twelve feet from left to right. A series of letters and symbols was stamped into the metal, divided into four square sections. Each section contained a coded message, all but one of which had been cracked and translated. The fourth code remained a mystery, known only to the artist and, according to legend, the director of the CIA.

Allan Bernatto stood in front of the copper statue, gazing up at the strange symbols that adorned its surface. Clad in a black trench coat, he held an umbrella in one hand and a steaming cup of coffee from the nearby cafeteria in the other. He stood with his back to her, but he spoke before she entered his field of vision.

"You're late, Freeling."

Rebecca didn't bother glancing at the slim platinum watch on her wrist.

"Sorry, Allan. Rain slowed me down." She stood next to him and glanced at the fourth section of the Kryptos panel. This was the code that no amateur or CIA cryptographer had been able to translate. "Taking a crack at the fourth code?"

Allan gave a short laugh, more of a grunt than an expression of humor. "You know how much this thing cost? Fucking ridiculous." He looked down at Rebecca, raindrops beading on his small, round glasses. "Walk with me."

Rebecca looked up and tried to read his eyes. As always, they were as dark and unyielding as the metal wall before them. She shrugged and nodded.

They turned and walked down the pathway leading out of the courtyard. The older man didn't say a word as their footsteps crunched across the pebbled path. Gradually, the sound of the rocks beneath their feet became louder than the chattering of their coworkers in the courtyard. He cleared his throat once.

"Where are we on the Kusaka situation?" His voice was low and even, as emotionless as the navigation system in her car.

"Sir, with all due respect—"

"No," he interrupted, "don't do that."

"Don't do what?" Even as the words left her mouth, she knew it was a futile gesture. She already knew how this conversation was going to go.

"I don't care about your 'due respect' or your opinions on the matter, or why you don't think we should get involved. I don't care if you like me, or hate me, or you think I'm the fucking Antichrist. I assigned you a task. I'm on a tight timeframe here. What do you have for me?"

Rebecca stopped in her tracks, forcing Allan to shuffle a bit before turning to glare at her. "May I be blunt, sir?"

He nodded.

Rebecca took a breath. "I do not have the access required for the task you've assigned me. The assets you want to deploy in this situation require an extremely specific skill set. Language skills, deep cover background, regional knowledge ... I've exhausted the normal pool of outside talent, and no one comes close."

Allan looked at his watch. "I've got a meeting with Homeland in ten minutes. Give me your pitch."

Rebecca stifled a laugh. Working for Allan had taught her new meanings of the word "arrogance."

"I don't have a pitch, Allan. I'm just not sure—"

Allan held up a gloved hand. "Just tell me what you want, Freeling. What's it going to take to get you to do your job?"

All humor left her face as her features hardened into an icy stare. The man knew how to get a rise out of her.

"All right. I need higher clearance to find the kind of talent you're looking for. I need access to records that are closed off to me right now. And I need Ethan working point for me on this. That's what it will take to get this done in the timeframe you've given me."

Allan nodded and looked towards the shiny buildings in the distance. Although he seemed disinterested, she knew him better than that. The far-off look in his eye was risk analysis. He was weighing the odds and planning his countermoves in case things went south.

"All right, fine. As of now, you are head of a new task group I'm starting. The Extra Departmental Assets Group, or some other bullshit name we come up with. High-level clearance. Minimal oversight. Ethan has access to any and all files he needs. Just get someone suitable in Tokyo by the end of the week. I don't care who it is. I don't even want to know who it is. Just get it done. Are we clear?"

Rebecca opened her mouth, but no words came out. Of all the possible outcomes of this meeting, a promotion was one she had never considered. Finally, she settled for a firm nod.

"Good. Don't bother keeping me posted.... I'll be keeping tabs on you."

He turned and walked off into the rain. Rebecca bit her lip, turning Allan's words over in her mind. She mentally replayed the conversation word by word. It occurred to her that a promotion at the CIA could be a curse in disguise.

Maximum clearance and minimal oversight ... just enough rope to hang herself.

CHAPTER FOUR

After forty-eight hours in Bang Kwang central prison, Thomas Caine ranked it near the top of his list of godforsaken hell holes. Eighty acres of stinking, sweat-stained concrete and metal surrounded him, and the air was thick with sewage and despair. He wasn't sure which smelled worse. He knew he had seen worse.... He had suffered pain and captivity the likes of which most people could never imagine. But Bang Kwang, the legendary "Bangkok Hilton," was a close second.

As he swatted a fly off his sweat-drenched forehead, he felt optimistic. True, conditions were bad, abysmal even. But in a place like this, a place of sickness, violence, corruption ... how far away could death be? How long could he realistically expect to suffer before infection, or a cold metal blade in the dark, ended his horror for good?

He shook his head, trying to clear his mind. *You've survived worse. You didn't give up then. You can't give up now.*

But why not? he asked himself.

His gaze drifted across the courtyard. Men were everywhere, like bloated, lethargic vermin infesting a long-dead corpse. Some talked in groups, smoking cigarettes they had bought off the guards with favors and contraband. Others played cards or flipped the pages of moldy, faded paperback novels.

Across the cement square, near a group of old picnic tables, a dozen or so prisoners lined up. An older man sat at the table with a worn leather satchel full of rusted tools. One by one, the men stepped up and opened their mouths, allowing the old man to peer in, examining their teeth.

As Caine had learned at mealtime the day before, the old man's name was Narong. He had been a carpenter before murdering both his wife and her lover. He had set fire to a van they were using for one of their romantic trysts. He claimed not to know they were both inside it at the time. The trial didn't go his way.

However, the fact that his cousin was an oral surgeon officially qualified him to act as the prison's dental services provider. They even let him carry his old tools. Prisoners requesting dental care lined up at his table. They were responsible for acquiring their own cups of alcohol to sterilize Narong's implements.

Caine looked away as Narong lowered a pair of pliers into a shivering, emaciated prisoner's mouth. Screaming filled the air. It was not an unusual sound in Bang Kwang, and the guards paid no attention.

Caine felt a prickling on his neck. He once again scanned the yard, drinking in the details. He watched Narong tugging at his pliers, the grimace of pain on his patient's face. The guards kept their backs to him and the other prisoners, studiously avoiding the horror show playing out behind them. *Why are they all looking away?*

A man emerged from the pack of prisoners, his leg chains jangling with each step. In seconds, the man closed in, and Caine knew what the prickling was: the sixth sense of a killer, recognizing impending violence. He had been sent here to disappear. It only made sense Lau would send someone to finish the job.

Caine, like every other prisoner, wore irons and chains around his ankles. There was just enough play for him to step forward and balance on his rear leg. He brought his hands up in front of him, palms open.

The assassin blinked, surprised to see his target advancing instead of moving away. Only an inch or two shorter than Caine, muscles bulged beneath his prison rags. Caine swore at himself for not noticing him sooner.

A tattoo of a scorpion danced across the thick cords of his shoulder and neck. It was the symbol of a Chao Pho, a local gang of mixed Thai and Han Chinese ethnicities. They controlled organized crime in Thailand's cities. Caine had a working relationship with the gangs, and he paid them a percentage when operating in their territory. But this was obviously not personal. Just business.

Scorpion made a rapid, twisting motion with his left ankle. The iron manacle clicked open and fell to the ground. Caine barely had time to register the movement before the big man pivoted on his left foot. Then, Scorpion launched his right leg into a powerful spinning heel kick.

Caine instinctively tried to execute a defensive kick. He raised his right foot, but then heard the clink of the chain surrounding his ankles pull taut. Cursing, he turned his body to the side, trying to pivot out of the way, but it was too late. Scorpion's heel smashed into his chest.

Caine's back slammed into the ground with a loud crack. Coughing and sputtering for air, he immediately assumed a defensive ground position. Covering his face, he rolled left and right, blocking blows where he could with his foot. The chain around his ankles made this almost impossible. He would have to get back on his feet if he hoped to survive.

To relax his spasming diaphragm, he took a deep breath. His instincts began to take over. Time seemed to slow down. He sensed the other prisoners circling them, cheering the fight on. They did not register as a threat, and his mind muted their bloodthirsty cries to a dull background roar. But the buzzing still tingled at the back of his neck.... There was another danger nearby.

Caine rolled to his left, towards one of the old battered picnic tables that dotted the courtyard. He allowed momentum to carry his body under the table. A blunt stick hit the dirt where his head had been a moment earlier. Another prisoner had joined the fight, this one tall but lanky and malnourished. After a few days on the prison diet, Caine could see why. The new attacker wielded a prison guard's baton. He, too, had been freed from his leg irons. Lau must have paid the warden a pretty penny to arrange this hit.

Caine popped up on the other side of the table. He slid back into his defensive position: hands raised, legs apart, one foot farther back for balance. He stared down his attackers. His emerald eyes were calm, and he did not blink.

The two men split up, each moving around a different side of the table. Caine launched towards Lanky first, moving as fast as his leg chains would allow. He surprised his opponent with his reckless advance.

Lanky bellowed and raised his weapon over his head. As the baton swung down, Caine used his left arm to divert the force of the blow. He swung his right arm and landed a vicious punch on Lanky's jaw. Before the stunned man could retreat, Caine grabbed his wrist and yanked him forward. He wrenched the baton from the man's weakened grasp.

Stepping back, he swung the club up between Lanky's legs. As the painful blow struck, he raised his elbow and dropped it with all his weight on the back of Lanky's neck. The man hit the ground like a sack of flour.

Caine dropped to his knees beside him, slamming the baton into the small of his back. Lanky's eyes popped, but instead of a scream, only a hissing breath escaped his lips. His fingers clawed at the dirt. He dragged himself away from Caine an inch at a time. Caine let him go. He stood up and focused his attention on Scorpion.

The big man charged towards him, his mouth open and rolling like a rabid animal. His meaty left fist launched forward in a punch. Caine stepped back, avoiding the powerful blow while rapping the man's knuckles with his baton. The big man yelped and attempted a follow-up punch with his right hand. But the pain from Caine's counterattack had thrown him off balance, and Caine dodged the clumsy strike with ease.

Scorpion shifted his weight, and Caine saw the signs of another left-right combo. He didn't have to plot his next move. It was like listening to music. He simply knew which notes should finish the tune.

Sure enough, Scorpion launched forward again with his left fist. Caine whipped his left arm in front of him, knocking the blow wide and leaving his attacker open. Stepping forward, Caine slammed the baton into Scorpion's gut. As the big man gasped and bent over, Caine clubbed him on the back of the neck and the giant crumpled to the ground.

Caine hesitated for a second, staring at the now-defenseless inmate. *Get it done!* the voice in his head roared. *If you don't make him an example, these guys will never stop coming.* He knew what to do, knew it was necessary. Still, he waited.

Scorpion groaned and began to pick himself up. Caine blinked, and the voice in his head took control. He straddled Scorpion's head. With a quick jerk of his ankle, Caine wrapped the chain between his legs around his enemy's neck.

Caine threw himself to the ground and pulled with his legs. Scorpion gasped as the chain grew taut around his bulging neck. He thrashed his body, struggling to loosen the chain. Caine threw all his weight into the stranglehold. Strong, fat fingers clawed at his ankles, but Caine grit his teeth and ignored the pain. After a few moments, the man stopped moving. Caine heard the death rattle leave his enemy's throat, a last gasping wheeze.

Caine relaxed his legs and let go. He staggered to his feet and surveyed the crowd that had gathered around him.

The other prisoners were cheering. They exchanged money, cigarettes, and drugs as they paid off their bets on the fight. Judging by the amount of money changing hands, Caine guessed he had not been expected to win.

He looked down at Scorpion's bloated corpse. He thought of how different a dead body looked from its living, breathing incarnation. After a person died, the stillness of death became like a new state of reality. The memories of it walking, talking, and living were like echoes, whispers in the wind that grew fainter with every passing second.

He looked around and saw Lanky had managed to drag himself under the picnic table for shelter. He wasn't moving, but Caine could tell he was still alive.

That's okay. One is enough. This time.

As the crowd parted, he saw Narong, still standing by his table, still holding the rusty pair of pliers. The old man grinned, raising the old tool in a jaunty salute. Caine could just make out the small, white tooth in the pliers' grip. His emaciated patient nodded and clapped his hands. Blood and saliva dripped from his mouth.

That was the last thing Caine saw before the guards forced their way through the crowd and began pummeling him with their batons. He made no move to resist. He sank to the ground and let the blackness fall over him like a blanket, numbing the pain of their blows.

When he fell unconscious, he was smiling.

CHAPTER FIVE

Rebecca sighed and leaned back in her office chair. As she massaged her temples, the plastic clicking of computer keys filled the air. It sounded like the mocking chatter of a high-tech rodent.

She returned her attention to the pile of dossiers spread before her. Assassins, mercenaries, disavowed agents ... a grim cast of unsavory players covered her desk, a collage of dark, bloodstained history. Each sheet of paper detailed the secret career of a highly trained killer. These assets were used discreetly by the CIA, but never appeared in official agency records. They were independent contractors in the world of espionage.

Across from her, Ethan's fingers scurried over the keyboard of his custom PC rig. Twelve liquid-cooled processing cores sifted through mountains of data. Every now and then, a promising dossier filled his screen. These were printed and added to the ever-growing pile of paper on Rebecca's desk. But each time she read them over, something wasn't right, some element was missing. What Allan was asking for, the timeframe he had given her ... only the perfect candidate would have any chance of success, and so far, that candidate was proving elusive.

"Ethan, at the very least, I need someone who can speak Japanese, for God's sake!"

Her information specialist didn't even look up from his keyboard as he printed up another batch of options. "Hasn't exactly been a hotspot for us lately, you know? Speak Arabic, welcome aboard, pop the champagne. Speak Japanese? Enjoy your tentacle porn. Know what I'm saying?"

She threw several useless dossiers in the trash.

"Uh, aren't you supposed to shred those?"

"Let's just burn the office down. It will be easier in the long run."

The problem, she thought, was that Ethan had it exactly right. For at least the last fifteen years, CIA asset recruitment had focused on the Middle East with a laser-like intensity. True, they had successfully infiltrated cells of Al-Qaeda and similar extremist groups. But the agency now found it difficult to rapidly mobilize elsewhere in the world.

She stood up and stretched her arms above her head. "This operation is going to crash and burn. And Allan set me up to take the fall. The Extra Departmental Assets Group is bullshit.... This whole thing is a big red bull's-eye painted on my ass."

"My ass, too, boss."

A soft electronic chime sounded from Ethan's computer. "Hold the phone ... what do we have here?"

Rebecca walked over to his desk, leaning over his shoulder. "What have you got?"

"Curiouser and curiouser ... I've been running traces on old aliases ... you know, fake identities, backstopped covers that we provided. Sometimes these freelance players are so far removed from their original identities, it's easier to track down the alias, right?"

"Yeah, I get it. What's so interesting about this one?"

Ethan looked up over his shoulder. "Do you mind? Personal space."

Rebecca bit her lip and took a step back.

"Okay, so if any official agency runs a check on one of these IDs, I get a flag here. And a fingerprint ID check was just submitted to Interpol by the Royal Thai Police for one Mark Waters."

"Who the hell is Mark Waters?"

"That's the point.... He's no one. Mark Waters was a deep cover identity we created. And the fingerprints the Thai police have on file match ours, so we know it's the same asset, but it's not supposed to be active. Whoever was assigned this identity, he's using it on his own now. And according to this file, he's been arrested by the Thai police for smuggling, racketeering, and ... looks like arms dealing."

Rebecca grabbed a chair and sat down next to Ethan. The young man shifted uncomfortably, but she ignored him.

"Who the hell is this guy? Show me."

Ethan's fingers danced over the keys. "Ladies and gentlemen, I present Mr. Mark Waters...." The Interpol file on the screen faded away, replaced by a CIA personnel dossier. The photo showed an attractive man in his thirties. He had short brown hair and intense green eyes. "Also known as ... Thomas Caine."

Rebecca gasped.

Ethan looked up at her, his eyes peering over the rims of his chunky black glasses. "According to our files, he's supposed to be dead. You know this guy?"

Rebecca stood up, brushed back her long red hair, and stared at the screen. "Yeah. I knew him."

"Well, obviously he's alive and kicking it in Thailand. What's his deal?"

"Officially, he was one of our best deep operators. He was posing as an arms dealer, to make a connection with the White Leopard drug cartel in Afghanistan. According to his handler's report, he went rogue. Killed his partner and disappeared with a shipment of guns and heroin. Then he resurfaced and tried to sell it on the black market. When the White Leopards found out who he really was, they killed him and took back their drugs."

Ethan nodded. "Okay. And unofficially?"

Rebecca paused for a moment, staring at the pixilated photograph.

"Unofficially ... I knew him. I debriefed him once, after an operation. We ... became close."

"How close?"

Rebecca didn't answer. She returned to her desk, shoved aside the white sea of dossiers and personnel reports, and grabbed the folder Bernatto had given her.

"Bury that report. I don't want any other internal system flagging it."

Ethan laughed. "Right! So you're saying you want me to hack every computer inside the CIA?"

"And Interpol if you have to."

She dialed her desk phone and waited for the operator to pick up. "Just do it, Ethan. Kill that report."

"Science and Technology, Special Activities Division," said a voice on the phone.

Rebecca cradled the receiver against her shoulder as she stuffed files into her leather briefcase. "Yes, video archives please? I need any footage we have on Thailand politicians. Something compromising. I need to lean on someone."

"Who exactly do you need to lean on?"

"Anyone tied to the warden of Bang Kwang prison."

She hung up the phone, grabbed her coat off the back of her chair, and eyed Ethan. "When they deliver the footage, send it to my phone. And Ethan, not a word of this, to anyone. Do you understand? Especially not Bernatto."

Ethan stopped typing again and looked up. His eyes looked wide and concerned behind his thick glasses. "Well, where are you going to be, if anyone asks?"

Rebecca slung her bag over her shoulder and hurried out of the office. "Tell them I'm visiting an old friend."

CHAPTER SIX

Genki Ink was a small tattoo parlor on Takeshita Dori, a pedestrian street in the trendy Harajuku area. The shop had a reputation for quality work, but its bosozuku gang clientele tended to scare off more casual customers. A small group of these gang members lounged outside the shop. They smoked cigarettes and ran combs through their greased hair as they watched the crowds go by.

Inside, the air smelled of sweat, mixed with the antiseptic sting of alcohol. The heavy electronic buzzing of tattoo guns was constant. Not even the Japanese punk rock music blasting from the shop's speakers could drown it out.

In the rear of the shop, the gang's leader, a Japanese man in his late twenties, lay face down on a table. He was shirtless, and his body was already covered with ink, a mix of various tattoo styles. His thick black hair was pushed up into a sweeping, shiny pompadour. A tattered black leather jacket hung off a chair next to him. The name "Sonny" was stitched across the back in bright red letters.

The jacket, tattoos, and hairstyle were the hallmarks of the bosozuku, the speed tribes. These motorcycle and street racing youth gangs served as a breeding ground for future yakuza. Sonny was a senpai, the head of the gang known as the Crimson Scorpions.

Sonny grunted as the needle buzzed back and forth. The red patch of ink beneath his skin grew darker and darker. He actually found the pain of the needle relaxing, in a strange way. Like a hard shiatsu massage, it hurt, but it was a welcome pain. His head lolled on the table as the artist continued working on the elaborate scorpion shoulder tattoo. The deep bass of the shop's punk music, the pulsing, painful warmth of the needle ... after a long night of drinking and partying in the Roppongi bars, he nearly fell asleep.

As Sonny's thoughts turned to dreams, he let his mind wander to the future. He pictured his eventual transformation from a bosozuku senpai to a yakuza kobun. At twenty-nine, Sonny was old for a bosozuku. Government crackdowns on the yakuza families had lowered the demand for new members. Enrollment opportunities were limited, but Sonny knew his turn would come soon.

He'd turned the Crimson Scorpions into the most respected gang in the Kanto region. He had prioritized their profitable activities: stripping stolen cars for parts, theft, low-level street drugs, and muscle for hire. He ran the gang like a business, making sure his members contributed to the bottom line and stayed out of trouble. Honor and pride had their place, of course. But it was the money he brought to the table that would secure his position in the yakuza.

The door to the tattoo shop swung open with a jingle, but Sonny paid it no mind. He was still contemplating his future: a life of flashy suits, sports cars, and beautiful girls at his beck and call. He dreamt of drinking sake from the cup of his *oyabun* and earning the respect and admiration of his brothers. Ignoring the common men who called him *"burakamen"* ... outcast. He had friends and relatives who had joined the yakuza. He was aware on some level that his dreams were fantasies, that the life had its hardships as well. Blood, tears, and loss were no strangers to those who moved up in the gangs. But, for now, he was content to dream.

Lost in his thoughts, Sonny paid no attention to the enormous man who'd entered the parlor. Clad in a black suit, his massive size eclipsed nearly all the light from the shop's front windows. Two other men, dressed in identical black suits, flanked him.

Bobu.

The artists were so engaged in their work, no one even looked up as one of the men began lowering the shades of the parlor windows. Bobu surveyed the store, his milk-white eye finally settling on Sonny. No emotion whatsoever crossed his features as he approached. His associates drew Glock 19 automatic pistols tipped with silencers. As they made their way to the back of the store, they opened fire.

The silencers turned the explosive shots into loud but muffled coughs. One of the tattoo artists, a girl with purple hair wearing a tattered concert t-shirt, looked up and gasped. She watched as her coworker, only a few feet away, collapsed to the floor in a crumpled, bloody heap. The tattoo artist barely had time to register what was happening before the gun coughed again. A bright red hole burst open between her eyes.

Wrenched from his daydreams, Sonny's head shot up just in time to see a half-naked, mohawked patron sprint for the front door. He almost made it before a bullet to the back of the head dropped him cold.

Sonny gaped at the senseless slaughter. He looked up as a shadow descended over his table. Bobu stood over him, gazing down. His scarred, warped features were like something from a nightmare.

The guns unloaded two more shots, and the tattoo artist next to Sonny fell backwards, crashing into a cart filled with tattoo ink and supplies. The ink spattered across the floor, mixing with his blood to form a psychedelic splatter of color next to his dead body.

The sudden burst of violence was over as quickly as it began. The buzzing of the tattoo needles was gone. Without their cricket-like hum, the shop felt quiet and empty, despite the loud music blasting from the speakers.

Sonny threw his body up into a sitting position on the tattoo table. The shock of the attack had caught him off guard. Those precious seconds he had wasted gawking would mean the difference between life and death.

His reached for the pearl-handled switchblade knife he stashed in the inner pocket of his jacket. It didn't make much sense ... four inches of slim, sharp steel against a barrage of gunfire. But it was all he had.

His fingers just brushed the rough leather of the jacket when he felt a crushing pressure around his wrist. Bobu had swooped down, grabbing his outstretched arm with one of his thick, meaty hands.

Bobu followed through with a strike, slamming his other hand into Sonny's neck. The huge man pressed forward, carrying Sonny through the air and smashing him into the wall behind the tattoo table. Sonny's vision blurred as his skull cracked against the wood. The impact knocked several sheets of tattoo flash art to the floor.

Despite the sudden exertion, Bobu's breath was calm and measured. He held Sonny against the wall, the bosozuku's feet kicking and flailing several inches above the floor. His massive, hideous face hung inches in the air in front of Sonny's. He sized up the squirming gangster with his milky eye and smiled.

"You are bosozuku?" he asked. "You wish to be yakuza?"

Sonny swallowed his panic, struggling to maintain his bravado in the face of this monster. Sonny had led gangs in turf wars and violent beatings. He had killed his enemies, watching their faces as they died. He squinted, knowing that fear showed first in the eyes.

"Who the fuck are you?" He was grateful to hear his voice didn't waver. "Do you know who you're messing with?"

Bobu barked a command, and one of his associates stepped forward, holding a cell phone in front of Sonny. On it was a digital photo of a girl. The expression on the girl's face was strange. She looked haunted. Lost. To Sonny, she looked like a fallen angel.

Bobu twisted his lips into a reptilian smile.

"I apologize for the inconvenience. We are looking for this girl. It is vital that we find her. You wish to be yakuza, yes? You wish to be part of a *ninkyo dantai*, a chivalrous organization?" Bobu spat the words, as though the phrase left a bitter taste on his tongue. "Then you must help us. You must help Japan."

"What the fuck are you talking about, man? I don't know that bitch! Man, my boys are gonna mess you up!"

Bobu kept smiling, but a wave of malice seemed to ripple across his features.

"Your boys? You mean the two-bit punks outside, preening and grooming for the Lolita harlots that walk this street? Please, let me summon them for you."

Bobu nodded, and one of his henchman disappeared from view. He turned back to Sonny. "Nihon. Japan. Our island. Our home is dying, my friend, from the worst cancer of all. Weakness. And you are part of this weakness, this sickness that is strangling our home. Just as I once was.... Ah, your associate has arrived."

Bobu moved his massive head. His lackey had returned from his errand. In his left hand, he held a metal hacksaw. In his right hand, he held the severed head of Sonny's second-in-command, one of the bosozuku he had stationed outside to stand guard. Both dripped blood onto the scattered papers and debris strewn across the floor of the tattoo shop.

"Look, man, I can help you! I've got people, I'm senpai...." Sonny didn't even care that his voice quaked. All pretense of courage and defiance drained from his features. He knew the man could see the fear in his eyes. There was no hiding it.

Bobu laughed. The sound was deep and guttural, like wind blowing through a dark, wet cavern.

"You are a weak, insolent child, a parasite who dreams only of sucking the blood of a diseased, cancerous host. You wish to be yakuza? I was once yakuza. And I tell you, they have lost their way. They flaunt their tattoos and cheap suits and gold-plated sports cars. They squabble over money and territory. Meanwhile, all around them, Japan is dying. The real enemy grows stronger and stronger."

Sonny struggled, but Bobu squeezed his throat tighter. "Let me see the picture.... I ... I think I know her. I can help!"

Bobu reached his free hand over to a tattoo needle on the counter next to him. He held it up, staring at it, fascinated.

"This instrument ... this is not even the proper tool for a yakuza to receive his tattoos. It should be *irezumi*, the traditional way. Done by hand, using needle and chisel. The time, the pain ... that is the price you pay for the beauty. The honor of proving your conviction."

The big man shook his head and laughed again, looking back at Sonny. "The honor of strutting around like a peacock in heat. Bah! I was yakuza once, but as you can see, I have renounced those convictions. Our scars mark us now. They show that our devotion is to a higher cause. And make no mistake. We will restore Nihon to its rightful place in the world. We will flush out the weakness, just as I had to flush the poison from my veins. But first, we must find this girl. She was working as a hostess at a club in Roppongi. Tiger Velvet. The other girls there say you were her client. They saw her leave with you."

Sonny nodded. "Yeah, yeah, some bitch at some club. Let me see. I'll help you find her."

"I gave you one chance. You refused. Now, you say you want to help us? Like a true yakuza, you must prove your convictions. I have no more time to waste."

Bobu plunged the tattoo needle into Sonny's right eye. A brief spurt of clear fluid burst from the wound, followed by a stream of crimson blood.

Sonny's shriek echoed through the room. Bobu and his men stared as his cry of pain turned to a pathetic sob.

"Said I'd help, man. I'll help! I'll do anything."

Bobu raised the needle again. "I am glad. You have one more chance. And one more eye."

CHAPTER SEVEN

Rebecca wiped her brow as she paced back and forth in front of the iron fence. The plants and flowers of the garden before her filled the hot air with a sweet scent, but they couldn't mask the stench of sweat and sewage. The combination was nauseating, like rotten fruit.

The garden occupied a tiny strip of land, no more than a meter across, before it was cut off by another set of bars. It was a tiny sliver of beauty trapped in a filthy metal cage. A private little paradise for no one's eyes.

Normally, neither visitors nor prisoners were allowed here. But Rebecca's visit was abnormal in every way.

The guards who had escorted her hurried away as quickly as possible. She felt like a witch or some kind of boogeyman. And that was fine by her. *Whatever works....*

The muted shriek of metal grating against metal came from deep within the bowels of the hellish prison. Then footsteps. Distant at first, they grew louder along with another sound: the jingling of a chain dragging along concrete.

And then he was there, standing in front of her, on the other side of the far fence. He was little more than a meter away, but ages of unanswered questions stretched between them.

He stared, unblinking, body perfectly still. She remembered how sometimes his stillness could unnerve her, as though he were dead inside. Then he would touch her face, or stroke her hair, or make some other human gesture. She would laugh and smile, no longer able to see the shadow that had so unnerved her, as if it were an optical illusion.

She nodded, not sure why, but feeling it was the appropriate response to seeing a living man she'd believed to be dead for so long.

"Well," she said.

"I knew someone would come," he said, his voice soft, but sharp, like a paper-thin knife, "but I didn't expect it to be you."

Rebecca bit her lip. "Who did you expect?"

Caine shrugged. "Anyone but you."

"You're supposed to be dead."

He smirked. "You sound disappointed."

Rebecca dug a plastic band from her purse. She pulled back her hair, heavy and damp with sweat, tying it into a loose ponytail.

Caine watched like a cat watches birds play on the other side of a window.

"Your hair is longer," he said.

Rebecca's face flushed. The two sets of bars cut the man before her into disjointed slivers, like reflections in a house of mirrors.

"My hair is longer?" Her voice rose to a strangled shout. "All these years, that's all you can say? I wake up, and you're gone. I mean, disappeared, completely out of my life. And now ... Tom, what the hell happened to you?"

Caine paused, then looked away. A muscle in his neck quivered. "That's not my name anymore. I don't know why you're here, but you should leave."

"No, Tom, that is your name. That's why I'm here. You're why I'm here." Rebecca's slim, porcelain hand gripped a metal bar. "Mark Waters was the asshole you were pretending to be. A drug dealer, who traded guns for heroin to terrorists. Is that who you are now? Is that who you decided to be?"

"No, that's who the United States government decided I should be. It served their interests, and I paid the price. Trust me, they got the better end of the deal."

Rebecca had to force herself not to step back from the bars. His voice—cold and raw with hatred—was like a blade of icy steel stabbing at her. She shivered, despite the intense heat.

Caine smirked again. "Now, I serve my own interests. I've earned that. So how about you drop the jilted lover act and tell me what it is you want?"

"I want the truth, damn it!"

Caine chuckled. "Then you may need to reconsider your career path."

"Fine. Screw the truth then. I'll just assume you are what your file says you are. A traitor and a disgrace."

"And dead. Let's not forget that."

"Well, if you're not interested in debating the truth, neither am I. Besides, I don't think it will be too long before the facts reconcile themselves. People don't last long in here. The locals call this place 'The Big Tiger.' Know why?"

Caine didn't answer.

Rebecca finally felt like the conversation was on equal footing. She took a step closer. "Because it eats men alive."

Caine held up the manila folder in his hands. "And this is what, exactly? My ticket out of here? A favor I do for you, in exchange for my freedom?"

She nodded. "I can fill you in on the details later, but the elevator pitch is in there. Arinori Kusaka is a prominent Japanese businessman with fingers in every technological pie there is. Works with all the major Chinese factories and has close ties to many government officials. He's also a CIA asset, whose intelligence has been instrumental in thwarting several industrial espionage and cyberterrorism attacks sponsored by the Chinese government."

Caine flipped through the dossier, scanning the photos and reports in the folder with a lazy detachment. "You want me to take him to a hostess club?"

Rebecca ignored him. "Kusaka claims he has knowledge of an imminent terrorist attack that will take place on U.S. soil within the next seven days."

"Well, good thing you're all such close friends then," he said without looking up from the folder.

"Kusaka has a daughter, mid-twenties, mother unknown. Apparently, she's fallen in with a bad crowd. Gangs, yakuza wannabes, that sort of thing. She stole some money and papers from his safe about a month ago and disappeared. Nobody's seen her since then."

Caine continued flipping pages in the file. He sighed. "Why on earth are you getting involved in this? Japan run out of cops and private eyes?"

"According to the report, Kusaka hired four private eyes to find her. The body of one was found in Tokyo Bay. The other three simply disappeared without a trace. And Kusaka claims the authorities are burying the case due to yakuza corruption in the department. Bottom line, Kusaka refuses to release his intel unless we help him find his daughter. And like I said, we're on the clock. We have seven days, including today, to make this happen."

"And you believe this intel is real? You trust him?"

"Doesn't matter what I believe. Bernatto believes him, and he's calling the shots."

Caine's head jerked up, and his eyes zeroed in on hers. The dark shadow of death that lay just beneath his handsome exterior glowered with menace. "Bernatto? Allan Bernatto? He's your boss?"

"Director of HUMINT. He's placed me in charge of a new group, Extra Departmental Assets Liaison, or some other bullshit title. Basically, I get this done, or it's my ass."

Caine dropped the folder on the bench next to him. "And a disgraced traitor in a Thai prison is the best you could do?"

She looked down at her taupe leather flats. "I was hoping you could tell me something, anything...."

"Hoping I was innocent? No, that's not it. You were hoping I could sell it to you. Because deep down, you didn't believe it, but you want to. So you can use me. Like Bernatto."

She looked up. "What do you mean?"

"Bernatto was my handler on Operation Big Blind, the op that got my partner killed. The op where he sold me out to the White Leopard clan."

"Bernatto sold the heroin? He actually used agency assets to facilitate a personal drug deal?"

Caine turned his back towards her. "I'm not saying anything. Get someone else." He shuffled away.

"Tom, wait!" She moved along the fence, trying to keep him in sight. "Tom, just tell me what happened! Please!"

The clink of his chain grew quieter, then disappeared. She heard the metal crash of a gate slamming shut. He was gone.

She was alone again in the courtyard. The garden was quiet, save for the buzzing of insects and the distant sounds of men, and metal, and pain.

CHAPTER EIGHT

Caine opens his eyes, and he is back. Back in the crumbling stone basement. Back where the harsh sunlight pierces through the cracks in the rock. The thin slices of light burn so bright, they are painful to look at in the darkness.

The chain of the rusty cuffs is slung over a hook in the ceiling. His wrists ache, and the rough metal bands have rubbed his palms raw. His feet dangle about a foot above the sandy floor. Every muscle in his body is taut and screaming. He cannot remember the last time he has slept. But nor does he seem to be fully awake. A prisoner now, his state of mind hovers somewhere between life and death.

He has no idea where he is. His captors have moved him several times, always covering his face with a dirty hood. He does not know when they will come again. All he knows are the lies he has to tell. The truth is forbidden. His life, his suffering, is nothing. He has to tell his lies. That is how he can win. The only way left to him.

He has lost the ability to see emotions in his captors, though he knows they are there, hidden in the men's shadowed features. Hatred, of him. Horror at the atrocities they inflict upon him. Fear.

Flickering glances of doubt. Tiny reminders that these are not demons, not monsters from hell. Human beings are doing this to him.

But he can't see them anymore, those minute glimpses of humanity. Maybe they were never there to begin with, just a trick of the light.

He opens his mouth to laugh, but no sound comes. There is no sound at all. Not the creaking of his chains, not the rats scurrying from the sacks of rotten grain in the corner ... all is silent.

Caine opens his mouth again, trying to make a sound, any sound. He shouts for help. He cries out his name, but nothing comes out, not even a dry croak. It is as if a heavy blanket has been laid over the entire room and no sound can escape its smothering embrace. But if he can't speak, how will he tell his lies? How can he win the game?

He hears footsteps on the stairs. In the unnatural silence, each step echoes like a gunshot. He twists and shakes, struggling to free himself. More blood spills from his ravaged body. Crimson droplets strike the sand beneath his feet.

CRASH. CRASH. CRASH. They are close now. He cannot see them, but the sunlight blinks and shifts as they descend the stairs.

And Caine knows one thing. When they come, the pain will start again. And it will feel like forever. Until the next time. And then forever will begin again.

He screams. Not for help. Not in pain. He screams just to scream. But there is no sound.

Caine woke up screaming.

He was laying atop a mattress of tattered, soiled blankets. The cell designed for two prisoners now housed eight men. They had to sleep lying head to toe across the floor. Their elbows and shoulders touched, skin rubbing against sweaty skin. The stench of the open toilet wafted through the still air. A single lightbulb filled the room with a pale, flickering glow.

Caine had found sleep nearly impossible for the first few days, but now exhaustion and hunger had dulled his nerves. Tonight he'd finally managed to plunge into a deep trance before the nightmare woke him.

The other men in the room grumbled and moaned, pulled from their slumber by his screams and thrashing. But no one uttered a word of complaint, not after his violent display in the prison yard.

Caine sat up and rubbed his aching shoulders. He had known the nightmares would come, just as surely as he had known Lau would send his killers. And he had known someone from the agency would come looking for him, once his alias popped up on their radar. But seeing Rebecca again.... *It had to be someone. It just happened to be her. She didn't come for you. She came to recruit an asset.*

And Bernatto. He had avoided thinking about the man for years. He had buried the past, with all its pain and betrayal and death. He'd even buried his own name. He had lost himself in his false identity, eking out a meager existence among the smugglers, pimps, and other entrepreneurs of the street. Hiding.

No, surviving, he countered. He almost believed it. But after seeing Rebecca, surviving no longer seemed like enough.

He took a deep breath. Stepping carefully, he picked his way across the carpet of bodies lining the floor. He stepped on a few elbows and fingers along the way, but again, no one confronted him. They grunted and shifted out of his way.

When he reached the wire mesh gate, he pounded it with his fist, sending a metallic clang echoing through the prison. "Guard! Get over here."

Mumbled complaints and curses drifted from the other cells, as footsteps traipsed down the hall.

"*Aow a-rai!*" the block guard barked. "What do you want?"

"The lady left me a file. I want to see it."

The guard stared at Caine for a few seconds. Had he overplayed his hand? Whatever leverage Rebecca had over the warden to set up her secret little meeting, maybe it was played out now.

The guard muttered a curse, then shouted down the hall to his partner as he unlocked the door. The other guard arrived and yanked Caine from the cell. "Let's go," he said in a thick Thai accent.

Caine looked back into the cell as the door swung closed. Its dark shadow moved across the other prisoners. They were a tangled mass of bodies, contorted into whatever space was available. Then the door slammed shut. Even under the glare of the buzzing lightbulb, the room seemed lost to impenetrable darkness.

They were the damned. He realized how close he had come to joining them. How childish his earlier refusal had been.

Twenty minutes later, he sat on metal chair in a stark, empty room. A small metal desk was bolted to the floor, and an ancient rotary phone hung from the wall. As he flipped through the pages of the file, a strange sensation flowed over him. He felt neither awake nor asleep. Alive nor dead. The place in his nightmare, where the pain lasted forever ... he knew he was not there. But neither had he truly escaped. Not yet.

Rebecca had given him the rundown on Arinori Kusaka, but Caine suspected there were details being withheld from him.

Details ... there were always details, hiding in the shadows. And knowing Bernatto, he would not have told Rebecca everything.

The criminal underworld and the intelligence community both operated in a never-ending sea of intel and data. The movements of high-level players like Bernatto and Kusaka left ripples and eddies. If you looked hard enough, you could just barely see them or, rather, the absence of information they left behind. Caine felt himself sinking into those dark currents now.

He flipped another page in the file to find a beautiful girl staring back at him. The photo was black and white, but he could tell her hair was lighter than most Japanese girls, an auburn brown. Her skin was starkly pale, almost pure white on the glossy photo paper.

She was reclining on her side, propped up on her arms on a small bed. The details of the room were blurry, but Caine guessed it was a flat or apartment, perhaps a friend's or boyfriend's. But her eyes ...

Caine could not imagine anyone looking at a lover with such haunted intensity.

Hitomi Kusaka.

Or so he assumed. The pictures were simply labeled "Hitomi." There was no other information about her in the file.

He leaned back in his chair. *That's wrong. Rich bastard like Kusaka, with enough juice to pull favors from the goddamn CIA, but no birth certificate for his daughter? No family pictures or outrageously expensive birthday parties or vacations abroad? No paparazzi photos of her cavorting at nightclubs or stumbling out of limousines?* He supposed they could be paranoid, privacy conscious. But it still felt off.

He sighed and looked around the empty, dingy room. This was probably the most pleasant thirty minutes he'd experienced since arriving at this prison.

Hell with it.

There was a business card taped to the front of the file folder with Rebecca's name and phone number on it. Nothing else. Caine picked up the ancient phone and listened to the dial tone for a moment, turning the dark possibilities over and over in his mind. With a shrug and a sigh, he dialed the number on the card.

"Hello?"

"It's me."

Rebecca paused. "Change your mind?"

"Maybe. Does Bernatto know about this? Does he know I'm involved?"

"No. He doesn't know I approached you. He doesn't want to know. He wants a deniable asset in case this blows up in our face."

"All right. Fine. I'm in. Fifty thousand. Half up front. In cash."

Rebecca was quiet for a moment. He could hear her soft breathing through the phone.

"Why didn't you come back?" she asked. "If you didn't do it, if Bernatto sold you out, why didn't you come back to prove it?"

He thought for a moment, unsure how much to reveal to her. She was tenacious, he knew, and that could be dangerous. "I did come back," he said. "It didn't work out. And if I stayed, someone would have gotten hurt."

"You mean me? Did Allan threaten me?"

"It doesn't matter. None of it matters; it was all bullshit. I killed people, and I thought I was making the world safer, better. But all I was doing was making people like Bernatto richer."

"This matters, Tom. If Kusaka's intel is real, lives are at stake. I have to know you can do this, that you're not just going to disappear again."

He thought for a moment. "I won't. Not until it's done. Fifty thousand, twenty-five up front. Cash."

"No." Her voice became cold and hard. "Not on this job. You get paid when you find her. Then you can crawl back under your rock if you want. I'll send a car for you tomorrow morning."

"You don't trust me?"

"Not yet."

He smiled. "Smart. And Rebecca?"

"What?"

He looked around the small, drab room.

"Send the car now."

"I will."

Caine listened to the static on the phone for a moment, then hung up. He walked back to the table and picked up the picture of Hitomi.

He wondered who she was looking at. He had a feeling he would soon find out.

CHAPTER NINE

It was about 5:00 p.m. when the plane landed at Tokyo Narita International Airport. It took another hour to clear immigration.

In the men's room, Caine splashed cold water on his face and scrubbed his skin. Then he ran damp fingers though his messy hair, slicking it back. He eyed his reflection in the mirror. The face staring back at him looked weary, on edge. There was a hollowness to his features, a shadow that seemed to hang over the raw, tan skin of his face. His eyes twitched like those of a predatory animal, caged for far too long.

He knew he was giving off bad energy, allowing the darkness inside him to creep its way onto his face, into his voice. Back when he had been operational, he could turn on and turn off the dangerous parts of his psyche, put the killer in the box until he was needed.

But now ... Lau's setup, the fight in the prison, seeing Rebecca again after all these years ... there was no box. The scars on his soul, only just healed, were torn open again. The darkness was out, for all to see—and that was dangerous. People keyed into that vibe, whether by training or simply an instinct for self-preservation.

Caine had caught the hesitation in the immigration officer's eyes as he handed over his carefully forged passport and visa. Luckily the official had decided it wasn't worth his time to stop a lone American tourist with no criminal record.

He took a deep breath. He hadn't been on mission in years. His body and mind were not sharp, he knew. Not at their peak. But they were good enough.

As he turned away from the mirror, he caught a look in his own eyes, a look he recognized. It was the same haunted, intense stare of the girl in the picture. Hitomi.

He stopped in the shopping concourse to buy some clothes and other basics with the credit card Rebecca had provided. They had both agreed it was a bad idea for him to return to his apartment, in case Lau had people watching for him. Instead he'd travelled in some old clothes from a bug-out bag stashed at a local bar.

He didn't like using the card. He knew it was a data point. It could track his purchases and location, but he figured she already knew where and when his flight arrived. He wasn't giving up any new details.

The glass doors leading out of the baggage area opened with a rush of air. Caine carried his lone suitcase and shopping bags out onto the sidewalk. He took a deep breath. The smell of the air filled his brain with hazy images. He had spent two years here, most of it pretending to be someone else. The images in his mind flashed past, like a movie playing on a warped, translucent screen ... a jumble of memories and lies. He couldn't remember which was which anymore.

As he joined the taxi line, he pulled out the phone Rebecca had given him. It was an older model from the agency, but still global and encrypted. And, of course, completely trackable. *None of which matters*, he thought. *I'm going to use it only once.*

He dialed the number she had given him from memory. The phone rang twice before she picked up. He sighed and waited for her to speak the recognition code, as they had arranged.

"I take it you landed. How was the flight?"

"Okay. The food was bad, and I already saw the movie. But I bought a book in the airport. Have you read any Basho?"

"No. I'm more of a Murakami fan." The responses were all correct. The names of the authors they used signified that neither party was speaking under duress or suspected others were listening in.

"Do you have an update for me?"

"No, the deadline is the same. Four days. And keep in mind, the home office didn't approve these expenses, so it's vital these negotiations are successful."

Great. Typical Bernatto. The higher-ups at the CIA hadn't approved his little favor for Kusaka. Probably didn't even know he was in Japan.

"I'll do my best," he said. "And Rebecca?"

"Yes?"

"Next time you hear from me, it will be a different number."

"What? That's not—"

He hung up on her, popped the back off the phone, and removed the battery and SIM card. Then he dropped the bundle in a trash can as he walked past. He would keep her informed of his progress, but he had no intention of letting her, or anyone else at the CIA, track his movements.

He walked up to a waiting taxicab. As he approached, the rear door automatically swung open, powered by a motor. For some reason, this strange little detail made him smile. He left his bags on the sidewalk, but watched to make sure the attendant placed them in the open trunk.

The driver, an older man, looked back and blinked. "Park Hyatt, *Onegai shimasu*," Caine said.

The cabbie smiled, his eyes wide with surprise. Caine's Japanese was not fluent, but it was better than the average tourist. As the car pulled away from the curb, he realized his instructions were the first time he had spoken the language since....

He halted that train of thought. Instead, he took in another deep breath of the cold night air. Here, far from the metropolitan center of Tokyo, the countryside consisted of rolling hills, dark against the moonlit sky. The air smelled of trees and grass and damp earth. It was invigorating. Caine closed his eyes and cleared his mind.

The past is in the past. Deal with it later. You're working now.

He opened his eyes and focused on the rearview mirror. He scanned the traffic behind them, looking for headlights that seemed too close or matched their movements. From time to time, he would look at the cars that drove alongside them. He searched for warning signs that they were being followed, but each car seemed to pursue its own, independent path. Each driver was moving towards their own destiny in the dark, cold night.

Occasionally, he would take interest in a driver or passenger, a pretty girl or a young man with glasses, flowers on the passenger seat next to him. He wondered where they were going, what waited for them at their destination.

If only you could answer that question for yourself.

The cab ride from Narita to Metro Tokyo was normally about an hour, but Caine requested several stops along the way. First, he asked the driver to pull into the parking lot of a convenience store. "*Chotto matte,*" he apologized. *Just a moment.*

With practiced ease, he rubbed his eyes and tilted his head down as he entered the store and walked past the counter, obscuring his features from the domed security camera.

The clerk, a younger man maybe in his early twenties, greeted him with the traditional welcome: "*Irashimasee.*" He didn't even look up from his manga as he said it. Caine approached the newsstand in front of the shop window. He flipped through a few magazines, letting himself dissolve into the background of the store.

Another man came in, wearing a suit and tie. He trudged over to the glass cabinet of cold drinks and grabbed a strange-looking beverage, whose label read "Pocari Sweat." Then he made his way up to counter. Business as usual.

Caine looked up from his magazine to scan the parking lot outside. He was looking for cars that lingered too long—people standing alone, watching the parking lot or his cab. But he saw nothing that aroused suspicion. Cars came and went, people finished their drinks and left. Only his taxi remained in the parking lot, its engine quietly humming.

He dropped the magazine back into the rack, returned to the car, and the driver pulled back into traffic. Caine requested two more random stops, but there were no issues. The confused, inquisitive glances from the driver made Caine smile. He was sure the man was beginning to wonder just who was in his cab.

It was a little after eight when they pulled into the circular driveway of the Park Hyatt Tokyo. A valet stood next to the cab, even though the rear door opened automatically. Caine handed the driver the credit card Rebecca had given him, knowing it would electronically place him at the hotel. The driver handed it back, along with his bill. As he signed the small piece of paper, he started to add in a sizable tip for the driver. Then he remembered that tipping was not the norm in Japan. He shrugged and signed for the larger amount anyway. The driver looked at the total, then looked back up, confused. Caine smiled. "*Gokuru samadeshita.*" *Thank you for your trouble.*

He slipped out of the cab and went around back to grab his bags from the porter. The driver sped off. Caine looked up at the hotel.

Three gleaming towers pierced the night sky, each taller than the next, like a series of steps. Each tower was capped by a sparkling glass pyramid, traced by glowing neon light. They were brilliant spears of metal and glass, piercing the dark purple sky. It was beautiful, but Caine had no intention of sleeping anywhere the agency could trace him.

He checked in at the front desk and let the porter bring his bags up for him. The room was spacious, modern, and luxurious. He barely even looked at it as he threw his belongings on the bed.

He pulled out a roll of black electrical tape, which he used to block the security hole in the door. He wasn't planning to stay there, but no sense in giving that away. Next he threw some of his new clothes and a few essentials into one of the larger shopping bags.

He left the room, slipping a toothpick into the doorjamb as he closed the door behind him. When the door clicked shut, he broke off the stub of wood he held in his hand, leaving the other half of the stick wedged invisibly in the door frame. If anyone opened the door to search the room, the tiny fragment would fall, and alert him if he returned.

He had to laugh. The people he was protecting himself from, the people who had tried to kill him in the past, were part of the largest, most well-funded intelligence agency on the planet. They had spy satellites, remote surveillance drones, and an unlimited army of operatives at their disposal. And he was relying on toothpicks and hotel switches for protection.

He took a combination of elevators and stairs down to the lobby, slipping out through a side entrance. He avoided the main driveway and taxi line. Instead, he walked a few blocks north and managed to flag down a cab on Minami-dori.

He had the cab drop him off just outside Kabukicho, a common destination for lone male tourists. He walked around the neighborhood for a bit, re-acclimating himself with the city's frenetic heartbeat. He made sure he looked like just another tourist, window-shopping, taking in the lights and sounds. He walked past the twin red arches that led into the infamous red light district, but he didn't pass through.

When he was certain no one was following him, he caught another cab to the Shinjuku Prince Hotel.

In his emergency stash he'd kept a spare wallet, complete with ID and credit cards under the name John Wilson. The cover wouldn't hold up under intense scrutiny, but for three to four days, it would serve his purpose.

It was 10:30 p.m. when he finally rode the elevator to the fourteenth floor of the Prince. The hotel towered in the Tokyo sky. The building was a thin slab of black granite, like an ancient monolith, watching over the city. It was not as fancy or ostentatious as the Park Hyatt, but it was known for its spectacular views of the city.

Caine stepped into his room and drew back the drapes. The lights of Tokyo spread out before him, a rolling carpet of stars, twinkling, flickering, burning, and dying. They surrounded him, taking up his entire field of vision. There was no other city like it. No other place on Earth felt so alive. It was like watching evolution on fast-forward.

He locked the door behind him and taped over the security hole. He considered dragging the dresser in front of the door, but he was just too tired.

He collapsed on the bed and looked around the small room, his vision blurry. It was nothing like the spacious, luxury suite he had left at the Hyatt. But it was anonymous. No one knew he was here. He was hidden. Invisible. Safe.

And that was the greatest luxury of all.

Within minutes, he was sound asleep. No nightmares disturbed his rest. Instead, he dreamed of dark, haunted eyes. They were waiting for him in the sea of light, just outside his window.

CHAPTER TEN

Rebecca wiped her brow and took several shallow sips from her water bottle. She had begun her run early, leaving the lobby of the Bali Hai Bay hotel at 6:00 a.m. She had been out only an hour, but the temperature was already in the high eighties and climbing. The humid air made the park trails and walking streets feel like a sauna, and her sleek body glowed with a sheen of sweat.

She had circled around the hotel and then made her way down the Bali Hai pier and back. The pier was of recent construction, part of Pattaya's efforts to attract family tourists. The pristine, white beams jutted out over the teal sea water. An array of bright, colorful fishing boats were docked at the various berths along the way. Few tourists ventured out so early in the morning, and she was grateful to have the serene beauty of the ocean to herself for a short time. But even the stunning view couldn't distract her thoughts from one uncomfortable subject...

Caine.

She was still processing the series of events that had brought him back into her life. One moment, he was a memory, a shadow, dead to her and the world. The next, he was standing in front of her, staring at her with those intense green eyes. She shivered in spite of the heat and humidity. The anger in those eyes, in his voice ... something had happened to him. Something not in his file. Something so bad he preferred the anonymity of death rather than seek her out. Rather than confide in her.

Operation Big Blind. His last mission. The file said Caine had been working a long-term deep cover operation, posing as an arms dealer and international criminal operating out of Japan. Through his association with the yakuza, he was able to forge connections to Aydin Turel, a Turkish arms dealer. Turel was believed to be the primary weapons supplier to a collection of fundamentalist terror groups in Afghanistan and throughout the Middle East.

Turel was simply a step along the way in Caine's mission, which was to identify and eliminate key players in the White Leopards. The Leopards were an upstart drug cartel operating out of the southern Kandahar region of Afghanistan. Their drug money was believed to finance numerous extremist terror groups in the area.

The yakuza linked Caine to Turel. Caine gained his trust, then set him up for a CIA rendition. All standard procedure. After a short but brutal stay in a black site prison, Turel was ready to play ball. He vouched for Caine and introduced him to the Leopards.

A meet had been set, complete with merchandise samples. Caine and his partner, an operative named Tyler, were both there when something had gone wrong.

Intel was sparse on what actually happened. All anyone knew for sure was Tyler was reported killed, and Caine had dropped off the grid. Turel's guns and the Leopards' heroin disappeared with him. It had been a simple matter to connect the dots. Caine was a highly trained operative. He was a living, thinking weapon in the war against terror. A machine. And sometimes machines malfunctioned.

Bernatto had been Caine's handler at the time. His final analysis of the operation was that Caine had played the various parties, including the CIA, and gone rogue. He had killed Tyler and taken the guns and drugs for himself, to sell on the black market.

In a follow-up report, Bernatto's intel suggested that the Leopards had tracked Caine to Indonesia and killed him in a retaliatory attack. General consensus around the CIA was, true or not, it was a tidy end to the story of a traitor. Caine was either dead or soon would be. He had too many enemies to survive for long as an independent operator. He was no longer a concern.

Rebecca remembered the night she had heard the news. The emptiness in the pit of her stomach. Sitting alone in her cold, silent DC apartment as she had sifted through the reports over and over. She had searched in vain for something, anything that could refute Bernatto's claims. But she had arrived at the inescapable conclusion that the man she had fallen in love with, the man she had shared laugher and memories and even her body with ... that man was a cypher.

His past, his background, family, friends ... all just shadows. She knew so little about him. She had never truly known Tom. And back then, she had thought she never would. He was gone. All she had left were a series of slim reports filled with damning accusations. Sketchy, fleeting glimpses of a stranger.

Now here she was. Thailand. Japan. Caine.

That look he'd given her, the anger and betrayal in his voice. That, she knew, was real.

By the time she reached the air-conditioned lobby of her hotel, she had made a decision: she was going to use this operation to uncover the truth about Caine, Bernatto, and Operation Big Blind.

On her way to the elevator, she noticed a man sitting in a lobby armchair, playing with his cell phone and reading a newspaper. She felt a ping in her subconscious. The man was young, late twenties, and white. Blond hair, blue eyes, chiseled features. He was wearing a Hawaiian print shirt, khaki pants, and work boots. The boots looked odd. She would have expected sandals or flip-flops this close to the beach.

She made a note to keep an eye out for him. Strange taste in footwear wasn't enough to set off her mental alarms, but she would have to be careful moving forward. This mission was off book.... She had no backup, no support. And if Caine's story was true, then Allan Bernatto was even more dangerous than she'd thought.

As the steel elevator doors clamped shut, she realized that, if that was the case, she had stumbled upon a secret Bernatto needed to keep hidden ... a secret he'd already sacrificed two CIA agents to protect.

CHAPTER ELEVEN

Caine sat in front of the small pachinko machine and twisted a pink plastic wheel, feeling vaguely ridiculous. The machine was covered with pictures of kittens and ice creams cones, and emitted a nonstop cacophony of electronic chimes and sugary pop music.

Earlier that morning, after a workout in the hotel gym and a traditional Japanese breakfast, he had made some phone calls to his old contacts. Yakuza bosses and lieutenants he had done business with, smuggling counterfeit jeans and purses through his operation in Thailand. Most seemed surprised to hear he was still alive. News of Lau's takeover must have travelled fast.

Like all criminals—himself included—they were a suspicious, paranoid bunch, and they all sounded vaguely uncomfortable to hear from him. The conversations were polite, but terse. Until they could figure out what exactly happened in Thailand, no one was going to give him what he wanted: a sit-down with Isato Yoshizawa. Isato was the *oyabun*, or leader, of the Yoshizawa clan, a powerful yakuza family based in Tokyo. They ran the local bukuto gambling trade in Kabuki-cho and other neighborhoods.

There was protocol to observe, in Japan more than most places.

Business deals could take weeks to close. Social meetings—to exchange business cards, share drinks, give gifts—were all part of the complex process. Each step followed its own rules of etiquette. In the underworld, things moved at a faster pace, but the principles were the same. There was an established order, a way of doing things. There were rules.

Caine didn't have time to wait. So he planned to change the rules.

As he twisted the pachinko wheel left and right, a stream of tiny metal balls poured into the machine. The wheel altered their speed, making them drop faster or slower, but the flow never ceased. Each tiny metal sphere would fall down the length of the machine, bouncing off a pattern of metal rods along the way.

If the speed and angle of the ball were just right, it would spill out an exit hole, into a plastic bin. If the ball hit a "jackpot" bar on the way down, it would trigger more balls to come pouring out, increasing the player's total ball count, and triggering flashing lights and music to emit from the machine.

The object of the game was to accumulate as many balls as possible in the winning bin. By hitting multiple jackpot bars, the final ball count could far exceed what the player started with.

Caine had chosen this particular machine not for its confectionary charm, but because it sat under a 360-degree security mirror. By looking up, he could observe the long, narrow room behind him. It was filled with flashing lights, blinking machines, and curiously sullen Japanese men who seemed to take no joy whatsoever in the lively, noisy game they were playing.

He continued twisting the plastic wheel, then stole a quick glance at the security mirror. Pachinko was mostly a game of chance and, like all games of chance, an underworld of gambling had sprung up around it. In this section of Shinjuku, pachinko gambling was controlled by the Yoshizawa clan.

That was why he was here.

Sure enough, a few minutes later, a pair of Japanese men sauntered into the parlor. They were clad in shiny sharkskin suits, their white silk shirts opened down to the chest. Their long hair was slicked back with pomade. A variety of chains and jewelry hung from their necks, and tattoo ink peeked out from either side of the open V across their chest.

Yakuza.

The two men made no effort to avoid jostling the gamblers as they navigated their way through the crowded room. Instead, the men and women at the machines shifted in their chairs or stood up and moved aside to make room.

The men stared at Caine as they walked past. His was the only Caucasian face in the parlor, so he knew he stood out. Caine smiled at them. One of the yakuza scowled, but the other returned his smile, an exaggerated leer, and dropped his hand to the left side of his waistband. Brushing aside his coat, he casually revealed the butt of a gun.

Caine watched as they walked past the redemption booth, where the manager of the parlor sat reading a manga. He put it down and bowed as the men walked past. They ignored him, disappearing through a red curtain hanging in the back of the room.

A loud, blaring buzzer and a blast of Japanese pop music distracted Caine. One of his balls had hit a jackpot bar. A stream of winnings cascaded out of the machine. The LCD screen burst into white light, then faded to black. A computer-generated graphic of an anime girl stepped onto the screen.

Her hair was neon green and spiked into a mohawk down the center of her exaggerated head. Floor-length pigtails spun and twirled as she danced to an upbeat pop song. The character picked up a microphone, belting out the lyrics in chirping, high-pitched Japanese. A heavily accented announcer spoke over the singing: "Ladies and gentlemen, Masuka Ongaku!"

The machine's light show flashed in time to the music. Caine shook his head and stood up. Only in Japan.

Caine pushed the call button at the base of his pachinko machine. A few moments later, an attendant came out from behind the curtain, grabbed his winning bin, and escorted him to the manager's booth. The young man dropped the bin on the counter, next to others Caine had accumulated throughout the day. The manager was once again buried in his manga. He looked up as a few errant balls rolled across the counter and fell to the floor.

He stared at Caine for a second, then dumped the balls into a funnel behind the counter. A computer counted the winnings and spat out a receipt from the cash register when it was finished. The man tore it off, read the number at the bottom, then handed it to Caine.

He turned and looked at the shelves behind him. Rows and rows of cheap electronics, random household items, and bizarre souvenirs stretched up to the ceiling. The mirrored wall behind multiplied them into a never-ending kaleidoscope of shoddy goods.

The manager stood on his tiptoes to reach a slim box on one of the higher shelves. Caine looked it over as the manager set it down. The writing on the box was in Japanese kanji, but the picture showed a DVD player of some kind. Caine placed his hands on the counter and stared the manager in the eye.

The manager squinted back, scratched behind his ear, then sighed. He produced several small, colorful plastic cards from a hidden spot under the counter and fanned them out on the glass countertop. He nodded his head towards the curtain in the back of the room.

Caine picked up the cards. "*Arigato gozimasu*," he said, dipping his head in a slight bow. At the back of the parlor, he parted the red curtain and stepped into a small concrete room.

Water dripped from a leak in the ceiling, creating a puddle on the floor. The attendant who had collected his winnings sat on a stool, slurping down some instant noodles from a Styrofoam bowl. At the end of the room, a wooden jam propped open the metal fire door. The attendant didn't even glance up from his meager meal as Caine walked past him and out into a long, narrow alley.

As he walked, Caine looked up at the edges of the buildings that towered over the narrow alley. His mental alarm bells were ringing. It felt like a good place for an ambush, but he saw no sign of any snipers above him.

He continued down the narrow passage. Ahead he could see flashes of green cabs and pedestrians, passing where the alley connected with the street. Just a few feet away was an entry to his right, a metal door painted over with several coats of thick, industrial grey paint. It was completely unmarked save for a small metal panel set in the center.

Perfect. The local tuck shop.

Gambling on pachinko was illegal in Japan, but the parlors, with a little help from the local yakuza, had found a way around that. Prizes could not be exchanged for cash in the pachinko parlors themselves, but winners could bring their tokens to hidden spots like this one. The yakuza bought back the prizes for cash and took a percentage of the winnings. They played the role of the "house," and, as usual, the house always won.

Caine stood to the side of the door, making sure it opened outwards and towards him. He knocked on the metal panel.

Nothing happened.

He knocked again. "Hey!" he shouted. "*Anta nana?*"

He heard the metallic fumbling of a latch on the other side of the door. The panel opened and a metal drawer slid out. Caine reached over and dropped his pachinko tokens in the drawer.

After collecting the winnings, the panel opened again, and the drawer slid back out. Caine grabbed a stack of yen from the drawer, slipping the thick wad of bills into the inner pocket of his blazer.

"Hey," he shouted in Japanese. "That's not enough. What are you trying to pull here?" It wasn't true, but he knew he had to get their attention if he was going to move up the chain to Isato.

A deep voice shouted back, "*Kiraina hito hanarete iku!*"

Caine couldn't help but smile. The voice had told him to go away, then called him an asshole.

"Give me the rest or I call the police!" Caine demanded.

He heard more fumbling behind the door, the sound of a latch turning. He pivoted his body towards the door as it swung open halfway. He used the momentum of his turn to launch a powerful kick at the door.

He heard a grunt of pain as the heavy metal door crashed into the person behind it. Caine immediately grabbed the edge of the money drawer, then yanked it backwards, ripping it from its socket.

The door bounced back open from the impact, and Caine stepped forward, kicking it open further. A man in a black suit staggered before him, blood gushing from his now-crushed nose.

Caine noticed two things right away. First, this man was not one of the yakuza who had walked past him in the pachinko parlor. And second, whoever he was, he was reaching across his blood-spattered shirt and slipping his hand into his jacket.

Caine charged forward, swinging the metal drawer in a powerful arc. The drawer knocked the man's hand away from the gun, then cracked into his chin. His head snapped back, blood spraying through the air.

He tried to take a step backwards, but Caine grabbed the man's shirt collar and pulled him in close. He drove his knee into the man's groin twice, while slamming the metal drawer into his left side, striking the solar plexus.

As the man crumpled, Caine heard a sharp crack.

Someone was shooting at him.

Using the incapacitated man to block the shots, Caine hunched low and surveyed the situation. At the far end of the room, another man in an identical black suit ducked behind a desk. Caine grabbed his hostage's weapon as the other man popped up from behind his cover.

Crack! Crack! The other man fired again. The sound was loud but muffled, like someone clapping in a soundproofed room.

Caine felt the impact as the bullets slammed into the human shield he held in front of him. His hostage was deadweight now, and he couldn't hold him up and still shoot. He let the body drop to the floor with a thud.

He was in fight mode now, his senses accelerated. Caine watched his assailant stand up from behind the desk in slow motion.

Caine hurled the drawer at him. The heavy chunk of metal flew through the air, smashing into the other man's shoulder as he raised his gun to shoot. The impact threw off his aim, and Caine felt the bullets slice through the air next to his ear. He held his ground, raising his own pistol in front of him in a double-handed grip.

Crack! Crack! Crack! The pistol barked in his hands. Three crimson holes burst open in the man across the room.

And just like that, it was over.

The room was silent, save for the distant sounds of traffic and the creaking of the metal door. It swayed on its hinges, open then closed. Open then closed.

Caine was panting. For a few seconds, he just stood there, looking around the room, observing the details.

He was surprised to discover four dead bodies in the room. In addition to the two men he'd fought, the two thugs who had passed him in the parlor were also splayed across the floor. Their clothes were riddled with bullet holes. Blood was everywhere. On the desk, on the floor, on the walls ... everywhere.

Caine took another breath, then kneeled next to the first yakuza. He patted the body down and removed a small but heavy Kimber automatic pistol, a wallet, and a cell phone.

He did the same with the other bodies. The other yakuza carried a similar cell phone, but was armed with a Spyderco folding knife. The other two men carried no ID or cell phones of any kind, just identical Beretta pistols fitted with silencers.

As Caine searched the body behind the desk, he noticed some scarring peeking out from under the lapel of his white shirt. Caine ripped it open, revealing an ugly pink mass of tissue that extended across the man's chest and up to his shoulder.

It looked like burn marks of some kind ... chemical or acid, maybe.

As he stood up, Caine realized the scars were in the same position as where a yakuza tattoo would be.

On the floor next to the dead man was a blue satchel, filled with yen notes. The safe behind the desk was open. It looked like someone, either the yakuza or the black suits, had been cleaning it out when the other party surprised them. Caine thought for a second, then grabbed the satchel. Using a handkerchief from one of the dead yakuza, he wiped down the weapons and phones, and put them back on the bodies.

He kept the knife, one of the phones, and one of the Beretta pistols for himself, stuffing them into the duffel bag. He opened the door a crack, looked left and right, then stepped out into the alley. He glanced back at the bloody scene behind him. Whoever came next to collect their winnings would receive quite a shock. Would they remember the tall Caucasian man who had gone before them?

Caine felt a tightening in his gut. Events were set in motion now. The clock was speeding up.

As he stepped out into the street, he spied a dark grey sedan about a block away. Something about it set off his radar. The windows were tinted so he couldn't see who was inside.

He paused and turned to look into a shop window, pretending to peruse the goods. As he stared at the rows of Masanuga sunglasses, he watched the sedan's reflection in the glass. Its engine was running. After a few seconds, it pulled away from the curb and joined the afternoon traffic.

Caine continued down the street, making a few random stops and turns along the way. The sedan did not reappear.

He pulled the yakuza's cell phone out of the duffel bag, dialing the number he had been calling earlier. A gruff Japanese voice answered. "*Hai?*"

"It's Waters. I need to speak to Yoshizawa-san. Immediately."

"I told you, Mr. Yoshizawa is a busy. He does not want to speak with you. Do not call here again."

"Check the number I'm calling you from. Trust me, Yoshizawa will want to speak with me." Caine slung the heavy duffel bag full of cash and weapons over his shoulder as he crossed the road.

"Tell him I have something that belongs to him."

He hung up, then dialed Rebecca's secure line from the cell phone.

After the electronic beeps that signaled a secure connection, the call went to voicemail. He thought about leaving a message, but decided against it.

He hung up and pushed forward into the crowd of Japanese pedestrians.

CHAPTER TWELVE

The Nagi Golden Gai ramen shop was small and cramped. Patrons had to wait outside until the chef called to them from a tube in the door. They were then directed to a vending machine to purchase tickets for the food they wished to order. Caine's selection—made from soy sauce, pork and chicken stock, and an astounding quantity of boiled sardines—nearly scalded his tongue as he swallowed a spoonful of broth. He savored the taste of vinegar and fish, then grabbed a clump of thick noodles with his chopsticks.

He turned towards the curtain that covered the entrance. Two men without tickets entered the cramped dining area. He knew they weren't here for the famous ramen. They were here for him.

One of the men looked like a J-pop idol. His hair, skin, and suit were all sleek and flawless. The other was older, his face like gnarled leather, his eyebrows white and bushy. The skin around his throat hung in folds. As they came closer, Caine recognized the world-weary face: Koichi Ogawa, one of Yoshizawa's most trusted aides. He looked up from his bowl and smiled.

"Koichi? Is that you? Goddamn, you look like shit, man!"

Koichi gave a thin grin, but the smile didn't travel to his eyes. The young man said nothing. He glanced at Caine with disinterest, then tapped the shoulder of the diner next to them. When the pudgy man saw who stood behind him, he mumbled, "*Sumimasyn*," and scurried away, back up the stairs to the street. Steam rose from his unfinished bowl of ramen and wafted into the heavy air.

Caine gestured to the empty chair. "Please, have a seat. Best shoyu ramen in Tokyo."

The young man laughed but did not sit down. He grabbed a pair of chopsticks, plucked some noodles from the abandoned bowl, and swallowed them with a loud slurp.

Koichi grimaced and rested an arm on the back of the empty chair next to Caine. His hands were calloused and dry, and Caine noticed one other odd detail.... Koichi was missing a finger. His pinky had been lopped off at the second knuckle.

"You said you have something for us, Waters-san?"

Caine took a long sip from an ice-cold bottle of Kirin beer. "I said I have something for Mr. Yoshizawa. I will give it to him."

Koichi nodded and peered at the duffel bag next to Caine. Caine shifted his arm, moving his hand closer to the slit he had cut in the bag. Inside, his gun sat loaded and ready.

"Very well," said the old man. "Follow me, please."

Caine sipped one last spoonful of his ramen, then stood up with the bag at his side. He gestured to the exit with his free hand. "Please, after you." They headed up the stairs, Caine sandwiched between the two yakuza men.

The late afternoon sun had taken on a hazy cast, slowly losing ground to the shadows that crept across the streets and buildings. Everything seemed tired and dreamlike in the receding light. The crowds had thinned out, and the streets were as close to empty as Tokyo got.

Koichi led the way to a maroon Toyota Crown sedan, a luxury vehicle that rivaled BMW and Audi imports. Caine whistled. "Very nice, Koichi! Coming up in the world, I see."

"It's not mine. Get in."

Caine got in the passenger side of the Crown. He watched as the younger man walked over to a black Nissan GTR sports car, parked ahead of them in the street. Known as a Skyline in Japan, its low, athletic stance and aggressive, straight lines resembled a hungry, black animal, a predator waiting to pounce.

As Koichi slid into the driver's seat, the GTR roared to life and tore off into the street, tires squealing. The smell of burnt rubber lingered behind. Caine moved the bag to his right side and slipped his hand into the slit. He felt the comforting weight of the Beretta in his fingers.

Koichi shifted the car into gear and pulled into traffic. Unlike the raw, menacing aggression of the GTR, the Crown's engine was smooth and powerful. It navigated the shadowed streets like a cruise missile wrapped in a mink coat.

"Who's the kid?" Caine asked.

Koichi looked over at Caine. "I'm surprised you don't remember. I'm sure you still have the scar."

"That was Kenji-kun?!" He shook his head. "I didn't even recognize him!"

Koichi kept his eyes on the road as the sedan cruised through the streets. "It's been years. He grew up. Things change."

Caine looked out the window as they drove. Evening was settling in. He could just make out the flashing lights of the Shinjuku bars and clubs through atmospheric haze.

"Some things do, but some things feel exactly the same."

He loosened his grip on the Beretta in the duffel bag. But he kept his hand close.

The drive through the city was uneventful. Once or twice, the hairs on the back of his neck tingled; he could have sworn they were being followed. But when he checked the rearview mirror, he was never able to catch sight of any pursuers.

He did spot a grey sedan, similar to the one he had seen outside the pachinko parlor. He saw it only once, and it was a common style of car, but it felt wrong ... and he knew to listen to his instincts. It followed their path for a few blocks. Then Koichi made a right turn, and the sedan continued straight. Caine flicked his eyes up to the mirror several times, but it did not reappear.

Thirty minutes later, Koichi drove them through the Roppongi intersection, past the Almond Coffee Shop. Caine noted that its famous pink-and-white striped awning was now housed in a modern, renovated building rather than the old one he remembered.

Koichi guided the luxurious sedan off the main road, into a labyrinth of tiny side streets and alleys. The car's tires rumbled over the uneven stone pavement. Finally, the car lurched to a stop, next to a red curb. Large signs stated "No Parking" in Japanese, but Koichi ignored them.

"*Ikimashou*," he said. "He is waiting for you."

Caine stepped out, looking up and down the alley. Loading docks and metal gates lined both sides of the dark, narrow street. A few small utility trucks and older cars were parked along the curb, but no one else stood outside. He spotted the black GTR parked ahead of them and smiled. *The kid can drive.*

As Koichi walked around the front of the car, Caine slipped the pistol out of the duffel bag and into his rear waistband. It was a calculated risk. They might search him, but he knew they would definitely look in the bag. Money was magnetic to these people.

Koichi stepped up to a large metal garage door and rapped three times with his knuckles. The door lifted with a grinding squeal. Two heavyset, scowling men stood on the other side. They nodded their heads, and Koichi turned to his guest.

"After you, Waters-san."

Caine stepped through the open gate into a large, bright room. It looked like a garage, but the concrete floor was covered with circular blue plastic pools, the kind suburban couples put in their yards for kids to splash in. The sound of running water echoed through the space.

Caine walked over to one of the pools and looked in. It was filled with clean water, and a clear hose snaked up from the floor into a large aquarium filter. Swimming through the bubbling water were five of the largest koi Caine had ever seen. Their metallic scales shimmered in hues of gold, red, and cream. They looked up at him, their eyes dark and mysterious, seeking only food.

An elderly man shuffled between the pools, looking down at the fish and murmuring in a soft, gentle voice. He wore a blue windbreaker and a tan baseball cap perched above his wrinkled brow. From time to time, he tossed fish food into the pools from a silver bucket.

Caine turned as Koichi stepped up next to him.

"Nice fish. Is that guy talking to them or himself?"

"He is singing to them. He believes it makes them grow larger."

"Looks like he's right."

Koichi turned his gaze back to the fish. "Waters-san, I must respectfully ask you to turn over your weapon. Then I will take you to see Mr. Yoshizawa."

Caine sighed and slowly slipped his hand into his waistband. Koichi didn't even flinch. Caine handed him the pistol.

"Careful with that gun. It's definitely hot."

Koichi nodded, then directed Caine to a door at the other side of the room.

The small, dark room beyond was lit by a single overhead lightbulb. The old floor creaked as Caine walked towards a table and chair. The walls were bare, except for a large hanging plaque of carved yew wood. Its intricate, chiseled lines depicted koi swimming up a waterfall and through an elaborate, temple-like gate. It was ornate and beautiful, and seemed out of place in the dark, spartan room.

Sitting in a chair beneath the carving was a short but stocky man, his face hidden in shadow. When he leaned forward, the light revealed black eyes glittering beneath a stern brow. His suit looked like it cost more than most people's cars.

Isato Yoshizawa.

Kenji Yoshizawa stood in the darkness behind him. He stepped forward and nodded at Caine.

Caine nodded back and walked over to the table. He did not sit down. He set the duffel bag of money down on the table in front of the elder Yoshizawa.

"This is for you, Yoshizawa-san."

The old gangster did not even look at the bag. His eyes remained focused on Caine's face.

"Waters-san. I did not expect to ever see you again."

Caine cocked his head. "Really? Somehow, I always knew I'd come back." As soon as the words left his mouth, he had no idea why he had said them.

"And so you have returned to Japan rob me?"

Caine's jaw hardened. "Rob you? Way I remember it, you're in my debt. *Giri*, right?"

Yoshizawa made a hissing noise as he sucked air in through his teeth. He shook his head. "*Baka Gaijin!*"

Caine smiled and pretended he didn't know the meaning of the insult. "Look, Yoshizawa-san, I recovered this from two men who were knocking over one of your Shinjuku parlors. I was there hoping to find Koichi, or one of your guys, and I stumbled across them. I figured bringing this money and information to you was the least I could do."

Yoshizawa sighed and gestured to the table. Caine sat down. Kenji leaned down close to his old man, whispering into this ear. The old man nodded and muttered a response only his son could hear.

"Kenji will have Koichi check your story, but I can already see in your eyes it is true."

Caine watched the young man leave. "He's grown. Good-looking boy."

"Yes. He is strong and smart. Certainly smarter than me. Too smart to waste his time in a dark, moldy old storage room like this. Kenji, I left some papers on my desk for you to address. Let me know if there are any problems."

Kenji stared at Caine for a moment, then turned and walked off into the darkness.

After Kenji left the room, Caine turned back to the old gangster. "So, why did you really ask him to leave?"

"I do my best to keep him away from all of this. And besides, I don't like discussing my obligations in front of others. I suspect you too have secrets you'd rather keep for now."

Caine shrugged. "I'm an open book."

Yoshizawa laughed. It was a brief, dry cough. "Please, do not insult me. Kenji may be smarter, but I am still no fool. The only reason you are still alive is because of the debt between us."

Caine moved his hand to his chest, rubbing the old scar beneath his shirt and jacket.

"Yeah, that debt feels pretty strong when it gets cold at night. Aches."

"Then we have much to discuss. First, tell me about these men you encountered."

Caine shrugged. "Local muscle. Black suits, automatic pistols. One strange thing, though."

Yoshizawa stroked his chin with his thumb and forefinger but did not blink. Caine continued. "Their bodies were burned or scarred somehow. Like they were covering something up. Yakuza tattoos, maybe?"

The old man nodded. "Yes, I have encountered these men before. They call themselves 'Tokyo Black.' They are a splinter group from the Shimizu family, our most powerful rivals. They hate their own family as much as us, feel that the yakuza has lost its way. They wish to return to the old ways, the ancient days of the secret societies."

Caine raised his eyebrows. "Secret societies?"

"*Hai.* For as long as Japan has had contact with the West, there have been those who have wanted to turn back the clock, to restore the old ways of feudal Japan. The Black Dragons fought to keep the Russians out of East Asia in the 1900s. And the Dark Ocean Society is even older than them. Groups like this have always had ties to the military, the government, even the yakuza."

Isato paused. He looked at Caine uncertainly. "These men, they swear allegiance to someone you are familiar with ... Bobu Shimizu."

Caine leaned forward. "Bobu? Wait, you mean the big guy, from—"

"Yes," Isato said, interrupting him. He turned his head and stared at the empty space where Kenji had stood earlier. "The man from that night, at the *izakaya*. The last time you were in Japan."

The old gangster sighed, and turned back to face Caine.

"I don't have all the details. From what I can gather, after his release from prison, Bobu killed his brother, Tetsuo, head of the Shimizu clan. There was some kind of power struggle between them. Then Bobu and his followers declared war on both the yakuza and the Japanese government, for failing to enforce hardline policies against China and others they see as enemies of Japan. They recruited as many of Shimizu's people as they could, then filled their ranks with the dregs of other families."

"And the scars?" Caine asked.

Yoshizawa made the sucking sound with his teeth again. "As I said, these men hate the yakuza as much as they hate the government. But they are all former yakuza themselves. To rise in the group, they must sacrifice their yakuza ties. They burn off their old tattoos with acid or welding equipment. Those who survive the pain are admitted to the inner circle and work with Bobu ... and whoever is behind him."

"How do you know someone is behind him?"

"Bobu is a thug, just muscle. He could never organize something like this. There must be someone pulling the strings."

Caine nodded. "Then it seems I've done you a great service today."

"What is that? Given me two bodies to clean? A bloodbath at one of my business establishments?"

Caine's eyes blazed in the dim light. "I've returned your money and identified your enemies. In addition to my other gifts."

The old gangster slammed his fist down on the table. The sudden, harsh movement startled even Caine.

"Enough! I know my obligation, and I have no wish to prolong it. Why have you come here? What do you want?"

Caine pulled his phone from his jacket, tapped the display, and slid it across the table. On the screen was a picture of Hitomi. "I'm looking for this girl. I need to find her. Quickly. I need your help."

Yoshizawa looked away from the phone but returned his gaze after a few seconds. "What would I know of this girl? Who is she?"

Caine hesitated, then shrugged. Yoshizawa would find out sooner or later. "Her name is Hitomi. Hitomi Kusaka."

"Kusaka? Arinori Kusaka?"

Caine nodded.

"I was not aware Kusaka-san had any children. At any rate, what would I know of a spoiled daughter of a wealthy man like Kusaka-san?"

"Yoshizawa-san, I need to locate her. I can't say any more. If you can help me find her quickly, I will consider your debt repaid."

The old man squinted at him and leaned back in his chair. "Why would you do this? What is she to you?"

"She's just a job. Someone wants her found, and I said I would do it."

"That's your only reason? Because you said you would?"

"Isn't that reason enough?"

Yoshizawa nodded and stood up. "I will make inquiries. Koichi will take you back to your hotel. Wait there."

Caine stood up as the old man turned away. "Why don't you let Kenji take me back? I'd love to see what that Skyline of his can do."

Yoshizawa shuffled into the darkness, shaking his head. He raised his hand in a dismissive gesture. "No, Waters-san. Koichi will take you."

There was the creak and bang of an old door opening and slamming shut, and then Caine was alone. He stood there for a moment, then turned and walked back the way he had come, to the light, the singing old man, and his fat, hungry koi.

CHAPTER THIRTEEN

Koichi was quiet as he drove Caine back to the hotel. Caine wondered what he was thinking but did not ask. He didn't want to break the silence.

When they neared the hotel, Caine pointed at the blinking red entrance sign to Kabukicho. "Drop me here. I'll walk back."

Koichi eased the car over to the side of the road. Caine tensed as the gangster slipped his four-fingered hand into his breast pocket. Koichi handed a small phone to Caine. "We will call you on this. Keep it with you."

Caine took the phone and got out of the car. He shut the door and watched as Koichi disappeared into the evening traffic. Then he flipped open his old cell phone and called Rebecca. After giving the proper sign-in credentials, he left her a voicemail. "I may have a lead. Need intel on Japanese nationalist-slash-domestic-terror group, goes by the name of Tokyo Black. I'll be in touch."

He hung up. As he walked back towards his hotel, he turned the evening's events over in his mind. He was fairly certain Yoshizawa knew something about the girl. He would not have offered to help otherwise. Caine also suspected that Yoshizawa knew "Mark Waters" had been an assumed identity ... a phantom designed to build credentials and a history in the Asian crime syndicate. Furthermore, the wily old gangster was smart enough not to ask who he really was.

The only question was whether he could trust Yoshizawa to help him and pay off his debt. Or did the old criminal consider his obligations null and void?

As he mulled over the possibilities, Caine felt the familiar tingle on the back of his neck. He ducked into the nearest well-lit store. It was a tiny Japanese sex shop cluttered with glossy images of schoolgirls and geisha, AV movie flyers, and rubber genitalia. An old woman behind a glass counter nodded and smiled.

Caine smiled back and picked up a magazine. He slid several hundred yen across the counter. "Keep the change," he said as he peered out the door. No one had followed him in. The woman jabbered at him, trying to force his change on him, but he ignored her. He rolled the magazine into a tight tube, then headed back out onto street.

As he walked, his sense of being watched increased. He stopped again and leaned against a wall, flipping through the pages of the magazine. Every now and then he glanced up, taking in his surroundings like quick snapshots. Woman in a blue dress. Two scrawny young guys. Old man with a camera. Nothing definite, nothing that pinged his inner radar.

Then he saw it. Across the street, a grey sedan with tinted windows pulled into a loading zone. There were hundreds of cars like it in Tokyo. But Caine knew this one was here for him.

He rolled up the magazine again and continued walking. As his eyes flicked across the mass of faces up ahead, he caught sight of a Japanese man in a grey suit. He was taller than the average Japanese male. His posture was perfect; his gait balanced. The man was walking slower than the rest of the crowd, occasionally stopping to peer in shop windows.

To Caine, he stood out. He felt wrong.

Forward tail, Caine thought.

Caine waited until the man turned and walked forward again. Then he ducked into the first doorway on his right. A dark stairwell led to a basement of some kind. Faint music drifted up as he descended into the shadows. Once his eyes adjusted to the dim light, he saw a red curtain at the end of the stairs. He parted the soft velvet with his arm and surveyed the bar beyond.

Dark wood, warm candlelight, and plush upholstery met his gaze. A woman's voice sang softly in the background. The notes of slow acid jazz floated over the murmur of hushed conversations.

As Caine took a seat at the bar, a young bartender slid over to take his order. He was a good-looking kid. He looked to be in his early twenties, with an intricate, spiked haircut. It looked like a work of modern art. "What can I get you?" he asked in English.

"Johnny Walker Blue, rocks."

Caine swiveled the chair to watch the entrance, but the curtain did not part again. Keeping one eye on the door, he assessed the various faces scattered across the room. They were young, hip, and blandly attractive. Most were Japanese, but he spotted a few Caucasians here and there.

The bartender set his drink down on a cocktail napkin. Caine paid cash, never taking his eyes off the entrance. The song ended, and, for a few seconds, he could make out the low, staccato chatter of men and women talking. The language was Japanese, but the sounds were the same as every bar in every part of the world.

The music started up again. He felt a puff of hot breath by his ear. A woman's voice, quiet but not a whisper, spoke.

"Are you waiting for someone?"

Caine swiveled around so quickly he almost spilled his drink. Sitting on the stool next to him was a Japanese woman with thick, lustrous hair that fell down past her shoulders in a gentle wave. Somehow he hadn't noticed her sit down. Very few people could sneak up on him, especially when he was on the lookout for danger. He feigned confusion; he was just a tourist who had consumed one drink too many.

The woman nodded towards the curtain. "I noticed you watching the entrance. You didn't even see me sit down. I thought you might be waiting for someone."

Caine shook his head. "No, not at all. Just spacing out, I guess."

The woman tilted her head and gave him a curious look. "Oh ... too bad. I was thinking how nice it would be to have someone waiting for me like that." She smiled, but it looked wrong. More like a trap than a flirtation. When she blinked, he felt like he was being scanned by a pair of cold, black camera lenses.

"Since you're alone, why don't you buy me a drink?"

Caine imitated a drunken leer, taking in her long legs, small waist, and the gentle swell of her breasts beneath the lace of her cocktail dress. When she crossed her legs, he could just barely hear the rustle of the fabric as it slid against her creamy, coffee-colored thighs.

"My pleasure," he said. He figured the woman was either what she appeared—a bored, lonely single looking for a free drink—or perhaps a prostitute. But there was another possibility. If the man outside had been a forward tail, Caine might have been made. The car, the tail, they might have been herding him to this location. In which case, his best option was to play the situation as normal as he could. Make them think they had the wrong man.

And normal men, alone in a bar, did not refuse drinks with beautiful women.

He gestured for the bartender and smiled at the woman. "I love this kid's haircut. Maybe I should get one."

She giggled, a light titter like most Japanese women. But again, the eyes were hard and cold. There was an intensity there she was unable hide.

"I don't think it would suit you." She reached up and brushed a stray lock of hair on his forehead into place. "That style is too young."

Caine laughed as the bartender approached. The woman ordered in Japanese, and he hurried off to make her drink.

"Are you calling me old?"

"No, not old. But not young either."

Caine sipped his whiskey, the cold ball of ice clinking against the side of the glass. "Just right?"

The woman shrugged. "Could be. What's your name?"

Caine thought for a second, taking another sip of scotch to mask the delay. He decided to go with the identity he had given the hotel. "John. John Wilson. And you?"

"Mariko." She gave her strange, forced smile again. The bartender returned with her cocktail, and Caine had it added to his tab. The young man nodded and moved away, leaving them alone at the bar. She took a sip of her drink, a light golden cocktail made with whisky, brandy, and apricot bitters.

"Thank you," she said. "It's delicious."

He slid enough yen to cover her drink across the counter, then turned his stool to face her.

"Mariko, it was lovely meeting you, but I'm afraid I must be going. My wife is waiting for me back at the hotel."

She sipped her drink.

"Liar. You're not married."

"What makes you say that?"

"I just know." She looked up at him, her eyes a pair of black holes in the dark space of the bar. Her pupils were singularities, their gravity pulling him in, deeper by the second.

He wondered if it was too late to escape. Had she trapped him here? Was this where he unraveled into a single frayed thread? Was this where it all fell apart?

"You don't like me?" she asked.

"I don't think I can afford you."

She pursed her lips. "With your friends, I wouldn't think that would be a problem. Assuming I was for sale, of course."

Dammit. Looks like option three. This meeting had been set up from the beginning.

"From what I hear," she said, her voice matter of fact, "Mr. Yoshizawa is quite generous to his close associates. Money, drugs, girls...."

Caine looked her in the eye, but her dark, black pupils gave away nothing. They merely studied him with mild curiosity.

"I'm sorry. I don't know who you're talking about. You must have me confused with someone else."

She took another sip of her drink. "That's certainly possible. Things can get very confusing, where these people are concerned. So, you don't know Mr. Yoshizawa?"

Caine said nothing.

The woman shrugged. "Then, as you say, I must have confused you with someone else. Do you play pachinko, Mr. Wilson?"

The pachinko parlor. The bodies....

"I'm sorry, Miss...?"

Her lips curled into a bitter, sarcastic smile. "Smith."

Caine smiled back. "Mariko Smith?"

She nodded. "Yes. I know it's a rather dull name, Mr. John Wilson. But at least it's simple. Easy to remember."

Caine stood. "Well, Ms. Smith, I'm afraid I really do have to go. Enjoy the drink."

"I will. Thank you. I hope we can run into each other again."

"Somehow I doubt that, but you never know."

As he turned away, she whispered into his ear, "*Ja, Mata.*" See *you later.*

He looked her over one more time. "*Sayonara.*"

As he walked back to the curtain and up the dark stairs, he hoped the goodbye was as final as he intended.

He stalked the streets surrounding Kabukicho for nearly an hour, but saw no signs of the Toyota sedan, or the man in the grey suit, or Miss Mariko Smith and her lace dress.

CHAPTER FOURTEEN

Ethan eased back in his chair as the girl on his screen twirled around. Her skirt lifted up as it spun through the air, revealing the curves of her body underneath. Ethan moved closer to the screen.

"Oh baby, that is beautiful. What's your name again?"

"I'm Ashley," she said in a breathy voice. She was employed by a one-on-one video chat service Ethan liked to use when he felt the need to relieve stress. It ran a little over two dollars per minute, but the cost was immaterial, of course. He had hacked their billing software. All his charges were forwarded to a secretary at the EPA who had stood him up on a date once.

"What do you want to see next?" Ashley asked.

Ethan gulped as her fingers crawled up her inner thighs....

BEEP! BEEP! BEEP!

He jumped in his chair as the small black window covered the images on his screen. Red letters typed out a short message:

SECURE CONNECTION REQUEST. RF-07716. STATUS: MOUNTAIN

"Crap," Ethan muttered. Ashley and her lovely behind snapped off his screen. He initiated a homemade program that tagged the video call with a virus. In a matter of seconds, all records of the exchange erased themselves from the chat company's servers.

He turned his attention to the chat window that had interrupted his fun and tapped a response on his keyboard.

SECURE CONNECTION INITIATED. DR-23748. STATUS: ORIOLE

The black box was replaced with another video chat window. Rebecca stared back at him with a curious look on her face.

"Ethan, you okay? You look a little red."

Ethan laughed as he adjusted his glasses and ran his fingers through his hair. "Yeah, yeah, boss. All good. Just working on some, ah, some reports."

She glared at him suspiciously. "Right. Look, are you alone? Is this connection secure? I mean, airtight secure?"

"Yeah, definitely. End to end encryption, my own algorithm. What's up? Your guy find the girl yet?"

Rebecca looked hesitant. "No, not yet. The op is in progress. But there are some ... irregularities. Some things I need you to look into. Off the books."

Ethan cracked his fingers like a pianist and grinned. "Off the books is where I do my best work. Ask and you shall receive."

Rebecca nodded and looked off screen for a second. She bit her lip, then turned back to Ethan. "Okay, two things. One is intel for the op. I need you to see if you can dig up any mention of a group called Tokyo Black. Splinter group from the yakuza, but politically oriented. Rightwing, nationalist leanings. Check the usual sources. Propaganda websites, extreme rightwing politicians, hate crime records, you know."

Ethan scribbled the words on a notepad on his desk. "Tokyo Black. Sounds like a punk rock band. What else?"

"Ethan, this is sensitive. You have to be careful. Do you understand? No one can know about this."

Ethan blinked, then smiled. "Come on, Rebecca, you're freaking me out. But look, I'm the Digital Ninja. I live in the internet's shadows. If I don't want someone to see me digging, they won't see me digging. It's that simple."

"Right. Except, you were caught once. That's why you work for me."

"I wasn't caught; I was entrapped. There's a difference. And you may be a pain in the ass for a boss, but you beat life in federal prison."

She nodded. "Okay. The operative we found, Thomas Caine. Bernatto doesn't know about him, right?"

"Nope. I purged all records of his arrest like you said. He hasn't turned up on anyone's radar but ours."

"Good. I need you to look into his last assignment. Operation Big Blind. Some things don't add up."

Ethan sighed. "Rebecca, that was what, eight or nine years ago? God only knows how much that intel was massaged, cut, redacted. Even if I can find anything, verifying it will be next to impossible. No one wants to dig up that skeleton again."

"Impossible? Even for the Digital Ninja?"

Ethan laughed. "This Caine guy got under your skin, huh?"

"Ethan, please. It's personal."

"Okay, okay, I'll see what I can do." Rebecca opened her mouth to speak, but he cut her off. "Yes, yes, I'll be careful. I'll be an invisible wind, a shadow in the night, a—"

"Ethan," she interrupted.

"Yeah?"

"Don't ever watch porn in my office again."

He gulped. "Right. Sorry, boss."

Rebecca smiled as she reached forward to sign off. "Thanks, Ethan." She tapped some keys, and her image disappeared from the screen.

Ethan sighed and leaned back in his chair. He shook his head before tapping away on the keyboard once again. He opened a new secure connection. Once he had received the proper call sign-in, he typed another short message.

SHE'S DIGGING. WE NEED TO MEET.

Birds chirped and squawked as they soared above the thick forest trails of Theodore Roosevelt Island. Ethan was no nature expert, but he was pretty sure the brown bird circling overhead was a hawk or some other avian predator. He watched as it lazily drifted by the clearing where the remains of an old manor house lay sunken in the ground.

He huffed and puffed in the cool air. The island was accessible only by foot, via a small bridge on the Virginia Bank, and he was unaccustomed to traversing such distances. The forested island served as a monument to Theodore Roosevelt's love for nature and the untamed wilderness. No cars and bikes were permitted anywhere on the grounds, and there were no roads—only long, winding dirt trails, pounded to a smooth surface by decades of use.

He shifted his backpack on his shoulders as he peered down into the sinkhole. It was covered in vines and tangled weeds, but he could spy signs of cracked, weathered fieldstone lining parts of the sunken pit. The house had belonged to some old banker named Mason. A fire had destroyed it long before the United States government took ownership of the island. Years of weather and neglect ate away at the remaining walls and structure. This hidden foundation was all that remained of the old house, save for an occasional fragment of old china washed up by the rain.

He heard footsteps crossing the grass and vegetation behind him. A tall man in a black overcoat approached.

Bernatto.

Ethan stood in silence and jammed his hands in his pockets as Bernatto walked up to him. For a few moments, they stood together, staring into the deep hole.

The hawk soared above, a dark shape against the blue sky. There were few other visitors on the island this late in the afternoon. The shriek of the bird rose above the distant rumble of traffic on the Roosevelt Bridge.

Bernatto turned and stared at Ethan. "Well?"

"You said to let you know if she started digging, if anything seemed out of the ordinary."

"Get to the point, Ethan. If you called me, something must be up. Don't waste my time."

"Look, we had a deal right? I do this for you, act as your eyes and ears on this op, and then I'm out. No more cyber-crimes unit. No more ratting out my old hacker friends, no more restricted computer access. I'm free to start over."

"You did the right thing, Ethan. Everyone deserves a second chance. This is an important operation. I need to make sure everything goes according to plan. You help me take care of this, I'll take care of you."

"Good. Something's got Rebecca spooked. She's asking about some kind of Japanese terror group, something called Tokyo Black."

Bernatto stared at him. "Go on," he said, his voice low and flat.

"Well, I don't know how they fit in with this girl you want found, but I dug up some information about them. They're like the Japanese version of our wack job militia groups, you know? Some yakuza guy got radicalized in prison. Gets out, comes home, decides the yakuza have lost their way. Feels like they've lost touch with their roots, they don't represent Japan anymore, or the Japanese people.

"So, he puts a cap in his brother's ass, takes over the family chapter, and turns them political. Low-level, domestic stuff. Kidnappings, extortion, a few bomb threats at government buildings. They say they want to unite Japan against China and their other common enemies. Japan is destined to be the Asian superpower, that kind of stuff. They start turf wars with the other yakuza families, steal their money, weapons ... anything to keep the group running."

Bernatto nodded. "Fascinating, but that sounds like Japan's problem, not mine."

Ethan pulled a manila folder from his backpack. "There's more. I

93

know you didn't want details on the asset. Deniability, right? See no evil, hear no evil?"

Bernatto glowered at him, his teeth clenched. Ethan handed him the file folder.

"Right, well, this guy we found ... I think you should take a look. I've never seen anything like it. Aside from his operational record, half of which is blacked out, he's a ghost. No background, no history, no military record, nothing. It's like he just popped up at CIA headquarters one day and started killing people. For all I know, he's a freaking terminator robot you guys built."

Bernatto took the file but didn't open it. He looked out over the dark hole of the old foundation and squinted. "What's the asset's name?"

"He surfaced in a Thai prison under the name Mark Waters, but that was just a cover ID. Rebecca said his real name is Thomas Caine. You know him?"

Bernatto nodded and opened the file, flipping through the pages without reading them. "Oh, yes, I know Thomas. Mr. Caine is a very dangerous man."

"Sure. Well, he's a spook, right? So now, Rebecca is digging into this old operation of his. Something called Big Blind. She asked me to go through a bunch of files about it. It's full of holes, man. Lots of conclusions, lots of supposedly dead people. But no bodies. No evidence. Lots of black marker, you know what I mean?"

Bernatto folded the file in half and slid it into his inner coat pocket. "Is this everything?"

"I mean, that's all I found on Caine. The Big Blind files are on Rebecca's office computer."

Bernatto looked up at the hawk. "Do you know why I picked this spot, Maslin?"

"Old dudes love to walk?" Ethan grinned.

"This island is a sanctuary. A peaceful, idyllic monument to nature." Bernatto held out his arms and took a deep breath. "But did you know that after the U.S. government took over this island from the Mason family, it was used as one of the first weapons testing sites in America?"

"They didn't mention that in the brochure."

The old man smiled and went on. "In the Spanish–American War, they used this island as a testing ground for the electrical ignition of dynamite. For the late 1800s, that was cutting edge weapons tech. Way ahead of its time."

"Yeah, real bleeding edge."

"Underneath all this beauty and nature, there's death and decay," Bernatto said. "Behind peace, there is war, and blood, and sacrifice. Always."

Ethan stepped back. "Look, man, that's all I got. We had a deal so I called you, but I have to get back."

Bernatto laughed. "Like you said, I'm an old man. I have a taste for history. Indulge me, for a minute. You see those fieldstones down there? Did you know Mason, the original owner of this island had them imported from Scotland? He said he always wanted his homeland beneath his feet."

Ethan leaned over the pit. "Really? Seems like a lot of trouble for your basement."

Bernatto clamped a gloved hand around Ethan's mouth and slid a black tanto blade knife out of his coat. He thrust the straight, flat blade forward, punching the weapon into Ethan's struggling body. The young man screamed, but Bernatto's vise-like grip across his face muffled the sound.

The blow didn't strike any major organs, but the wound gushed blood, pumped by Ethan's panicked heart. Bernatto whipped out the blade and placed it along the soft flesh of his victim's throat. He sliced left to right, then kicked the body forward, into the hole.

There was a loud crack as Ethan's head struck one of the broken stones. His body rolled over, and his glazed eyes rolled back in their sockets. Blood continued to bubble and flow from the gaping throat.

"George Mason wasn't Scottish, you idiot," Bernatto hissed.

He wiped the blade clean on the dirt and pocketed the knife.

Then he walked back towards the footbridge that connected the island to the mainland.

As he passed the island plaza and the majestic bronze statue of Teddy Roosevelt pointing towards the sky, he pulled out his cell phone. "Hello? Yes, I need to book a ticket on your first flight out to Pattaya, Thailand."

CHAPTER FIFTEEN

The *izakaya* pub in Osaka is dark, smoky, and loud. Caine throws back a glass of sake. The rice wine is expensive, and he knows it is a waste to shoot it like cheap tequila. But the Japanese men surrounding him all laugh and cheer. *"Banzai!"* they shout. Caine laughs and slams the tiny glass down.

The surface of their table is buried in empty glasses, bottles of liquor, and food. Platters of takoyaki octopus balls, tempura, udon noodles, grilled meats ... it is a small feast to celebrate their partnership and the profitable deal he has brought to them.

Isato Yoshizawa sits next to Caine. He's chosen an expensive navy blue suit and a white silk shirt for the occasion. Most of the gangsters in Caine's company have shed their jackets and unbuttoned their shirts. But not Isato. He is the oyabun. He commands respect.

Across from them is Koichi, indifferent to the ruckus around him. Caine finds him impossible to read but feels distrust in the old man's stare. Caine gestures and makes a joke, but the pub is so loud he can't even hear his own words. Shaking his head, Koichi gets up from the table. Two of his lieutenants stand and follow. He lights up a cigarette and navigates his way through the crowded bar.

Caine leans over to Isato. "I don't think he likes me."

The oyabun smiles. "Give him time. Koichi is old-fashioned. He is wary of working with barbarians."

Caine shrugs and pours another finger of scotch into Isato's glass. "Well, I'm glad you're more open-minded."

"One must stay current or become obsolete. I want the next generation to inherit a strong family. Still, it is difficult for old gangsters like us to catch up."

Caine senses movement at the front of the izakaya. Some sort of commotion. Isato's smile fades as Caine's hand dips towards the opening in his suit. A small child bursts out of the crowd near the entrance and runs towards Isato, smiling. Caine sighs and his hand falls back to his side. He knows this boy. It is Isato's son. Kenji Yoshizawa.

The effect on Isato is mesmerizing. The stern old man transforms into a proud, grinning father. Caine watches as Isato lifts the boy up on his lap while a stately Japanese woman rushes towards them. Rioko, Kenji's maiden aunt, bows slightly to Caine, then deeper to Isato.

"*Gomenasai!*" Rioko says. "He ran out of the hotel room. I had to chase after him!"

Isato laughs, tousling the young boy's hair. "He knew we were just talking about him! My son is a smart boy, eh?"

At the far end the izakaya, the manager and some of the patrons stare at the child with disapproval, but no one says a word. Isato whispers something into the boy's ear, and his face turns pensive. Isato kisses Kenji on the cheek, then shifts him off his lap, handing him to Rioko. The boy takes her hand, and they push their way towards the front of the izakaya.

"What did you say to him?" Caine asks.

Isato sips his scotch, hesitant. Finally, he answers. "I told him he was the future, both for me and for the yakuza. And that, someday, he would know what that truly meant."

Caine shakes his head.

"Heavy stuff."

"Not for him. He has my blood. And my love. There is nothing he cannot do."

Caine holds up his glass. "To the future." The pair clink glasses and drink.

As the aunt leads her nephew to the exit, Kenji looks back at Isato. The old man smiles, and Kenji breaks free of Rioko's grip.

Time seems to slow to a crawl.

A figure appears over Rioko's shoulder, a mountain in a grey sharkskin suit. His black hair is swept back into a small, tight bun, like a sumo wrestler. Half his massive face is covered by a snarling tiger tattoo. Caine has never met this man, but he knows who he is from the CIA briefing reports. Bobu Shimizu. A member of the rival Shimizu crime family, and brother to the Shimizu oyabun.

Bobu settles a cold, lifeless gaze on Isato, then shoves Rioko out of the way. He is holding a gun.

As Caine struggles to his feet, his reflexes dulled by alcohol and a lack of sleep, Kenji runs to his father. Isato stands and opens his arms wide, oblivious to the danger. Bobu aims the gun, and Caine runs to intercept Kenji, pushing hapless bystanders out of his way.

Isato looks up and locks eyes with Bobu. Their faces freeze in snarls of mutual hatred. Bobu's thick finger tightens on the trigger. Kenji runs into the line of fire. The boy skids to a stop, frightened by the angry look on his father's face.

Caine slams into Kenji. He grabs the boy and pivots around, putting himself between the boy and Bobu.

Bobu fires. The gunshot reverberates like an explosion in the small bar.

Caine gasps as the bullet tears into him. He falls to the ground, clutching Kenji in his arms. The terrified child kicks and screams, trying to get away. Caine holds on, despite the bullet wound in his shoulder. He winces in pain, but he does not let go.

Koichi and his men rush back in. The bar patrons scream and scatter for cover as Koichi draws a gun of his own, aiming it at Bobu.

Isato rushes over and pushes Koichi's gun hand up towards the ceiling.

"No, you idiot! No more shooting! Get Kenji out of here!"

Koichi grabs Kenji from Caine's arms. Caine's field of vision narrows. A black haze closes in from all sides.

The last thing he remembers is Bobu glaring at him in a cold rage. His tiger tattoo seems to roar with deadly fury. The combination of the man's ferocious face and grim stare is horrifying. He reminds Caine of an *oni*, the red-skinned demons that deceive and devour humans.

As Bobu turns and flees the bar, Caine falls into the sweet embrace of unconsciousness.

Caine woke from the dream slowly, tentatively. He willed himself to consciousness. The darkness lifted, replaced by a dim light creeping between the curtains of his hotel room. He felt like a man pulling himself out of quicksand. One step at a time.

He sighed and rubbed the sleep from his eyes. All the nightmares of his past seemed to be returning one by one. Their dark touch lingered on his mind.

Caine forced himself out of bed. After a brutal workout in the hotel gym, followed by breakfast and a scalding hot shower, he felt like he had finally escaped the lingering unease left behind by his dream. *Not a dream*, he thought. *Memories*. He rubbed the small white scar on his shoulder. The past had left its mark on him. It would not let him forget.

With nothing else to occupy his time, he flipped on the TV and watched the news. All the stations were reporting the same story. The prime minster of Japan had given a speech criticizing China for military escalations surrounding the Senkaku Islands. The speech was in Japanese, but a flat, monotone English translation chased his words.

"Both sides recognize that they have different views regarding the tense situations arising in recent years in the waters of the East China Sea, including those around the Senkaku Islands. But we do not consider this a territorial dispute. There can be no dispute over facts, and it has been acknowledged again and again that these islands are the sovereign territory of Japan. Rather, we believe there is a dispute over the causes behind the recent growth in tensions around these islands. And for this, we feel it is clear that provocative activities by China are to blame."

According to the newscaster's recap, the U.S. Secretary of State was flying in to mediate a sit-down between officials of Japan and the People's Republic of China. Caine shook his head and turned off the TV. *Unbelievable. All this over a bunch of uninhabited rocks in the middle of the ocean.*

A buzzing sounded from the nightstand next to his bed. There was a text message on the phone from Koichi: "We have information for you. I will pick you up at 8:00 p.m."

He erased the text.

CHAPTER SIXTEEN

The tiny internet cafe by the beach was simple, clean, and fairly busy. A few local teenagers, a vacationing businessman or two ... the clientele was typical for a spot like this.

Rebecca scanned the crowd one more time. Nothing seemed out of the ordinary, so she reached into her woven beach bag and removed a black USB dongle. Turning back to the computer in front of her, she inserted the device into a port on the machine. An icon popped up on the screen, and she double clicked it.

The tiny USB device instantly created a secure link to the network she used to reach Ethan. For the third time that day, she opened the black window and tried to initiate a chat.

SECURE CONNECTION REQUEST. RF-07716. STATUS: ARCHIPELAGO

She took a sip of her Singha, pretending to be just another well-to-do professional on holiday. The cursor blinked silently on her screen.

There was no response.

Shit.

She glanced around the cafe one more time. Certain no one was observing her, she yanked the dongle from the computer and the chat window blinked out of existence. Rebecca deleted her history on the machine, then got up to leave.

Outside, bikini-clad girls ambled down Soi 5, heading for the beach. Neon green and yellow motor scooters buzzed along the road, gleaming in the overhead sun like shiny beetles humming through the air. In her tank top, shorts, and oversized tortoiseshell sunglasses, Rebecca blended into the throng of beachgoers. The gold bangles and woven bracelets adorning her arms jingled as she walked.

After the air-conditioned chill of the cafe, the sudden blast of afternoon humidity felt good on Rebecca's skin, but her face was still contorted in a troubled scowl. Ethan could be flaky, but it wasn't like him to just disappear like this. *Hell*, she thought, *the guy practically lives in front of a computer.*

She was just about to try calling him again when the phone rang inside her bag. She picked it up, expecting to see a message from Ethan. Instead, it was an unfamiliar international number. Japan. Caine.

"Hello?"

"It's me," said Caine.

Rebecca was annoyed to find herself comforted by the sound of his voice.

"I figured. Still reading that Basho?"

"No, I finished that one. Figured I'd try the Murakami book you recommended."

"Can't promise you'll like it," she answered. "New number. You must be going through a ton of burner phones."

"Yeah, well, privacy has its price. And it may be cheaper than the alternative."

She nodded in silent agreement. "Any luck with the girl?"

"I have a lead. I'll let you know if it pans out."

"Good. The clock is ticking. Did you get the info I forwarded you?"

"Yes. Tokyo Black. Your report jives with my intel here."

"How are they involved?"

"I'm not sure they are yet, but our paths have crossed." Caine paused. "You sound stressed. Everything okay?"

"I'm fine." She sighed. "It's probably nothing, but...."

She trailed off, unsure what exactly to say.

Caine's voice cut in, sharp as a knife. "But what? What's wrong?"

"My information specialist. Ethan Maslin. He's a hacker the FBI busted a couple years ago. He cut a deal to work for the CIA."

"What about him?"

"Well, he sent me the info on Tokyo Black yesterday. The files I forwarded you." She paused, listening, but there was only silence and static on the other end of the phone. "And I haven't been able to reach him since then. I'm sure it's nothing, but—"

"It's not nothing," Caine cut her off. "These hacker guys love to brag. Did he tell anyone about this operation? Did he tell Bernatto that I was your asset?"

"No, of course not. I had him delete all the records. And I'm telling you, Bernatto doesn't want to know."

"Don't be so sure. Is that everything?"

"Yes. Well, maybe. I don't know. Yesterday I saw this guy at my hotel. Something about him felt off. I don't know why, but he felt military to me."

"Rebecca, this Maslin guy ... what else did he dig into besides Tokyo Black?"

Rebecca looked down Soi 5. She saw a group of three men moving towards her. They looked to be a mix of ethnicities, probably Thai and Indonesian. They were wearing khaki pants and cheap t-shirts. One of them had a limp, and another had a colorful tattoo on his arm. The tattooed man stared at her as they came closer. The street behind them simmered with rippling waves of heat.

Rebecca turned to her right and headed down the beach road, away from the cafe.

"What do you think, Tom? I had him look into Operation Big Blind. That report is bullshit, and we both know it."

"Dammit, I told you—"

"You told me a lot of things, Tom. Maybe if you would just tell me the truth, I wouldn't need to go looking for it myself."

"Rebecca, I didn't tell you because you were better off not knowing," he snapped. "Why the hell do you think I stayed away in the first place?"

"It's a lie, isn't it? You didn't kill Tyler. You didn't take the drugs and the guns. Bernatto did and set you up to take the fall."

Caine sighed. "We can talk about it later. Right now, you have to get out of Thailand. Get your ass in a cab and go straight to the airport. Leave your things, just go."

Rebecca looked behind her. The three men continued down Soi 5, past the beach road, laughing and catcalling at pretty girls as they went by. They didn't even look in her direction. She took a deep breath and realized her heart had been racing.

"Tom, we're on mission. Bernatto may be dirty, but this intel is real. We can't just—"

"I'll handle it. Just get the hell out of Thailand. If Bernatto knows you're there, it's not safe. Promise me."

"Maybe you're right. I'll go. But keep me informed."

"I will, I promise. Contact me when you're somewhere safe."

He hung up.

Rebecca stepped out into the street to hail a cab. A few seconds later, a small blue taxi weaved its way through the beach traffic and pulled up to the curb. As she got in, she debated if she should go back to the hotel to get her things. Then she remembered the sharp edge to Caine's voice. It was fear. He was afraid for her.

"Airport, please."

The driver smiled. He was missing a tooth. "U-Tapao airport? Take about forty minutes in this traffic. Fifteen-hundred baht, okay?"

"That's fine."

She cracked her window, letting the warm breeze wash over her as they pulled away from the corner. She felt her heartbeat slow down. It was the fear in Caine's voice that had triggered her rush of adrenalin.

Was it possible? Was Bernatto a traitor?

There is another possibility.... Maybe I'm only seeing what I want to see. Maybe Caine was guilty. Maybe he was playing her; maybe he had been all along.

She knew that, in her profession, the truth was a luxury. Exotic, hard to obtain, and not without expense. But she was determined to seek it out, no matter what it cost.

The taxicab sputtered to a stop at a four-way intersection. The road ahead was blocked by a mass of traffic. Idling engines and honking horns replaced the gentle sound of waves crashing on the beach. Rebecca craned her neck out the window but couldn't see past the blockade of cars.

"What's wrong? Why are we stopping?"

The driver shook his head. "Look like accident. I bet you it's another tour bus. They crash all the time. Roads very bad here, miss. Eighty people die here every day in traffic accidents!"

"Is there another route we can take?"

The driver tapped some buttons on the smartphone suction-cupped to the windshield. "Let's see how bad it is.... Maybe we take side street and loop around."

Rebecca watched as the driver called up an alternate route. The car shuddered as he put it back into gear. "Okay, bingo! Hang on; we need to turn around." He looked over his shoulder, and the car whined as he backed up.

Rebecca saw his eyes go wide and his jaw drop before she heard the brakes screeching. She had just enough time to turn before the hood of a huge black SUV filled the rear windshield.

The impact crumpled the rear of the taxi and launched her forward into the air. For a fraction of a second, she felt weightless, as if she were hovering above the rear seat of the taxi. She heard the sound of shattering glass and squealing metal. Then her head struck the back of the driver's seat. The impact snapped her back, and she collapsed on the rear floor of the vehicle. Shards of glass rained down on top of her.

Blood streamed from a gash on her face. She tried to move her head, but the muscles in her neck screamed in pain. She called out to the driver.

"Are you okay?" Her voice was a hoarse croak.

There was no response.

She heard sirens in the distance. They grew closer. Within a few minutes, flashing lights reflected across the shattered windows of the vehicle. She heard voices, footsteps. Grinding metal.

How did they get here so quickly?

The crumpled door to her left ripped open. She felt strong, firm hands grasping her, pulling her from the wreckage. The hands lifted her onto a stretcher. The sun beamed down overhead, an uncaring orb of fire, bleaching the scene of the accident in a curtain of white light. She squinted, unable to look at it.

"I'm okay," she mumbled. "I'm fine. I have to go."

A man in a paramedic uniform leaned over her. He lifted her eyelids open and shined a small flashlight into her pupils, first left, then right. He nodded, then buckled a nylon strap tight across her abdomen.

She tried to resist as he buckled similar straps around each wrist, but she knew her efforts were pathetic. She felt a needle slide into her arm. "Wait..." she said, her voice faint and weak.

The paramedic looked down at her. The sun cast a halo of fire behind his head, reflecting on his blond hair. She had seen him before.

It was the man she had spotted at the hotel.

He spoke into a small microphone at his throat. "Package is secure. Condition stable but injured."

As her vision faded to black, she realized two things. She had finally discovered the truth: Bernatto was obviously dirty. Caine had been right.

And he had been right about something else as well.

She was in terrible danger.

CHAPTER SEVENTEEN

Caine stood outside the Shinjuku Prince Hotel. The night air was crisp, and he zipped his leather jacket a bit higher. Around him, an anonymous crowd of businessmen, families, and tourists came and went. The lights of Tokyo glittered against the night sky.

He tried to keep his mind off Rebecca. He should have known she would investigate his old file. He chided himself for revealing as much as he had. If Bernatto knew he was alive, knew that he had spoken to her....

He stopped that train of thought before it could consume him. Right now, he had a job to do. Rebecca was leaving Thailand. With any luck, by the time she got to safety, this would all be over. And if Bernatto did suspect her, then Caine's best course of action was to get his hands on something Bernatto wanted. And right now, for reasons unknown, that was Hitomi.

He checked the watch on his wrist. It was 8:15 p.m. He remembered Koichi being more punctual.

A guttural roar emanated from the street below, so loud it drowned out the taxicabs and limousines idling by the hotel entrance. Tires squealed around the corner, and a black sports car streaked towards him. Caine took a step back as the vehicle zoomed up to him and screeched to a halt.

The driver's door of the black GTR swung open, and Kenji stepped out, smiling. "Hey, man. Heard you liked the car...."

"She's a beast all right. What happened to Koichi?"

Kenji grinned like a Cheshire cat. "He'll meet up with us later. Here...." Kenji tossed him the car keys. "Why don't you drive? See what she can do."

Caine looked at the keys, then back at Kenji. "Your dad know you're here?"

Kenji walked around to the passenger door. "Anyone ever tell you you ask too many questions?"

Caine smiled and slid into the driver seat. "Occupational hazard."

He pushed the ignition button on the dash, and the engine roared to life like a snarling tiger.

Kenji looked over at him. "Yeah? What occupation is that?"

"Now look who's asking questions."

Caine depressed the brake and moved the shift lever into position. Stepping on the gas, he revved the engine to 4,000 rpm. Kenji smiled with approval. "Looks like you know what you're doing."

"Sometimes, kid. Sometimes."

Caine released the brake. Six-hundred horsepower shot through the car's transmission in the blink of an eye. The GTR launched forward, tearing out of the hotel driveway.

"Head north," Kenji said. "Follow the Chuo main line."

Caine downshifted and sped past a local tofu delivery truck. "You want to tell me where we're going?"

"Ikebukuro. We got word your girl went to see a *yonigeya* there."

"A what?"

"A *yonigeya*. It means 'fly by night arranger'. They help people in trouble disappear."

Caine kept his eyes on the road. "What kind of trouble?"

Kenji fished a toothpick out of his pocket and wedged it in his teeth. He rolled it around absentmindedly as he looked out the window at the passing lights. "Oh, you know. Loan sharks. Gangsters. People like that."

Caine was silent.

"Anyway," Kenji continued, "when they get in too deep, a *yonigeya* can help them smooth things over. In extreme cases, they pose as window washers or lawn workers. They enter a house and smuggle their clients out of town. Set them up with new lives. Obviously the yakuza keeps close tabs on such people." Kenji pointed to a traffic sign as the GTR streaked past it. "Take the next exit."

Caine drifted right and sped up a ramp onto a winding freeway. The glowing lights flicked by faster and faster as the car got up to speed.

"Kind of like a private witness protection."

Kenji nodded. He looked at over at Caine. "You know, I have to say, I never thought I would see you again. I wasn't that young, but I barely remember that night."

Caine maintained his forward gaze, scanning the road. "You were young enough. And I'm sure you were in shock."

The young man nodded. "Yeah, sure. I've heard all the stories, though. I mean, you took a bullet for me. I feel like I should at least, I don't know, thank you or something."

Caine gave Kenji a quick glance. "Kenji, that was a long time ago. Forget it; you don't owe me anything."

"How can you say that? I might not be here if it wasn't for you. You know Koichi, he felt so guilty he cut off his own finger. My dad didn't even ask him to; he just did it. Said he should have been there, but he wasn't. You were."

Caine shook his head. "No matter how much time I spend here, there are some things I will never understand about this country."

Kenji laughed. "Yeah, right? I understand it, though. Honor, duty ... all that samurai bullshit. I grew up hearing stuff like that from my father nonstop. This great legacy that was going to pass down to me, like it passed from his father, and his father, and so on and so on."

"That's a lot to lay on a kid's shoulders," Caine said. "Looks like you went your own way though."

"I didn't have a choice. After that night, you know, the one who was really in shock was my dad. Suddenly, everything I'd heard my whole life ... leading the yakuza, being the next oyabun, honoring the family ... that was all over. Like that." Kenji snapped his fingers. "He's kept me at arm's length ever since."

Caine shot Kenji another quick glance. "Kenji, you can't blame your father for being concerned. He almost lost you. Of course it was a shock."

Kenji stared at him, his eyes wide and intense, probing. "Have you ever felt like that, though? Like your whole life, everything you believed was true, everything you thought was going to happen ... it just disappears, in less than a second. You don't know exactly how or why. You just know it was taken from you. Do you know how that feels?"

Caine swallowed. When he spoke, his voice was thick and heavy. "Yes, I do."

Kenji looked away from Caine and stared out the window. "I went to the best schools, got the best grades. Got a Western education. I've successfully managed all my father's legitimate finances. Hell, if he'd let me, he could make more money from investing than all this petty yakuza bullshit. But he loves it. It's his family."

"Kenji, you're his family."

"True. But that night, it was like, his family was split in two. And if push came to shove, if he had to choose...."

Kenji's voice trailed off. "Whatever. Anyway, I'm glad I got the chance to thank you. But there's always one thing I wanted ask."

Caine nodded. "Go ahead."

"What made you do it? I mean, you met me, what, three or four times before that night? It's not like you and my dad were friends or anything. You took a freaking bullet for me! Was it to impress my dad? Did it help make your deal or something?"

Caine sighed. "Kenji, I don't know. I can't say why I did what I did. I just reacted and did what came naturally. At that moment in time, I didn't think about it. But I thought about it later. I thought about it a lot."

"Yeah?"

"Yeah. And believe me, if anyone should be thanking anyone, it's me. Look, you must realize, this life, people like me and your father, it's not all fast cars and duty and honor and parties. Sometimes, too many times, we have to do things that ... well, things that can haunt you. Things we would rather forget. But we can't."

"*Kurayami no haji wo akarumi ni mochidasu na,*" Kenji said.

"I'm afraid your English is a lot better than my Japanese." Caine kept his eyes on the road as he weaved around some slower-moving traffic.

"It's an old saying. It means you must keep the shameful things you've done in the dark. Not expose them to the light. Keep it buried, inside."

Caine nodded. "I have a lot of secrets buried in the dark. But what I did that night ... that's something I don't have to keep buried. It takes my mind off things when the darkness gets to be too much. And I'd gladly do it again, in a heartbeat."

Kenji nodded. "Well, thank you."

"You're welcome." Caine looked over and smiled. "You father really doesn't know you're here, does he?"

Kenji looked away. "No, he doesn't. Just one more thing he doesn't know about me."

Kenji didn't speak again, and they drove on through the night in silence.

CHAPTER EIGHTEEN

By the time Caine and Kenji reached Ikebukuro, a light rain began to fall across the sprawling district. Caine slowed down, cautiously maneuvering the powerful sports car through the congested city streets. As the raindrops spattered on the pavement, the roads became sleek and reflective, like long ribbons of black satin.

They drove past the Ikebukuro station, the third largest train station in the world. Caine had to marvel at the size of the place. Buildings in Japan always seemed smaller in scale than their Western counterparts. But here, the buildings were massive. The Seibu and Tobu department stores, the towering Sunshine 60 entertainment complex ... everything was bigger, larger than life. Their glowing lights reflected off the wet pavement, bathing the car in flashes of red, green, and purple neon as they passed. It was like driving through a galaxy of bright, colorful stars.

As they circled around the station, Kenji provided brief, simple directions. Soon they reached the outskirts of the area where the lights were just as bright, but almost entirely red. They had entered Ikebukuro's unofficial Chinatown, a small enclave that had sprung up north of the station. Signs for Chinese restaurants and businesses hung from balconies and beckoned from dark basements.

Kenji led them down a dark alleyway behind a small office building, just off the main street. Each floor of the building housed a different business. The signs were in Chinese, but the occasional English word—such as "Passport" or "Laundry"—was printed in bright yellow letters.

"This is the place," Kenji said.

Caine slowed the car to a stop. They got out, and Caine followed Kenji down the alley and around to the main street.

The building they were parked behind was flanked by similar structures on the left and right. A street-side cafe filled the ground floor of the left building. It sat beneath a huge red sign, with blinking Chinese characters.

Koichi sat on a stool at the cafe, eating a bowl of dumplings. Caine recognized them as *xiaolongbao*, Chinese soup dumplings. Each delicate pouch of dough was filled with cooked pork and a delicious sweet broth.

Koichi looked up at Caine and Kenji. "What took you so long?" A trickle of broth dripped from his mouth, which he wiped away with a napkin.

Caine smiled and looked around the packed cafe. Several Chinese and Japanese patrons sat at the counter, all devouring the same pork dumplings. They ate at a rapid pace, scooping up the little pouches and sucking them into their mouths with loud slurping noises.

"The news keeps talking about tension between Japan and China," Caine said. "But you both seem to have the same lousy table manners."

Koichi stood up and tossed some yen on the counter. "What do I know about politics? I just like the dumplings." He nodded at Kenji. "Here, you can finish."

"But—" Kenji began, but Koichi gave him a stern look.

"If your father knew you were here with me, he would take another finger. That would make things very difficult in my line of work."

Kenji sighed and sat down in front of the steaming bowl. "*Hai.* Have fun."

Caine and Koichi walked through the misty rain towards the center building. Kochi spoke to him in a low voice. "Ikebukuro is Kyokuta-Kai territory. The Yoshizawa clan was in a feud with them, but Isato brokered a peace several years ago. Now, our mutual business is too profitable to squabble over such things."

"Well, I'm glad you're one big happy family now."

"When Isato put the word out about this girl you're looking for, one of their members said she had been seen visiting the yonigeya here. They keep an eye on his office in case he tries to help someone skip out on a debt to the Kyokuta."

"Fly by night arranger. So, if this girl was looking to run, who was she running from?"

Koichi gave him a thin-lipped smile. "I assumed from you, Waters-san."

Caine shook his head. "I don't think so."

Koichi opened the door, and they walked into a small, dirty lobby, its Formica floor yellow with age. Next to the elevator sat an old Chinese man in a frayed brown windbreaker, eating from a plastic bowl. Between slurps of noodles, the man spoke a few words in Japanese, and Koichi nodded. "He says the elevator is broken."

"Stairs it is."

Koichi opened a stained white door with a crumpled lunar calendar tacked to the front. Behind the door they found a flight of rickety wood steps. As they started up the stairs, Caine felt a tightness in the pit of his stomach. They were entering unfamiliar territory.

"Any chance I could get my gun back?"

"I thought you might ask, Waters-san." Koichi reached behind and pulled the Beretta Storm from his waistband. "Careful. As you said, this gun is hot."

Caine slid out the magazine to confirm it was loaded. Then he slammed it back in, racked the slide, and flipped the safety off. He noticed Koichi had drawn a small Colt defender pistol from inside his jacket. Caine could see where the stub of his pinky finger ended, unable to circle around the small weapon's grip.

"Koichi, Kenji told me about that night, what happened. I'm sorry about—"

Koichi sucked in air through his teeth, making a hissing sound. "Now is not the time, Waters-san. And you have nothing to be sorry for."

"Right. Okay, let's just say when this is over I owe you a drink."

"When this is over. Now, the man we are looking for has an office on the fourth floor. His name is Naka."

They continued up, passing the second floor without incident. As they reached the third floor, the stairwell door burst open. Caine's hand shot towards his waistband but stayed there. A young Chinese man stumbled down the stairs, holding the hand of a giggling girl in a short, sparkling dress. As she brushed past them on the stairwell, she muttered something in Chinese and the man laughed.

Caine looked at Koichi, and the older man shrugged. "There's a massage parlor on this floor. She thinks we're cops. Bad for her business."

They continued up the stairwell. Caine's eyes narrowed and focused. His movements became smooth and graceful, like a stalking cat. He was a predator now. And this man, Naka, was his prey.

The fourth floor was dark and deserted. Doors flanked the short hallway to their left and right. They were marked with Chinese characters, but Caine had no idea what they said. Koichi pointed towards a single door facing them at the far end of the hall. The door was unmarked, but a frosted glass panel was set in the center. Caine couldn't make out any detail behind the window, but he could tell the lights were off inside.

Caine turned the knob. The door creaked open.

As they stepped into the room beyond, Koichi reached for a light switch. Caine put his hand on the old man's shoulder to stop him. He pulled a small penlight from his leather jacket and flicked it on, keeping his hand cupped over the bulb. He let the small pinprick of light dance over the office as their eyes adjusted to the darkness. Koichi grunted, and they both drew their weapons. Caine crept along the wall, keeping to the edge of the room.

"Looks like someone had the same idea we did," he said.

The beam of the flashlight revealed overturned chairs, open file cabinets, and papers littering the floor.

The office had been ransacked.

A safe in the wall, behind a now-empty bookshelf, hung open. Its contents were strewn across the floor like confetti after a New Year's Eve party. A massive mahogany desk—a bit too grand for its dingy surroundings—sat in front of a large window. Through the window, Caine could see the Ikebukuro lights in the distance. They twinkled behind the dark, jagged skyline of the buildings across the street.

Caine and Koichi crept past a glass partition in the middle of the office. A small sitting area lay behind the frosted glass. A pair of cheap sofas, their vinyl surfaces marked with stains and cigarette burns, flanked a small coffee table. A cracked ceramic ashtray perched on top of a stack of magazines. It was filled with butts and ash. Caine bent down and sniffed. Koichi gave him a strange look.

"Smoked recently," Caine whispered. He looked up, noticing a small closet door in the corner. The Japanese writing on the wooden door said "Supplies." Caine pointed to his eyes, then the door. Koichi nodded and held his gun out as they stalked forward.

They flanked the door on either side. Caine reached down and twisted the knob. The door swung open about an inch, and something heavy shifted. The closet door crashed open. Caine stepped back, Beretta pointed at the door. A large object toppled over and fell into the room with a thud.

Koichi gasped. It was a body.

Caine knelt down and examined the corpse. It was a Japanese man in his thirties. His ripped, tattered clothes hung off him like rags on a scarecrow. His face was unrecognizable. It was covered in cuts, bruises, and some marks Caine suspected were burns.

"He was tortured," Caine muttered. "Who the hell did this, Koichi? What's going on here?"

Koichi shook his head. "Waters-san, I swear I have no idea. Someone didn't want him talking to us."

"So, who knew we were coming here tonight?"

Koichi looked back and forth between the body and Caine. "I don't know. I must call Yoshizawa-san."

"Wait," Caine said. "Let's get our facts straight first. I'll search the body. Check the desk. See if you can find anything on Hitomi."

Koichi headed over to the desk. He rustled through papers as Caine dragged Naka's corpse into the center of the room. He patted down the body. The man's wallet was still in his back pocket. Caine flipped it open and found the usual contents: a driver's license, some random business cards, and a few thousand yen. "They left his money," Caine said. "This wasn't a robbery."

"Was there any doubt?" Koichi answered back.

Caine patted down the man's pockets again. He looked around the floor of the closet. There was nothing there other than boxes of printer paper and other supplies. The bottoms of the boxes were soaked by a thick pool of blood.

"Koichi, I don't see this guy's cell phone. He has to have one, right?"

"This is Japan. Three-year-olds have cell phones. Maybe he left it in his desk?"

Caine heard a click, and the room filled with light. Koichi had turned on a desk lamp. Caine blinked. The light was dim, but in the dark office, it was almost blinding. As his eyes adjusted to the light, Caine saw a diffuse red glow sparkle across the frosted glass divider.

It could be nothing ... a trick of the light? Perhaps his eyes were still adjusting to the sudden brightness? But as Caine stood up, he felt the familiar tingle and knew to trust his instincts.

He stepped out from behind the divider, raising the Berretta in a double-handed grip. He aimed the weapon towards Koichi and pulled the trigger.

CHAPTER NINETEEN

BLAM!

Koichi looked up in shock as Caine's gunfire blasted over his shoulder. The bullet pierced the window behind him, sending a spiderweb of cracks through the large pane of glass. Koichi raised his gun towards Caine, but before he could even aim, a second shot rang out. This time the retort was quiet, distant, from across the street. The window exploded into a shimmering curtain of falling glass shards.

"Get down!" Caine shouted.

Koichi dove to the floor, revealing a pencil-thin beam of red light tracing through the office. Caine fired again, and the desk lamp exploded in a shower of sparks. Once again, darkness engulfed the room.

Koichi cursed in Japanese as Caine crawled across the floor, dragging Naka's corpse behind him.

"That shot, Waters-san. You scared the hell out of me!"

"I saw the laser sight. There wasn't time to warn you. I figured cracking the glass might throw off his aim."

"I just thought you were a bad shot."

"By the way, this may not be the best time, but you should know my name is not Mark Waters."

Koichi and Caine flanked the window, keeping low. "I thought as much," Kochi said, "but is there something else you prefer I call you?"

Caine thought for a second, then shrugged. "Not really."

The sniper's beam continued to dance across the room. It drifted through the darkness like a cobra, swaying in the air before delivering a killing strike.

Caine shoved Naka's body across the floor to Koichi. "When I give the word, let's give this guy something to shoot at. Understand?" The old man nodded. Caine waited until the laser sight disappeared again. "Okay, now!"

Koichi gripped the man's body by the scruff of his neck and heaved the corpse up onto the windowsill. The laser sight blinked back on and darted towards Naka's body. Caine peered around the corner of the window. He saw the flash of red across the street, on the rooftop of another building. Its blaze gave away the sniper's position, huddled behind a rooftop air conditioning unit.

The shooter fired again, the bullet thudding into Naka's dead body. Koichi hissed as the impact knocked the corpse backwards. Before the body even hit the ground, Caine stood and aimed his gun towards the roof of the building across the street. The laser sight snapped towards him, but before it could settle, Caine opened fire. He emptied the Beretta's clip in a wide pattern, sending a hail of bullets at his hidden enemy.

The laser sight dipped down as the sniper took cover. Caine dropped back down below the level of the windowsill. Koichi peered around the corner of the window. "He's moving!"

Koichi opened fire. Caine turned and saw the dark figure on the roof burst into a sprint. Koichi's bullets kicked up tiny explosions of dust at the fleeing man's feet, but the shots did not hit their mark.

"*Kono Yarou!*" the old man cursed, his face twisted into a snarl. "The little shit is heading for the fire escape!"

"Give me your gun! Do you have another clip?"

Koichi looked at him in disbelief. "I'm not running away from this piece of shit coward!"

"Kenji is still downstairs! You have to get him out of here!"

Koichi's face clouded. He handed over his pistol and an extra clip of ammo he pulled from his shoulder holster rig.

"You're right, Waters-san. Good hunting."

Caine grabbed the gun and ammo and jammed them in his waistband. He sprinted towards the emergency exit on the other side of the room. He threw open the door and found himself high above the dark alley behind the building. The metal stairwell creaked and shook as he ran out onto the balcony. To the right, he spied a water pipe running parallel to the fire escape. Without hesitating, he grabbed the pipe and stepped off the fire escape.

The rusty metal pipe was slick with rainwater, and he slid faster than he was expecting. The peeled, flaking paint tore and bit at the skin on his hands. He grit his teeth and grabbed the pole tighter, slowing his decent as he neared the ground.

When he hit bottom, he fell from the pipe and rolled across the pavement. Gasping for breath, he staggered to his feet and drew the Colt. As he ran around the corner of the building, he ejected Koichi's spent clip and slammed in the new one.

He burst out onto the street and jogged towards the other building. His hands were bloody and sore, making it hard to keep a firm grip on the pistol, but the pain was worth the head start he'd gotten on his adversary. He could see the dark figure across the street, just making it to the bottom of the fire escape.

Next to the office building, a bewildered Kenji waited alone behind the now-abandoned dumpling stand. "Hey, man, what the hell is going on?" he yelled. Caine ran past him into the street, splashing through the puddles that filled the cracked pavement.

Caine raised the pistol, taking aim at the dark figure now dropping to the ground. Traffic screeched to a halt as cars skidded around him on the wet streets. Before he could fire, a sleek red car streaked in front of him, blocking his shot. The man jumped into the passenger seat, and the car sped around the stopped traffic.

Caine swore until he realized he still had the keys to Kenji's GTR. He turned back to the young man. "Koichi's on his way down. Go with him!"

"Yeah, but what about my car?"

Caine ignored him as he sped back to the alley.

CHAPTER TWENTY

The black GTR tore out of the alley like a stealth fighter, screeching into the wet city streets.

Caine was just in time to see the taillights of the getaway vehicle as they sped away from the building and rounded a corner. He stepped on the gas. The engine's growl shifted to a high-pitched wail as the powerful car pursued its prey.

He clenched his jaw as the steering wheel vibrated in his hands. The GTR's tires squealed as he drifted around a corner, but they held their grip on the slick, wet pavement. His quarry's rear lights grew closer, as the two vehicles raced towards Ikebukuro station.

Caine realized he was chasing after the new Acura NSX, a 550-horsepower supercar. His Nissan maintained a slight edge in power, but the Acura was more nimble ... and at these speeds, the slightest mistake would cost him his target. And quite possibly his life.

Closer to the train station, the NSX shot through an intersection. It looked like a curved stiletto perched on massive racing wheels, and all heads turned as it flew by. Caine growled as the light changed. A crowd of shoppers and pedestrians wandered out into the street, heading for the mall on the right.

He jerked the wheel to the side. The car smashed through a thin metal railing dividing the highway from the lanes to the left. It crumpled the barrier as if it were cardboard. A shower of sparks shot up in the air behind him, as the car caught and dragged a twisted scrap of metal along the ground. Caine turned the wheel again and swung around the crowd of people with inches to spare. He had just enough time to make out the shocked expressions on their faces as they watched him blaze past.

The car shuddered as the metal fragment dislodged and fell to the ground. The maneuver had cost him distance, but he could still see the Acura ahead. It sped around more traffic and pedestrians, then darted towards an exit off the freeway. Caine followed. Glancing down at the dash, he saw the speedometer creep towards ninety miles an hour. He caught a brief glimpse of a street sign before it became a blur in his rearview mirror; they were heading towards the Yamate Tunnel.

Part of the Shunto Expressway, the eighteen-kilometer underground tube was monitored by traffic cameras at regular intervals. Caine knew it would not be long before they attracted the attention of the police. For a moment, he considered giving up the chase. If he were arrested, Rebecca would not be standing by to bail him out again. Plus, Bernatto would learn that Caine was alive, if he hadn't already.

Instead, he stepped on the accelerator, closing the distance between him and the Acura. His instincts drove him to pursue. The people in that car had known he would turn up at Naka's office, had been waiting there for him. There was a good chance they had been the ones to search the office, which meant they might have Naka's cell phone—the next link in the mysterious chain that led to Hitomi.

He had to follow.

The Acura sped right, entering the twisting, banked curve of the tunnel entrance. Caine slid the GTR to the shoulder of the road, speeding past the commuters waiting their turn to enter. The road dipped down. Caine's stomach fluttered as his car dove into the tunnel opening and the dark, rainy night disappeared behind him.

The tunnel was massive. Its grey concrete walls were illuminated by orange bursts of light that flashed overhead. The roar of the GTR and the high-pitched whine of the turbo-charged Acura merged in an unholy mechanical scream. As they shot past the traffic at the entrance, the cars behind them slowed to a crawl. For a brief second, they were alone in the tunnel, like two shiny bullets racing down the barrel of a gun.

Here on the smooth straightaway of the tunnel, Caine's powerful GTR had the advantage. He closed the gap, pulling up next to the Acura. He saw the driver glance over at him, his brow furrowed in determination. Caine turned his eyes back to the road. A sea of blinking red taillights filled his view; they had caught up with the tunnel traffic.

The Acura broke away, darting around a group of slower-moving cars. Caine braked to avoid slamming into a Toyota van. He jammed his fist down on the horn as he jagged left and right, looking for an opening in the traffic. A white Mercedes driven by a perfectly coiffed young lady pulled over, letting him pass. She gave him the finger as he sped by.

Up ahead, he spotted the Acura's distinctive taillight bar. The traffic had forced its driver to slow down as well. The car's racing tires squealed as it swerved around a green-and-white taxicab. The cab slammed on its brakes, letting the Acura zip past. Caine darted left, barely sliding past the stopped vehicle. He heard the sound of metal grating against metal. His passenger-side mirror flew off as it scraped against the side of the cab.

He breathed a quick sigh of relief, then stamped back down on the gas. As he gained on the Acura, the traffic ahead slowed to a stop. Up ahead, two lanes of the tunnel merged into one. The single lane crawled forward to the left. A barricade blocking some road construction closed off the right lane. Beyond the barricade, the tunnel branched off into an exit.

Caine sped around a motorcyclist riding a Kawasaki crotch rocket. He was now neck and neck with the crimson Acura. They were running out of room, the split in traffic just a few hundred yards ahead. Caine chanced a quick glance at his adversary. The driver was staring straight ahead, not watching him. Caine clenched his jaw, braced himself, and threw the wheel to the right. The GTR slammed into the Acura at triple-digit speed. Both cars wove back and forth as they struggled to regain control. The GTR's all-wheel drive regained its grip first, and he slammed into the Acura again.

Both cars drifted right, towards the barricade. With a crash of splintering wood, they exploded through the barrier and charged down the closed tunnel exit. The unfinished section was barely lit at this hour. Between the pools of darkness, Caine saw flashes of construction equipment, stacks of metal pipes, and piles of debris.

Caine's car shuddered as the Acura swerved over and slammed into him. *Well, all's fair,* Caine thought as he struggled to keep control of his vehicle. The Acura slid towards him again. His rear wheels began to fishtail as the two cars crashed together. When they separated, bits of metal and trim fell from the cars and clanged behind them on the pavement.

In the hazy orange glow of the work lights up ahead, Caine saw a forklift. It was parked in the center of the unfinished exit lane. He straightened the GTR out and charged towards it. The driver of the Acura glared at him and sped up, keeping pace beside him. Caine looked over to see the driver jerk the wheel towards him again. But this time, Caine was ready.

He stepped on the gas and jagged right. The two cars scraped sheet metal, but Caine was able to keep his position. They continued speeding towards the forklift. He saw the menacing twin metal prongs of the lift platform, suspended in the air like blunt metal fangs.

He wove back and forth, keeping his distance from the Acura. *The timing has to be perfect,* he thought. He watched the Acura's driver, saw him glancing back and forth between him and the road.

He straightened the car out and relaxed his fingers on the wheel, anticipating his enemy's actions. *Now!* his brain screamed.

As the Acura driver once again jagged the wheel to the left, Caine slammed down on the brakes with both feet. The car shuddered, its anti-lock system struggling to engage. As Caine's speed plummeted, the Acura slid left into empty space and shot in front of him.

Before the other driver could react, Caine slammed back down on the gas. In less than a second, the speedometer shot back up to triple digits. Caine's car lurched forward and rammed into the rear of the Acura. The other driver struggled to control the car as it surged forward from the impact.

As Caine spun his wheel to the left, he sped past the Acura and saw the driver look up in horror. The NSX plowed straight into the forklift. As the two metal bodies collided, the twin prongs of the lift sheered the roof off the sports car. With a horrendous metal crash, the body of the car crumpled. The mass of fused metal flipped over into the air, slamming back down with an echoing clang.

Caine winced at the sound. He hit the brakes, his car skidding to a stop. He took a deep breath and removed his hands from the steering wheel. He waited until they stopped shaking. After a few seconds, the adrenalin racing through his body subsided.

He opened the door and jogged over to the wreckage. The stench of gasoline and burning metal assaulted his senses. He knelt down next to the remains of the Acura. It was almost impossible to tell where the sports car ended and the forklift began.

Caine peered into what remained of the cabin. The blades of the forklift had punctured the front airbags. The white cloth of the bag draped over the driver, concealing his mangled face. A light dust of talcum powder covered his clothes. Caine patted down his body but found nothing of interest. The man had been wearing a black suit, and his arms were scarred and burned but the wounds weren't fresh.

He moved on to the passenger. The man wore similar clothing, now ripped and torn. Caine opened his shirt, revealing the same burn marks on his shoulder and chest. He was certain now. These men were Tokyo Black.

Reaching into the man's jacket, he found two cell phones that had survived the crash. He slid them into his pocket and looked back at Kenji's car. The beautiful GTR's black paint had been scraped off on the passenger side. Long red streaks from the Acura's paint ran the length of the dented and dinged metal body. The vehicle could be easily tied to this crash.

"Sorry, Kenji," Caine muttered to himself.

He drew his pistol and fired a barrage of shots into the gas tank. A stream of clear fluid began to puddle beneath the car. Caine picked up a piece of burning debris from the Acura and hurled it at the gathering liquid. The gasoline ignited. Within seconds, flames engulfed the GTR. A thick cloud of toxic black smoke filled the tunnel.

Caine passed through a nearby evacuation door into a narrow, dim corridor. As he closed the door, the car exploded in a cloud of orange flame behind him. The fire crawled towards the Acura, consuming both the wreckage and the bodies inside.

CHAPTER TWENTY-ONE

The sun warms her back as Rebecca jogs along the wooded trail. The autumn leaves rustle in the air above her, whispers of red and orange. When she looks around, the colors are all she can see. Is that a tree? An old windmill ahead? The details fade, lost in a shifting haze of muted brilliance.

Then Caine is there, waiting for her at the end of the trail. She can just make out the green of his eyes. She runs towards him, fighting to catch a glimpse of him through the veil clouding her vision. Her feet pound along the path, but the carpet of dead leaves absorbs all sound. Is she getting any closer? She can't tell. His voice calls to her.

"Rebecca, it's time to wake up."

She blinks, and everything changes. The mattress underneath her naked body is firm and warm. Caine's hands cradle her gently. Dawn's first light drifts in through the window. The autumn colors are replaced by the chocolate silk of her duvet, the soft white of her cotton sheets. Caine is next to her, behind her, perched above her. She rolls over and stares into his eyes.

He looks troubled. She caresses his cheek. "What is it?"

He looks away. "I have to go soon." His voice is quiet. Hesitant. "I won't be able to see you for a while."

She tilts his face back towards her. "Is it a mission?"

He smiles, but the lines around his eyes are tense. He always looks awkward when he has to tell her the truth. "You know I can't talk about it."

She looks at him, confused. The words and the colors are jumbled in her mind. Nothing makes sense.

Chocolate brown, bright orange, crimson blood, soft white.

She rolls over. Her arm reaches out, but her fingers brush against cold, empty sheets. His body is gone. *He was just there*, she thinks.

Where has he gone?

"Rebecca, it's time to wake up."

"I have to go."

"A disgrace and a traitor."

"If Bernatto knows...."

Rebecca's eyes fluttered open.

Towering before her stood the man who had dragged her from the wreck. She was sitting, her arms pinned behind her.

Before she could process her surroundings, the man swung out his arm and slapped her face. Her head swung to the side from the impact. She struggled, attempting to shrink away, but she was tied to a metal office chair. She blinked and moaned in pain.

"That's fine, Mr. Douglas. She's awake."

"Allan!" she gasped. He was standing to her right, his hands jammed in the pockets of his pants. "What the hell are you doing here? What's going on?"

He was slouching, and dark circles hung beneath his eyes. "Ms. Freeling, I won't insult your intelligence so please don't insult mine. In point of fact, I have to say you've impressed me. You really did find the perfect asset for this operation. I couldn't have done better myself." He paused, considering her carefully. His lips curled around nicotine-stained teeth. "That's about as high a compliment as I can give."

Rebecca took a long, slow breath. As Bernatto spoke, she reviewed her circumstances, taking in the little details that surrounded her. Concrete walls. Water dripping from the ceiling, mold. The air was warm and dank. They were still in Pattaya. She could smell the humidity.

Bernatto watched her with tired, calm eyes. "Take your time, Ms. Freeling. Look around all you want. That's what you were trained to do, after all. Scan, process, assess. Glad to see you were paying attention."

Allan's enforcer, bored by the conversation, turned away. He stepped in front of a rickety table and began cleaning an assortment of pistols with a wire brush.

"Allan, what the hell is going on here? Why are you—"

Allan's eyes clouded with annoyance. He raised a hand in the air, like a frustrated parent scolding a toddler. "Please, Ms. Freeling. You know exactly why I'm here."

"Allan, I don't. I—"

"Thomas Caine."

She shook her head. "What are you talking about? Caine is dead."

Bernatto smiled, but there was no humor in his face. "I know Caine is your asset. Deniability is not the same thing as ignorance, Ms. Freeling. I've followed every step of your operation. I've had Mr. Douglas here tailing you since you arrived in Thailand. And I confirmed my intel with Ethan before I removed him from the playing field."

Rebecca blinked back tears. She used her anger, her hatred of the man standing before her to keep her voice steady. "Removed him? Like you removed Jack Tyler? Like you tried to remove Caine?"

"More successfully, I can assure you. But, in the end, it seems everything worked out for the best. As I said, Caine is the perfect asset for this mission. His background, his experience ... perfect."

Rebecca struggled at her bonds, shaking the chair. "So everything Caine said was true. You set him up. Betrayed him. You're a liar, a murderer, and a traitor!"

Allan's face flashed with rage, and his arm twitched. Rebecca braced for the strike, but his anger faded as quickly as it surfaced. It was soon replaced by his usual emotionless gaze. "I'm no traitor. Everything I have done has been for the good of my country. No matter how myopic, bloated, and unrecognizable it's become. And Caine ... my dear, whatever you may think, believe me, you know nothing about Thomas Caine."

"I know you framed him, hung him out to dry, and tried to have him killed."

Allan nodded. "All true, I suppose, but Caine is not the man you think he is. Do you have any idea how much blood is on his hands? How many lives Caine has ended? How many operations—black, unsanctioned, wet, whatever term you want to use—he has participated in?"

"What are you talking about? I've debriefed plenty of operatives. He's no different than—"

"You're deluded, Rebecca. Caine is nothing like other operatives. Everything about him, even his official work with the CIA, was part of his cover. He was a member of a very special group, a team of specialists with superlative skills. All handpicked by me. Trained by the best, to be the best. One-hundred-percent loyal. One-hundred-percent dependable. And as always, one-hundred-percent expendable. When I saw an opportunity to remove him from play and create a benefit for myself and the program, I took it. That was my directive."

Rebecca struggled in her bonds. "You goddamn son of a bitch!"

"Fine, I'm a son of a bitch. A cold-hearted bastard. In my job, I have to be. But let me ask you this: you were in a relationship with Caine, weren't you? Don't bother denying it. I know it's true."

Rebecca stared at him, eyes molten with fury.

"The morning he left you, the last time you saw him before I sent him to Japan ... you must realize, he knew that he was leaving the country. He knew he would be under deep cover, that he would be away from you for years. Did he say anything to you about it? Did he even say goodbye?"

Rebecca said nothing. There was nothing to say. On this, if nothing else, she knew Bernatto was right.

"Make no mistake," he said. "Caine is as cold as they come. You may think you know him. Maybe you loved him, maybe you even got under his skin a little. But Caine will always be part of my world. Not yours. So let's stop wasting time and drop the pretenses."

Rebecca glared up at him. "Fine, let's drop the pretenses. What the hell is this mission about anyway?"

"It was supposed to be about preparation. About getting a step ahead. For once, not getting caught with our pants down."

"Seems to me like it's about covering your ass."

"Let's just say, in this case, my interests and the interests of the country are aligned. Have you ever heard the expression 'Thucydides's Trap'?"

"Allan, please, this is insane. It's not too late to stop this."

"You don't know your history, Rebecca. It is too late. Thucydides was an ancient Greek historian. Wrote the history of the Peloponnesian War. The conflict between Athens and Sparta. You know, the Iliad, Trojan horse? Christ, weren't you a poli-sci major?"

"What on earth does that have to do with anything?"

"The rise of one nation's power will inevitably cause fear, and eventually war, with the already established power. That's the Thucydides's Trap. He was talking about Athens and Sparta, but it's proven true again and again throughout history.

"Today, China is Athens, and the United States is Sparta. War is inevitable. And we are not remotely ready for it. Every day, China conducts cyber-attacks on United States servers. It strengthens its economies, expands its borders. And what do we do? Engage in trade talks and ogle their cuddly pandas."

Rebecca tried to hide the gears turning in her brain. "War with China? What does that have to do with this girl? Why is she so important?"

Allan barked a short, wheezing laugh. "The girl? She's meaningless. Just some black sheep daughter of a very wealthy, very compromised asset. But the information she has ... she probably doesn't even know she has it. But that's the key. That's what this operation is about. Whoever gets it first will have leverage over the other party."

"What information? Leverage over what?"

Bernatto gave her an uneasy look. "The situation on the ground has changed. My risk of exposure has become untenable. But Kusaka and these deformed fanatics he's working with ... they refuse to listen to reason. I have to bring them to heel, get them under control, or they'll destroy everything."

"Kusaka was working with you all along? And what about this terrorist attack we're supposed to be preventing? Was that all a lie, too?"

"I never lied to you, Ms. Freeling. I do have intel regarding an imminent terrorist attack on United States soil, one that will entail a significant loss of life. I should know. I helped plan it."

Rebecca stopped struggling and stared at Bernatto. "And you say you're not a traitor?"

He shrugged. "That depends on how simple your worldview is. You work for the CIA, not UNICEF. I would expect more from you."

"This missing girl, the information she has ... it exposes you?"

Bernatto nodded. "Yes, but it can also help me with Kusaka. Force him to back off, until the time is right."

"What about me? Why am I still alive?"

Bernatto pulled a chair away from the crumbling desk and sat down to face her. He stared at her over the rim of his glasses.

"I would think you'd have guessed already. You're my insurance policy."

"Insurance for what?"

"To make sure Thomas Caine does his job and finds that girl before Kusaka does."

CHAPTER TWENTY-TWO

A curved panoramic window dominated an entire wall of Arinori Kusaka's office. The twinkling lights of Tokyo's Sumida district spread out before him like jewels against the black velvet curtain of night. But his focus rested on an enormous structure thrust into the sky: the Tokyo Skytree tower.

At 634 meters, it was the tallest tower, and second tallest structure, in the world. The observation decks on its top floors contained a glass-enclosed viewing gallery, restaurant, and gift shop. At night, LED lights illuminated the tower, making it glow a dark purple. The color reminded Kusaka of the ripe plums he had devoured in his youth.

Although his firm had no direct hand in building it, Kusaka still swelled with pride when he saw it. It was a marvel of Japanese engineering. Strength, elegance, beauty ... to him, the tower symbolized all that he loved about his country.

Kusaka shifted in his chair. The curved glass warped his reflection like a funhouse mirror. A solid and sturdy man in a pin-striped suit stared back at him, his hair so grey it was almost white. Although he was close to seventy years old, his skin was devoid of wrinkles or age spots, and he kept his full head of hair cut military short. His face was round and full, giving him a playful, mischievous expression when he smiled, which he did often. He knew it caused his enemies to underestimate him, both in business and in other endeavors. He used that to his advantage, of course.

When the intercom on his desk beeped, he swiveled away from the window. It was late, and he had sent his secretary home for the evening. He pressed a button on the intercom.

"Come up."

He poured a glass of 1960 Karuizawa single malt from a bottle on his desk. The precious liquor cost over half a million yen per bottle and had been difficult to find. To acquire it, he had sent his assistant to a small bar in the town of Karuizawa itself, near the base of the Asama volcano. The bar owner hadn't wanted to part with his only bottle, but Kusaka made him an offer for five times what the whisky was worth. His assistant said the bar owner wept as he completed the transaction. Kusaka drank it neat, straight from a crystal tumbler. He savored the sweet, oaky taste, its creamy notes of vanilla rice milk and salted butter caramel.

A monitor on his desk showed a massive man entering the private elevator on the ground floor. Kusaka glanced at the man's hideous, scarred face. Bobu's blind white eye stared back into the camera. Kusaka took another sip of scotch. Bobu was insane, but he was still useful. Things were moving quickly now. This was the critical moment, the moment that would define success or failure—both for himself and Japan.

The elevator door in his office chimed and slid open. The huge man entered the room.

"Bobu Shimizu," Kusaka said. "To what do I owe the pleasure?" There was a hint of impatience in his voice.

Bobu stood in front of Kusaka's desk and bowed. Kusaka paused for a second, just long enough to ensure Bobu paid him the proper respect. Then he nodded. "Sit, sit. Would you like a drink?"

Bobu waved his hand. An uncomfortable, tense expression clouded his features.

"No. Thank you," he demurred. "I am here to apologize. We have failed."

Kusaka took another sip. "Do you at least have the girl?"

Bobu cleared his throat. "No, not yet, but we were able to recover the cell phone from her *yonigeya*, a man called Naka. Before he died, our man accessed a text your daughter sent him. She is scheduled to meet him tonight at the Millennium Dome. I have sent some men there to find her."

Kusaka swallowed his drink, allowing the taste to slowly drip down his throat. As he smacked his lips, he slipped his hand into the open drawer of his desk, his fingers curling around a pistol.

"Shimizu-san, I told you before. Do not refer to this whore as my daughter." Kusaka set the gun down on his desk, with a casual gesture, as if he was holding a stapler or a pen. "Don't make me tell you again." Kusaka looked up at Bobu and smiled.

Bobu bowed his head. "Apologies. But there is more. This man, Mark Waters ... the *gaijin* is hunting the girl as well. He is working with the Yoshizawa family."

Kusaka began polishing the barrel of the pistol with a cloth. "What of him?"

"I have seen him before, years ago. Back then, the Shimizu and Yoshizawa clans were engaged in a gang war, a dispute over territory. This *gaijin* was there the night my brother sent me to kill Isato Yoshizawa."

Kusaka's eyes twinkled. He was still smiling. "Oh? What happened?"

"Things went wrong. Isato's son, Kenji Yoshizawa, got in the way of my shot. This man, Mark Waters, took a bullet for him. He saved the boy's life."

"Interesting. It is no coincidence he is here now. There are other forces at play here, forces you are unaware of. Do not underestimate this man. He is more dangerous than any of Yoshizawa's soldiers."

Bobu bowed again, deeper this time. "*Hai!*"

"Now, is the plane on time?"

Bobu checked the watch that bulged against his massive wrist. "Yes, it should have landed twenty minutes ago."

Kusaka nodded. He finished his whisky, then poured himself another glass. He held up the gun, letting the polished black barrel glint in the light. The pistol was long and sleek, with a slim, tapered barrel. The oval-shaped butt was fitted with grooved mahogany grips. "Have you ever seen a gun like this, Bobu?"

"Not in person. It's a Nambu, yes?"

"Mmmm," the older man grunted. "Nambu Type 14. Officer's pistol in World War II. It fires an 8mm, .320 bullet. Look at it ... beautiful. Reliable. Accurate. Adopted for military use in 1925, which is how it got its name ... 1925 was the fourteenth year of the Taisho Emperor's reign."

Bobu gave a thin smile. "Before my time."

"Yes, but a patriot like yourself should be familiar with our glorious history. At any rate, this pistol was my father's. He bought it himself, when he was promoted to officer."

"Then you must be honored to carry it."

Kusaka sipped his whisky and stared at the gun. He did not look at Bobu.

"I was born after my father returned home from the war. He was young, entered the army at sixteen years old. When the war ended, he returned to Osaka, opened a shipping company, and took a wife. She was a local girl, pretty, but not beautiful. We lived in a small house outside the city.

"Our life was comfortable. But even as a young child, I knew something was wrong with my father. There was an invisible barrier between him and myself, a wall I could not even understand, let alone break down. He always seemed to be looking in the distance at something I could not see. Something I was afraid to see, based on the look in his eyes.

"One day, my father and I were alone in the yard. My mother

had gone into town to do the shopping. Believe it or not, I even remember what she was planning to cook that night. Nikujaga stew." Kusaka shook his head. "I can't remember half the women I've slept with in this life, but I remember what my mother was planning to make for dinner that night, decades ago."

Bobu sat in silence. Kusaka continued.

"At any rate, I was playing with a ball. Kicking it around, pretending I was playing football. My father was sitting in a chair under our cherry tree, sipping cold barley tea. I kicked the ball under his chair and pretended I had scored a goal. Cheering my own victory, I ran over to him. I was desperate for his attention, desperate to break through that awful, cold wall of what I took to be indifference. 'Father, did you see my goal?' I asked.

"He turned and looked at me—or, rather, looked through me. I saw no love in his face. No affection or anger. No joy or hatred. His face was that of a dead man. A sleepwalker. 'I watched men play football once before,' he said. 'During the second Shanghai incident in 1937. That's what the politicians called the battle. An incident.'

"He looked down at my little red ball, next to his feet. He was just sitting there, but he was shaking, ever so slightly. I was afraid then. I knew something was wrong, but he continued speaking, in this flat, empty voice.

"'I was captured with my squad,' he said. 'One by one, they led each soldier to a bamboo cage. When they locked the cage, the man inside could not move. He was trapped, stuck sitting on a wooden stool, with his head sticking out. Just from the neck up.' My father paused, then looked up at me. 'Then, they took a sword. A huge, curved sword. And then....'

"My father drew his finger across his throat. He didn't smile. He wasn't making a joke. He was telling me, his eight-year-old son, about watching men being beheaded by Chinese soldiers. The story went on....

"'And do you know what they did then?' he asked me. 'They watched the heads topple down from the men's necks. They watched them roll across the ground. Then the children ran up, laughing, singing. They kicked them. They kicked the heads. They used the heads for footballs. They played football. They kicked them in the dirt streets until the faces wore away....' I remember his voice trailed off then. He said something else, but I could not hear his words.

"And with that, he stood up and kicked my red ball across the yard. Then he walked into the house. I didn't chase the ball. I didn't follow him. I didn't know what to do so I just stood there. I thought if I said a word, if I made a sound, something terrible would happen. Then I heard a noise. Like an explosion, but softer. Something between a car backfiring and a champagne cork popping. You see, at that age, I didn't know what a gunshot sounds like. It doesn't sound like it does in the movies."

Bobu shifted in his chair. "No," he said. "It doesn't."

"I ran into the house. As I walked through the kitchen, I heard two more explosions. I was crying, shivering with fear as I stumbled into the bedroom. And there he was. My father, laying face up on a tatami mat. A pistol in his hand. He had fired two shots into his gut, but they hadn't killed him. So the third shot, he fired into his mouth. The blood ... that's the only image I remember after I found him. The blood was everywhere. I could smell it. It smelled like burning copper."

Kusaka hefted the pistol in his hand, contemplating it. "Such a strange way to kill oneself, don't you think? Almost like a modern version of seppuku. An honorable suicide. This pistol. My father's pistol. This is the gun he used to take his life. I've kept it all these years. As a reminder."

"Of the brutalities of war?" Bobu asked.

"No," Kusaka answered. "The price of inaction. I could have stopped my father. I could have run into the house. I could have embraced him. I could have done anything. Instead, I just stood there, trembling, while my father, a soldier, a patriot, suffered ... and finally took his own life. The only honorable way out that he could see."

Kusaka picked up his drink. His face was taut, grim, but as he sipped the warm amber liquid, his features softened.

"Japan has lost much over the years. We both know it. We are each patriots, in our own way. Our country grows weaker every day, while China, and others, prosper. We cannot wait for help from the West. My allies there have become weak-willed, fearful. If Japan is to become strong, to once again be the dominant power in the East, then we must not give in to fear. We must act."

Bobu stood and bowed again. "*Hai*. It will be done."

Kusaka nodded. "A war is won a single victory at a time. Find Hitomi. Return my property. Then the plan will move forward."

Bobu turned to leave. Kusaka swiveled in his chair. He stared out at the beautiful purple light of the Skytree. "And Bobu?"

"Yes, sir?"

"I am quite certain you will once again cross paths with the *gaijin*, Mr. Waters. I am also quite sure that is not his real name. Whoever he is, I believe this is destiny. You have an opportunity to take action and correct your previous failure."

He did not turn around, but he could sense Bobu's bow. "When we meet again ... he will die."

Bobu turned and left. As the elevator closed, Kusaka picked up the Nambu pistol and aimed it at the tower on the other side of the glass. He lined up the top of the tower's observation platform, positioning it between the notched sites at the rear of the pistol. He pulled the trigger, and the gun clicked. It was empty.

He pulled the trigger two more times. Once for each bullet his father had fired into his body.

CHAPTER TWENTY-THREE

The small green taxi waited to turn into the massive Tokyo Dome complex. The sprawling entertainment center was only a short distance from Ikebukuro, but traffic clogged the expressway. Caine stared out the taxi's window. He watched a Ferris wheel across the way spin in a lazy circle, lifting its passengers high into the night sky. The lights of a roller coaster streaked past, circling around the Ferris wheel as it rumbled along its track.

"Is there another route we can take?" Caine asked in Japanese.

The driver shook his head. "Sorry ... big concert at the dome tonight. Masuka Ongaku. Traffic is worse than usual, and that's bad, if you know what I mean." The driver chuckled to himself.

Caine handed a wad of yen to the driver. "Here. Just let me off at the station up here. I'll walk the rest of the way." The driver maneuvered the cab over to the side of the road. Caine got out and followed the signs directing pedestrians towards the dome.

The driver rolled down his window. "Sir, wait! This is too much!"

"Sorry, I don't have time for change!" Caine pushed his way past a crowd of teenage girls with bright, dyed hair. They clutched small, colorful stuffed animals, and anime characters adorned their t-shirts and bags. Caine paused to look at the huge posters lining the walking route he'd chosen. They were advertising for the evening's concert, and the picture looked familiar. He pulled out Naka's cell phone and flipped through the text messages.

He located the conversation with Hitomi. Her avatar was an anime character's face. Big eyes, neon green hair, black leather clothes. It was the same design as the posters. Masuka Ongaku. "Looks like I'm in the right place," he muttered as the crowd swept him along.

It took about fifteen minutes to reach the dome. The massive structure arching up into the sky was nicknamed "The Big Egg" for its curved, oval shape. Rows of colored lights ran up the side of the building, gleaming lines of purple, green, and yellow. An enormous circle of white neon rimmed the top, and just below, huge glowing blue English letters spelled out "Tokyo Dome."

Caine could hear the distant thumping of music; the concert had begun. Throngs of eager concert-goers gathered around the dome's entrances. They poured into the narrow doorways like bright colored sand spilling through an hourglass. As he approached, Caine noted the rectangular metal detectors and the security personnel. They were checking bags and purses for drugs, alcohol, and weapons. He scanned the crowd but saw no sign of dark suits or scars.

Caine peeled off from the crowds and headed for the back of the dome. He knew the men he had chased in Ikebukuro had probably reported in before he'd caught up with them. If Tokyo Black was hunting this girl, too, they would be here as well, or at least on their way.

What was so important about this girl? he wondered. What did this group want with her? Was it a kidnapping plot? It didn't feel right. Everything about this girl was a mystery. Yet the CIA had sent him, at no small expense, to find her. And this Tokyo Black group had proven itself willing to kill, and die, to track her down. Caine knew he was missing a vital piece of the puzzle.

But Hitomi was not the only one whose life hung in the balance.

Rebecca had been digging at his past, uncovering secrets Bernatto had killed to keep hidden. If he caught wind of her investigation, if he was on to her....

Enough, Caine told himself. The best way to protect Rebecca was to find what Bernatto wanted before someone else did. He had to focus.

As he circled the building, the crowd thinned out. The pounding bass from inside grew louder. The thumping tones echoed from the open doors of a cargo dock, where workers were busy wheeling in food supplies on metal carts.

Koichi stood to the side of the huge, open doorway, illuminated by the harsh glow of a work light. He was smoking a cigarette, watching the workers go about their business with an air of bemusement.

"All this work for fake concert. What a waste," he said as Caine approached. He flicked his cigarette to the pavement and ground it out beneath his heel.

Caine surveyed the workers, looking for signs of burns or scars. "What do you mean fake? Sounds pretty real to me."

"You never heard of Masuka Ongaku?"

Caine shook his head.

Koichi shrugged. "Come on," he said. "You'll get a kick out of this."

Caine followed him into the loading dock. "Did you drop off Kenji?"

"Yes, he is with his father. Safe. He did ask about his car, however."

Caine's jaw clenched in a tense smile, but he kept his eyes focused on the hallway ahead. "Right. About that...."

As they approached the door to a service corridor, a pair of security guards flanking the entrance intercepted them. Koichi gave them a harsh glare, and they stepped aside. "Please enjoy the concert, Mr. Ogawa," one of them said, shouting to be heard over the music. The two guards bowed. Koichi opened the door, and they made their way into the dome.

"What was that about?"

"The Yoshizawa family has ties to the construction company that built this place. And they own the company that staffs the security here. Naturally, as a sign of respect, the dome lets us attend whatever concerts we wish."

"Naturally," Caine smirked. "Here, take a look at this." Caine handed Koichi Naka's cell phone, showing him the text conversation with Hitomi. "These numbers here ... that's where Naka and the girl are supposed to meet right?"

The old yakuza nodded. "*Hai.* Box seats, upper level. Follow me."

Koichi threw open a set of double doors at the end of a sloped corridor. He and Caine stepped into the interior of the Tokyo Dome. It was like being born into a world of exploding lights and sound. The music was deafening, a high-pitched, electronic pop song. The singer's vocals were warped, cartoonish squeaks. She sounded like a cross between a digital synthesizer and an opera singer, a musical instrument from the future.

Looking down from the mezzanine level, Caine saw the crowd beneath them sway to the music. The dark figures surged up and down to the frantic beat. A sea of neon green glow sticks waved in the air, a synchronous pulse of light rippling through the crowd. Caine's focus drifted through the chaos of light and sound, settling on the stage.

He had never seen anything like it. Masuka Ongaku looked like her pictures. Literally, exactly like her pictures. She appeared to be a glowing anime character. Her backup band was hidden away in the shadows on the stage. Caine could see they were real people, hunched over keyboards, pounding on drums, jamming on electric guitars.

But Masuka herself was something else ... she was a living, dancing, anime cartoon come to life, with giant blinking eyes, a tiny mouth, and an impossibly pert figure. As she danced and performed, her glowing green hair shimmered in slow motion, like a serpentine dragon snaking through the hazy air.

A halo of glowing light radiated from her slim body. Her image had to be computer generated, but her movements seemed to have depth and weight to them.

"What the hell is that?" Caine shouted into Koichi's ear.

"I told you. Fake concert. The name Masuka Ongaku is a play on words. In English, it roughly sounds like 'Musical Mask.' It's a hologram, projected on stage. The fans can download her software onto their computers, phones, whatever. They write the songs, sing them into a microphone. And the computer sings them back in Masuka's voice. The company that owns her licenses the songs they like from the fans."

Caine shook his head. "Unbelievable. Let's get this over with."

They climbed a steep set of stairs, and Koichi led him through another set of doors. Once again, the music dropped to a deep, thumping beat, reverberating through the walls.

"The box seat from the text is this way," said Koichi. Caine followed as they circled around the upper level of the dome. Here, the crowd thinned out and looked wealthier. Rich young mistresses walked arm in arm with their corporate boyfriends. Parties of older men in expensive suits laughed, as they drank sake and beer while standing at small circular tables.

It looked like every other exclusive concert Caine had seen. Only at this one, the star performer literally did not exist.

The numbers on the doorways they passed were going up. Caine forced himself to tune out the noise from the concert. Box number 25B was just a few doors down when he grabbed Koichi's arm. "Look!" he hissed. "There."

Outside the box seat entrance stood a pair of men dressed in black suits, eyeing the crowd passing before them. One of them turned to watch a pretty girl in a pink dress walk by. As his jacket flared open, Caine spotted the butt of a pistol hanging from a shoulder holster.

"Let me guess," he said. "That's 25B?"

Koichi nodded, and they backed up until Caine was certain they were out of sight. He perused the remaining crowd on the upper level, but no one else stood out. To his left was a door marked "Maintenance."

He looked over at Koichi. "You sure you're up for this?"

Koichi's lips curled as a look of distaste crossed his face. "I promised my oyabun I would assist you until the girl is found."

Caine nodded. "Okay then. I have an idea."

"I can't believe you got drunk on our shift! Do you want to get us both fired?" Koichi continued berating Caine in Japanese as they made their way towards box 25B. They were both dressed in the same purple smocks the rest of the dome staff wore, and he pushed a plastic cart full of cleaning supplies ahead of him.

Caine kept his head bowed as he shuffled along next to the older man. "*Hai*! Yes, sir. Sorry, sir," he answered in broken Japanese. He was carrying a spray bottle of cleaner in one hand and a sopping wet towel in the other.

The two men stiffened as they approached. Koichi smiled and waved his hand. "I am so sorry to inconvenience you. My *gaijin* partner here passed out and forgot to clean this box before you arrived. Please forgive his laziness. I will make sure he remedies his mistake immediately and gives you the Tokyo Dome experience you deserve."

The two men looked at each other. Caine could make out the telltale red scars on their necks as they twisted their heads and whispered in each other's ears. "Go away. You are disturbing our employer," one of the guards replied with an angry sneer. "You can clean up later, when he's done with the box."

"Sorry, sir, Dome policy. All box seats must be cleaned before customers arrive." Caine slurred his words and pretended to stumble forward.

"Leave now, or the next janitor will be cleaning your blood off the floor."

"Okay, okay." Caine raised up his hands in defeat. "We'll just have to clean up out here." He saw the flash of recognition pass across the man's features, but it was too late.

He lifted the spray bottle and fired a blast of liquid directly into the guard's face. The Tokyo Black soldier screamed in pain as the caustic liquid splashed into his eyes. He drew his gun and swung it blindly, struggling to aim the weapon at Caine.

Before anyone in the surrounding crowd noticed the commotion, Caine swung the wet towel like a whip. The heavy, soaking rag snapped through the air, striking the man's face with a loud slap. He stumbled backwards, blinded and in pain. It took him a second to realize he had allowed Caine to get too close.

And a second was all Caine needed.

Caine rushed forward and yanked the gun out of his grip. Meanwhile, Koichi had burst into motion, driving his cart towards the other sentry. The weight of the cart slammed into him before he could draw his gun. The momentum knocked him back through the door. Koichi kicked the cart forward, knocking it and the guard back into the darkened room.

Caine stepped through the door, pushing the blinded guard in front of him. Inside the dark room, he spotted a third Tokyo Black member. The man was looking up, entranced by the overwhelming music and a bright light hovering in the room. He whirled around as the two guards stumbled backwards and fell to the ground. "What the hell?!" He reached for his gun.

Caine dropped to his knee, the guard's pistol in his hands. Behind him, he heard the sound of Koichi kicking the door shut. Caine tuned out the chaos assaulting his senses. Then he fired.

Six tiny explosions crackled through the room. His bullets found their targets, two in each enemy. The three Tokyo Black members lay on the floor, blood seeping from fatal wounds.

Koichi surveyed the carnage. "I enjoyed that," he confessed with a sheepish grin.

Caine stood up and took a deep breath. "I didn't know you had a sense of humor."

Koichi looked surprised. "I wasn't joking."

Caine looked through the glass windows. There was no sign that anyone had heard the gunshots over the thumping bass of the concert. He then turned his attention to the rest of the room, a small, luxurious box seat.

Dim lights set into the ceiling illuminated several cushy chairs perched on a sloping platform, overlooking the concert below. A small bar ran along the wall, and various bottles of liquor sparkled in the shifting light. A laptop sat open on the bar, a colorful screensaver dancing across the screen.

In the center of the chamber was a circular table, its top slanted at an angle and covered with a strange, shimmering material. The hovering light that had so engrossed the third guard beamed down from the ceiling.

There was no one else in the room.

Caine turned to Koichi. "Okay, where the hell is she?"

"Maybe they got to her first."

"No. I am here." A voice echoed through the room.

It was an artificial, robotic chirp. It sounded familiar. Caine turned back to the table. The lights in the ceiling had rotated and pivoted. They were projecting an image down through the hazy air. The shimmering film on the table reflected the image upwards, giving it the illusion of a three-dimensional object. Caine stared in surprise. He was standing face to face with Masuka Ongaku herself.

He reached out, letting his hand drift through the image. It looked solid, real, but his hand passed through it as if it were a reflection in the still water of a pond. Masuka's head seemed to turn and follow his movements, as his hand cut through her incorporeal body.

The image laughed, a squeaky, girlish giggle. "You can't touch me. I'm a digital ghost."

Koichi drew his pistol and stood next to Caine. "They must have installed these projectors in the box seats for the concert. Anyone could be using the Masuka software." He did not take his eyes off the glowing image as he spoke.

"It's not anyone," Caine answered back. "It's her." He turned and looked at the laptop on the counter. "Hitomi Kusaka? Is that you?"

The Masuka hologram brushed a shimmering strand of neon green hair from her face. She looked up at him with huge, luminous eyes. "Maybe. Maybe not. Who are you?"

"Hitomi, please listen. We're here to help you. There are dangerous men looking for you."

The image of the girl spun around in the air, her short, black skirt twirling around her. She looked back at Caine over her shoulder. "You think I don't know that? Why do you think I downloaded this software? Where is Naka-san? He was supposed to help me."

"Naka is dead. Hitomi. The same people who are after you killed him. We have to find you. We can help you; we can keep you safe."

"I doubt that. Those men you just killed. They are the ones who killed Naka?"

Koichi stepped to the door and stood guard as Caine followed the hologram with his eyes. "Yes. Or other men like them. They call themselves Tokyo Black."

The image of Masuka turned back to face him and nodded. "*Hai*. I know who they are. They work for my father."

So that was it ... the missing piece of the puzzle clicked into place. Arinori Kusaka was linked to Tokyo Black. And this girl, his daughter, could somehow tie him to the group's activities. But what could Bernatto's angle be in all this? Rebecca said Kusaka was a CIA asset. Was Bernatto simply protecting a valuable source of intelligence? No, Caine thought. It had to be more than that.

Caine forced himself to silence his racing thoughts. He could untangle the whole mess later. First, he had to find the girl. Before Tokyo Black did.

"Hitomi, please listen to me. We can talk about all this later. Mr. Naka is dead, and these men have tracked you this far. They won't stop now, and you can't run forever. Please, let me help you."

"You never answered my question," the cute voice chirped. "Who are you?"

Caine paused for a moment. He wasn't sure how to answer. It had been so long since he had told anyone the truth. He was surprised how difficult it was.

"My name is Thomas Caine." Koichi looked at him in surprise. Caine shrugged and gave a half-smile, then turned back to the hologram. "I realize you don't know me, but you saw what I did to these men. I have skills, training, and I have friends we can trust. I'm your best shot at getting out of this alive. Please, let me help you."

The hologram paused. For a moment, it seemed frozen, unmoving. Caine wondered if the projection software had suffered a glitch. Then a flicker of light ran through it again. Masuka's long neon hair bobbed and drifted with life. Her eyes blinked. She sighed, and her petite shoulders slumped. The effect of the artificial character acting so human was unnerving.

"Very well. I'm tired of running anyway. You can't outrun my father's money. It just goes on and on, forever."

"Hitomi, where are you?"

"I'm in Shinjuku. I rented a room at a karaoke bar called The Space Age. I logged into the laptop in the box seat remotely."

She gave him the address. Caine committed it to memory and turned to Koichi. "Twenty minutes away," Koichi muttered.

Caine nodded and looked back at the hologram. "Okay, we're on our way. Stay where you are. Don't open the door for anyone else. Not police, not your father, nobody. *Wakarimas ka?*"

"*Hai.*" The image of Masuka nodded, indicating she understood. Caine found the cute bobbing head and swirling green hair a bizarre contrast to the gravity of the situation. "Please hurry," she chirped.

The projector lights hummed and dimmed, then shut off with a click. As the image disappeared, Caine grabbed the guns from the bodies on the floor and handed one to Koichi. The old yakuza stared at Caine as he jammed it in his waistband. "Thomas Caine, eh? That your real name?"

Caine nodded.

"Why did you tell the girl that? You didn't have to say it in front of me."

Caine's green eyes blazed as the shimmering lights from the concert danced across his face. "It's like she said. I'm tired of running."

Koichi gave a thin smile and opened the door. "Somehow, I don't think we're through running for the night."

CHAPTER TWENTY-FOUR

Koichi's face twisted into a frown as they navigated the labyrinth of service corridors back downstairs. "Wait ... Caine-san, is what that girl said true? Is Arinori Kusaka behind this Tokyo Black group?"

At every bend, Caine scanned the deserted hallways warily. "Your guess is as good as mine. I knew something was wrong about this job. I guess this was it."

"If that's the case, then this girl ... she is not missing. She is running. And Kusaka wants her back from some reason. A man like this ... you have made a powerful enemy."

Caine curled his lips in a grim smile as they pushed through a set of swinging doors. "Yeah, I seem to have a knack for that."

The older man shrugged. "At least this enemy is one we share. Once Isato learns Kusaka is behind the attacks on the Yoshizawa clan, he will throw the full weight of his empire against him."

"Just what I need ... a gang war on top of everything else." Caine halted as they reentered the sloping service corridor. Several cleaning carts were tipped over in the hallway. He turned and spotted a dark puddle seeping out from under the door of a maintenance closet.

"Get down!" Caine shouted. The words formed on his lips before he even realized the puddle was blood.

Caine slid to the ground and rolled behind one of the overturned service carts. The doors ahead of them swung open. Two Tokyo Black men with KG-9 machine pistols stormed into the corridor. A hail of bullets ripped through the air. The short, perforated barrels of the machine pistols glowed with muzzle flash as they pumped out round after round. Koichi fell to his knees and scrambled for cover. He grunted in pain as a gash of red ripped open across his thigh. Once tucked behind a cart, he drew his pistol and returned fire.

Caine popped up to join in the barrage, firing a quick double tap towards the men at the end of the hall. They fell back behind the swinging doors.

"Is there another way out of here?" Caine asked.

"Back the way we came. From the concert floor, we can get to another exit."

Another hail of bullets exploded through the hall. One struck the cart inches from Caine's face. A shard of plastic shrapnel sliced across his cheek, opening a bloody cut. He blindly returned fire, hoping to keep the men from advancing further.

He turned to Koichi. "You okay?"

"*Daijobo desu.* I'm fine; it's just a scratch."

Caine heard the mechanical clicking of the men reloading behind the doors. "Okay, look, we have to split up. One of us has to get that girl and get her back to Isato. It's the only place she'll be safe."

Koichi shook his head. "I'm not limping back to lick my wounds. We go together."

Without warning, another barrage of bullets burned through the air above them. Chips of paint flew off the walls and fluttered to the ground like snow.

"Very noble," Caine snapped. "But if we both stay here, it's over."

A strong, chemical smell filled the air. It smelled familiar. Caine examined the cart he was using for cover. He rummaged through the cleaning supplies and stuffed garbage bags. Finally, he located the source of the odor: a punctured bottle of bleach leaking across the floor.

Caine glanced over at Koichi. "Cover me!"

Koichi sat up and fired a stream of bullets into the doors. The Tokyo Black men ducked back.

"We can't hold this position much longer, Caine-san."

"Just give me a few seconds!" Caine grabbed the bottle of bleach. He tore open the closest garbage bag and searched through the debris that spilled onto the floor. Grabbing an empty plastic water bottle, he removed the cap and filled it a quarter full with bleach. He mixed the bleach with a few more cleaning chemicals from the cart. The caustic liquid sloshed into the bottle, stinging the scrapes and cuts on his hands.

The Tokyo Black men reached around the doors, blindly firing into the hallway. Bullets ricocheted though the passage. The air filled with a fine cloud of dust as the walls began to crumble. Koichi popped up and blasted another round of bullets at their attackers. "Caine-san, I'm almost out! Whatever you are doing, it better be quick!"

"Just a few more seconds," Caine muttered through clenched teeth. Moving back to the garbage, he found a foil wrapper, clinging to the uneaten remains of a hot dog. He tore the foil into small pieces, crumpled them into balls, and dropped them into the bottle of chemicals. He sealed the cap and shook the bottle.

Nothing happened.

The Tokyo Black men opened fire again. The bullets thudded into the cart, sending a spray of cleaning supplies and debris into the air.

Caine shook the bottle again. "Come on, damn you!"

Caine focused his eyes on the bottle with laser-like intensity. Inside, the cloudy liquid was still, unmoving.

Then he saw it.

The sodium hydroxide in the bleach began to react with the

aluminum. The liquid churned and foamed, filling the clear water bottle with a thick white smoke.

"I need cover now!"

Koichi leapt up, firing a wild series of shots towards the partially open doors. As the Tokyo Black men ducked for cover, Caine rose up and took aim. He threw the bottle towards the doorway. It arched through the air, crashing down just in front of the doors. It rolled down the slope, behind the two gunmen.

For a split second, Caine saw the bottle swell and distort. The thin, clear plastic struggled to contain the expanding gas and heat generated by the chemical reaction. Then, with a loud crack, the bottle exploded.

The two men turned, startled by the sudden noise. Within seconds, they were surrounded by a white cloud of noxious, burning vapors. Coughing, they stumbled backwards, desperate to escape the makeshift tear gas that stung their eyes and lungs.

As they crashed through the doors, Caine and Koichi stood up and fired. The Tokyo Black men's bodies jerked and twisted with each bullet hit. Then they fell to the ground, dead.

Koichi coughed and fanned the air as the burning smell drifted towards them. "Nice trick."

"Something I picked up in Afghanistan."

They checked their pistols. The clips were empty. They moved forward to search the dead bodies. The KG-9s were almost empty as well, but each man carried a Beretta pistol in a shoulder holster. Caine and Koichi armed themselves, then passed through the swinging doors.

The loading dock was a stunning scene of slaughter. Workers' bodies littered the ground, and the stench of blood was thick in the air. Koichi gaped at the carnage. "These men ... they are insane! To kill like this, all to find this girl?"

Caine shook his head. "There's more going on here. Kusaka's not just involved with Tokyo Black. He has ties to the CIA, China ... whatever he wants, it's bigger than Hitomi, maybe even—"

The familiar explosion of gunfire cut Caine short. Four more Tokyo Black men came storming down the corridor behind them. Caine dropped to one knee and took aim. As the men poured through the doorway, he opened fire.

His rapid shooting dropped two of the men, but the survivors surged into the room. One took cover behind a metal freezer. The other charged Caine, screaming and opening fire.

Caine rolled behind a steel rack of serving trays for protection. Koichi stood his ground, raised his arm, and fired. A bright red hole opened in the thug's forehead as he fell.

Koichi nodded his head towards the freezer. Caine nodded back and began to creep towards the edge of the room.

Koichi called out to the hidden assailant. "Any more of you parasites crawling around? No? Just you then?"

The Tokyo Black man leaned out, but in the split second he needed to take aim, Koichi opened fire. Bullets sparked off the metal freezer, and the man ducked back without getting off a shot.

Caine crept along the dark, shadowy edge of the room. He could just make out the furtive movements of his target, wedged between the wall and the freezer.

Koichi fired off another pair of shots, the sound echoing in the tiny metal canyon behind the freezer unit. The shots had the desired effect, keeping the thug's attention focused forward. Caine aimed his pistol. He had the man in his sights.

Before he could fire, the man lurched forward. Caine squeezed his trigger, but the shot clanged off the metal pipes of the freezer. He cursed and spun around, moving back towards the center of the room. Before he cleared the freezer, he heard two sounds: the clanking metal of the loading dock door echoing through the room. And then a single, lonely click.

The sound of a gun jamming.

As he ran out from behind the freezer, he saw Koichi, struggling to pull back the slide on his pistol. The Tokyo Black man fired from the hip, sending a spray of bullets through the air. Koichi spun and dove to the ground, but he was too late. Bright splashes of red tore through his body as he hit the ground and rolled. He did not get up.

Caine darted over to him. "Koichi!"

He brought his pistol to bear on the Tokyo Black soldier, but he knew in his heart he had made a mistake. The other man would pull the trigger first, and his life would end on this cold, dark loading dock floor.

But instead of the spray of a submachine gun, he heard three single shots ring out in rapid succession. The Tokyo Black man crumpled to the ground like a puppet whose strings had been cut.

A woman's voice echoed through the room. "Security Bureau. Drop your weapon. Put your hands on your head. Do it now, please."

Caine turned and saw a woman staring back at him over the barrel of a pistol.

He blinked. He recognized her. She was wearing a slim pair of jeans and a leather jacket, instead of a fancy cocktail dress. But he was certain it was the girl he had met in the bar.

"Mariko Smith?"

"Officer Murase, if you please. Do as I say, Mr. Wilson. Or Mr. Waters, or whatever you're calling yourself now."

Security Bureau, Caine thought. *Japan's version of the FBI.* He dropped his pistol to the ground and turned to Koichi. He felt the older man's neck. There was a pulse, but it was weak.

"He needs medical attention."

She nodded. "I've already called it in. Paramedics will be here any minute, along with the police. We have to leave. Now."

Caine squinted at her. "Why is that, Officer?"

Mariko ignored his query. Instead, she reached into the pocket of her jacket with one hand. She used the other to keep her pistol aimed at Caine's head. She pulled out a set of plastic wrist cuffs and tossed them on the floor in front of Caine.

"Put those on, please."

"Officer Murase, I'm getting the distinct sense you don't trust me."

"Small wonder. Just about everyone you've encountered in Japan has ended up dead. Now stop wasting time. One way or the other, you'll be leaving here. It will be better if you leave with me than the Tokyo Metro Police."

Caine looked back at Koichi. He was unconscious but breathing. He looked back at Mariko. "Are you arresting me?"

Mariko's dark eyes locked with his, unblinking. "That depends."

"On what?"

"On who you really are and what you're doing here. But once the regular police show up, I won't have a choice, will I?"

Caine sighed. "There's always a choice. Just not always a good one."

He picked up the cuffs, slipped them over his wrists, and tightened them with his teeth.

He stood up. "Mariko Murase, pleased to meet you. I'd shake your hand, but...." He held up his cuffed hands.

Mariko stepped forward, keeping the gun trained on him, and spun him around. She kicked the pistol on the floor away from them and did a quick frisk. After confirming he had no other weapons, she marched him to the to exit.

"So, what should I call you?" she asked.

"It doesn't matter, as long as you listen to what I have to say."

CHAPTER TWENTY-FIVE

Rebecca lifted her head. She had passed out again, a remnant of the drugs in her system. Whatever Mr. Douglas had injected her with, it was potent. But now her vision was clear.

Her arms were still shackled to the chair behind her. She looked around the empty room, then twisted and pulled at the restraints. She heard her bracelets jingle together and breathed a sigh of relief. They had missed something. It was a small comfort, but it was something.

Okay, she thought. *Remember your training. Scan, analyze, assess.*

They were still in Pattaya. A basement. She sniffed the air—dank, humid. The mold on the walls indicated they were near the beach. A dark corridor led off to her right. She could hear the droning of a television off in the distance. The basement had to have at least two rooms, maybe more, judging by the size of the hallway. Her brain clicked through the principles she'd absorbed in her CIA orientation classes. First rule of escape: change your circumstances.

"Bernatto! Allan, please," she cried out.

She heard a sigh and the creaking of springs from down the hall. Then footsteps. She counted the seconds in her head. As Allan entered the room, she did some quick mental calculations. He was about twenty-five feet down the hall. Mr. Douglas stepped into the room behind him and took up a position next to the door. Bernatto stared down at her.

"What is it, Ms. Freeling?"

"I'm getting the sense this is going to take a while."

"And your point is?"

"Unless you want this hole to smell even worse, I'm going to need a bathroom break."

Bernatto looked at Mr. Douglas, who shrugged. He turned back to Rebecca, his eyes lingering for a second on her chest. She suppressed a shiver of revulsion.

"You can hold it. Shouldn't be much longer now. One way or the other."

She looked at up at him, her eyes feeble and pleading. "You don't know that. Caine hasn't called in yet, has he? Please, Allan, it's not my fault you abducted me from a coffee shop. This place does have a bathroom, doesn't it? You can wait right outside. Where am I going to go?"

Bernatto sighed and turned to Mr. Douglas. "Take her. Don't let her out of your sight."

The operative smiled and stepped over to the table full of guns. He picked up an HK pistol, loaded a clip, and racked the slide. He held it in a loose grip as he walked behind her. "It would be my pleasure."

He unlocked the cuffs, and she felt the warm tingle of blood flow returning to her wrists.

"Stand up, please. Nice and slow."

She did as he said. Her eyes drifted to the table full of weapons and equipment across the room. She forced herself to look down as the man grabbed her arm.

"Let's move," he said, his voice rough and low.

Whoever Mr. Douglas was, he was good. He had the weathered look of a freelance contractor. Black Water, Delta Blue, or one of the other private military firms the United States government used to farm out off-the-books work.

In her experience, those men came in two models. Rugged, natural-born warriors, burned out by their time in the Armed Forces. These men knew no other life than to fight for a cause they believed in.

And the others ... killers looking for an excuse. The ones the military could not wait to get off their roster once the initial fighting was done. The ones who liked it, who couldn't get enough of it. Some might have called them broken men, but the truth was, they had never been whole in the first place.

There was something about Mr. Douglas that made her think he was the latter. Maybe it was the way he looked at her. He seemed to stare through her, as if she were already a ghost—a temporary piece on the chessboard, one he would enjoy removing when the word was given.

He was good. But he had made a mistake, she reminded herself. He had missed her bangle.

He gave her a gentle push forward, towards the corridor. As she stumbled into the dark hallway, the sound of the TV grew louder. A newscaster was speaking in English, discussing the growing tensions between China and Japan, and the Senkaku Islands dispute. The U.S. Secretary of State was scheduled to mediate talks between both countries tomorrow.

She paused. Could that be what this was about? Was Bernatto involved in the talks in some way? As they walked past the television, Bernatto broke off and entered the dark room. She heard the squeak of springs as he sat down on whatever moldy piece of furniture he had scrounged up.

Mr. Douglas spoke from behind her. "Keep moving, please. The bathrooms are up ahead." Her eyes had adjusted to the darkness, and she saw the door at the end of the hallway, ahead of them. When they reached the door, she stopped. There was silence for a moment, then

Mr. Douglas's voice, pleasant, but with the steely undercurrent of a knife's edge. "After you, Ms. Freeling."

Rebecca turned around, a look of disgust on her face. "Does this place have spiders?"

Mr. Douglas took a step backwards, keeping the gun trained on her. "Do you have to go or not?"

The doorknob turned in her hand with a rusty clicking sound, and the door creaked open. The room was pitch-black. Damn. No windows. Again, she felt the gentle push on her back. She stumbled forward. "I can't see a thing," she said. "How do you expect me—"

She heard a click, and the room filled with a green, flickering glow. An old fluorescent light hung from the ceiling, surrounded by spiderwebs, mold, and chipped paint. The rest of the bathroom was just as filthy. The stinging scent of urine was overwhelming.

Spattered patches of black and brown mold colored the walls. A large, dark spot marked where the wall buckled inwards, most likely caused by water damage from a broken pipe behind the warped drywall.

Mr. Douglas shut the door behind them and tilted his head towards the stalls. "Let's go."

Rebecca stared at him for a second. "Um, would you mind waiting outside?"

"Yes, Ms. Freeling, I would. I'll be right here, in case you see a spider." His thin lips curled into a smile.

She shrugged and turned towards the toilet stalls. One had a bent, mangled door that hung open. The other stall's door was missing. Judging by the mangled metal of the hinges, it appeared to have been ripped off.

She chose the stall with the door and closed it behind her. She gagged, the stench of urine magnified in the tiny space. In the flickering light, she could see his feet, standing at attention outside the stall door. Which meant he couldn't see her body. At least he had given her that much privacy.

His second mistake.

She dropped her shorts down to her ankles for his benefit. With slow, silent movements, she slipped one of her bangles off her wrist. It was large, thick, and hinged in the middle. Unlike her other jewelry, this one was cheap and hollow. She had used this hidden cavity inside to her advantage. She tilted the unhinged bangle, and a tiny black canister slipped into her hand. It was thinner than a tube of lipstick, and featureless, save for a red button on the top and a tiny indented nozzle on the side.

She took a deep breath. The man standing outside her stall was an experienced killer. She had training, but she knew she was not in his league. She was an analyst. A desk jockey. Mr. Douglas lived in a different world. So did Caine, she realized. Bernatto had been right about that.

"Ms. Freeling, we have to get back."

She pulled her shorts back up and fastened them. She took another deep breath. Bernatto seemed confident that this would be wrapped up soon. If she waited any longer, whatever he was planning would come to fruition. She couldn't allow that to happen. She had to get free, call for help, call Caine.... She had to act.

She palmed the canister and placed the bangle back on her wrist. She spoke to hide the clicking noise it made as she shut the hinge. "I'm sorry, I can't go with someone watching me like this." She then reached forward and quietly unlatched the stall door. "Could you please just stand outside for a few minutes? I'll be quick, I promise!"

She heard footsteps approach the stall door. He instinctively knew something wasn't right. Men like him had an operational awareness, a sixth sense for when things were wrong. She was counting on it. She sat down on the toilet seat, raised her feet off the ground, and positioned them in front of the door.

"I'm afraid that's enough," Mr. Douglas said, his voice tinged with annoyance. "For your own safety, Ms. Freeling, I think we'd better go back."

She heard the metal scrape of the stall door pulling open. Everything seemed to be moving in slow motion. Her doubt and fear swallowed her courage in an inky black maw of darkness. Every action she imagined taking ended with a bullet in her head and Mr. Douglas staring at her lifeless corpse.

Then she thought of Caine. He had left her, true. He had lied to her. Maybe she had never truly known him. Maybe she still didn't. But she knew he had been betrayed. He had suffered torture, he had been branded a criminal, a traitor ... and she had believed all the lies. The man responsible was down the hall, watching television.

Whatever else he might be, Caine had proved himself a survivor. Now it was her turn.

Her mind snapped back into focus. The door moved a fraction of an inch. As it cleared the doorframe, she lashed out with her legs. All the days she had run, all the early morning hours she had spent pounding the pavement ... every mile, every foot, every inch she had pushed herself to complete ... she focused all of it into one powerful kick.

The door exploded outwards, smashing into Mr. Douglas and his outstretched arm. He stepped backwards, avoiding the full force of the blow, but the impact was still enough to throw him off-balance. His gun hand dropped to his side as he blocked the swinging door with his left forearm.

Rebecca lunged forward. She swung her right arm towards the operative's face. The swing was wide, clumsy. She was off-kilter, her muscles paralyzed with fear and exhaustion. She stumbled as she moved in close for the blow.

Mr. Douglas had already recovered from the bruising impact of the door. He grabbed her arm in midair, stopping her fist inches from his face. He yanked her forward. "Ms. Freeling, that was foolish. But I appreciate your spunk. It will make the rest of our activities so much more satisfying."

Rebecca opened her fist, revealing the tiny black canister. She closed her eyes and depressed the red button with her thumb. The hissing jet of compressed gas filled the air, and Mr. Douglas screamed.

In less than a second, the blast of red pepper spray inflamed his eyes, nose, and throat. As his hands flew to his face, Rebecca broke free of his grasp and dove backwards as fast as she could. In the small, dingy bathroom, the cloud of spray had already expanded to fill the air. She could feel the sting of it in her eyes and nose. But it was nothing compared to the point-blank blast she had delivered to the man's face.

She coughed and stood up. Through squinted, tearing eyes, she saw the operative grabbing and clawing at his face. He stumbled backwards towards the door. She reached down and grabbed the filthy porcelain cover of the toilet's water tank.

Hefting the brick-like slab in her hands, she swung it down on Mr. Douglas's head as hard as she could. The blow connected with a dull thud. Something between a grunt and a scream emerged from the man's mouth. He dropped to the concrete floor. His body twitched and jerked, as his mouth struggled to form words.

The white weapon in her hands was now streaked with blood. She hefted the weight over her head. Her arms shook. She saw Mr. Douglas turn and look up at her, a snarl of pain and anger replacing his usual cold, calm stare.

"Satisfied now, asshole?" she hissed.

She dropped the porcelain cover on his face. The impact shattered the white brick into several fragments. A geyser of blood erupted from his crushed nose. His body went limp. Rebecca grabbed the gun from his lifeless hands. She tumbled off the safety and checked to make sure it was loaded.

It was.

She took a deep breath. Her legs buckled, and she almost lost her balance. She steadied herself. *You're not out of this yet*, she thought.

She aimed the gun at Mr. Douglas's unmoving body.

No, she thought. If Bernatto hadn't heard the commotion, he would certainly hear a gunshot. Right now, the element of surprise was the only thing she had on her side.

She had to get out before Bernatto armed himself and made it back to the bathroom. She turned and kicked at the buckled, collapsing wall. Plaster and drywall crumbled to the ground. She kicked again, harder. Cold, dank air wafted in where a small black hole opened up. The air smelled of mold, rust, and sewage.

   Rebecca smiled.

CHAPTER TWENTY-SIX

Mariko led Caine past a row of delivery trucks in the parking lot, careful to keep out of sight. Caine heard distant screams coming from the dome. It was impossible to tell if someone had discovered the grisly scene they'd left behind or if it was just the general commotion of the concert. As they walked, Caine twisted his wrists back and forth, working to loosen the plastic restraints. Mariko had checked their tightness, but a couple millimeters could make all the difference later.

"I suppose I should thank you for saving my life." Caine flashed her a charming smile.

She ignored him and scanned the parking lot. "Keep walking."

"Where are we going? And why is a PSB officer in such a hurry to leave a crime scene instead of waiting to file a report with the police?"

"*Damare!*" she hissed. "Quiet. I can't hear myself think. Do you always talk this much?" She shoved the pistol in his back, prodding him forward.

"Sorry. Guns make me nervous."

She led him to a parked Toyota. It was a grey sedan.

"That car looks familiar...."

"It should. I've been following you since your first night in Kabukicho. Get in."

She opened the rear passenger door, and Caine slid into the car. A Japanese man in rumpled clothing waited in the driver's seat. He looked fit, despite the lines of age in his face. Caine recognized him at once. He was the forward tail, from the night he met Mariko.

A scowl settled onto his face when he saw Caine. He turned to Mariko as she sat next to him. "What the hell are you doing, bringing him here? Are you crazy?"

She closed the door with a thud. "He knows something. Drive."

The man shook his head and started up the car. As they pulled out of the parking lot, Caine could see a row of police and ambulance lights flashing in the distance. The lights cut a path through the standstill traffic.

Mariko turned around to face him. The harsh glow of the neon and streetlights outside reflected across her face.

"All right, Mr. Wilson. I'm listening. Talk."

"Call me Tom."

She said nothing.

"I can't tell you everything.... To be honest, I don't know everything. But I can tell you that all of this, the yakuza, Tokyo Black, the fighting, it's all over one girl. Her name is Hitomi Kusaka. She's Arinori Kusaka's daughter, and she's in danger."

Her eyes narrowed. "Arinori Kusaka? The businessman? You're certain he's involved?"

Caine wondered if had said more than he should. Her entire demeanor had changed at the mention of Kusaka's name. He'd struck a nerve.

"Your turn," he said. "Why have you been following me?"

She bit her lip as she glanced over at her partner, then back at Caine. "I've been investigating links between the yakuza and certain rightwing groups. Groups that have potential to commit acts of domestic terror."

"Groups like Tokyo Black?"

"*Hai*. Exactly. Japan has always had organizations such as these. The Red Army, Aum Shinrikyo. Death cults, secret societies. But Tokyo Black ... I've never seen anything on this scale before."

"What the hell do they want? Who's pulling their strings?"

Mariko shrugged. "They're radical conservatives. They claim that Japan has allowed itself to become weak, subservient to other nations. Particularly China. It began as a gang, in Fuchu Prison. A man named Atsutane Yuasa started it, after he was sent there for a gas attack on a subway in Osaka. One of his followers in prison was a man named Bobu Shimizu."

Caine leaned forward. "Bobu Shimizu? Tetsuo's brother? Big guy? Tattoo on his face?"

"Yes, although he no longer has the tattoo. Before he was yakuza, Bobu was a low-ranked sumo wrestler. He hurt himself a few times in the ring, got addicted to painkillers. From there, he moved to heroin. He was Atsutane's cellmate in Fuchu. Atsutane helped him clean up, got him through the withdrawal. Bobu left prison addiction-free, but he became fanatically devoted to Atsutane's teachings."

Mariko paused. "Now, your turn. Who are you really? When you popped up on our computers as Mark Waters, I thought maybe you were brokering another arms deal with the Yoshizawa family."

Caine shook his head. "No, that's not why I'm here. I told you, I'm looking for this girl, Hitomi. Tokyo Black wants her as well."

"And what will you do with her if you find her?"

"I'm not here to hurt her. That's all I can say for now."

Mariko was silent for a moment. She glanced at her partner. He gave her a quick, uncertain look. He muttered something in Japanese, but Caine couldn't catch his words. She turned back to Caine.

"This girl, Hitomi Kusaka. She is interesting to me for two reasons."

"Why's that?"

"First, I have suspicions that Arinori Kusaka has been secretly funding Tokyo Black. In my investigation, I uncovered evidence that he was funneling money to them through his numerous companies. When I presented my findings to my superiors, I was suspended. They said I had acted without permission, exceeded my authority."

"So that's why you were in such a hurry to leave the Dome."

A frown crossed her face. She looked away. "Kusaka-san is a highly respected man. He has political connections, friends in the government. I was foolish to make such an accusation without more proof. I should have waited until I had evidence that could not be ignored or explained away."

"Sounds to me like your superiors are dirty. Wouldn't matter what evidence you had. Either way, your hunch was right. Hitomi said she's running from her father. She said Tokyo Black works for him."

Mariko reached into the back pocket of her jeans. She pulled out a folding knife and flicked it open. The passing lights glinted off its blade.

"That is the second reason this girl interests me."

"Her father's connection to Tokyo Black?"

Mariko reached out and sliced the plastic restraints on Caine's wrists.

"No, not just that."

Caine massaged his wrists as the blood began to flow back into his hands and forearms.

"Okay, what then?"

"According to official records, Kusaka-san has no children."

Caine and Mariko walked down the busy Shinjuku sidewalk, while her partner parked the grey sedan around the corner. She sauntered confidently ahead of him, as if they had been working together for years. Caine found her sudden trust in him strange, and remembered the flash of emotion she had betrayed when he had mentioned Kusaka's name.

Something about her story was bothering him....

She pointed to a neon sign two blocks down the street. "That's the address you gave me. The Space Age. Very popular karaoke bar."

Caine nodded. "Mariko, before we go in, I have to ask.... If you're suspended right now, why are you still after Kusaka? Is this personal?"

"My duty is to protect Japan. If Kusaka is a danger to this country, I must stop him."

"Isn't it also your duty to obey your superiors?"

She glanced over at him, a curious look on her face. "Is that what you do?"

Caine laughed. "Not exactly."

Mariko stopped walking and turned to face him. "You are familiar with the *47 Ronin*? The famous samurai story?"

"I think I saw the movie."

"The ronin began as samurai. They became ronin, masterless warriors, when their lord was assassinated. They vowed to find the killer and avenge him. But the shogun, hoping to preserve peace, ordered them to stand down."

"What happened?"

"They waited a year for the perfect opportunity to strike. Then, under cover of darkness, they raided the assassin's castle and clashed with his army. Eventually, they fought their way to their lord's killer and beheaded him."

"And they lived happily ever after?"

She shook her head. "No. Justice was served, and their lord could finally rest in peace. But they had still disobeyed the orders of the shogun. He ordered that the men commit seppuku, the ritual suicide of the samurai."

"So, did they make a break for it?"

She gave him a strange look. "No. Don't you see? Even though they had avenged their lord, the men were still ronin. By committing seppuku, the shogun gave them the chance to die as samurai. Their honor was returned. Balance was restored."

"That's a nice fairy tale. But it still sounds pretty personal to me."

She paused. "Remember the man I told you about, the one who started Tokyo Black?"

Caine nodded. "Atsutane Yuasa. Bobu's mentor."

"I barely remember ... I was just a little girl. But that subway attack ... the one he planned. I was there when it happened. I survived. But my mother...."

She shuddered. "I ran out the door of the subway car. We were going to the dentist, and I was scared. I was causing trouble. My mother tried to stop me, but it was too late. I saw her looking through the glass; she was terrified for me. A policeman found me crying on the platform. He brought me to the next stop, but that was the train they attacked. She never made it to the next station. Nobody on board did."

There was something in Mariko's voice ... a tiny quavering, a slight dip in volume. Whatever it was, it cut through Caine's hardened shell. After a lifetime of fighting and violence, Caine had seen more death and despair than he cared to remember. He knew the wounds of grief and loss could cut far deeper than any physical pain.

His face softened. "I'm sorry."

"What about you?" she asked. "Is your interest personal?"

Caine nodded as they reached the club.

"Definitely personal," he said.

They passed through a set of glass doors and entered an elevator under a flashing neon sign.

CHAPTER TWENTY-SEVEN

Mr. Douglas sat up and gasped for breath. The dank, dingy air of the bathroom filled his lungs and cleared the haze from his eyes. The sting of the pepper spray still lingered, but that was secondary to the throbbing in his head. He gingerly explored the damage. His blond hair was matted with blood, and he felt a tremendous lump just behind his left ear.

"That goddamned bitch," he muttered.

He had been careless. Bernatto's file said the target was a bureaucrat. Basic field training only, no operational experience. He had underestimated her. He should have followed operational procedure, instead of relying on a file given to him by another bureaucrat. After all, that's what Bernatto was, no matter how deadly and thorough he may have seemed.

The girl was smart. Tenacious. She had played both of them.

He wiped the dripping blood from his face, flinging spatters to the floor as he stood up. Immediately, a wave of nausea hit him. He stumbled to the sink, leaned over, and dry heaved. After a few minutes, it passed. He took a deep breath, wiped the spittle from his lips, and stared at his face in the cracked mirror. The damage looked severe and he might have a concussion, but he had suffered worse.

In his reflection, he noticed the large, dark hole in the wall behind him. She must have broken through the drywall.

He checked his watch. He hadn't been out long, which meant she couldn't have gone far.

He patted down his pockets. She had his pistol.

Fine, he thought.

He strode out into the hall. He walked past the dark room where Bernatto was watching TV. The older man called out to him.

"Everything all right?"

"No," he answered. "She's on the move."

He kept walking. Bernatto raced into the hallway and followed him as he entered the room where his weapons were organized.

"What are you talking about? How could you let this happen?" Bernatto shouted.

Mr. Douglas clenched his jaw and grabbed an identical HK pistol to the one Rebecca had stolen from him. He loaded it, racked the slide, and slipped it into his shoulder holster. Next he slung an HK MP5 submachine gun around his neck. He slid several spare magazines of ammo into pouches on his belt.

"She hasn't gone far. I'll take care of it."

"Listen to me. I need her alive. Do you understand? Alive!"

Mr. Douglas stopped and stared at Bernatto. "Right now she is alive. Should I stand down? Or do you want me to pursue? If I pursue, I will do my best to deliver her alive. But I think we both would agree her death is preferable to certain other outcomes."

Bernatto lowered his gaze. "Fine. Go. Do what you have to."

Mr. Douglas added one more weapon to his arsenal ... a collapsible spring baton. He whipped it through the air a few times, testing its heft, then slid it through a loop at his belt.

"Trust me, I prefer alive as well. For now."

He strode from the room as Bernatto cursed under his breath. He checked his watch. Time was running out.

Scrapes and bruises covered Rebecca's arms. She winced as she dragged herself forward through the darkness. The crawlspace was only a few feet tall and pitch-black. Occasionally, she would run into a twisted shaft of iron rebar jutting from the ceiling.

The narrow, dark space was silent, aside from the occasional drip of water. She had half-expected to hear the frantic scuffling of a pursuer ... Bernatto or even Mr. Douglas. She realized that, in her haste to escape, she had forgotten to check his pulse. Was he dead? Or just unconscious?

She shook her head and moved forward another inch. It was too late to second-guess herself now. Either he was dead or he wasn't. And she could sooner picture Mr. Douglas rising from the dead than Bernatto crawling after her in this filthy crawlspace himself.

She froze when a rustling sounded above her and chips of drywall and other debris drifted down. The rustling grew louder. Someone was moving around up there.

She had no idea what kind of building she was in or the layout of the place. Was there a subfloor directly overhead? she wondered. The sound grew closer, and she struggled to turn over in the tight space. She looked up, peering into the darkness above her.

BANG!

The shot exploded through the air next to her head, sending a shower of dust and debris into her eyes. She screamed and clawed her way forward.

BANG! BANG!

Two more shots rang out, each one closer than the last. She could feel the sizzle of hot air as a bullet streaked past her ear.

This time, she didn't scream. Instead, she pulled the HK pistol from her waistband. She could feel her heart racing. She could almost hear it thumping in the tiny, dark crawlspace. She slowed her breath and steadied her hand. Aiming the gun at the floorboards above her, she squeezed off two shots.

The explosion was deafening in the enclosed space. She ignored the ringing in her ears and moved forward again. Her body twisted around the iron rebar that blocked her progress.

More bullets rained down from above. The shots came at a slow, steady pace. The bastard was honing in on her movements, tracking her by sound. Well, two could play that game. She returned fire, using the bullet holes above her as a guide.

Her head slammed into something solid. Another bullet smashed through the floor, just missing her knee. She unleashed a wild barrage of bullets at the floorboards above her until she heard a muted grunt of pain.

The sounds above stopped. Exhausted and panting, she twisted her body around to face the barrier. Her fingernails clawed at the drywall. It was soft, rotted from mold and humidity. Pivoting her legs around, she began to kick at the wall. A clump of soggy plaster shifted and crumbled to the floor. She could make out a small black hole, darker than the rest of the shadows surrounding her. She kicked again and again, until it was large enough to squeeze through.

She crashed to the ground, her clothes covered in dirt and grime. Her hair was damp and streaked with filth. She stood up and looked around, holding her pistol out in front of her. She was in a cavernous concrete room. A row of windows ran along one wall, vanishing into the darkness. They were boarded up from the outside, but shafts of moonlight penetrated the cracks.

The ceiling above her was a maze of pipes and industrial lighting. All the bulbs were shattered. A fine dust of broken glass sparkled on the floor. A few rusted oil drums lay scattered about the chamber. The writing on the barrels was in Thai, but the black stick figures and universal symbol for fire needed no translation.

She was in some kind of industrial building, she realized. An abandoned oil refinery or maybe a chemical plant. That meant they would be on the outskirts of the city. Far from the crowds. Far from help. She took a few tentative steps out into the darkness.

A barrage of gunfire nipped at her heels. She yelped and charged forward. The gunfire followed her, kicking up puffs of dust and powdered glass. She dove for cover, but the attack persisted. The bullets ricocheted off the concrete column she hid behind and danced around the room.

Then the gunfire ceased.

Rebecca bit her lip and peered around the edge of the column, trying to get a bead on the shooter. Near the hole she'd made was an air vent just below the ceiling. Squinting in the darkness, she could just make out a shadow shifting behind the vent.

She gripped the pistol with both hands and spun out from behind the column. She fired. Her bullets sparked against the metal of the vent. She ducked back behind the column as another burst of automatic weapon fire streaked towards her.

She spun her head around, searching for something, anything she could use. On the floor behind her were scraps of cloth and rags, most likely makeshift blankets from homeless squatters. Empty tin food cans littered the ground.

A burst of red light filled the room, blinding her. A sizzling, hissing sound filled the air. She dropped down to a crouch and closed her eyes for a second. A familiar voice echoed out of the darkness. Bernatto.

"Rebecca, this is pointless."

She blinked her eyes open. A bright pinpoint of red light flickered in the center of the room. Bernatto was using signal flares to illuminate the area.

Keeping the column between herself and the air vent, she kicked one of the metal cans out into the room. It clanged across the floor for a brief second before it was struck by another explosion of gunfire.

As the can danced through the air, Rebecca charged to the next column. She caught a glimpse of a shadowy figure in a doorway. Bernatto raised his arm, and Rebecca saw the brief muzzle flash of a pistol. She darted to safety behind the column. The bullet ricocheted off the concrete floor behind her.

The room once again fell silent, save for the sizzling flare in the center. She was just outside its radius of light, hidden in shadow behind the other columns.

A loud crash and the clatter of falling metal echoed in the space. *The air vent!* She risked a quick glance and saw the dark figure of Mr. Douglas drop to the ground.

She fired, sending several quick shots his way. He ran and took cover behind another column. He was limping. One of her shots from the crawlspace must have found its mark. She could not resist a slight smirk of satisfaction.

"Rebecca, think this through," Bernatto said. "You're alone out here. You're outnumbered. You're out of options. I don't want to hurt you. In fact, I need you alive. Don't make this harder than it has to be. Put down your gun, and let's work something out."

"Like you worked something out for Tom?"

She darted towards another column. More gunfire rang out from behind her. She heard a flurry of footsteps as Mr. Douglas moved to another column.

Bernatto tossed another flare. It landed close to her, shrinking her cover of darkness to a sliver of shadow. She fired several rounds towards the door and a double tap towards Mr. Douglas's position. In the darkness, she knew she was firing blind, hoping to hold back the inevitable.

She ducked back behind the column and scanned the room again. She searched for another door, an air vent ... any way out of the impossible situation facing her now. She saw more evidence of squatters. Dirty old clothes. A filthy plastic doll missing its arms and legs.

A second voice called out into the darkness. It was Mr. Douglas.

"There's something else you should keep in mind, Ms. Freeling. I've been keeping count, you see. You're down to one bullet. And there's two of us. This is a fight you can't win. So take a second, think it over. Then do what Mr. Bernatto here says. I promise I'll go easy on you."

The icy tone of his voice gave Rebecca the feeling that his version of "going easy on her" would be less than pleasant. She ejected the magazine from her pistol and checked the load. He was right ... the magazine was empty. That left her with a single round remaining in the chamber. She choked back a curse.

She slammed the magazine back in the pistol. She could hear Bernatto's footsteps growing closer. He ignited another flare and tossed it towards her. It rolled to a stop a few feet from the column she was hiding behind.

As its blood red glow chased away her shadows of concealment, she spotted something she had missed in the darkness. A makeshift cooking stove. It was little more than a homemade valve and a length of metal tube, attached to a small canister of propane gas. The contraption sat in a rusted shopping cart. A thin sheet of bent, charred metal served as a cooking surface.

Two sets of footsteps moved closer, and Bernatto called out to her. "This is bigger than Caine, bigger than you. We're talking about America's future here, Rebecca."

Rebecca grabbed the flare and slid over to the shopping cart on her hands and knees. *Just keep, talking you bastard.*

She tossed the metal grill aside and grabbed the propane tank. She forced herself to be careful as she unscrewed the metal hose from the makeshift burner. As she worked, she heard the two men advancing towards her.

"Rebecca, this is your last chance," Bernatto said. "Work with me. We can do some good here, I promise you. Just hear me out."

A part of her knew what she was attempting was crazy ... suicide, even. But as far as she could see, Mr. Douglas was right. This wasn't a fight she could win. Unless she changed her tactics.

A barrage of gunfire exploded behind her. She ducked down low, but a red-hot pain lanced through her back. She cried out and fell to the ground.

Her breath turned to a series of ragged gasps. She could feel hot blood pooling beneath her back on the cold concrete floor. She hugged the fruits of her labor to her chest, as if she were clinging to life itself.

The shadowy outlines of Bernatto and Mr. Douglas stepped out from behind two columns at opposite ends of the room. The figures sharpened as they moved closer. Mr. Douglas's perfect, cherubic face and cold smile made him look like a fallen angel in the hellish red light. Bernatto's angry scowl was amplified by the shadows that moved across his face. He was the fallen angel's master, the devil himself.

She tried to roll away, her brain jumbled with panic and fear. The pain in her back, the numbness in her torso ... she realized she couldn't move her legs.

She was paralyzed from the waist down.

"Rebecca, I'm disappointed. This is foolish."

Mr. Douglas stopped six feet away from her. "I'm not disappointed, Ms. Freeling. I'm just curious. One bullet left ... what do you do? Shoot me? Shoot Mr. Bernatto? You know, when I was in the SEAL teams, we always saved one bullet for ourselves, just in case. Maybe this bullet has your name on it. What's it gonna be, Ms. Freeling?"

Rebecca choked back her tears. She was damned if she would let them see her cry. She let her arms fall to her sides. The small, dirty white canister rolled out of her arms, stopping just a few feet away from Mr. Douglas.

The flare was tied to the top of the canister with the length of metal hose. Its red glare burned away the shadows; in its crimson light, she saw Bernatto's features shift from an annoyed scowl to shock. She had just enough time to smile before he turned and ran for the door.

Mr. Douglas lifted his MP5, but he was too late. Her gun was already aimed straight at the canister. She pulled the trigger.

A massive fireball filled the room, lifting her and the two men and tossing them through the air. She caught a glimpse of Mr. Douglas's face as the fire tore at his flesh. Then she fell to the ground. She felt as though all the air had been sucked from the room.

The darkness spun around her as she slipped into the cold, black space of unconsciousness.

CHAPTER TWENTY-EIGHT

The interior of The Space Age karaoke bar was quiet and subdued. Brief flashes of loud music would drift through the dark hallways, as customers entered and exited their private rooms. But when the doors closed, the only sound came from the quiet movements of cocktail waitresses and hosts. They glided through the corridors, balancing trays of empty glasses, bottles of sake, and platters of deep-fried snacks.

The hostess at the door bowed to Caine as they entered.

"*Irashimase.*" She greeted him with a flirtatious smile. "Do you have a room reservation?"

Caine smiled back. "We're meeting a friend. *Arrigato gozimasu.*"

The hostess bowed again. Her eyes flicked over to a new set of customers entering the busy bar behind them. Caine and Mariko stepped into the labyrinth of dark hallways and muted music.

Caine looked up at the numbers above the private karaoke rooms. "Back this way." They pushed past a crowd of drunken party girls and made their way to a red leather door. Caine scanned the crowd. From the corner of his eye, he saw Mariko making her own assessments. *She's a pro,* he thought. *Might be difficult to shake her loose if I have to run with Hitomi.*

He pushed the thought to the back of his mind. He would deal with that later. For now, she seemed like she could be useful.

Once they were satisfied they had not been followed, Mariko nodded to Caine. "It's clear."

He opened the door and stepped into outer space.

A high, curved ceiling rose above the dark room. A hidden projector beamed an image of stars and planets onto the dome above, while an eerie song played. The effect was startling and realistic, like a miniature planetarium.

Caine closed the door after Mariko. If the strange room fazed her at all, she didn't show it. She looked up as an image of Saturn streaked above them.

"Hitomi?" Caine called out into the darkness, shouting over the music.

The song's volume dipped. "I am here."

Caine didn't recognize the girl's voice. Then he remembered: when they last spoke, Hitomi had been using the Masuka Ongaku avatar. Her voice was no longer a robotic chirp. It was softer, human ... a curious combination of bored and scared.

Caine looked around. Unlike other karaoke rooms he had seen, this one was circular. Chairs were arranged around the walls, and the musical lyrics were projected on the ceiling, amidst the stars and planets.

His first glimpse of Hitomi was just a bright outline. He saw a halo of light, surrounding the dark shadow of a feminine form. She was sitting in front of the room's projector.

"Who is she?" Hitomi asked. Caine looked back at Mariko, as she took a step forward.

"My name is Mariko Murase," she said. "I'm working with the *Keisatsu Cho,* Public Security Bureau."

Hitomi's shadowy form twisted in her chair. "Then you work for my father, whether you know it or not."

"Hitomi," Caine said, "we're here to help. You can't keep running. You said so yourself. These men chasing you are dangerous. It's only a matter of time until they find you. Unless we can stop them."

"I was almost free of him. Then you showed up. For all I know, you led them to me."

Mariko pressed a button on the wall. With a quiet mechanical hum, metal blinds rose up from the floor, uncovering the windows and revealing the city outside.

A shaft of darkness crawled across the room, chased away by the glow of the colorful lights outside a large, curved window. Hitomi appeared in the reflection as the darkness receded to the edges of the room.

She looked different from her picture. A bit older, maybe twenty-one or twenty-two. Her hair was no longer a rich, dark brown. She had dyed it a pale, almost silver blond, and it shimmered in the glow of the city outside.

Her skin was pale as well, either from makeup or hiding indoors. Her eyes were soft pools of brown in the luminous white landscape of her slim face. Slashes of dark eyeshadow gave them a strange, alien look, like the lifeless eyes of a kabuki mask.

She wore a white sequined bustier and a long matching skirt. The shimmering fabric clung to her body, stretching as she crossed her legs. Expensive-looking heels adorned her tiny, pale feet. She had unbuckled their ankle straps, and one of the shoes dangled as she bounced her foot up and down.

She looked like a ghost, a pale figure of death sitting alone in a dark room.

"Not exactly playing it subtle, are we?" Caine remarked.

The girl smiled and sipped a cocktail.

"I'm hiding in plain sight. My father knows what I look like. A more extreme look makes men like him and his followers uncomfortable. Maybe they will not look at me so closely this way."

Mariko stepped forward, looking the girl up and down.

"Who are you?" she asked. "Who are you really?"

"You know who I am."

"Arinori Kusaka has no children," Mariko snapped. "I don't have time to play guessing games with you, girl!"

Mariko stormed forward and swiped Hitomi's cocktail glass off the chair. The girl flinched as it shattered against the wall.

"Mariko!" Caine grabbed her by the arm. She shrugged out of his grip and turned back to Hitomi.

"People are dying. Kusaka has this city in a chokehold of corruption and bribery. Whatever he is planning, it is dangerous. It must be stopped. I must stop him. And you WILL help us. Do you understand me?"

An angry glare replaced Hitomi's peaceful gaze. "Kusaka-san is my father." She spat out the words, as if they tasted bitter on her tongue. "He may not acknowledge it any more than you do, but it is the truth just the same. You think I am playing a game? You don't know anything about me. You don't know what I had to do to get here. What I went through to find him. And now, what I've had to do to escape."

"If Kusaka-san is your father, you must be one of the richest girls in Japan. Why would you want to escape?"

Caine stared at the two women. There was a severity about Mariko that bothered him. He was beginning to get the feeling there was more to her interest in Kusaka than she had told him. As they argued, he moved to the window and surveyed the street below.

"You know nothing," Hitomi said. "I was not born here. This is not my home. And he does not see me as his daughter. He sees me as...." Her voice trailed off.

Caine saw a stream of flashing red lights in the distance. They formed a long line in the street and were heading straight for the intersection where The Space Age bar was located.

"Mariko?" Caine called over his shoulder. "Did you report in to your superiors before we came here?"

Mariko looked back. "No, why?"

"We've got a problem. Look."

She stepped over to the window. The line of lights was closing in. It was a row of police cars, snaking in and out of traffic, making a beeline for their location.

"*Kuso*," she cursed. "It must have been my partner, Taro. He's worried he'll be suspended, too, for helping me. I should have known he'd crack. Now he'll probably get a commendation."

Caine hit the button on the wall, and the blinds began to close. "Hitomi, we have to go."

The girl stood up. "It's my father, isn't it? I told you he'd find me."

"No, it's the police."

She sighed and draped a black leather jacket over her shoulders. "I keep telling you, it amounts to the same thing. Money, power, connections ... my father is Tokyo. Do you understand? He controls everything in this city."

Caine touched her shoulder, guiding her towards the door. Mariko poked her head out into the hallway.

"It's clear. Let's move."

They headed for the exit. "Hitomi, I know your father is a powerful man. But he doesn't control everything. Or everyone."

Hitomi looked at him as she stepped out into the corridor. She stared into his eyes, tilting her head slightly. Her pupils were wide and dark. She was clearly on something.

"You look familiar to me," she said in a dreamy voice.

"You saw me at the concert, on your camera, remember?"

She shook her head. "No. It's not that. It's your eyes. They look like mine. I can see the pain in them."

She touched his face with her slim hand. Her fingers were cold. "Pain and betrayal. You have suffered these things. Haven't you?"

"Yes," Caine said. "I have."

She looked away. "Then you should know better than to think we can escape my father. There are some things no one can escape."

She turned and followed Mariko out into the hall. Caine paused for a brief second, wondering what she meant. Then, as the sirens grew closer, he stepped into the darkness outside.

Behind him, the projected cosmos of twinkling stars and spinning planets continued to dance across the ceiling.

CHAPTER TWENTY-NINE

The tiny blip on the air traffic control screen pulsed brightly. Natsumi sipped her coffee as she watched the green dot inch closer and closer on the radar screen. She grimaced. The black liquid in her cup had turned cold and bitter.

"Looking good, 1168. Maintain this approach vector. Please transmit IDENT code now. Repeat. Please transmit IDENT code now."

Haruki, her handsome assistant controller, leaned over her shoulder and set down a fresh cup of coffee.

"*Arrigato,* Haru-kun. It's been a long day. My shift was supposed to end an hour ago, but this one is a real pain in the ass."

The young man smiled. "Oh, someone important?"

Natsumi shrugged. "We'll see. All I know is they made me give this flight double the normal clearance. Had to move all other flights into the next safe zone." The terminal next to her screen began to beep and flash numbers. The plane was sending its IDENT code, identifying the flight. Natsumi submitted the code to the tower control for clearance.

They waited a few minutes, staring at the screen as the blip began its final approach to Tokyo Narita Airport. Then the terminal flashed again. Natsumi squinted at the result. "Well, well, what do you know..."

"What?"

Natsumi turned to her mic and once again spoke in English. "Roger that, 1168, IDENT received. You are cleared to land. Please follow the approach coordinates I am sending you now. Thank you, and good evening."

"Well, who is it?" Haruki asked.

Natsumi took another sip of her coffee and smiled. "U.S. State Department flight. Wasn't on any of the logs. Apparently, the Secretary of State is making a last minute visit to Tokyo."

"Oh, that's interesting. I wonder what she's doing here?"

Natsumi stood up and stretched. She grunted in pain as she arched her back, then she slipped on a worn wool coat. "I have no idea, but once that plane's on the ground, something very important is going to happen."

The young man's eyes were wide. "Really? What's going to happen?"

Natsumi smiled. "My shift is going to end, and I am going to go home."

A sea of photographers swarmed behind the barricades guarding the C-32 aircraft. The plane was long, sleek, and gleamed in the runway lights. A woman dressed in a stylish grey business suit stepped out onto the stairs that led to the tarmac.

United States Secretary of State Janet Kelson waved to the reporters. A phalanx of Secret Service agents stood at attention, scanning the crowd from the ground. Two more flanked the secretary and her aide, a petite younger woman named Susan Clifford. The entourage followed as she descended the steps to meet the greeting committee of Japanese officials and a ranking U.S. Naval officer.

She bowed, then shook each of their hands in turn. The press continued snapping photos as she moved down the line. When she got to the Naval officer, she omitted the bow and gave his hand a firm shake. She leaned in closer. "I hope they didn't drag you out of bed for this, Captain."

The military officer smiled. "No, ma'am. I was just stationed here last week. Still haven't adjusted to the time difference."

"That's what hot sake is for." She turned and faced the crowd one more time. The Japanese officials stood by her side, posing for another series of photographs.

After a few minutes, one of the Secret Service agents led her away from the flashing lights and reporters. They walked over to a waiting limo. The chauffeur opened the door, and she climbed in. Susan followed after her.

The door closed, and Janet's mouth gaped as she uttered a loud yawn. "How long is the drive to the hotel?"

Susan pulled out an enormous smartphone and tapped on it with a stylus. "Two hours in current traffic."

Janet shook her head. "Can't even take a nap, or I'll be up all night. Do you have my briefings?"

Susan handed her a stack of manila folders. "Here's everything we have on the Chinese and Japanese officials. You'll be meeting them for breakfast at the embassy, then traveling by helicopter to the islands."

Janet nodded. "A little light reading."

Susan smiled and consulted her phone. "Looks like rain tomorrow. Make sure you bring your trench."

"Lovely. I hope that's not a bad omen."

The limo pulled away from the airport. Janet began to flip through papers as they turned onto the freeway. This would be a useful trip, after all. She figured the United States could use some diplomatic good will after all the turmoil in the Middle East. A few pictures with the local officials, a quick helicopter ride to a series of rocks not worth fighting about. Whatever China and Japan decided about these islands, she knew this could be a perfect PR opportunity for the United States.

Even better, if she could play the diplomacy game just right, she could strengthen ties to both China and Japan. The United States would be seen as a fair, impartial ally to both.

But it would require finesse. The last thing America needed was to be pulled into a pointless conflict between China and Japan. Even a diplomatic squabble such as this could have long-term economic repercussions.

At first, she'd been annoyed when the U.S. ambassador was hospitalized. The car accident was terrible in terms of timing, and she resented being ordered to take his place at these talks. The flight to Tokyo was thrown together last minute, and the long trip was more than a tad inconvenient.

But now she was beginning to see the situation as an opportunity. An opportunity for peace. And an opportunity for personal advancement.

A new song played over the limo's stereo speakers. As she flipped through the files, she began to hum along.

CHAPTER THIRTY

The cell phone rang and rang until once again the voicemail picked up. It was the third time Caine had tried to reach Rebecca. He knew she was traveling, but she hadn't checked in on the airphone as they had agreed. He had hoped maybe he would catch her at a connection airport, but so far he hadn't had any luck.

Something was wrong.

He sat on the bed of the rundown love hotel and rubbed his face. The day's activities had taken a toll. As the adrenalin of this latest brush with disaster subsided, he felt his body groaning in protest. Tired, beaten, battered ... he knew the signs. He could not keep going like this forever.

The walls of the cheap room were paper-thin. He could hear the shower running in the bathroom, where Hitomi was cleaning, and hopefully sobering, up. Mariko paced back and forth in front of the closed blinds. She stopped and pulled them aside. She stared out the gap for a second, surveying the neon lights and crowds of people walking down the busy street.

The bed was round, bubblegum pink, and—Caine noted with amusement—equipped with an assortment of vibration settings. The sheets were gleaming satin. Looking up, he saw a circular mirror recessed in the ceiling. His reflection looked distant and alone, adrift in a vast sea of shimmering pink.

Mariko noticed him looking up and gave him a grim smile. "It's been a long time since a man's taken me to a place like this."

"Hey, you picked it."

She shrugged. "Our options were limited. At least here, we could check in by computer. No one to see our faces if the police or Tokyo Black come looking for us."

Caine gazed at her, drinking in the details. Smooth skin. Dark, lustrous hair. Her body promised warmth if one could just get past the darkness that lay behind her icy, calculating stare. She was beautiful, and it had been a long time since he had allowed himself to appreciate a woman's beauty.

But Caine knew attraction could be a dangerous weapon. It could make him lower his guard, ignore risks, or fail to notice obvious signs of danger. He reminded himself to stay sharp.

The mission, whatever it was, was not over. Bernatto, Kusaka, Bobu ... it seemed he added a new name to his list of enemies every day. He wondered if Mariko was an ally, or if her name would soon be counted among those who wanted him dead.

Mariko stared at him for a second, then walked over, and sat down on the bed next to him. He found his eyes drawn to the curve of her ear, framed by the sweeping black line of her hair.

"You're wondering if you can trust me," she said.

Caine looked her square in the eye, searching for truth in the dark sea of brown and black. "Mariko, we barely know each other. And back at the bar, you came at the girl pretty hard. I get the feeling you're not telling me something."

For the first time, her cold, black stare began to thaw.

"I ... yes, there is more. For you as well. This man, Bobu ... you have a past with him?"

Caine nodded. "You could say that. A few years ago, the Shimizu and Yoshizawa clans got into a pissing match over territory. You know, typical yakuza stuff. Old school. Bobu was sent to take out Isato Yoshizawa. Send a message. A young boy, Isato's son, got in the way. I was there, and I ... I couldn't just let it happen. I blocked Bobu's shot. I took the bullet. Isato and the boy lived. Bobu was caught by the police, went to jail. The Shimizu clan fell into decline."

Mariko's eyes narrowed. "What on earth were you even doing there?"

"It's a long story, and I can't really talk about it."

She stared at him for a second. Then she nodded and looked away.

"What I told you before, about my mother ... her death left a hole in my family. My father was never the same after she was gone. He became distant, turned to drink. The doctors said it was the alcohol that killed him. But the look on his face ... it was grief that consumed him. I could see it plain as day."

Caine put a hand on Mariko's shoulder. A tremor ran through her body. "My younger sister, Emiko ... I wasn't there for her. She wasn't like me. She was gentle, fragile even. She couldn't face the pain alone. She went down a path ... I did not approve of. Drugs, boyfriends. *Toroburu* ... trouble. We fought. I said things that were unkind. We did not speak again for several years.

"A few weeks ago, she left me a message. She said she needed to talk. I was busy pursuing this case. I was determined to expose Kusaka's links to Tokyo Black. It was all I could think about; it was an obsession. If I could cut off their funding, I could cripple them once and for all. I could...." Mariko's voice trailed off. She looked up at Caine. Her voice wavered. "I never called her back."

"What happened?" Caine asked, his voice low.

"Several days later, park rangers found a girl in Aokigahara Forest. She was dead. Massive drug overdose. Aokigahara is a beautiful place. The Sea of Trees. People go there to end their lives. It is known as the Suicide Forest."

"I've heard of it."

Mariko's almond-shaped eyes glinted with held-back tears. "The girl they found ... it was Emiko. My little sister. A death in that forest, it is no accident. You understand?"

Caine nodded.

"She went there to end her pain. In my country, it is not always an easy thing to ask for help. Emiko tried to reach out to me. I didn't call her back. I wasn't there for her. I couldn't...."

"I'm sorry," Caine said. "You can't blame yourself." He knew the words would not help, but what else was there to say?

Mariko shook her head. "As a young girl, I cheated death. Now, it is seeking me once again. A man ... a sick, disturbed man kills my mother and hundreds of others. He dies in prison. But he was like a black stone tossed into a quiet pond. The ripples of his actions spread and tore my family apart.

"Now, years later, Bobu, his apprentice, returns to seed more hate and destruction. It is a circle of death. As if his spirit is reaching out for me from the grave."

Caine gripped her shoulder. She looked up, her eyes moist and wide. "No, Mariko, these are just men, not spirits. I've known men like this all my life. Fought them. Killed them. Even worked with them, when I had to."

Mariko nodded. "I know they are just men. I know. That is why I kept investigating Kusaka, even after I was suspended. He is the head of this thing. His money is this thing's lifeblood. It is keeping Tokyo Black alive."

Her eyes hardened, and she stood up, shrugging away Caine's hand. She shivered and crossed her arms. Her voice dropped to a whisper. "I will stop them. Kusaka, Bobu Shimizu. I'll go to hell itself and stab this cult's founder in his black heart if I must. But I will end Tokyo Black. For my family. And for Japan. That is my duty."

A small, quiet voice spoke out. "I am sorry about your sister."

Caine and Mariko turned to find Hitomi staring at them. She was wrapped in a white terry bathrobe provided by the hotel. Her silvery hair was wet and glistened in the light. Standing in the dim room, soaking wet, her makeup washed away, she looked young, frail, and ethereal.

Mariko's voice was calm but firm. "Hitomi, I'm the one who should apologize. When I saw you tonight, you reminded me of Emiko, in a way. I was not there for her. That is my shame. I'm sorry I took it out on you."

Hitomi looked down. "You fight for her now. She is lucky to have a sister like you."

"Why is Kusaka so determined to find you?" Caine asked. "What do you have that he wants?"

Hiromi sighed and sat down on the bed. "At first, I thought he just wanted me back. As I said, he does not see me as a daughter. I am his property."

Mariko walked over to Hitomi and began to stroke her hair with a towel. "What do you mean?"

"I was born in China. My mother was ... my father, Kusaka-san, paid her. For her body. For pleasure. He visited her many times on his business trips to Beijing and Shanghai. I grew up hearing that my father was a rich, powerful man, a king in Japan.

"When my mother died, I used every penny she had saved to come here. I did not have a passport. I was nothing in China ... a ghost. I paid men to smuggle me here. I owed them money so I worked in their clubs and bordellos. I pleasured men as my mother had. And then I found Kusaka-san. My father. I went to him, hoping that he would save me from the monsters who had brought me here."

"Hitomi, I'm so sorry," Caine said. Living in Thailand, he had heard many stories of girls looking for a way out, smuggled around the world, hoping for a better life. He had even come up against traffickers himself. He knew such stories rarely had happy endings.

"My father was the biggest monster of all. He bought my contract out from the Chinese gangs. I thought my dreams had come true. But I did not go to live with him in his mansion. Instead, he sold me to the Shimizu family. They put me to work in their clubs. And my father, he...." Her voice trailed off.

Mariko looked over at Caine and slowly shook her head. Caine's entire body simmered with anger, but he said nothing.

"He does not see me as his daughter," Hitomi said. "He says I remind him of my mother. That is how he sees me. Sometimes, I would be delivered to his house for a night. Once, I saw him hiding papers and computer equipment in his safe. He took pictures of me, sometimes. I knew the pictures were in the safe. I just couldn't stand it, knowing that they were there.

"One night, he got very drunk after ... after he was finished with me. He forgot to lock the safe. I took what was inside and left. I thought I could blackmail him. That he would be ashamed of his actions, and he would pay me enough money that I could go home."

"It wasn't the pictures, was it? On the drive?" Caine asked.

Hitomi shook her head. "I don't know. I tried to hook it up to a computer at an internet cafe, but it wouldn't work. It is in code or something. I couldn't access it. And now, these men. I have seen them before ... the one with the burned face?"

"Bobu," Caine hissed.

Hitomi nodded. "My father sent me to him once." She shuddered. "He is just as big a monster as my father. He believes what he is doing will restore Japan, somehow. Make the country powerful again. He's crazy. And my father has sent him to find me.

"He has been chasing me all this time, killing all those people...." She began to sob gently. Her body shook, softly at first, then harder. Mariko grimaced, then held her in an embrace.

"I needed money, quickly. I worked in the soaplands, hostess clubs, anywhere I could. There was a bosozuku boy who had a thing for me. His name was Sonny. He introduced me to Mr. Naka. The yonigeya was going to help me leave the country once I had saved up enough to pay him."

She gripped the sheet next to her in her slender fingers. "Now Naka-san is dead," Hitomi said through her tears. "I have no more money, no passport. There's nowhere left to run. Bobu will find me."

"We're not running," Caine snarled. "We have something these men want. That means we have leverage."

Hitomi shook her head. Her eyes were wide with fear. "Leverage? Are you crazy? Does the rat have leverage over the tiger just because the tiger wants his meat?"

Caine stood up. "Sometimes it's not about who has the biggest teeth, Hitomi. It's about who goes for the throat first."

"Where is the drive now?" Mariko asked.

Hitomi wiped the tears from her face. "It's at the Hotel Riverside, in Asakusa. It's a capsule hotel. I left the drive in a locker there."

"Then that's where we're going," Caine said. "Hitomi, you'd better get dressed."

The girl nodded and padded back to the bathroom. When the door clicked shut, Mariko turned to Caine.

"What are you going to do?" she asked.

"I was just hired to find her. I never got any instructions beyond that."

"And now?"

"I have no idea. But judging by the people who are after it, whatever is on that hard drive must be dangerous. I'd feel better if it was in our hands."

"I'd feel better if it was in my hands," Mariko said. "I'm still not sure what your involvement is here."

Caine nodded. "Yeah, I'll let you know when I figure that out myself." He pulled out his cell phone and dialed another number.

"What are you doing?" Mariko asked.

"Calling for backup." He turned away from her as a voice on the other end of the line picked up. "It's me. I need to speak with Yoshizawa-san. Tell him I need a favor."

CHAPTER THIRTY-ONE

Kenji Yoshizawa whistled a catchy K-pop tune as he walked through the Roppongi warehouse. He felt a strange current in the air, a nervous energy. The yakuza thugs scattered around the large room puffed away on their cigarettes and spoke in hushed and hurried tones. They watched him pass with hard, silent stares, then returned to their conversations. His father's men were on edge. Something was happening.

He shook his head as he watched the old man in the blue windbreaker shake food into the plastic pools covering the floor. The koi farm was one of many investments he'd advised his father to dump. As usual, Yoshizawa-san refused to listen to him. Kenji could show him charts and graphs all day. He could show the business's lack of profits, the rising cost of supplies and real estate, and a million other statistics. If his father wanted a business location to conduct his yakuza meetings, why not at least make it a successful business?

But his father would ignore the charts, the graphs, and Kenji's statistics. Instead, he would rattle on about old stories or superstitions. Like the legend of the koi who, after a hundred years, managed to swim up a waterfall and through the dragon gate, despite mocking demons impeding its progress. The ancient gods were so impressed, they transformed the koi into a powerful dragon with gleaming gold scales.

Kenji knew there were no gods handing out dragonhood, in Japan or anywhere else. Those who craved power were not rewarded for hard work or perseverance or swimming up waterfalls. Power belonged to those who were smart, strong, and ruthless enough to take what they wanted, no matter the risks.

Tonight, he promised himself, he would take what he wanted. No charts, no graphs ... things would be different this time. Tonight his father would listen to reason. He would make him listen. The family's future was at stake. And this time, it would take more than handguns and cheap suits to secure their future.

Kenji approached the old man who sang to his fish in a quiet, gentle voice. He vaguely remembered coming to the warehouse as a child and seeing the same old man, singing the same old song, as he sprinkled food into the water. He realized he had no idea what the man's name was.

"Hey, does that song really work?" Kenji asked. "Does it make the fish grow bigger?"

The old man gave him a thin smile. "Oh, I don't know," he croaked. "Who can say? They're just fish, after all."

Kenji laughed. "Then why do you sing to them? Do they like it?"

The old man shrugged. "I like it. And they don't seem to mind. You see that one there, the blue one?" The man pointed to a stunning blue-and-white koi who was swimming in tight circles, away from the other fish. Its scales looked like trails of sapphires and diamonds sparking in the water.

"What's so special about that one?"

The old man smiled again. "The colors ... the blue and white. He is you, the son. The red koi are the mothers. And the black ones are the fathers. Blue koi represent the role of sons."

"Why is he swimming all alone?"

Frowning, he leaned in closer. "That's a good question, young man. Perhaps his parents were removed from this pool. Maybe they were sold."

Kenji smiled. "Well, at least this place makes some money then. Later, old man."

As he strutted away from the pool, the old man watched him go, then looked back at the blue koi. The fish continued lapping its small section of water. The man frowned again, shook his head, and resumed his singing.

Kenji made his way to the dark back room. The two beefy men guarding his father's office nodded and moved aside to let him pass. The heavy metal door clanked and clattered as it rolled up into the ceiling. Kenji nodded to the men and continued into the dark corridor that lay beyond. He heard the door lower behind him, hitting the concrete floor with a clang that echoed through the air.

Up ahead, a single dim light gleamed through an open doorway. He could hear his father's short, muted sentences. He rounded the corner and entered the dim office. Isato sat behind his desk in the far corner of the room. He was on the phone, his mouth set in its usual impatient scowl.

Kenji grabbed a chair from the center of the room. It was the same chair Waters had been sitting in only a few days earlier ... the beginning of the recent insanity. He dragged it in front of Isato's desk and waited for his father to finish his conversation. The single light swayed overhead.

"*Hai.* Yes, I understand. Very well. I will welcome having you in my debt for a change. When this is over, you and I will have a long discussion about your involvement with this family." He slammed the phone down and looked up at Kenji over the rim of his glasses.

"Kenji, welcome. I didn't realize we were meeting this evening. It's a bit late to go over finances, isn't it?"

Kenji leaned forward in his chair. "That was Waters-san, wasn't it?"

Isato took off his glasses and began to clean them with a cloth he pulled from his suit pocket. "Yes, although Koichi tells me that's not his real name. I assumed as much."

"His name is Thomas Caine, Dad. Did you know he was working for the American CIA the last time he was here?"

Isato slipped his glasses back on. "And how would you know that?"

"You may not realize it, but I do my part to take care of this family as well. I'm not just an accountant."

Isato dismissed him with a wave of his hand. "Bah, I keep telling you, leave the yakuza stuff to Koichi and the others. You're more useful to me in the boardroom than the streets."

"Where is Caine now?" Kenji asked.

"That's not your concern," Isato said. "Now, do you want to go over numbers or not?"

"Come on, I owe the guy. I just want to make sure he's okay."

Isato looked at him long and hard. His beady black eyes seemed to look through Kenji's face, into the dark space behind him. For the first time in his life, Kenji got a sense of how his father's enemies and underlings might feel, faced with that penetrating stare.

"Kenji," Isato said, "you don't get to be my age in this business without learning how to spot a lie. Now what is this all about?"

Kenji sighed and leaned back in his chair. "Jeez, Dad, it would just be nice if, for once, you could at least act like you trust me. I was helping him earlier tonight. Koichi and I took him to see Mr. Naka. Or at least what was left of him."

Isato slammed his fist down on his desk and cursed in Japanese. "Dammit, Kenji! I told you to stay away from him! Koichi knew about this?"

"Take it easy, man. You'll give yourself an aneurysm. I just gave him a ride; that's all. You may be the oyabun, but I'm the oyabun's son …. Koichi has to respect me, too, right?"

"Kenji, it's not about respect. I want to keep you away from all of this. You spend your days in meetings and office buildings and coffee shops. You have fancy cars, expensive clothes, beautiful girls. Why on earth do you want to waste your time in a barren, boring, dark, cold warehouse like this? This isn't your world. You don't belong here."

Kenji nodded. His face looked pale in the harsh light. "You don't think I belong here, I know. Ever since that night, you've done everything in your power to keep me away. But this ... this warehouse, the men outside, your two-bit scams and pachinko halls and massage parlors ... this is everything in this world that you love. And you keep me away from it. Separate. Because you don't think I'm good enough."

Isato shook his head. "No, Kenji, it's because I want you to be better than this."

"I'm your son," Kenji said. "This is your life, and I'm not a part of it."

Isato shook his head. "I don't have time for this right now. I promised Waters-san ... Caine, as you say ... that I would send him assistance. Koichi's wounds are not as bad as I feared, but he's still not up to a fight, which means I need to find someone else I can trust."

"You still haven't answered my question. Where the hell are they going? Maybe I can help."

"You've done quite enough. They're going to the capsule hotel in Asakusa. This girl he's been searching for, whoever she is, left something valuable there. Why this is my concern, I have no idea."

Kenji leaned back and smiled. "You're right. It's not your concern. You've done enough."

Isato shook his head. "Kenji, you may understand numbers and finances better than I ever will. But in my business, those things are nothing next to honor. I cannot buy my men's respect with money—not any kind of loyalty that matters, at any rate. I have to earn it by my actions. Part of that is keeping my word. Paying back my obligations."

Kenji nodded. "Okay, let's say you're right. You have an obligation to Caine, but you also have an obligation to this family. A greater obligation, wouldn't you say?"

Isato stared at Kenji again, his dark eyes squinting. He said nothing.

"Listen to me," Kenji said. "Trust me now. Do not call in your men. Do not help Caine. You've done enough. Trust me, and this family will prosper beyond your wildest dreams."

"What are you talking about?" Isato asked. "What have you done?"

"I did what you do. I have insured this family's success. In my own way."

Isato reached out and began dialing the phone on his desk. "Kenji, I don't know what you're talking about. I suspect we will have a long conversation about it shortly. But, for now, I gave my word. I intend to keep it."

Kenji gave his father a cold smile. He pulled a sleek, black pistol from his jacket and aimed it at Isato's head. The old man looked up and found himself staring into the dark, circular barrel of the gun. If he was afraid, he didn't show it. His expression remained blank and smooth as slate. Inscrutable.

"Father," Kenji said. "Put down that phone. Now."

Isato did not put down the phone. "What do you think you are doing?"

"I'm making this family rich. You put me in charge of your finances, remember? And like you said, I know numbers. I just put in a short order for all your China-based investments. In less than twenty-four hours, if everything goes according to plan, this family will have made hundreds of millions of dollars."

"According to whose plan? Yours?"

"Does it matter? I'm telling you, I will make our family richer and more powerful than you could in a lifetime of this yakuza bullshit! Now, for once, would you please just listen to me!"

"It was you, wasn't it?" Isato said in a low voice. "You have been working with Tokyo Black, with Bobu Shimizu. Do you realize who this man is? What he almost did to you and this family?"

"I work for Arinori Kusaka. Bobu is just another crazy gangster with something to prove. Once we no longer need him and his followers, we'll eliminate him. Tokyo Black will scatter, and the Yoshizawa family will be rich enough and powerful enough to stomp out the remains of the Shimizu clan. Dad, just listen to me, this will work. I will give you everything you've ever dreamed of."

Isato shook his head. "No. Not like this. I'm sorry, Son."

Kenji laughed. "Sorry." He lowered the gun and stood up, pacing back and forth in front of his father's desk. "What are you sorry about, Dad? For letting me be raised by nannies and girlfriends and aunts? For shipping me off to America the second I turned sixteen? For making me an accountant and giving my legacy away to Koichi or one of these other apes you've got working for you?"

"Yes, Kenji, I am sorry for all that. And I am sorry I failed you as a father. If you think I would work with the man who almost murdered my own son ... or these terrorists who have turned their backs on their family and traditions ... if you think I would do that for any amount of money, then I have taught you nothing about what it means to be a man. You know nothing about honor. And you know nothing about me." Isato put the phone to his ear and finished dialing the number.

Kenji stared at him for a second, his eyes wide with surprise. For a split second, he realized that he had been wrong. Nothing had changed. His father still hadn't listened to him, would never listen to him. Everything he had worked for, all his hopes of proving his worth and earning his family's respect, were about to vanish with a single phone call.

He blinked, and the corner of his mouth twitched. He snapped the gun back up and aimed it at his father.

Then he pulled the trigger.

Kenji's ears were still ringing from the gunshot. He felt disoriented, dizzy. The smell of smoke, blood, and gunpowder turned his stomach.

He still held the gun, clenched in a tight grip. His hand was shaking.

His father slumped onto the floor. Kenji ran over to him.

"Oh, fuck. Fuck! What did I do?! What the hell did I do?" he muttered as he helped his father sit up on the floor. Blood gushed from a hole in the old man's neck. A deep red stain spread across the collar of his crisp white dress shirt.

Kenji heard banging from outside. The rolling metal gate was locked from the inside, but he knew it wouldn't keep Isato's guards out for long.

"Boss, *daijobo desu ka?*" the men cried, their voices muted by the heavy metal barrier. "Are you okay?"

Isato coughed blood. Kenji turned to him, his eyes wide and pleading. "Dad, I'm sorry. I didn't ... I just, I needed you to listen! You never listen."

Isato regarded Kenji with half-closed eyes. "I'm ... I'm sorry, Son. I'm an old man. Perhaps I was too set in my ways. But it's not too late for you. Listen to me, one last time...."

The banging on the metal door grew louder, but Kenji held tight to his father. "This business with Kusaka and the Shimizu family ... it is shameful. It dishonors you and this family. Promise me you will stop it. Immediately. Promise me that, and I will rest easy."

"Dad, you don't understand! I did all of this for you. For the family. This is my legacy!"

"Promise me!" Isato hissed as his eyes began to flutter closed. "My soul is black enough with my own sins. Don't make me face eternity with this on my conscience as well. The failure ... the failure to raise my son with honor."

Kenji held Isato in a gentle embrace. His lips quivered as he spoke, but his words were as hard as steel. "No, Father. It's too late. And I am not a failure. You will see."

Isato sighed and slumped back to the ground. One last breath wheezed from his body, and then he was silent. Gone.

Kenji stood up. He looked at his hand, and it stopped shaking. He found new resolve in his father's words. He would show him. Even in death, his father would see.

He would not fail. This was his time. His time to lead.

He heard the metal scrape of a crowbar being inserted under the rolling door. Time was running out. He had to use this tragedy to his advantage. He turned the gun towards his left arm and placed the muzzle against the fabric of his expensive black suit. Gritting his teeth, he pulled the trigger.

Once again, his ears rang as the explosive gunshot echoed throughout the room. He screamed as a white-hot pain engulfed his arm. The screaming and clattering noise outside intensified, but he could barely hear it over the ringing in his ears.

He stumbled over to the office's rear entrance, to the side of Isato's desk. He locked the door, took a step back, and kicked at the doorknob. The wood splintered and gave way as the door flew open. He fired another shot into the hallway, then slid the gun back into his waistband. "Help!" he screamed in Japanese. "He's getting away!"

He slid down to the cold concrete floor and lay next to his father. He clamped one hand over the wound in his arm, staunching the dark blood that seeped from the bullet hole. He glanced at his father's corpse. Even in death, the eyes stared at him with an accusing glare. Half-open, cold, judging.

He looked away.

There was a metallic crunch, and the door rolled open. His father's bodyguards poured into the room. Two of them ran to Isato's side and checked his pulse. Another helped Kenji to his feet.

"Is he okay? That's my father! Talk to me, damn it!" Kenji shouted.

The man checking Isato looked up and shook his head. "I'm sorry." Another guard put an arm on Kenji's shoulder. "Thank God, you're all right. What happened? Who did this? Was it the stinking Shimizu clan?"

Kenji shook his head. "No. It was the *gaijin*. And I know where he is going. Get the men ready. We move now."

The guard hesitated. "*Hai*, if you please, I will contact Ogawa-san. He will—"

"No," Kenji said with a firm voice as he dusted off his clothes and straightened his blood-soaked blazer. "Koichi is not the oyabun's son. I am. My father is lying there dead, and you want to talk?"

"No, of course not, but it's just—"

Kenji grabbed the man by his lapel and yanked him close. With his other hand, he thrust his pistol under the man's chin. The gun shook, as a tremble of pain from the bullet wound shot through his arm.

"We move now. The *gaijin's* going to Asakusa. We will follow him, and I will kill him. Is that clear?"

The guard looked up at him, fearful, desperate. "*Hai*, I understand, but Koichi is the second-in-command. He—"

Kenji pulled the trigger. The back of the man's head spattered across the lightbulb hanging from the ceiling.

The other guards stared at Kenji. Strange red shadows swayed back and forth across the room.

"Koichi is second-in-command. I am the new oyabun. It is my birthright. Does anyone else here disagree?"

The men looked down at the dead guard and back at Kenji.

No one spoke.

Kenji smiled.

"Good. Now, first things first. I understand I need a new car."

CHAPTER THIRTY-TWO

Caine peered out the windshield of a tiny Toyota Aqua. They had stolen the teal green hatchback from an alley around the corner from the love hotel. On the way to the Hotel Riverside, he made a quick stop at a small, rundown convenience store. He chose one with just a few cars in the lot.

Using the blade of the Spyderco knife in his jacket, he unscrewed the license plate of another Toyota parked in the dark, lonely lot. Then he swapped it with the plate from the Aqua. It wouldn't fool an inquisitive cop if he ran the numbers, but it would deter anyone searching for the Aqua's plates. Better safe than sorry, in case the owner reported it stolen before he could ditch it.

They were now parked across the street from a short, nondescript grey building. The capsule hotel had no neon lights or giant billboards proclaiming its existence. The tiny capsules actually occupied the upper floors of another hotel, whose entrance faced the busy street. From the alley, there was nothing to distinguish it from any other building in the area.

Down the building's side ran a red banner advertising the going rate for one of the tiny capsule rooms stacked in rows inside the hotel. For a small sum of yen, travelers and businessmen could stay the night in one of the tiny capsules. Then they could shower in the morning, eat a quick breakfast in the cafe, and be on their way home. Or more likely, head back to work after a night of heavy drinking.

Mariko sat next to Caine, in the passenger seat. She scanned the alley for signs of danger. Hitomi curled up in the backseat, listening to music on her cell phone through a pair of wireless headphones.

The headphones were topped with tiny triangles that looked like ears. Perched on Hitomi's head, they made her look like a strange, ghostly cat. Her eyes peered out at something unseen out in the dark night.

Caine shifted in his seat. "Isato said he would send backup," he said. "They should have been here by now."

Mariko gave him a sideways glance. "Imagine that. Unreliable yakuza criminals. Maybe you need a higher class of friend."

"From what I've seen, they've been more reliable than the local police."

Mariko made a sound somewhere between a sigh and a grunt, and continued to look out the windshield.

Caine turned around. "Hitomi, are you sure this is the place?"

She looked up at the grungy building and nodded. "Yes, this is where I was staying after Sonny put me in touch with Mr. Naka. I paid cash and rented the capsule for a couple weeks. I figured no one would find me here."

"It's not the worst hiding place," Mariko observed. "Anonymous, quiet, low-key...."

"From what I remember, the capsules don't lock, and you have to check out every day. Where did you leave this drive?"

"There are lockers on the women-only floor. They are outside the showers. I left it there. I still have the key. I paid the manager extra, told him I would be gone for a while. I think he was sweet on me."

Hitomi handed Caine a small locker key, which hung from a circle of curled pink plastic. "There is a combination lock on the door to the women's floor. The code was ... let me see ... press the one and nine buttons, then the five and three buttons."

"Got it," Caine said. He took the key and started to get out of the car.

"Where do you think you're going?" Mariko asked.

"I'm going in. I have a feeling backup's not coming."

"Didn't you hear her? It's a women-only floor."

Caine looked down at her. "Trust me. I've managed to infiltrate tougher spots than a women's bathroom."

"You're going to cause a fuss. There could be women showering up there! I should go."

Caine checked his watch. "At this hour? I doubt it. Besides, I need you to keep an eye on her."

"And what happens when a half-naked woman goes screaming to the manager that she was peeped by a dirty *gaijin* pervert?"

Caine smiled. "Every job has its perks."

He shut the door and jogged across the street to the building's shadowy side entrance.

"*Buta*," Mariko hissed to herself. Hitomi giggled. Mariko turned back to face her. "What's so funny?"

"You like him," Hitomi said in a small but confident voice. "Don't you know anything about men?"

"What do you mean?"

Hitomi stared at Caine as he crossed the street and entered the door in the alley next to the hotel.

"That one ... he is not right for you. Too much pain in both of you. There is no healing there. You and he are like two sides of the same coin. You may touch, but you can never stand side by side."

"And just how do you know so much about him?" Mariko asked.

She shrugged. "I know how to read men. It's in their eyes. When this is finished, he will leave here."

Mariko nodded. "Maybe that's not so bad," she said.

"Maybe you will get the chance to find out," Hitomi replied with a sly smile. Then she turned to look out the window, staring into space. Mariko could hear the faint music playing from her headphones.

She looked back towards the empty street and waited.

―――

Above the side door in the alley hung a small green sign with white kanji writing. In English, the words "Capsule Hotel" flanked the larger Japanese characters.

Caine checked the alley one last time, ensuring he was alone, then pulled the door open. He found himself in a concrete stairwell. On the second floor, he passed through another door and stepped into a tiny lobby.

The once-white counter of the reception desk was stained a dull grey by age and cigarette smoke. Behind the desk were rows of tiny lockers for personal belongings. A glass cabinet was stocked with toiletries, sake, and other sundries for sale. A wrinkled piece of paper outlining hotel policies was taped to the counter.

The lobby was empty and silent except for the sound of television playing in a back room. Moments later, the wrinkled old desk clerk shuffled out front to greet him. The man mumbled to him in Japanese, and Caine could not quite catch what he said.

Caine pulled out his wallet and lay some yen down on the counter. The old man nodded and took the money. Reaching under the counter, he pulled out a small bundle and set it down before Caine. It was a locker key and a toiletry kit, balanced on top of hotel pajamas. The man gestured with his head towards a curtained changing booth to the left of the desk. Caine grabbed the bundle, thanked the man, and headed into the changing area.

The changing room, like the rest of the hotel, was small. There was just enough room for the two wooden benches that sat in the center of the room. They were surrounded by about forty metal lockers.

Caine located the locker number on his key. He opened it, took off his shoes, and put on a pair of foam slippers. They were comfortable but completely impractical if he had to run. But the last thing he wanted to do was attract attention, and this was the standard custom for these sorts of hotels.

He left the pajamas in the locker and headed back out. The old man saw that he was still dressed in his street clothes. He shrugged but said nothing.

On the fourth level, Caine found the first of the capsule floors. The dim hallways were narrow, barely wide enough for two men to walk side by side. Brown industrial carpet covered the floor, and it stank of cigarettes and sweat.

On either side of the corridor, the capsules themselves were stacked in rows of two. Each unit was a small plastic cell, just large enough for a grown man to lay down or sit up. A thin mattress covered the floor, and a small TV monitor hung from the ceiling. Some people jokingly referred to them as "coffins" due to their narrow, rectangular shape.

Caine padded down the hall, pretending to look for his unit. As he walked, he checked the ceiling out of the corner of his eye. He didn't see any security cameras.

Most of the capsules had thin bamboo shades drawn over the entrance. Caine could hear the snoring and grunting noises of the men inside.

He found his capsule. He had rented it only for cover, but he decided he could spare a few minutes to try Rebecca one more time. He had still not been able to report in, and she might have more information for him.

He climbed the short metal ladder to the second row of capsules and slid into his small plastic room. It was white, sterile, and reasonably clean. He turned on the TV and set it to a channel that displayed only late-night static. Then he dialed Rebecca's number.

The phone rang three times before it picked up. No one spoke.

"Hello?" he said. "It's me. I finished the Murakami book."

He could hear faint static on the other end of the line.

Then a voice. A man's voice.

"I don't have the proper response, Tom. You've got me there." The voice was raspy and strained, but Caine still recognized the man on the other end of the line."

"Allan Bernatto."

"Yes, Tom, it's me. Glad to hear you're still alive."

"Well, Allan, I find that a bit hard to believe. The last time we spoke, you sent a hired killer to finish me off."

"It was nothing personal, Tom. We're all expandable in the end. You know that."

Caine felt trapped by the smooth plastic walls of the tiny room. They were closing in, growing smaller and smaller, giving his rage nowhere to go. It simmered in the small, hot room.

"What are you doing with this phone?" he snapped. "Where's Rebecca? If you've hurt her, I swear I'll—"

"You'll do what, Tom? I'm not in Japan, so making threats just makes you look weak at this point. Did you find the girl?"

Caine clenched his teeth. Bernatto was right. There was nothing he could do, but every muscle in his body had one desire: to reach out and strangle the voice on the other end of the phone. He took a deep breath. *Get it under control*, he told himself.

"No," he said calmly, "that's not how this is going to work. First, I want to talk to Rebecca."

Allan sighed. It sounded like a wheeze. "I suppose I could lie, but sooner or later, I know you'd demand proof of life. The truth is, I don't have her. Not anymore. I don't know where she is now. I don't even know if she's alive. She caused quite a ruckus in her escape."

"Then we have nothing to talk about."

"Did you find Hitomi? Did she give you the drive?"

So Bernatto knew about the drive all along, Caine thought.

"What's on the drive, Allan? Why do you want it so bad? Leverage against Kusaka? You know who this girl is? What he's done to her?"

"Arinori's perversions are none of my concern, but there is

certain information on that drive ... information I provided him that I need to get back."

"What information?"

"Arinori and I were working together on something—something big, something that could benefit both our countries. But he's taken it too far. I need to limit my exposure."

Caine sat quiet for a moment, processing Bernatto's words.

"This terrorist attack ... it's real, isn't it? You planned it with Kusaka? Some sort of false flag operation. What's the target, Allan?"

"I can't say any more. Call me when you have the drive. I can clear your record, Tom. I can fix things. You can come back home. Just work with me on this."

The person in the next cubicle grunted and rolled over on his mattress. He kept his voice a low hiss, so it wouldn't carry through the thin plastic walls.

"Here's what's going to happen, Allan. I'm going to get that hard drive. I'm going to stop whatever Kusaka is planning. And then I'm going to find you. Do you hear me? You better pray Rebecca is alive and well. Because if she isn't, nothing in the world is going to stop me from bleeding you out. You know what kind of man I am, Allan. And you know I can do it."

"Tom, wait. Just listen for a—"

Caine hung up the phone. He clenched his shaking fist to steady his nerves. After all these years, hearing Bernatto's voice brought back the years of suffering, the pain, the betrayal. In an instant, nothing else mattered. All he wanted to do now was leave Japan and find the man who had burned him, who had twisted him. The one who had made him a killer. Find him and make him pay.

Bullshit, said the inner voice, the one he could never silence. *Bernatto didn't make you a killer. You were always a killer. That's why he recruited you. You were just a weapon he used for his own ends.*

Caine ran his hands through his hair and breathed out slowly. *Enough.* He had a mission. Survival meant moving forward. Like a shark, forever swimming against a relentless current.

He raised the shade on his capsule and dropped to the floor. He thought about the push-button lock Hitomi had described, and reached back into the cubicle. He grabbed the small toiletry kit the manager had given him.

Then he made his way back to the stairs, heading for the top floor showers and Hitomi's locker.

CHAPTER THIRTY-THREE

Caine stood facing a plain wooden door in a small vestibule on the hotel's top floor. The doorknob sat below a push-button combination lock, just as Hitomi had described.

He glanced up again, checking the ceiling for security cameras. When he was satisfied that his actions were unseen, he pressed the small silver buttons in the order she had given him. He turned the doorknob.

Nothing happened. The door was still locked.

They must have changed the combination, he thought.

He unzipped the toiletry kit and removed a slim tube of talcum powder. He shook a small amount into the palm of his hand and knelt in front of the lock. A quick puff of his breath blew the powder into the air, coating the metal buttons with a thin film of white. He gently blew on the lock again to dislodge any lose powder.

His careful dusting revealed masses of fingerprints next to the various buttons. The buttons were numbered 1 through 5. The concentration of prints seemed heaviest at the 1 and 4 buttons. He pressed those two buttons simultaneously, then pressed the 2 button with his other finger.

He heard a soft click, and this time the door opened.

He did not walk through. Instead, he leaned forward to check the area.

He spotted the metal housing of a security camera, mounted to the ceiling on the other side of the door. Keeping his back to the wall, Caine slid into the room. As he moved, he made sure to keep the camera directly above him, staying out of its field of view.

A small cluster of red and black wires led from a hole in the wall to the back of the camera. He gave them a sharp tug, and they yanked loose, cutting off the video feed.

Unlike the men's floor, the women's section was not carpeted. The floors were smooth hardwood and much cleaner. The air smelled of perfume and deodorant. The grunts and snores from his floor were replaced by soft sighs, the rustling of sheets.

He was flanked by row after row, chamber after chamber of women, separated from him by only a thin shade of fabric. Caine realized how alone he had been the past few years. How long since he had truly connected with a woman. Now he was surrounded by them. He imagined their bodies tossing, turning, writhing under the thin white sheets, lit from all sides by the harsh, sterile glow of the capsules.

He thought of Rebecca, then of other women he had known during his exile in Pattaya. All touched by the pain and darkness following in his wake.

Shaking his head, he moved on.

He stepped past a row of cubbies stuffed with bathrobes, shampoo, and slippers. The floor changed from wood to a pale pink tile. He could hear the sound of someone showering around the corner.

Damn. Mariko had been right.

He could see the lockers on the other side of the shower stalls. Whoever was enjoying her late-night shower was out of view. Caine crept forward. As he crossed the communal shower, the woman came into view.

Her back was to him as he snuck past. He watched as the

droplets of water traced the curve of her thigh. She turned and threw her head back. A huge splash of water slapped the floor as she rinsed shampoo from a glistening dark mass of hair. The lather slid down her back, over her buttocks, and down her legs.

Caine tore his gaze away and moved on. The sound of the shower masked his footsteps, allowing him to make it to the lockers without drawing her attention. He turned the corner, putting himself out of her line of sight, and breathed a sigh of relief.

He found the number matching Hitomi's key. Inside were a few of her belongings ... a pair of slippers, some gum, a crumpled transit card. Caine pushed these aside and found a small, rectangular package. It was wrapped in a pink t-shirt, with a picture of Masuka Ongaku on the front. Inside the shirt was a silver metal device with black rubber bumpers on the edges.

Caine recognized the Iron Key drive immediately. He had used them before himself to transport sensitive information. They were built by a company in America, with funding from the United States government.

Iron Key drives contained high-level hardware encryption. They could also be set to shut down, or even erase, all onboard data if accessed by an unauthorized system. Whatever was on the drive, Kusaka was serious about keeping it secure.

But Bernatto's angle was still unclear. He said he needed leverage against Kusaka, that the man had gone too far. What did that mean, exactly?

A shudder of disgust ran through his body. He imagined the horrors Kusaka had inflicted on Hitomi. Was the evidence of his abhorrent perversions all he was protecting? Hitomi didn't think so, and Caine had to agree.

Kusaka had been a CIA asset, providing information through his Chinese industrial connections, but now he seemed to be working with Bernatto on something far more complex. What was their plan? What were they trying to accomplish? And why did they now seem to be at odds?

The hard drive he held in his hands was the key to answering those questions.

A woman's scream rang out. Caine tensed and slid the hard drive into his jacket pocket. He heard a man shouting in Japanese.

Caine peered around the corner and saw a man wielding a pistol. He was waving it in front of the naked, terrified woman. She was sitting on the tile floor of the shower, struggling to cover herself with her hands as the water cascaded around her.

The man looked yakuza ... flashy suit, slicked back hair, the usual signs. But Caine didn't see Tokyo Black scars. The thug pointed the gun at the woman and shouted again, asking her if she had seen a *gaijin* man on this floor. She shook her head no.

Caine stepped out into the shower area. "Hey!" he shouted. The gangster wheeled around and pointed his gun at Caine. The woman looked up, her eyes wide with fear.

Caine took a step forward. "Looking for me?"

The yakuza man grinned and stepped forward. He gestured with his gun. "Someone wants to speak with you, *gaijin*."

Caine shrugged. "That's fine. Lead the way."

The man circled behind Caine. "Downstairs. Move it ... nice and slow."

From the corner of his eye, Caine saw the man move towards him. He felt the muzzle of the gun brush against his left arm, and he knew it was time to act.

Caine shrugged his arm backwards, as if he were about to take a step. The movement was slight, but it shifted the angle of the gun backwards a hair, moving him just out of the line of fire.

As soon as he felt the gun shift, Caine's body exploded into motion. His left arm shot out, knocking the other man's gun up and away from his body.

Caine wrapped his hand around the wrist of his attacker's gun hand and twisted his body sideways. As he turned, he slammed his right elbow into the other man's face.

His victim spun around, blood streaming from his crushed nose. Caine drove his knee into the thug's groin.

The man grunted and pitched forward. As the air exploded from his attacker's lungs, Caine grabbed the barrel of the gun. With a quick twist, he yanked it free from the man's grasp. In one fluid motion, he swept the arm back, whipping the other man across the face with the pistol.

Then he lashed out with his leg and kicked the man forward.

The terrified woman screamed and scurried out of the way as the yakuza collided with the shower wall. Caine stepped under the spray of water and grabbed the man's hair. He slammed his face into the wall over and over again, until the man slumped to the ground, unconscious.

Caine stepped back, panting. The woman cowered in the corner, staring at the pulverized face of the man lying on the ground. When she looked up at Caine, her eyes glazed over with fear and shock.

Caine tucked the pistol into his waistband. He pulled off the man's blazer, draped it over the woman, and helped her to her feet.

"Here, put this on," he said. "*Dai jobo des*. Everything's going to be okay. Go back to your capsule. Stay there. Don't come out for anyone other than the police, you understand?"

The woman nodded, although Caine doubted she actually understood what he said. As she ran off, Caine kneeled down and tore open the man's shirt. There were no scars.

Instead, intricate yakuza tattoos covered the man's skin. One curled up his arm, featuring three koi fish. One blue, one red, and one black, swimming up a stream of water, through a wooden gate. Caine recognized the design at once.

The man was not Tokyo Black. He was a member of the Yoshizawa clan.

It looked like Mariko was right again. His alliance with Isato seemed to have dissolved. The old gangster had helped Caine find Hitomi. Maybe now he considered his debt fulfilled.

Caine checked the thug's pistol, making sure it had a full load, and headed for the stairs. He could no longer trust Isato and his yakuza. Rebecca was missing, or worse. And Tokyo Black had influence over the police.

The only two people he could count on now were waiting for him downstairs in a dark alley.

Caine snuck downstairs and slipped out the side door. As soon as he hit the pavement, he knew something was wrong. He couldn't say why exactly, but something about the thick night air, humid and heavy, felt off. The light mist that enveloped him hinted at the familiar scent of danger.

Maybe it was paranoia due to so many betrayals and surprises, but Caine had lived a life based on instinct and he didn't think twice about trusting his intuition now. He slid the pistol from his waistband and thumbed off the safety. He kept close to the alley wall and walked back to the street.

Peering around the corner, he saw several cars parked across the street, their headlights facing the alley. Shadowy figures approached, indistinct against the blazing backlight.

He heard the explosive blast of gunfire. He ducked back behind the wall as bullets sent chips of concrete flying through the air. He returned fire, shooting blind around the cover of the wall. Then, for a moment, there was silence.

A voice called out. "Waters-san, it's me, Kenji! Come on out, man. We need to talk."

Caine's eyes darted back and forth as he tried to make sense of this new information. Isato was a gangster, yes. He may have withdrawn his support, maybe even put out a hit on Caine to tie up loose ends.

But there was no way on Earth he would send his son. From everything Caine had seen, Isato went out of his way to insulate Kenji from his yakuza activities.

"Kenji?" he called out. "What the hell are you doing here?"

"Meet me in the middle of the street. Let's work this out before one of these ladies gets hurt."

Caine cursed under his breath. Hitomi and Mariko. Kenji must have surrounded them, got the upper hand.

He was torn. This was a no-win situation. He didn't have enough intel to know what was going on with Kenji. He knew the drive was the mission. Hitomi had led him to the drive. Mariko had helped. Now that the drive was in his possession, they were both expendable. Just as Bernatto had said—everyone was expendable.

The smart thing to do would be to head the other direction. Get out of the alley before Isato's men closed off the opening behind him. Take the drive, get somewhere safe, and plan his next move. Find out what happened to Rebecca. That was the right play.

But it didn't feel right.

He stood up. "Just you and me, Kenji. I get the feeling your family isn't too happy with me right now."

"Sure, man. Just you and me. For now."

Caine slid the pistol back into his waistband. He stepped out into the street, his hands held loosely in front of him, open and unthreatening. He took a few steps forward.

He could see Kenji, flanked by a group of eight yakuza thugs. Caine recognized a few of them as Isato's men. One had an arm draped across Mariko's neck, her hands tied behind her. Caine looked her in the eye as he walked towards the group, and she returned his gaze. She looked scared, but she lifted her chin and nodded slightly. She was ready to make a move if need be.

Behind the group of men, Caine saw Hitomi sitting in the passenger seat of a pearl white Lexus LFA. She turned to look at him, her eyes blank. They showed no fear, or regret, or recognition. Caine knew that look. He had seen it in the mirror many times. It was the look of someone who had made peace with death. Someone who longed for it. Because the alternatives that awaited them were far worse.

Not this time, Caine vowed.

Caine stopped walking and turned his attention to Kenji. The young man nodded and approached him.

"I hope this isn't about the GTR, Kenji. Sorry, you know how Tokyo traffic can be."

Kenji smiled. "Of course not. I was tired of that ride anyway. As you can see, Mr. Caine, I've already replaced it." He nodded back towards the Lexus.

"Call me Tom. I'm glad you know my name. It was getting awkward hearing you call me Waters-san all the time. So what's this all about?"

Kenji stopped in the middle of the street, ten feet away from Caine. He slid his hands in his pockets, arched his back, and smiled. "This is about family. It's about my father. Isato Yoshizawa."

Caine looked at Kenji warily. "Does he know you're here?"

"He doesn't know anything anymore. He's dead."

Caine gritted his teeth. So Isato was gone. The man had been a criminal, a killer for sure, but in some strange way, Caine had felt a kinship with the old man, a connection of some kind. Now that the connection was severed, he felt a pang of loss. "I'm sorry to hear that. I really am."

Kenji took a few more steps forward. He leaned closer and murmured, "I'm sure you are, Tom. I'm sure you are. Because, these men here, they're under the impression you killed him."

"What? Why on Earth would they think that?"

"Because that's what I told them."

"Kenji, what are you—"

Kenji cut him off. "I don't have time to explain it. You have something I want. Give it to me, and I'll tell them the truth."

Caine dipped a hand into his jacket. He saw the gunmen tense, but Kenji smiled and nodded. He slipped out the small silver hard drive and held it up so the others could clearly see it.

"You mean this, don't you? This is what Kusaka wanted. Now

you want it. You're working with him, aren't you? You're his mole inside the Yoshizawa clan."

Kenji reached out for it, but Caine pulled it back from his grasp. The young man's face flushed with anger, but Caine also glimpsed shock and fear there. The kid was in over his head. He was struggling to tread water in a situation that had escalated beyond his control.

"Kenji, what's on this drive? What is Kusaka planning? It's not too late. You can help me stop it. We can fix this."

"Are you fucking crazy? It's not too late? My father is dead. This is all I have now. If this doesn't work, then everything ... my father ... it was all for nothing!"

Kenji's features hardened. "I'm not gonna let that happen. Give me that drive, or I swear my men will shoot you down and I'll take it from your corpse. But first, I'll make the cop lady beg for a bullet in the head."

Kenji gestured at his men, and the man holding Mariko shoved her forward. She stumbled and fell to the pavement. Cursing, she blew her hair out of her face and stood back up. The gunman led her to the middle of the street, stopping just behind Kenji. The yakuza looked back and forth between the two men with a confused expression on his face.

Kenji held out his hand. "The drive. Stop wasting my time, and you can have her back in one piece."

"Hitomi, too."

Kenji shook his head. "She's not part of the deal. Kusaka has other plans for her."

"You disgusting little piece of trash," Mariko hissed. The gunman clubbed her on the back of the head, and she dropped to her knees.

Caine looked into Kenji's eyes. He saw pain, uncertainty, even fear. But he also saw neglect and determination. What he didn't see was a way out. He held the drive out to Kenji. "Your father would be ashamed of you, Kenji."

The young man grabbed it. "My father never saw my value and

look where it got him." He stared at the drive in his hands. "All this over a fucking hard drive. Unbelievable."

He turned around and walked back to his car. "Sorry, Tom," he called over his shoulder, "but from what I understand, you're a pretty coldhearted bastard yourself." Then he spoke in Japanese to his men. "Kill them both."

Caine went for his pistol, but before he could draw, Mariko whipped into action.

She leapt to her feet, crashing the top of her head into the jaw of the gunman who stood behind her. Keeping her body close, she pushed backwards, keeping his gun arm outside and to her right. She stamped down with her right heel, crushing the man's instep. He fell to his knees, yelping in pain.

As Caine's gun cleared his waistband, Mariko spun out of the way, giving him a clear shot at the yakuza thug. Caine fired two bullets into the man's shoulder, then aimed for his head.

Before he could pull the trigger again, a sudden explosion of light blinded him. A burst of wind ruffled his hair, and a deafening roar descended from above. The spotlights of a helicopter beamed down, sweeping back and forth across the area.

Kenji and his men were equally surprised by the arrival of the police choppers. "Let's move!" Kenji shouted. His men scattered.

Kenji dove into his white Lexus. The engine roared to life, and he tore down a side street. As he fled, Caine caught a glimpse of Hitomi staring at him from the rear window. A split second later, they were gone.

A line of police cars, lights blazing and sirens screaming, charged down the street. Mariko kicked the wounded yakuza's gun away from them and jogged over to Caine. "We don't have much time. Cut me loose!"

Caine pulled out his knife and slit her plastic restraints. The police cars skidded to a halt. Within seconds, a squad of men in blue jumpsuits and body armor surrounded them. They were wielding submachine guns, and a few were armed with sniper rifles as well. As the men began to fan out into assault positions, a loud speaker on the helicopter blared at them in Japanese.

"Mariko—" Caine began, but she interrupted him before he could finish.

"It's Tokyo Special Unit. Like your SWAT teams." She put a hand on his shoulder. "There's only one way this goes down where you live. Do you understand?"

Caine nodded. He handed her his pistol, kneeled on the ground, and put his hands on his head. As the assault team jogged towards them, weapons at the ready, Mariko pulled out her badge and held it up. She pointed the pistol at Caine's head.

"Thomas Caine," she said, "you are under arrest."

CHAPTER THIRTY-FOUR

There was no clock on the wall in the Tokyo Metro Police detention room. The walls were, in fact, empty of any decoration. Just four sterile white slabs. Still, Caine's internal clock told him it was morning. He had dozed off in fits and spurts since they'd locked him in here. During that time, no one had spoken to him or come to check on him. He had not seen a single soul.

They called it a holding room, not a jail. These rooms were for people awaiting interrogation. But the metal table bolted to the floor, the handcuffs chained to a loop on the table ... they told a different story.

He had not been charged with any crimes, but his situation here was every bit as bleak as before, when he sat rotting in the Big Tiger prison. And this time, it didn't seem like Rebecca would be coming to his rescue.

Rebecca ... his thoughts wandered to her. Had Bernatto lied on the phone? Had he killed her? Or had she escaped him? If she was free, why hadn't she made contact?

Caine shook his head to dislodge the dark thoughts from his mind. Mariko said she would talk to her boss, a director in the First

Public Security Division of the *Keisatsu Cho*. She was certain she could convince him there was new evidence of Kusaka's involvement in Tokyo Black. And that Caine was vital to the case against him.

Caine wasn't so sure.

He knew the corrupting influence of money and power. If Hitomi was right, then Mariko's superiors had been protecting Kusaka all along. They would turn a blind eye to any new evidence she presented. It was bureaucratic self-preservation. When a lie was uncovered, the lie simply grew bigger. It devoured whatever new truths came to light.

Like Hitomi had said, there were some things you couldn't escape. He had been a fool to believe otherwise.

The small red light of a security camera mounted in the corner blinked on and off. They were recording him. He wondered if Mariko was watching him right now.

Without warning, the door swung open. Two armed men in police uniforms entered and took up positions at either side of the door. He was about to have visitors. Maybe Mariko had some news. He allowed himself a flicker of hope.

A friendly looking man in a sharp business suit entered into the room. He sighed and took a seat across the table.

Arinori Kusaka nodded his greeting at Caine. His wide grin wrinkled the corners of his eyes as he studied Caine's face for a moment. The heavyset man spoke in a warm, gravelly voice.

"Not who you were expecting, I take it? Well, that's okay. I like to surprise people. Keeps life interesting."

Caine stared into Kusaka's eyes. "What do you want?"

The old man chuckled. "That's quite a question, isn't it? Well, let's establish the ground rules first. Look up there ... see the camera?" Kusaka pointed, and Caine looked at the camera again. The red light was no longer blinking.

"Normally they record everything that goes on here. Phone calls, interrogations, you name it. But me? I'm just a good citizen who has served his country. And I've contributed quite generously to the police department. So, as you can imagine, they accord me certain favors. Privacy is one of them. Access to interesting prisoners like you is another. That should tell you something."

"It tells me power corrupts just as much in Japan as anywhere else."

"Well, that's one way of looking at it, I suppose. It should also tell you that I find you interesting."

Caine shrugged. "Well, I don't like to brag...."

Kusaka slapped his hands on the table. "Since you've arrived in Japan, you've been quite a thorn in my side. And Bobu Shimizu's as well."

"Your choice in partners has caused you more trouble than I ever could," Caine said. "Bobu isn't exactly what I'd call stable. And Bernatto is a traitor to his own country."

"Funny, that's what your file says about you, Mr. Caine. That's about all it says, in fact. Bernatto told me you were a deep cover operative. That seems to be an understatement. In fact, your cover identities seem to have more history than you do. The fiction is more true than the reality."

Caine said nothing.

Kusaka sighed and leaned back. "Well, at any rate, you're right about poor old Bobu. That scar on his face...." Kusaka hissed and shook his head. "Strange man. But at least he's committed. His part in this will be over soon. And Bernatto? Well, he lost his nerve, tried to stop what we set in motion together. But now that the drive is back in my possession, he has no leverage. No way to extricate himself without exposing his involvement. He'll play ball now—for as long as I need him to, at any rate."

"All right, you've got me curious. What have you and Bernatto set in motion?"

Kusaka was silent for a second. When he spoke, his voice went flat. "For decades, I've watched my country sink into decay and submission. Our military presence in the Pacific has been neutered. Our economy continues to stagnate and fail. Our youth have lost their way. And in the mad scramble to hold onto whatever scraps we can, our values have been compromised. We have become a shadow of ourselves, just as you are a shadow of the man you once were. Weakened by pain and loss. Hiding, licking our wounds. Meanwhile, our true enemy grows stronger. Their power and influence increase with each passing day."

The chains around Caine's wrists clinked as he shifted his hands. "And who exactly is the true enemy? Because right now, I've got to tell you, I've kind of lost count."

"You joke, Mr. Caine. I like that. I like to tell jokes, too. It puts people at ease, makes them underestimate me. Oh, I'm not a vindictive man, but I like to think most of my enemies have fallen with a smile on their face."

Caine leaned forward. "Let's get one thing straight, Kusaka-san. You don't scare me. I've faced death, and I've faced pain. I've sure as hell faced men like you, more than I can count. Most of them are in the ground. So, if you came here to talk, then talk. If you came here to gloat, have your fun. But don't think for a minute you intimidate me."

"I see now why you've caused me so much trouble. You have the fire inside you. Like Bobu. And that girl, Mariko. You know what you are, Mr. Caine? You're a goddamn ronin! A true hero, right out of a fairy tale."

Caine shook his head. "I'm no hero."

"Whatever you say. As to your question, we don't have much time left, Mr. Caine. Let's just say that, as Japan has fallen, an old enemy has risen to new heights of industrial and economic power."

"China," Caine said.

"Yes, China. The United States and Japanese governments have done their dance of diplomacy and trade. Both are blinded by greed and willful ignorance. Each is afraid the other will seduce this powerful new ally and turn against the other. Meanwhile, China grows more and more powerful every day. And history tells us war is inevitable. And when war with China comes, as things stand now, we will both lose.

"Men like Bobu have the will to take action against this enemy. But protests and marches, beating up immigrant business owners ... that is not the way to defeat this enemy. He lacked the scope of vision necessary. I gave him that vision. And Bernatto shared my vision as well. He helped with the technical particulars."

"That's what's on the drive?" Caine asked. "Information from Bernatto?"

Kusaka smiled. "Ah, so you weren't able access the drive, were you? I was curious. I took great pleasure in questioning Hitomi about that. Now I know she wasn't lying."

"Where is Hitomi now? What did you do with her?"

Kusaka waved his hand in the air, dismissing Caine's concerns with the gesture. "Don't waste your time on Hitomi. That girl ... she's my one bad habit. The weakness I just can't kick. I suppose it's better this way. Now that she's back where she belongs, under my control, I can give her a proper goodbye."

"You know that's your daughter you're talking about?"

Kusaka's face flared with anger, and he pounded the table with his fist. "What do you know about it? You think she's the first girl to show up at my door? Desperate for money, for a better life? For the acknowledgement of my blood in her veins? She's another example of the cancer eating this country from the inside out!"

Caine watched Kusaka build himself into a seething rage. The old man's eyes stared forward, but they were no longer focused on Caine. It was as though Kusaka was looking through him, not even seeing him. Somehow he saw the object of his rage and anger instead.

"Just a half-breed whore!" he shouted. "I don't care who she is. I don't care what she is. All she means to me is—"

Caine lunged forward, cutting off Kusaka's rant in mid-sentence. Grabbing the metal ring in front of him, he swung his legs up into the air and slid his body forward on the table. The old man lurched backwards, but he was too late. Caine's legs clamped around his neck.

Kusaka gasped for breath. He strained to break free of the hold, but Caine locked his ankles and twisted his torso. Using his legs, he dragged Kusaka forward onto the table. Then he began to squeeze.

"I don't care who you are either," Caine hissed through gritted teeth. He clenched his legs tighter.

The door exploded open. Five Caucasian men wearing body armor and tactical gear stormed into the room. Caine looked up. *White guys, unmarked body armor, grey polo shirts ... definitely private security contractors*, he thought. Probably on the CIA's payroll.

"Jesus Christ!" one of them exclaimed. "What the fuck is this?" The Japanese official escorting them began shouting in Japanese.

Kusaka threw his body weight back and forth, struggling to dislodge Caine's chokehold. One of the contractors walked up to Caine, raised his rifle into the air, and slammed it down on Caine's skull. The blow snapped his head back, but he held his grip on Kusaka.

The contractor slammed the rifle down two more times, and Caine's body collapsed. He slumped down on the table, and his legs went limp.

The old man leapt up, coughing and gagging. One of the contractors helped him stand. "Are you all right, sir?"

Kusaka pushed the man away. "I'm fine," he sputtered, overcome with another fit of coughing. "Just get him the hell out of here. I'm sure you have your orders."

"Yes, sir," he answered and turned back to his men. "Secure the prisoner!"

Caine rolled over on the table. Blood streamed from the impact wound on his temple. He stared up at the man who had battered him and spit blood into the air.

The man leaned in close and whispered into his ear. "Bernatto says hi, asshole."

Then he clubbed Caine across the face one more time. Caine's vision went dark.

CHAPTER THIRTY-FIVE

Mariko flung open the door to office 257, the office of her superior. She marched up to his desk as his assistant rushed in behind her. "Excuse me," the flustered young woman said. "I told you Director Yamamoto is on an important call. You can't just—"

Mariko glared at the woman, and her complaints died down to a whimper. A middle-aged man with a long, gaunt face and thinning grey hair held a phone receiver to his ear.

His uniform's silver buttons and trim gleamed with a polished shine. Behind him, the windows of his office offered a breathtaking view of the morning sun as it rose over the bustling Tokyo metropolis.

Director Yamamoto looked at Mariko, then turned to his assistant. "It's fine, Hiro-chan," he said. "You can leave us."

He spoke into the phone. "*Hai*. I understand. The security team has been granted access to the prisoner. He will be placed in their custody. We will not interfere. Thank you, sir."

He hung up and shot a weary glance towards Mariko. "Officer Murase. Please, sit down."

Mariko did not sit. "Sir, you're turning over Caine without a debriefing? No questioning, no interrogation? I wasn't even allowed access to him, and he's my prisoner!"

"Sit down!"

The director's voice sharpened, but Mariko stayed where she was. "Sir, did you at least read my report? I've uncovered new evidence that—"

The director picked up a manila folder from his desk and shook it in the air. "This report, here? The one that details an illegal investigation into a prominent, respected Japanese businessman? A man who has provided our government with invaluable assistance? And a man who has made significant charitable contributions to this department?"

"Arinori Kusaka is a criminal, sir. I can prove he has associations with the Shimizu yakuza clan. He has provided financial backing to a violent splinter group of that organization known as Tokyo Black."

"There is nothing in your report that conclusively links Kusaka-san to this organization. And speaking of violence, it wasn't Tokyo Black that left a trail of dead bodies across this city over the last twenty-four hours. It was you and this American operative, Thomas Caine."

"That American is a material witness. He can link Kusaka to Tokyo Black and to other crimes involving his daughter, Hitomi—"

"Arinori Kusaka has no children, Officer Murase."

"She's illegitimate and living in Japan illegally, which has allowed him to pimp her out to the Shimizu sex clubs while he systematically abuses her in every way imaginable. This 'respected' man you're so intent on protecting? He's a monster who rapes his own daughter and funds terror and bloodshed on the side!"

Director Yamamoto sighed. He held out his hand and gestured towards the chair in front of his desk. "Murase-san, please. Sit."

Mariko allowed herself to sink into the chair. The director's voice softened and took on a fatherly tone.

"Even if your report could prove that these allegations are true, and we both know it can't, your investigation of Kusaka-san is unauthorized. You are suspended from duty. Any evidence or information in this report is inadmissible. The best I can do is start fresh and open a new investigation of Kusaka's possible yakuza ties."

The director pulled a sheaf of crisp white papers from a drawer. He slid them across the desk to Mariko. "And I can remove your suspension and allow you to resume active duty."

Mariko eyed the papers in front of her. "You would do that? I'd be back on the Kusaka case?"

The director steepled his fingers under his chin and paused for a second. "No," he answered. "Sign there and your suspension will be lifted, but I can't have you investigating someone like Kusaka-san based on a personal vendetta."

"Personal vendetta? This man is a threat to Japan! I have a duty to—"

"I read the report about Aokigahara Forest ... your sister. I'm very sorry for your loss, Officer Murase. I should have insisted you take some personal leave. It was poor judgement on my part. But now I'm sure you can see how it could appear that grief is clouding your judgement, that your personal feelings are motivating you to pursue Kusaka-san ... and this case."

Mariko was silent. Her intense glare seared into the director's eyes, but she didn't say a word.

"Please," he said, "consider my offer. You're a dedicated officer. There is nothing I would rather do than allow you to resume your duty and continue protecting the people of Japan. Take some time; put this all behind you. Then come back to us. In the meantime, I will assign an impartial officer to this case."

He set a monogrammed pen on top of the forms and pushed them a few inches closer to Mariko. "Sign the form. Resume active duty; let this go. It's for the best."

Mariko picked up the pen and stared at it. It looked expensive. "What about the American? What happens to him?" she asked.

The director leaned back in his chair. "That's above our pay grade, Officer. He's a rogue CIA operative, and he's wanted by his government for treason. Someone in the CIA has made a deal with the Japanese government to turn him over to a private security team for immediate rendition. I have no idea what they offered us in return, but I assume it must have been substantial. As it stands, I've been ordered not to talk to the prisoner or interrogate him in any way. All we have to do is release him to the security team."

The director paused and checked the dial of the Rolex on his wrist. "By my count, he should have left the building with them ten minutes ago. They'll remove him from the country, and at that point, he's no longer our concern. Problem solved."

Mariko tossed the pen on the desk and stood up. "Beautiful pen. Mont Blanc? Did Kusaka's blood money pay for that?"

"That's enough, Officer," the director answered in a curt voice. "Take the offer while it still stands, or you can consider your suspension permanent!"

Mariko nodded. "Maybe you're right. Maybe I do have a personal stake in making Kusaka pay for his crimes. But unlike you, my devotion to my duty is not for sale. Sometimes honor and duty can become personal, but that's not an excuse to turn away from what you know is right."

She stormed out of the office. As she left, she called back to Yamamoto, "And you're wrong about Caine. If the CIA gets him out of the country, our problems are just beginning."

CHAPTER THIRTY-SIX

Secretary of State Janet Kelson peered out her tinted window at the dreary weather. As the limo pulled up to the American Embassy in Asakusa, tiny droplets of rain drizzled down the glass. The dark grey skies did little to flatter the architecture of the embassy building. A heavy-duty iron fence surrounded the plain concrete structure. The building sat on a thin slice of land leased from the Japanese government. An American flag hanging from a lone pole fluttered in the slight breeze.

Her limo driver stopped at the main gate to present their credentials. The guard stepped into his tiny booth to confirm their information on his computer. All standard procedure. A few minutes later, he stepped back out and tapped her window.

Janet forced a smile as the window powered down. Her jet lag from the fifteen-hour flight made this simple act more of a challenge than she expected.

The guard handed her an ID badge. "Thank you, ma'am. Just making sure it's really you back there."

Her assistant leaned forward. "Thank you, Officer. I'm sure you're aware the Secretary has an important meeting at the embassy this morning. It's critical that we meet the other delegates in a timely manner. Will that be all?"

"Yes, ma'am." The gate swung open at his wave, and the limo cruised forward onto the embassy grounds. And just like that, she was now on United States soil. She had experienced this hundreds, perhaps thousands, of times in her diplomatic travels. But the feeling never failed to give her a warm sense of pride and patriotism.

She was proud of her country and proud of her role in its international affairs. She felt a surge of confidence. She was certain that the afternoon's talks would be a success. Rain or shine.

The limo stopped, and embassy staff stepped forward to open her door. Cool droplets of water spattered her designer trench coat as she got out of the car. The rain increased its staccato beat on the metal roof of the limo. She turned to Susan, who had exited the limo on the opposite side. "Looks like you were right about that rain."

Susan held up her enormous cell phone and smiled. "Thank the Google gods."

A man jogged up to them and snapped an umbrella open over Janet. Susan joined her underneath, and he escorted them to the building entrance. They were met by a handsome Japanese man wearing a tailored navy suit. A U.S. Diplomatic Service pin adorned his plum silk tie. He smiled and extended his hand.

"Welcome to Japan, Madam Secretary."

"Don't you look dashing, Peter? Always a pleasure."

Peter Takahara, the embassy's Deputy Chief of Mission, shook both their hands. Then he led them into the embassy building.

"Are the others here?" Janet asked.

Peter nodded. "They arrived a few minutes before you did. We've got China's Foreign Minister and Japan's Minster of Foreign Affairs. Both are complaining that they're hungry, but otherwise I'd say they're in good spirits."

"Well, I can't say I blame them," Janet whispered as Peter led them into the foyer.

They marched through a series of ornate, white columns that

circled the room. Beige settees surrounded a navy throw rug in the center of the room. An American eagle was woven into its fibers. One of the eagle's talons clutched an olive branch, the other a quiver of arrows. It stood ready, for peace or war.

As Janet entered the room, she had to stifle an urge to laugh. The Chinese and Japanese officials looked almost identical to each other. Both were tall, slender men in charcoal grey suits. Even their glasses were similar.

The Japanese minster stood a couple inches taller than his Chinese counterpart, and his skin was a shade darker. She shook his hand, then turned to the Chinese foreign minister. "Gentlemen, please, accept my apologies. I'm so sorry I'm late."

The diplomat's smile was thin, but he nodded. "Of course, Madam Secretary. After all, you did have the longest flight." Staff photographers darted forward to snap pictures as the officials greeted each other. They all shook hands and shared polite laughter.

"Well," Janet said, "I understand we've all managed to work up quite an appetite this morning. I've asked the kitchen to prepare a specialty from the American South. Biscuits and gravy. What do you say we save the photo ops for after breakfast? Then we can visit these islands on a full stomach."

The officials nodded their consent. Peter and Susan politely blocked the photographers as the three made their way to the dining room.

"I've never had this 'biscuits and gravy' you speak of," the Chinese official said. "Sounds a bit heavy for my taste."

Janet took the man's arm and allowed them to fall a few steps behind the Japanese minster. "Well, I'll tell you what. It beats the heck out of miso soup and cold fish."

The captain of the Grey Fox gazed down from the bridge at the empty main deck. The sparkling daggers of morning sunlight cut through the dark clouds above them, reflecting on the waves ahead.

The Kusaka Industries heavy freighter had set sail from Beijing. Their cargo hold was only at half-capacity. They were transporting a meager quantity of cheap cell phones and even cheaper t-shirts.

Per his instructions, he had altered the shipping manifest to indicate a full load. His men had cleared the top deck, leaving a long, empty expanse that stretched from the bridge to the pointed bow.

The captain chomped down on his cigar. Smoking was not allowed on the bridge of Kusaka Industries vessels, but he always lit a cigar before returning to port. It was an old tradition, one he expected to take with him to his grave.

After a few deep puffs, he turned away from the window. According to the ship's GPS navigation equipment, they were just inside Japan's territorial waters. The huge freighter was positioned between the Sea of Japan and the East China Sea. Several hundred miles west, out of sight on the distant horizon, lay South Korea and their insane neighbors. And south of that, the behemoth ... China.

Less than a hundred miles off their starboard bow sat the Senkaku Islands, the disputed rocks stirring up all the recent political turmoil.

The captain shrugged. He wasn't much for politics. Japan claimed the islands belonged to them. China rattled its sabers, and occasionally flew drones and fighter jets over the disputed territory.

The captain had seen his share of bar fights in the seediest ports of call all around this world. This latest eruption bore all the markings of two drunkards, posturing and puffing their chests for the crowd. They would throw a few half-hearted punches, then slink back to their beers.

All the captain cared about was getting paid. And taking on this extra assignment for Kusaka-san promised a lucrative payday indeed. He cracked his knuckles and smiled. In the next five minutes, he would make more money than he had all year.

He took another puff of his cigar and turned to the small group of men behind him. He had ordered all general crew to clear the bridge and wait below decks. Equipment inspection, he had told them. The only men left stood behind him, talking in low, quiet voices. They were all dressed in identical black suits.

He wasn't exactly sure who they were. They looked like yakuza to him—he had dealt with plenty of those types during his tenure in the shipping industry. But these men seemed different somehow.

They exhibited none of the bravado or swagger of the gangsters he had encountered in the past. These men were quiet, driven, and purposeful.

The captain cleared his throat and coughed. The men stopped talking and turned to face him.

"We're in position," he announced.

One of the men, a tall, slim figure who towered over him, nodded. He issued a quiet stream of orders to his comrades. The other men bowed and shouted, "*Hai!*" in unison. They cleared the bridge except for the tall man. He remained, standing next to the captain.

The two men watched as the doors of a large steel cargo container swung open. A few minutes later, a black missile-like form was wheeled out onto the empty deck.

Painstakingly refurbished and modified, the aircraft was a Chinese-made Lijian Mark 2. Also known as the "Sharp Sword," it was an unmanned aerial vehicle, or UAV for short.

The drone cast a sinister shadow on the freighter's empty deck. Its sweeping wings and bulging fuselage were covered by rubbery black, radar-reflective material. It resembled some sort of huge, predatory nocturnal bird.

The captain turned away from the window. "When do I get paid?"

The man beside him grunted but did not look away as his men scurried about the drone, preparing it for flight. "Soon. We will all receive our reward soon."

The tall man slipped in an earpiece. "Final check. Report," he said. The captain could not hear the response, but the tall man nodded.

"Begin final countdown."

His lips moved as he silently counted down from ten. The men outside maneuvered the drone into position. The empty deck of the ship stretched before it. Once the drone was in place, the men scattered and took cover behind the cargo container.

The countdown reached zero. The drone's engines flared to life, and the sinister black craft charged forward. It rapidly gained speed.

Although the Chinese denied it, many believed the Lijian Mark 2 was based on stolen American plans for the U.S. X-47B. Like that device, the drone was designed for aircraft carrier deployment. The Grey Fox was no aircraft carrier, but its upper deck was within operational tolerances for takeoff.

The drone screamed towards the end of the deck. The captain sucked in his breath. He watched as the craft tore across the metal surface. It charged closer and closer to the edge, and the churning sea waters below. *What if the damn thing falls into the drink?* he thought. *How do I get paid then?*

The drone was operating on autopilot. There was nothing the captain, or anyone else on board, could do to assist the aircraft. It would either take off and fly to its predetermined coordinates ... or it would not. His companion showed no trace of emotion as he watched the drone speed towards the end of the deck. At the last second, inches away from crashing into the ship's bulkhead, the drone lifted into the air. It soared above the ship's deck, rising into the clouds above.

The captain raised his fist in the air and cheered. "*Banzai!*"

The tall man nodded and spoke into his earpiece. "Takeoff successful. Prepare for phase two. For Japan."

The captain slapped him on the back. "Now we all get paid, eh?" he exclaimed with a wide grin.

"*Hai.* Now we have the honor of serving Japan with the ultimate sacrifice." The man keyed in a code on his cell phone and then slipped the device in his pocket. The men outside sat down on the deck and stared up into the dark, cloudy sky. They watched the drone shrink into a tiny black dot and then disappear into the haze.

"Hey, what the hell are they doing?" the captain asked.

The tall man slipped his hand into his jacket. "They are preparing."

"Preparing for what?"

"To be purified. By death."

A sudden, deafening explosion rocked through the ship. The deck shuddered beneath his feet.

"What the hell was that?" the captain screamed.

He grabbed the ship's radio. Before he could bring the microphone to his mouth, a second explosion shook the freighter. He could feel the ship listing already. Water had begun flood the cargo compartment. The ship's hull was compromised.

The captain depressed the talk button on the microphone. "All hands, all hands, abandon—"

Before he could finish his sentence, a gunshot rang out on the bridge. The captain gasped as the metal slug tore into his lung. He dropped the radio as he fell. Above him, the mic swung back and forth on its curled rubber cable like a pendulum. He could tell by its swinging pattern that the ship was tilted off axis. They were sinking.

The tall man now stood over him, balancing against the extreme angle of the ship. He was aiming a heavy pistol down at the captain. The captain held up a hand in protest.

The tall man fired again. A bloody hole opened in the captain's hand. The bullet tore through his flesh and buried itself in his chest.

His attacker knelt down to whisper, "You and your crew will also be purified. Together, we have raised the sword. Others will use it to strike the death blow."

As the captain's vision faded, he heard more muted gunfire, followed by screams. He caught a glimpse of the grey clouds outside the window before the ship lurched again and they slid from his view.

As he faded from the world around him, he thought of the drone streaking through the sky. An arrow of death, launched from the black heart of the underworld.

He hoped there was no underworld. No heaven. And, most importantly, no hell.

As the captain slipped in the final blackness of death, the stern of the Grey Fox dipped beneath the dark, churning water. The men on the deck and the tall man in the bridge sat with their legs crossed in the lotus position. Frigid water surged into the ship.

The tall man gasped as the freezing chill of the ocean struck his body, but he did not move. He looked forward, determined to stare death in the face as it came for him.

And death did come. The massive freighter disappeared underwater. Only the scattered flotsam and a few floating corpses marked the fact that it was ever there. Soon, the ocean's churning waves would disperse even these last bits of evidence.

High up in the clouds, oblivious to the death and destruction below, the drone continued its relentless flight towards Japan.

CHAPTER THIRTY-SEVEN

Caine awoke to utter blackness. His head throbbed and ached. He gasped for breath.

The darkness surrounded him. He realized he was wearing a hood. He couldn't see a thing under the sack covering his head. The smell of sweat and canvas triggered a surge of panic through his body. The hood reminded him of his days of imprisonment with the White Leopard clan.

For a few seconds, he was certain that he was back there, in the desert. Everything and everyone else was just a dream. The mission, Rebecca, Hitomi, Mariko ... they were hallucinations. Phantoms. The pain and the screaming were his only reality.

No, he thought. *That's in the past. Get a grip!*

The seconds ticked by, each one an eternity of panic and terror. But Caine grit his teeth and remained still, his body betraying nothing. Soon the fear receded from his nerve endings. He was back in control.

A gentle rocking motion and the muted sound of tires on pavement confirmed he was in a vehicle. He remembered the security team and Kusaka's smug, smiling face. He had almost killed the man in a stranglehold before the mercenaries had intervened.

They had beat him senseless, but they hadn't sedated him. Sloppy. A breach of standard rendition procedure.

Bernatto must have contracted these men in haste. He had made some kind of deal with Japanese intelligence. Gave them something they wanted in exchange for the sanctioned rendition of a burned agent. Once they got him out of the country, Caine knew exactly what would happen. He had run enough of these operations himself to know his future was bleak.

They would either shoot him or dump him in a black site prison, a place from which he would never resurface. Either way, he knew he had to act before they arrived at their destination. Every second he delayed was a second closer to his death.

Caine listened. He heard men rustling, breathing, grunting. They did not speak, but he was able to piece together a mental picture of their positions in the vehicle.

The driver sat in front of him, to the left. He could hear the man sigh and curse under his breath as they hit traffic. That meant they were most likely still in Tokyo.

To his right sat another man. He heard a soft metallic clacking coming from that direction. It was a quiet, rhythmic sound that matched the bouncing of the vehicle over the pavement. The sound was subtle, barely noticeable, but it was a sound Caine knew well.

It was an automatic rifle, clattering against its sling as the vehicle vibrated.

Caine pegged the man next to him as the one who had beaten him unconscious. It was impossible to be sure, but he had a gut feeling. Either way, he knew the man was armed.

Assuming another man sat in the front passenger seat, he was dealing with three captors. The other men would be in a second vehicle, most likely a blocker car traveling ahead of them. Their job would be to keep an eye out for any possible resistance.

Caine let the motion of the vehicle rock him backwards. Without appearing to move, he rolled onto his back and let his head loll against the side of the vehicle. Judging by the amount of space in the backseat, he assumed they were in an SUV.

He didn't much like his chances of taking out three armed men while blindfolded and restrained. But he didn't have much of a choice. If he was going to die, he would die fighting, not drugged up in some concrete bunker, lost in whatever country the CIA was farming its torture out to these days.

Caine tensed his muscles and prepared to make his move. The vehicle gained speed as traffic eased up. Then the brakes squealed to life, and momentum rolled him forward. He knew the man next to him would be off-balance as well.

Caine jerked his legs backwards. In one fluid motion, he slipped his feet through his tied arms. Before the man next to him could react, he lashed both legs out in a powerful kick. The blow cracked the man's skull against the side window.

"Holy shit! This fucker's awake!" a voice shouted from the front seat.

The man to his right grunted, then the jingle of the rifle strap rang out. Caine knew it was only a matter of time before the man clubbed him again or took a shot. Caine honed in on the metallic sound and kicked until he made contact with the rigid firearm. He drove it backwards and heard the man grunt again as the rifle smashed into his face.

How do you like it, asshole? Caine thought.

He rolled forward as the vehicle swerved back and forth. The driver reached back and struck him with a security baton. The coiled steel snapped across his back. A burning pain eclipsed all other sensations. The baton had struck his spine, square between the shoulder blades.

Caine collapsed to the floor of the vehicle. He twisted his body forward, shielding his vitals. The man to his right began stamping down on his back.

"You son of a bitch!" he roared, as his heavy combat boots battered Caine's flesh.

As the rain of kicks and blows continued, Caine's vision begin to blur. An arm wrapped around his neck and dragged his head up in a chokehold. A harsh whisper breathed in his ear.

"You know," the voice hissed, "we're supposed to get you out of the country before we do you. But hey, sometimes accidents happen."

Caine coughed as the man's forearm dug into his windpipe. His attacker's other arm pressed down on the back of his head, driving his neck forward. Caine became lightheaded as the hold reduced the blood flow to his brain.

He tried to pummel the man with his bound hands, swinging them up and over his shoulder. But his awkward position beneath the seat made it impossible to land a hit. With each passing second, his strength ebbed away as his brain began to suffocate.

The naked choke, a variation on a jiu-jitsu maneuver, was a dangerous hold. If applied past the point of unconsciousness, it could easily cause brain damage or even death. And Caine had the distinct feeling his assailant had no intention of letting him go.

Caine forced his weakened legs to lift his body up, sliding his head up his attacker's chest. When he felt the man's breath on his neck, he tipped his head forward. A split second later, he slammed it backwards. The back of his skull crushed into the man's face.

The mercenary howled in pain and loosened his grip. Caine let his body go limp. He dropped like a stone, slipping out of the stranglehold.

As he fell back to the floor, the edge of the hood caught on the man's forearm and pulled halfway up. A burst of daylight flashed into Caine's face. He squinted, struggling to focus on his surroundings. The blood rushed back to his head, and he felt even dizzier than he had when suffocating.

The vehicle continued swerving left and right. The driver swung his baton again, just missing Caine's face. The blow struck his shoulder with a loud crack. Caine winced, and it took all his willpower not to vomit on the floor. The pain, dizziness, and careening vehicle all conspired against his diminished senses.

He shook his head, and his vision began to clear. He caught a glimpse of the man next to him, hands covering his face as blood gushed from a broken nose. Then the front passenger twisted around and pointed a pistol at him.

He heard the click of the hammer and found himself staring down the barrel of Colt .45. He closed his eyes. Once the man fired, he wouldn't have even a second to feel the pain before his head exploded into a bloody pulp.

The explosion was deafening as the gun fired.

Mariko stepped on the gas and the grey sedan leapt forward. She wove in and out of the stop-and-go traffic, ignoring the angry beeps and shaking fists as she disrupted Tokyo's morning commute.

Up ahead, she saw the twin black SUVs. They were stopped in a line of cars waiting to turn onto the Shuto Expressway. Based on their route, she guessed they were traveling to Haneda airport. A private aircraft would no doubt be waiting there, ready to whisk them out of the country.

She jogged her steering wheel left. The sedan's underbody screeched as it jumped the curb. She flew past the stopped cars, made it through the light, and darted into traffic just behind the rear SUV.

She knew the move would draw their attention, but she no longer cared. She had to stop them before they made it to the airport. The longer they spent on the expressway, the more dangerous the chase would get.

The SUVs sped up once they reached the clearer lanes of the expressway. Then the rear vehicle begin to swerve back and forth. The swaying vehicle clipped the rear end of a delivery van as it chugged past them.

The SUV's rear windows were tinted dark black, and Mariko

could not see inside. But she knew what had to be causing the erratic motion: Caine was fighting to escape.

Her sedan surged forward and pulled up to the passenger side of the rear SUV. She saw the front passenger pointing a gun towards the rear seat. She could not see Caine in the back, but another passenger was struggling. She saw his back pressed against the rear side window.

Mariko slammed her car into the side of the SUV. Metal screeched against metal at seventy miles per hour. The larger vehicle drifted to the left.

She could hear the crack of a gunshot over the deafening collision. She hoped the impact of her ram had thrown off the gunman's aim.

The front passenger leaned out his window and took aim at Mariko. She jerked her wheel to the left again. He had time to squeeze off only two shots before the cars collided.

Mariko kept up the pressure, pushing against the SUV. The screeching metal of the locked vehicles sounded like the frenzied shriek of a rabid animal. She knew that, as soon as she let up, the man with the pistol would be gunning for her again.

Up ahead, the lead SUV slid out of position and moved in front of her. Men with automatic rifles leaned out the rear windows. The explosive blast of automatic weapon fire filled the air.

She ducked as the windshield exploded. Tiny fragments of safety glass caught in her hair. Bullets whined and screeched as they tore into the metal frame of the car.

She slammed on the brakes and dropped back behind the rear SUV. The big black vehicle was still weaving across the road, but at least it provided some cover from the riflemen. Then, a few second later, the vehicle straightened out and stopped swerving. It fell back in line with the lead SUV.

Now what? she thought. She knew she had to keep them off-balance, keep them reacting. Otherwise, it was only a matter of time before they killed both her and Caine.

She stepped on the accelerator and braced herself. Her sedan slammed into the vehicle's rear bumper. The SUV lurched forward and struck the vehicle in front.

The impact threw the riflemen off balance. The armed men were unable to recover as the vehicle exploded forward.

"*Yatta!*" she exclaimed. She had made an opening.

She charged forward past the rear SUV. As the forward vehicle straightened out, the gunman on her side raised his rifle. But before he could fire, her rear windshield collapsed into a sparking curtain of broken glass. The driver of the SUV behind her was shooting at her as well!

She ducked just as the lead gunman opened fire. More bullets tore through the car. It was only a matter of time before one of them found its target. Keeping her head low, she spun the steering wheel and hit the gas.

The front corner of her sedan slammed into the rear wheel of the SUV. The driver slammed on the brakes, but she forced her foot down even harder on the shaking accelerator pedal. The gunfire stopped, and she popped back up in her seat.

The SUV fishtailed in front of her and skidded sideways. The driver was frantically spinning the wheel, trying to regain control. But the corner of her sedan was still pushing the rear of the SUV forward, forcing it into the skid.

To her left, Mariko saw they were entering a cloverleaf exchange, a wide, sloping traffic circle that would carry them up and over the lower expressway. She pulled her pistol from her leather jacket and took aim at the driver's front wheel.

She fired. The tire exploded in a cloud of smoke and shredded rubber.

The SUV continued to skid straight forward, moving against the curve of the road. Mariko revved the accelerator again, pushing the vehicle forward even faster. Then she jerked the wheel to her right and darted away.

There was a split second of silence as the lead SUV tipped and flew into the air. Then gravity took over, and the huge metal body crashed back down onto the pavement. The frame twisted into a lump of crumpled metal as it tumbled over and over, rolling towards the edge of the overpass.

With a screeching roar, the SUV slammed up against the metal guardrail. The thin rail snapped under the weight of the heavy vehicle. It crashed through and teetered over the overpass.

As it fell down to the expressway below, the twisted metal ribbons of the severed rail caught in the rear axle. The vehicle lurched to a stop. It swung back and forth, hanging over the road below like a grisly pendulum of twisted metal.

Mariko's relief was short-lived. A quick glance in her mirror showed the rear SUV gaining on her. The front passenger was leaning out his window. He was now armed with an automatic rifle.

She screamed as a hail of bullets slammed into the rear of her car.

CHAPTER THIRTY-EIGHT

Back in the SUV, Caine had managed to pull himself onto the rear seat and pin the mercenary against the window. He had felt the impact as Mariko rammed the vehicle over and over. Her sudden attack had allowed him to use the other men's distraction to his benefit.

He twisted his head and saw the front passenger fire his assault rifle at Mariko's grey sedan. Caine grit his teeth and threw himself back to the floor of the vehicle. He tensed his body as the merc in the backseat recovered and began kicking at his bruised shins.

Ignoring the pain, Caine reached forward between the seat and door frame. His fingers wrapped around the seat release lever. He yanked it backwards.

The front passenger seat tilted back, driving the gunman's aim up and away from Mariko. The headrest slammed into the face of the merc in the rear seat, and Caine grinned with satisfaction as the man cried out in pain.

He swung his legs up and struck the jaw of the man in the front seat, knocking his head against the door frame. As he lifted himself to a sitting position, Caine saw Mariko's vehicle.

The sedan was riddled with bullet holes. He could see Mariko inside, as she drifted left and accelerated. She was trying to get out of the line of fire.

Caine paused for a split second. The man next to him lifted his battered face from the headrest and aimed his weapon at Caine's head. The front passenger recovered and begin to raise his rifle out the window. The driver turned the wheel, bringing the vehicle behind Mariko. He was lining up the perfect shot.

In that split second, Caine noticed one thing.

None of them were wearing seatbelts.

Without hesitation, Caine grabbed the belt over his left shoulder. Looping it over his arms and chest, he threw his body forward. His fingers curled around the vehicle's emergency brake. He yanked it upwards with every ounce of strength he had left.

The rear wheels locked. The tires shuddered and screamed as they bounced across the pavement. Everyone in the car, Caine included, was thrown forward. A white-hot dagger of pain lanced through his battered body, as the seatbelt jerked him backwards.

The driver's face smashed into the windshield. He fell back in a daze, his hands slumping off the wheel. The passenger dropped his rifle and reached over to grab it, but he was too late. They were traveling too fast. The wheel spun in his hands, and the entire vehicle lurched sideways.

Caine let his body swing from the seatbelt. He kicked the rear mercenary in the head again. The man smashed into the side of the car. He reached out for Caine, but he was fighting against gravity. The entire vehicle was tipping over in his direction.

Caine wrenched himself onto the seat and clicked the shoulder belt across his body. The pavement rushed up to meet them. The side windows exploded inwards, as the vehicle flipped and rolled.

Warm blood dripped down Caine's face. He wasn't sure if it was his.

The percussive beat of rain echoed through the cabin. Water droplets spattered off the shattered windows and mangled metal body of the SUV.

He was laying on his side. He struggled to sit up and found himself staring sideways out the shattered front windshield.

The rear mercenary was suspended in the air, pinned in place by the front passenger seat. His lifeless face was a collage of gashes and wounds. Droplets of warm blood dripped sideways from a cut in his forehead and struck Caine just below his eye.

No, Caine thought, *I'm disoriented.* The blood wasn't dripping sideways. The entire vehicle was sideways. It had stopped rolling and come to a rest on the pavement with the driver's side facing down.

He patted down his body. Waves of pain shot through his limbs as he applied pressure to several bruises and small gashes, but nothing appeared broken.

With a grunt, he unlatched the seatbelt. The aches and pains intensified as he moved, but he ignored them and began patting down the contractor next to him. He removed the man's pistol, an American made Kimber 1911, chambered in 45 ACP.

Using the butt of the pistol, he smashed through the spiderweb of cracked glass in the passenger side window. He held his head up, allowing the cool rain to soothe his battered face and wash away some of the blood. Then, bracing himself for another wave of searing pain, he crawled up and out the shattered window.

He dropped to the pavement and surveyed the wreckage. The SUV had flipped into the path of traffic, and a small pileup of cars surrounded him. Luckily, no one else seemed hurt.

Footsteps approached across the wet pavement. He spun around, raising the pistol in his still bound hands, but it was only Mariko. She jogged through the rain towards him, wet wisps of dark hair plastered to her face.

"*Daijobo desu ka?* Are you okay?"

Caine nodded. "Thanks to you. You saved my life."

Mariko brushed the hair from her eyes. "Kusaka's paid off my superiors. They offered to put me back on duty as long as I dropped this investigation. They think he's just a rich businessman trying to avoid a sex scandal. You're the only person I've met who knows that Kusaka is tied to Tokyo Black."

"So, in other words, you were just doing your duty."

She slipped a utility knife from her back pocket and cut through his bonds. "Of course. But if it makes you feel better, when this is all over, you can buy me dinner."

Caine nodded, then groaned in pain as he flexed his wrists. The muscles in his neck and arms burned. "Deal," he grunted. "Anywhere you want to go."

Mariko took his arm as they limped towards her battered grey sedan.

"We've got about five minutes before the police show up. And based on what I told my director to go do with himself, I don't think I'm going to be able to talk our way out of this."

Caine let her help him into the passenger seat. As he buckled the seatbelt, she slid in and started the car. The engine sputtered and wheezed, then roared to life.

"What's next?" she asked.

Caine was silent for a second. "Kusaka came to visit me, just before the security team showed up. Whatever he's planning, it has something to do with China. He sounded obsessed. He blames China's rise in economic power for all of Japan's problems."

Mariko maneuvered around the wreckage on the freeway and sped off down the expressway.

"Mmm," she said with a nod, "that's a common sentiment in Japan these days. We have always had an uneasy relationship with China. Many rightwing political groups feel our government has caved in to China's demands. That we have allowed our shame for our actions in World War II to allow China to flourish, at our expense. But that still doesn't tell us what he's planning."

Caine stared out the side window. "Right. Head for Roppongi."

Mariko looked over at him. "What's in Roppongi?"

He did not look back at her. Instead, he studied his reflection in the rain-spattered window. A ruin of cuts and bruises stared back at him.

"Apparently," he growled, "Kusaka and I have a mutual friend."

CHAPTER THIRTY-NINE

They parked in the alley outside the Yoshizawa koi farm. Caine drew his pistol and stalked towards the metal garage door.

"I thought we were visiting a friend," Mariko whispered. She drew her own weapon and scanned the alleyway for danger.

"Yeah, well, there seems to have been a slight misunderstanding. Just follow my lead."

Mariko nodded and took up a position next to Caine.

Caine rapped on the door, following the same knocking pattern Koichi had used earlier. For a few minutes, nothing happened. Then the door began to roll up. Caine held his pistol ready. But as the door rose, he found himself staring into Koichi's wrinkled face.

The man looked pale and withered, but his eyes burned with dark intensity. He was flanked on either side by Yoshizawa's yakuza soldiers. Greased hair, shiny suits. Definitely armed.

"Koichi! I thought you'd be in the hospital."

"I was. Then some of my men called to tell me about what happened."

Mariko looked Koichi up and down with surprise. "The hospital just let a gunshot victim walk? And the police didn't stop you?"

Koichi made a dismissive gesture. "Cops? Who has time to talk to cops? That's what lawyers are for. When the oyabun of a yakuza clan is murdered, his second-in-command can't just lay resting in bed, now can he?"

The old gangster maintained his stone-faced expression, but Caine could see pain in the lines around his eyes. He knew it was not from the man's injuries. "So it's true?" he asked. "Isato is dead?"

Koichi nodded and hobbled away from the door. Caine and Mariko followed as he led them past the pools of koi.

Despite the death of Isato and the chaos that had followed, the old man in the blue windbreaker was still there. He was still singing to the fat koi as they swam in their pools. The old man looked up as they passed. A grave, serious expression hung on his face.

Caine felt a strange emptiness in the pit of his stomach. Isato had been a criminal. The yakuza liked to project an image of modern-day Robin Hoods, rebels who stood for the people of Japan. But he knew most yakuza clans were involved in drugs, prostitution, arms dealing....

To rise to a position of power as Isato had, the man certainly had blood on his hands. But then again, Caine knew he had spilled his share of blood as well.

Caine couldn't say the world wasn't better off without a man like Isato in it, but he also couldn't deny there was something about the old man he had respected. And he was Kenji's father. They were bound together in a debt of honor that night, years ago. The old bullet wound in Caine's shoulder began to throb.

"I'm sorry, Koichi. I know he was like a father to you. But you must know I didn't kill him."

Koichi uttered a short, pained laugh. "Of course, I know. You think we'd be standing here talking if I thought you had?" The old man shook his head. "I wish you had killed him. That would be far less painful than the truth."

Koichi looked over at Mariko. "*Chotto Matte* ... she's a cop, right?"

"I'm suspended from duty," she said. "I'm just here as an observer."

"Then observe the fish," Koichi said to her. "They're beautiful, *ne*? Caine-san, come with me."

Caine turned to Mariko. "You mind waiting here?"

"Of course not," she answered, her voice polite but cold. Her shoulders stiffened, and she turned on her heel a little too fast.

As soon as Caine followed Koichi into the back room, two yakuza thugs took up sentry duty by the door. Mariko sighed and looked down at the bubbling pools of water.

She watched a fat white koi lazily beat its fins in the water. It looked up at her, black eyes glittering, wide mouth gulping. She remembered Hitomi's words in the car, outside the capsule hotel.

Two sides of the same coin, she had said. Always touching, but never standing together.

Kenji sat before them, sullen and slightly pale, tied to a chair in Isato's office. He looked up, and Caine saw his pupils were wide and dilated. He was in shock but otherwise appeared unharmed.

The room smelled of soap and bleach, and a large screen television now stood in the corner. Koichi limped over to Isato's desk and picked up a remote.

"Isato was no fool," Koichi muttered. "He used this warehouse to meet with rival yakuza, other crime syndicates, dirty cops. He had a security camera installed in that sculpture up there."

Koichi looked up at the large wood carving of the swimming koi, hanging on the wall behind Isato's desk. "Thing ran twenty-four, seven, just in case he needed leverage or a record of what was said. Take a look. I'll show you what I showed the men when they called me down here."

The old man clutched his stomach and groaned as he sat down in Isato's chair. Kenji looked away from the screen. Koichi pressed play.

Caine watched as the security footage played on the monitor. The video was grainy and washed out, but the images were clear enough.

He saw himself enter the room, as he had several days ago. Kenji walked out, as he and Isato talked. Caine blinked. It had only been, what, a couple days ago? It felt like another lifetime.

Koichi pressed a button, and the footage blurred as the images shifted to fast-forward. A time and date stamp in the top right corner of the monitor advanced to the previous evening. The footage returned to normal speed, and Caine watched as Kenji entered the room.

The audio was muted, but it was clear they were arguing. He saw Isato hang up the phone. Looking at the time stamp, Caine realized he had been on the other end of the phone call, asking Isato for backup. Now he knew why it never arrived.

On the screen, he saw Kenji raise the pistol. From the high angle of the camera, the image looked surreal and impersonal, like a video game come to life. He saw the explosive puff of the bullet leaving the gun as Kenji fired. Isato slumped over and fell to the ground. The video continued playing.

"Admit it, old man." Kenji spoke up. "You're getting off on this, aren't you? This is what you wanted all along. Now you're finally in control instead of just being my father's bitch."

Koichi pressed a button, and the TV went black. He did not look at Kenji.

"I would have given my life for you. Or your father. As for who will take control of this family, that is not for me to decide. I have reported your actions to the Yamaguchi-gumi. The heads of the families will meet and decide what is to become of the Yoshizawa clan. For all I know, they may disband our whole goddamn organization. Absorb us into another family."

Caine's voice was quiet. "Kenji, why? Why did you do it?"

"I was trying to do it for him." Kenji's eyes were wide, damp, pleading. "It was all for him. To show him I wasn't just an accountant, that I could help him."

Koichi slammed his fist on the desk. Caine was reminded for a brief second of Isato and his rare bursts of emotion.

"Help him? You helped him to the grave! You may have destroyed everything he spent his life building! If you were anyone else but the oyabun's son, you'd be chopped into little pieces by now. Do you have any idea what you've done?"

Kenji sobbed. "I didn't mean to. I just snapped. I thought this time would be different. I thought he'd listen to me. And when he didn't, it was like I wasn't even in the room anymore. Like I was watching as someone else pulled the trigger."

Caine turned to Koichi. "I need answers. Kenji has them. People are going to die if I don't get them. Do you understand?"

The older man grimaced and gave an uneasy nod. "I understand. Do what you have to."

Caine kneeled down in front of Kenji. A twitch of fear shivered through the young man's features as he looked into Caine's eyes.

"Kenji, what's your connection to Kusaka? What the hell are he and Bobu planning?"

For a second, Kenji's face flared with anger and determination. He stared hatefully at Caine and kept silent.

Caine did not blink. "I've been trying to keep the shameful things I've done buried, Kenji. Don't make me add more to the list."

Kenji's head rolled forward, and the determination drained from his features like a balloon deflating. His voice was quiet and meek. "I interned with Kusaka Industries during my senior year in the United States. When he visited his U.S. offices, he seemed to take an interest in me. Took me under his wing."

Koichi threw the TV remote against the wall. The young man jumped as it shattered into plastic shards and clattered to the ground. "You idiot! What are you, a schoolgirl? He knew who you were. He took an interest in you because he wanted influence in the Yoshizawa clan."

Kenji laughed. "Then he picked the wrong kid. You know better than anyone, my father never listened to me. Kusaka respected me more than my father ever did. Anyway, when Bobu was released from prison, Kusaka shifted his attention to the Shimizu clan. He helped Bobu splinter the clan and reshape it into Tokyo Black. He financed them, gave them direction. Used his government connections to keep them out of jail. He said he needed an army of pawns and Bobu's fanatics fit the bill. Christ, what those men did to themselves ... they're all fucking crazy!"

"But what does Kusaka want?" Caine asked. "What is this all about?"

The young man took a deep breath. "I don't know all of it, but one of his deep sea salvage operations recovered a damaged Chinese drone. They dredged it up in the waters between China and Japan. He's managed to keep his political leanings quiet, and he has powerful business connections to Chinese aerospace industries. He found out where it crashed and was able to recover it before the Chinese government did. They didn't report it missing because it went down in disputed territory. It's a prototype, some kind of advanced stealth technology."

Caine stared at Kenji in shock. "A prototype? Is it armed?"

The young man shook his head. "No, it wasn't carrying any weapons. But Kusaka-san had his engineers gut it. They ripped out any nonessential systems and packed the body full of explosives. Whatever that thing hits ... it's over, vaporized. It's just a big flying bomb now."

Koichi leaned forward in his chair. "So he's turned a billion-dollar Chinese drone into a high-tech kamikaze? And just what does he plan to do with it?"

"All I know is he's going to use it to attack a target in Japan. With all the tension between China and Japan right now over the Senkaku Islands ... I mean, the Japanese government is just looking for an excuse to take a harder stance against China. Something like this..."

"The match that lights the fuse," Caine finished. "But those drones use encrypted control signals. Even with his industrial connections, I can't imagine the Chinese government would give him access to those codes."

"That's where Allan Bernatto came in. Kusaka had already been working with him as a CIA asset, reporting on Chinese industrial espionage. Bernatto wanted the CIA to start taking Chinese cyberterrorism seriously. So he helped Kusaka. Apparently, he had a Chinese state-sponsored hacker stashed in a black site somewhere. Renditioned the guy out of Hong Kong. He got him to crack the drone's encryption."

"That's what was on the hard drive," Caine said. "Kusaka needed it back to control the drone."

Kenji nodded. "When Hitomi stole it, he flipped the fuck out. Tore up the whole city looking for her. And I guess Bernatto got cold feet. He said Kusaka changed the target, that it was too high profile now. He tried to get the drive back, pull out of the whole thing."

"So he had Rebecca send me," Caine said. "Once I found Hitomi and the drive, he would have sent in his private mercs to kill us both and take the drive back. Keep himself from getting exposed if the whole plan went south."

Koichi sucked air through his teeth. "So you're not just a traitor to this family, Kenji. You're a traitor to Japan as well. What was in it for you?"

"Once this thing blows up, China's economic relations with Japan and the West are gonna tank. I mean, even if they blame it on hackers or rogue terrorists or whatever … it's going to set back trade relations for years. Kusaka's shorted all his Chinese investments."

"And you did the same," Caine said. "You ran your father's finances. You shifted his money to short positions on the same investments, didn't you?"

"I would have made this family millions. Maybe even billions. Do you know what kind of power that money could bring? We could have absorbed the other clans. We could have—"

"Kusaka's going to murder innocent people and possibly start a war, just to satisfy his personal politics," Caine interrupted. "Your father may have been a lot of things, Kenji, but he wasn't a mass murderer or a traitor."

Kenji flinched.

Caine lifted his pistol and placed the barrel on Kenji's knee. "What's the target?"

Kenji shook his head. "I swear, I don't know. He never told me."

Caine cocked the trigger on the pistol. Koichi eyed him warily but said nothing. He grunted and turned away.

Kenji looked up at Caine, desperate.

"Kenji, you need to think very carefully. What is the target? Don't make me ask again."

"Look, I don't know, okay! What does it matter? He could attack anything ... the capital, a mall, an office building. All that matters is the news will report a Chinese stealth drone attacked Japan!"

Caine pressed the barrel harder into Kenji's knee. "Where is he?"

"He could be anywhere in the city! Bernatto didn't just give him the drone codes. He modified the piloting controls so they fit in a suitcase. He can't access the Chinese satellites, but once the drone is over the Tokyo metro area, all he needs is line of sight."

"Dammit, Kenji, you have to do better than that! People are going to die unless we stop him!"

"Caine-san, just a minute," Koichi said.

Caine turned towards him but kept Kenji in his peripheral vision. "Go ahead."

"The boy said Kusaka needs line of sight to control the drone once it reaches Tokyo?"

"That's right. That's all I know," Kenji stammered.

"That's actually more difficult than it sounds," Koichi said. "There are so many tall buildings in Tokyo. Even local radio and TV stations that broadcast from Tokyo Tower have trouble with blocked transmissions. If Kusaka and Bobu are using a portable transmitter, they'll need someplace taller than that. It would have to be taller than all the surrounding buildings. Otherwise, they'll break the line of sight between the transmitter and the drone."

Caine nodded. "Okay, sure. You have a place in mind?"

Koichi examined his cell phone. "Kusaka has offices all across the city, but his newest branch just opened a few months ago. It's in the Skytree Plaza, right across from the Skytree tower."

"Never been there."

Koichi nodded. "It's new, wasn't built when you were here last. But take a guess what the tallest structure in Tokyo is?"

"Sounds like it's worth a look."

Koichi stood. "As I said, the Yoshizawa family has been ordered to lay low until the council makes its decision. I am forbidden to send any of our men to help, but that doesn't mean I can't go with you on a sightseeing trip."

The old man stepped forward, then grabbed his stomach and groaned in pain. Caine hurried over and eased him back in the chair. "Koichi, you've done enough. Mariko and I will take it from here. You've got other things to worry about."

Koichi nodded glumly. "Damn it. Can't take a bullet like I used to."

"Jesus, how many times have you been shot, old man?"

"Lost count after the third."

Kenji's trembling voice rang out. "Listen, there's one more thing you should know."

"Speak up, kid," Caine said.

"Kusaka gave me a deadline to get all my trades in. Whatever he has planned, it's happening today. And soon."

Caine glared at him. "Soon? As in when?"

Kenji looked at the clock on the wall. His voice wavered. "Soon, as in an hour from now."

CHAPTER FORTY

Caine and Mariko sped down the expressway in silence. The skies overhead were a swirling abyss of black clouds. The rain had intensified, and droplets of water battered the windshield.

Mariko flipped on the windshield wipers of the new car Koichi had lent them. It was an economy car, nothing fancy, but the last thing they needed was to stand out and get pulled over by the police right now.

Koichi had also provided him with another firearm, a new Beretta PX4 Storm Compact. The pistol came with a range of adjustable back strap grips in its case. Of all the weapons he had used recently, it fit the most comfortably in his hand. He ejected the weapon's magazine and checked the slide as they raced through the rain towards Tokyo's Sumida district.

Mariko hissed a string of Japanese curses under her breath as she turned and exited the expressway. Caine couldn't quite make out the words, but her sentiment was clear.

"I take it your phone call with your partner didn't go well?"

"Ex-partner, you mean. And no, it didn't. He felt bad about

ratting us out before so he gave me a heads up that the Security Bureau has issued a warrant for my arrest. Yours, too, by the way."

Caine shrugged. "Well, it beats being executed by a private death squad."

"*Hiyowana okubykomon, ne!*"

"I don't know what that means, but it doesn't sound good."

She glanced at him from the corner of her eye. "It means coward with no waist."

Caine chuckled. "I think you mean spineless coward."

She nodded. "Yes, exactly. I told them what you found out, but I don't know if they will take the threat seriously. Even if they do, I doubt they would make a move before bringing me in for a debriefing. They'll have to get approval from the various security and intelligence chiefs. If what you say is true, there simply isn't time."

"We make quite a team," Caine said. "I'm wanted for treason. You're under arrest for defying your superiors. And Koichi's entire clan may be disbanded."

Mariko flashed Caine a bitter smile. "Now we truly are ronin. Masterless warriors. But we will still do our duty."

Caine slapped the magazine back into the Beretta and flicked the slide release lever on the pistol. The slide slid shut with a metallic click. He thumbed off the manual safety and tucked the gun into his waistband.

"Duty? No, that's not why I'm here."

"Why, then? You completed your mission; your superiors betrayed you. You could have left at any time. Why stay?"

Caine looked out the window and watched the raindrops trickle down the glass, each one following a unique, unpredictable path.

"First of all, there's Hitomi. Drone attack, terrorists, billions of dollars on the line ... in the middle of all that, no one else is going to care about one missing girl. Kusaka has her stashed somewhere. I'm to find her before this is all over. Assuming she's still alive."

Mariko's voice softened. "I see."

"And then there's Kusaka. I know Kenji is responsible for his own actions, but I just can't.... I've held on to the memory of what happened so long. It's the one thing that's kept me going all these years. And Kusaka took that and twisted it. Corrupted it. Now, it's just one more bad dream, something that will keep me awake nights."

"And you want to make him pay?"

"Call it what you like. I don't care if it's justice or revenge. I just want Kusaka out of this world. Whatever waits for people like us ... hell, bad karma, or just worms and dirt, I'm going to send him there."

"People like us? You are nothing like Kusaka," Mariko said. "You are a good man."

Caine shook his head. "No. I'm not. But for this, I won't have to be."

Caine looked up to see the massive Skytree tower looming before them. It drew closer and closer in the distance.

The tower was a slim, delicate-looking skeleton of steel. The graceful lines of its support structure swept up into the air, narrowing as they reached its apex. It looked almost too fragile to support the bulbous observation decks at the top, over a quarter mile above the city streets.

The clouds around the tower were grey and grim. To Caine, it felt like the sky and earth had somehow been inverted. When they ascended the tower, they would not be rising up, closer to the heavens. They would be descending, deep into the dark underworld of death.

After parking, Mariko used her police ID to bluff their way past the ticket line in the lobby. First, she informed the guards that Caine was an Interpol agent on loan to the Public Security Bureau. Then she battered them with a barrage of threats and insults when they failed to pay the proper respect. In the end, they bowed and ushered them through the security line, eager to get rid of them.

Safely ensconced in an elevator, Caine watched the floor

numbers flick past on an LCD screen. They rose at a dizzying speed. A recorded voice played over the elevator's speakers: "Next stop, Tembo Deck, floor 355."

It was still early morning, and the heavy rain had discouraged most tourists. They were alone in the glass box as it rose up the tower. The rain and clouds obscured the view. Caine saw only a dream-like landscape of partially hidden skyscrapers, protruding from the mist. The grey, rippling waters of the Sumida River snaked towards the complex. He could just make out the lights of boats, forging across the water, leaving cold, white trials in their wake.

The elevator began a gentle deceleration. Floor 340, 345, 350 ... finally, there was the soft hiss of brakes. "Floor 355, Tembo Deck," said the voice. The doors opened. Caine and Mariko stepped out.

They were immediately greeted by a Japanese woman in a hospitality uniform. "Welcome to Skytree tower," she said and guided them to the panoramic observation window that curved around the entire floor.

Caine nodded and smiled, but kept a wary eye on the small crowd as they ventured out into the lounge. He froze when he felt a slight tremble under his feet. "Is this thing moving?"

"Yes," Mariko said. "It was designed to move counter to wind and earthquake vibrations. Its flexibility makes the structure stronger. Japan is one of the most seismically active regions in the world. We have to design our buildings to withstand quakes and typhoon force winds."

Caine shook his head as he felt the subtle shifting of the floor beneath his feet. "Guess I'm glad we skipped breakfast then."

They cautiously walked the edge of the observation lounge. On any other day, Caine would have enjoyed the stunning view of the Tokyo skyline. Even through the rain and clouds, he could still see the massive city, stretching out in all directions. But today, he kept his eyes on the crowd. He searched for any sign of Kusaka, Bobu, or their Tokyo Black soldiers.

"The clearest line of sight would be from the upper observation deck, the Galleria. It's about a hundred meters higher than this point," Mariko suggested.

"Then that's where we go," Caine answered.

"We have to take a second elevator up. It's a more expensive ticket than this floor."

They followed the curved path to the other side of the lounge. There they found another attendant and a set of ticket machines next to a separate elevator. To avoid a scene, Caine purchased the tickets normally, and they stepped into the elevator.

"Next Stop, Tembo Galleria, floor 445," the elevator's voice chirped. One hundred meters sped by in a blur of clouds and raindrops. Then they slid to a smooth stop, and the doors parted. Another attendant greeted them as they stepped out onto the deck. A sign on the wall informed them that they were now 445 meters above the city.

The Tembo Galleria was actually two observation decks. The lower area was connected to the upper deck by a large, winding glass tube that curled up and around the tower. There was a gap between the two ends of the tube. From where they were standing, they could see the higher end, a flat glass window sixteen feet above them.

Caine and Mariko pushed their way past a small group of tourists returning to the elevator. A few sightseers snapped pictures of their friends, waving from the other end of the tube.

Mariko stopped and pointed to a map of the structure mounted on the wall.

"Look here. The Galleria tube leads up to floor 450. There's a maintenance corridor here...." She pointed to a spot on the map on a second observation deck, just past the exit from the tube. "That must be how you get to the roof."

Caine nodded. They began to walk up the tube when Caine felt the floors shift again. This time the motion was a sudden jerk, more pronounced than before. Mariko grabbed his arm to steady herself. Outside, the rain picked up in intensity. It pelted the glass windows surrounding them, like the patter of automatic weapon fire.

A woman's voice came over the loudspeakers. She began issuing instructions in calm, measured tones, first in Japanese, then in English.

"Ladies and gentlemen, due to wind velocity, the Skytree observation decks have been closed. Please make your way to the nearest elevator and descend to ground level. No new passengers will be admitted up to the tower observation decks at this time. *Arigato gozimas!*"

A group of tourists scrambled towards Caine and Mariko, eager to catch the elevator down. As the crowd engulfed them, Caine craned his neck. He struggled to look past them and see if anyone remained in the tower.

The crowd parted and moved on, leaving two men standing in the middle of the tube. They were dressed in dark-colored suits, their faces hard, their features sharp. Caine saw the telltale sign of scars, just below the collar of their shirts.

He was reaching for his pistol when the men turned and saw them, standing apart from the crowd at the elevator. They shouted in Japanese and ducked into a low shooting stance as they reached behind their backs.

Caine grabbed Mariko and dove for a small alcove along the inside edge of the tube. He fired three wild shots as he leapt through the air. They struck the glass behind the men. The bullets left tiny cracks in the thick, industrial glass, but the window did not shatter.

The crowd screamed and surged forward, as the gunfight erupted behind them.

"Everyone, get down!" Mariko shouted back at them. "On the floor, now!"

The two men returned fire, their bullets ricocheting off the edge of the alcove. Caine winced and shielded Mariko with his body. Sparks and chips of paint exploded around them.

"I don't need you to protect me!" she shouted.

"No, but I need you alive to cover me!"

Caine charged forward up the tunnel, firing as he moved. The men turned and ran, heading away from them up the tunnel, towards the upper deck.

Caine darted to the outer curved edge of the glass tube. He looked down and saw the gut-wrenching drop yawn beneath his right side. He jogged forward at a rapid but measured pace.

Mariko quickly followed behind him, keeping to the inner edge of the tube. She held her gun at the ready, sweeping back and forth as they moved forward in tandem.

They reached the end of the Galleria tube. To their right, a large opening led to the upper observation deck, 450 meters above the ground. Soft purple lighting slowly pulsed. The speakers overhead were silent. The only sounds they could hear were the muted screams behind them and the incessant patter of rain on the glass windows.

Caine and Mariko flanked the entrance to the upper deck and peered around the corner. A barrage of gunfire greeted them. To the left of the entrance, one of the fleeing Tokyo Black men had tipped over a display case of brochures. He was covering the tunnel exit.

Caine squeezed off a quick series of shots to return fire, then ducked back behind the entryway.

"The maintenance door is to the left!" Caine shouted. "The other one must have gone to the roof."

Mariko looked over at him and nodded. She dropped to one knee, peered around the edge of the entrance, and opened fire. "We have to make sure those people back there get down safely!"

Caine fired another volley of shots towards the Tokyo Black man. His bullets exploded through the wood case and paper brochures. A confetti of debris exploded into the air.

He checked his watch. If Kenji was right, they were running out of time.

"Then we split up. I'll take the roof. You cover me and keep any other Tokyo Black men away from the people. Now that the elevators are stopped, the only way to get to them is through you."

Mariko shook her head. "No, we do this together!"

"No time to argue. If anyone other than me comes down those stairs, shoot first!"

Caine leapt to his feet and sprinted through the entrance into the observation deck. To his right, he saw a grey door set into the wall with red Japanese letters across it. Underneath, in English, it said, "No Trespassing."

To his left, a few terrified civilians lay on the floor, covering their heads and crying. The gunman must have kept them from heading for the elevators to use as potential hostages.

Caine charged towards the maintenance door. From the corner of his eye, he saw a flash of movement and knew the Tokyo Black man had popped up from his cover. The man was aiming, drawing a bead on Caine's back as he ran towards the door. Caine didn't look back. He reached the door and gave it a shove.

It was locked.

Behind him, more gunfire exploded. Bullets hissed through the air and thudded into the wall next to him, mere inches from his head.

Mariko leaned around the corner, firing wildly at the Tokyo Black gunman. He turned his attention away from Caine and returned fire.

Caine pointed his gun at the door lock and fired two quick shots. The lock assembly exploded into a mangled shard of metal. He kicked the door open and hurled himself forward into darkness.

CHAPTER FORTY-ONE

As he paused for breath, Caine's eyes adjusted to the darkness. He was in a small concrete corridor. A door on his left led to several flights of metal stairs wrapping around the inner core of the tower.

He jogged up the stairs. The clanging of his footsteps echoed through the still air. After three flights, the stairs ended at another door. About twenty feet above, he could see the inner core of the tower. It narrowed and joined with the base of the antenna support structure. The door had to lead to the Galleria roof.

He recalled the view from the observation deck ... the seemingly unending drop through banks of clouds and the tiny spires of the buildings below. He readied his pistol, took a deep breath, and slammed his body into the door.

As soon as the door cracked open, an immense wind whipped it into the side of the structure with a loud crash. Caine darted outside, hoping the harsh noise would muffle the sound of his arrival. The wind drove the cold rain into his face, like stinging needles of ice.

He braced his body against the wind and examined his surroundings. The roof was a flat circular ring, like the observatory beneath it. A low chain fence ran around the outer perimeter, about fifteen feet from the center of the tower. Beyond the fence was a track, possibly for a motorized window washing cart or another maintenance vehicle.

The vastness of Tokyo stretched as far as his eyes could see. Without the glass between him and the impossibly high drop, he felt tiny and insignificant. His life was like a weak, flickering candle. A strong gust of wind could sweep him over the edge and snuff him out in a second.

The chain fence was nothing, just a minuscule barrier that stood between himself and a 1,400-foot plunge into the echoing screams of death.

Above him, latticework supported the huge broadcast antenna, which towered several hundred yards overhead. He could not see the top of the antenna. It pierced the clouds and disappeared into their dark, rolling folds of grey.

Caine stalked around the center pillar of the tower. A man hunched over a small table came into view. A tarp strung from the lattice of the antenna formed a crude tent over the man, a barrier against the rain.

Caine stepped closer, his gun out and ready. He recognized the man as one of the two from the confrontation in the Galleria tunnel. He was Tokyo Black ... but where were Kusaka and Bobu?

As he crept closer, he spotted the dead body of a security guard lying on the roof. A crimson bullet wound pierced the center of his forehead. His body was pushed up against large metal housing mounted on the track that ran around the roof. It was the size of a small utility shed and hung over the edge of the roof like a bird perched on a ledge.

Turning his attention back to the small table, Caine spotted the silver gleam of Kusaka's hard drive sitting next to an open briefcase. Wires ran from the drive to electronics equipment housed in the case.

Kenji said Bernatto had modified the drone's controls, that they could fit in a briefcase. This had to be it! From this high up, the portable transmitter could maintain line of sight with the drone anywhere in the city. Caine cocked his pistol and stepped away from the tower base.

"Put your hands up!" he shouted over the wind and rain. "Move away from the briefcase! Do it now!"

The man jumped and spun around. His eyes were obscured by large, dark glasses. A small antenna pointed up from the glasses, near his temple.

The man ripped the visor off his face and reached behind his back. Caine fired without hesitation; a double tap of bullets exploded into the man's chest. He rushed over seconds after the body hit the ground. He kicked the man's pistol away, and it clattered under the fence and over the edge of the tower.

Ripping the glasses off the man's face, he held them up to his eyes. He reeled as he suddenly found himself streaking through dark clouds at what seemed like a thousand miles per hour. He yanked the visor away from his face to regain his balance.

"What the hell?" he muttered. Slowly he brought the visor back up to his face. Again he was thrust through the sky at rapid speed, piercing the rain and clouds like a jet-propelled arrow.

He turned his head left, and the point of view rotated to follow him. The clouds rushed by him sideways now, as if he were looking out the side window of a jet plane.

His body staggered as he adjusted to the strange sensation. Digital readings surrounded the central image, filling his peripheral vision. Air speed, altitude, pitch, yaw ... all the information one would need to control a drone.

So that was how Bernatto had miniaturized the drone control package! He had virtualized it. It wouldn't be as precise as an actual control booth with real instruments. But for what Kusaka was planning, it didn't have to be. All they had to do was guide the drone to its final destination. Gravity would do the rest.

Looking to his left, Caine saw a red wireframe control stick superimposed over the image. He reached out his hand, but it did nothing. The image he was seeing must be the drone's forward camera. When he turned his head, the camera rotated. But the drone's course was unaffected.

He looked around at the readouts blinking at the borders of his vision. One of them showed a small topographical map. Course headings rapidly blinked in and out as they adjusted. Caine looked forward again. The drone's view was descending, lowering though the clouds.

He saw city streets come into view. Buildings rushed beneath him as if he were a giant predatory bird, skimming over the rooftops of the city, searching for prey.

The camera centered on the building up ahead. It was a dull grey slab with a helipad on its roof. A helicopter sat on the pad, its rotors idling. The fisheye view from the drone's camera was distorted, but Caine could make out tiny figures walking towards the helicopter.

The building's architecture was completely unremarkable, but Caine recognized it immediately. It was the American Embassy in Tokyo. United States soil, right in the heart of Tokyo.

The Secretary of State, the Chinese Foreign Minister, Japan's Minster of Foreign Affairs ... they were all meeting at the embassy to discuss the Senkaku Island dispute. And Kusaka was going to take them all out in one fell swoop, in what would look like a Chinese military strike.

The loss of life would be disastrous, and the repercussions could lead to war.

He reached for the digital control stick again, but it still had no effect. Tearing off the glasses, Caine examined the controls in the briefcase. Kenji had said the Skytree tower coordinates were preprogrammed into the drone. It would be guided to the final target from here. There had to be a way to order it back.

There! He spotted a red button marked RECALL. He slammed the button, and the machine began to beep.

He held up the glasses again and saw the view of the embassy rotate away as the drone changed course. It was returning back to the tower, back to its programmed coordinates.

He was slipping the visor into his inner jacket pocket when he felt, rather than saw, a motion above him. A subtle shift in light, the rustle of clothes barely audible over the rainfall. Whatever it was, he instinctively sidestepped and pivoted, bringing his gun hand up.

His quick reaction saved his life. A massive, shadowy form dropped to the ground, exactly where he had been standing. The falling body grazed his side, knocking him back a few feet.

Caine raised his pistol. The huge, dark shadow swung towards him, knocking the Beretta from his grip. A powerful arm slipped under his right elbow and yanked him forward. As he lost his balance, another arm scooped his right leg, lifting it upwards.

Within a fraction of a second, his entire body was lifted into the air and thrown backwards. He slammed down onto the roof. The impact radiated through his bruised, aching body like an electric shock. He grit his teeth and forced himself to roll backwards. He leapt up to a standing position.

Bobu Shimizu stood before him, blocking his access to the drone controls. Caine panted in the rain, plotting his next move. A single black eye, brimming with hate, glared back at him. The man was even larger than Caine had remembered. Naked from the waist up, his many scars and injuries painted a hideous tapestry across his body.

"Bobu Shimizu!" Caine shouted with a rueful smile. "I have to say, I like the new look. The face tattoo was a little off-putting."

"Thomas Caine." Bobu's deep voice easily carried over the rushing wind. "I never knew your real name until now. But ever since our first encounter, I have dreamed of facing you again."

"Really? Didn't go so well for you the first time."

"You are wrong. Everything went exactly as it should have. It was destiny. During my years in prison, I was cleansed by pain and fire, purged of my poisonous addiction. I found my purpose, a greater destiny than I ever could have imagined for myself as a two-bit gangster. I shall be the savior of Japan.

"And what of you? What have you done in the years since we first met? Hidden like a frightened child? Squandered your life in the shadows, watched as everything you believed in was proven a lie? All while carrying the mark of my bullet in your flesh. Now, once again you stand before me, and I have the privilege of facing you as my true self. I have become my destiny. There is nothing you can do to stop me."

Caine rubbed the old bullet wound. It ached and stung with pain. He pushed it harder, and the pain grew. It flooded his senses and washed away all traces of fear and uncertainty.

"Destiny, huh?" he said, shouting over the rain. "We'll see about that. Where's your boss, Kusaka?"

Bobu shrugged, his enormous muscles rippling at even the most minimal movement.

"Most likely in his mansion, enjoying his plaything. I do not pretend to understand his obsession with that girl, but I am no stranger to weakness. Our greater purpose shall purify him, and he will be forgiven for his failings."

Caine's eyes blazed with anger. "We'll have to agree to disagree on that."

The massive man stepped forward. The rain dripped down his exposed skin. Trails of water traced the glistening, pocked expanse of his burned and mangled flesh.

"The drone's already on its way back here," Caine shouted. "You've missed your window. The dignitaries will be boarding the helicopter any minute."

"Then I will strike them in the air. There will be plenty of time to locate them after I finish with you."

Caine pushed his rain-soaked hair out of his eyes and pivoted his body sideways. He raised his hands in front of him, beckoning his opponent to begin the assault.

Bobu's face twisted into a nightmarish snarl. The hideous scars that marked his face, the burned eye, and his massive frame made him seem more monster than man. And then, bellowing an angry roar, the monster charged forward.

CHAPTER FORTY-TWO

Caine fought the urge to back away from the freight train of flesh barreling towards him. He knew the point of Bobu's charge was to push him back, put him on the defensive. It would allow the bigger man time to put his greater reach and muscle mass to use.

Instead, Caine stepped forward and kicked Bobu's left knee. A shock ran through his body as the blow connected. Kicking Bobu's leg felt like kicking the trunk of an ancient tree. The huge man grunted and dipped forward as his knee buckled, but he did not go down.

Instead, Bobu used his forward momentum to swing a savage hook punch through the air. Caine ducked under the blow. As he moved, he lashed out and hit Bobu's exposed neck with a fast knuckle punch.

If Bobu felt the blow through the layers of sinew and muscle beneath his skin, he didn't show it. He spun around and drove his elbow into the back of Caine's head. The impact sent Caine's body sailing forward. His head struck the metal roof, and he collapsed next to the Tokyo Black man he'd gunned down earlier.

As his vision cleared, Caine noticed something about the man he'd missed before. A chunky black band was strapped around his wrist. A red LED light mounted to the plastic band was blinking. He snatched it off the man's wrist and rolled over, just in time to ward off Bobu's stomping foot.

Caine crossed his arms to block the blow, but Bobu's bulk and strength drove his limbs back into his chest. The kick knocked the wind out of him. Bobu grabbed him by the jacket and hoisted him into the air.

Caine gasped for breath. His arms flailed as he tried to grab hold of Bobu's arms, but his feeble grip slipped loose. Bobu lifted him over his head and tossed him through the air like a ragdoll.

Caine struck the chain fence. He rolled over it and landed on the track. He scrambled for purchase as he felt his weight shift. He was sliding over the edge!

He let go of the wristband, which fluttered into the air behind him. With both hands, he clawed at the metal edge of the track. His body swung to a stop. He found himself hanging on for dear life from the top of the tallest building in Tokyo. Beneath him, the dark clouds and city buildings spread out in a dizzying tableau. It was welcoming him, waiting for him to fall and assume his place in the mural of death.

Caine struggled to pull himself up, his knuckles white with exertion, his body wracked with waves of pain and exhaustion. He managed to raise his body a few inches, only to slide back down again. Peering through the falling rain, he saw Bobu approach the ledge. The hulking man stared down at him with his strange white eye.

"Do not fear death, Caine-san. In pain, you will be purified."

"Go fuck yourself," Caine spat back.

The big man threw back his head and laughed. Then he stomped down on the fingers of Caine's left hand. Caine screamed as the full weight of his body tugged on his right arm. His fingers began to slip on the cold, wet metal.

As he swung one-handed from the edge, he spied a long metal cable running down the side of the tower, about ten feet to his left.

He looked up and saw it was one of four cables running from the bottom of the metal housing mounted to the track. A window washing cart—that had to be what the track was for! If he could just move over a few feet....

Another wave of pain shocked his body as Bobu stamped on his right hand. Caine gasped and forced himself not to let go. Bobu smiled down at him as he ground his foot into the track, crushing Caine's fingers beneath his weight.

Struggling to maintain his grip, Caine slipped his bruised and bloody left hand into his pocket. Bobu tilted his head down. His hideous features curled into a curious smile. "How much longer can you hold on, Caine-san? Your life can be measured in seconds. What will you do in your last few moments on this Earth?"

Caine lurched his body upwards and drew his hand from his pocket. His fingers grasped the hilt of his Spyderco knife. In one fluid motion, he flicked open the blade with his thumb and stabbed the blade down into Bobu's foot.

Bobu howled in pain and stepped back. Caine let go of the knife and grasped the track with both hands. As Bobu yanked the blade from his shoe, Caine slid his body to the left, closer to the thick metal cables. He moved his hands as quickly as he could without losing his grip on the slick metal.

His feet dangled about thirty feet above the curved surface of the Galleria tube. On a small metal ledge connecting the tube to the outer wall of the observation deck, he spotted a tiny red light blinking on and off. Caine realized it was the wristband. It must have landed there after he dropped it.

As Caine hurried his pace, Bobu charged back towards him, now clutching a large pistol. He opened fire. Caine flinched as the bullets whizzed past his head. Then a familiar voice called out, "Security branch! Drop your weapons!" It was Mariko!

Bobu turned and bolted. The sound of gunfire rang out as Caine's grip began to slip. He swung his body, and his leg made contact with the cable. He wrapped both legs around it, then reached out with his left hand. Holding on for all he was worth, he looked down and nearly cried with relief. The window washing cart hung suspended from the cables. The mobile housing overhead held the winch mechanisms that raised and lowered it.

Caine slid down the taut metal wire like a fireman's pole. When he reached the cart, he fell inside and dropped to the floor. The cart was little more than a metal framework and a floor to stand on. But after hanging off the edge of the tower, it was a welcome safe haven.

Caine heard another series of gunshots. He looked up, but his view of the roof was blocked. The cart began to sway in the wind and rain. The metal cables whined as they shifted back and forth.

Caine spotted a simple control panel mounted to the edge of the cart. The panel consisted of two levers. One moved the cart up and down, the other side to side. He grabbed both levers, and tried to move the cart down towards the blinking red light. Nothing happened. The tower must have shut off power to the unit when they shut down the elevators.

Caine estimated the wristband was only about fifteen feet below him. As more shots rang out from the roof, he climbed up onto the edge of the cart. He balanced on the thin metal framework, using one of the cables to steady his body in the wind.

The cart hung about five feet away from the ledge. If he missed, he knew would never be able to hold onto the smooth glass side of the tube. He would slip over the edge and fall, 1,400 feet down.

The cart lurched again, and he grabbed the cable tighter. The tiny metal cage swung out, farther away from the tube. Then, like a pendulum, it swung back. Closer, closer....

Caine leapt from the cart. He saw a brief glimpse of the city far below, the image flashing in the gap between the cart and the ledge. Then he struck the flat metal surface and collapsed.

He slowly stood up on the narrow walkway that ran just above the spiraling glass tube of the Galleria. The metal ledge sloped downwards at a steep angle. To his right, he could see the Tembo observation deck through its enormous glass windows. The vast room was empty. Mariko must have escorted the hostages to the elevators before coming up to the roof.

To his left, a small metal lip that came up to his knees was the only barrier between himself and the drop below. The wind whipped through his hair, and he lowered his stance to steady himself. Scanning the walkway, he spotted the blinking light of the wristband. It was wedged against one of the windows' metal support beams.

He slid over to the window, grabbed the band, and wrapped it around his wrist. Then he reached into his jacket and pulled out the visor. He hoped everything was still connected wirelessly to the briefcase transmitter above. Taking a deep breath, he slipped on the glasses.

As the visor covered his eyes, his view changed to the drone's camera, swooping through the clouds. He was circling the tower in a wide, lazy orbit. A preprogrammed arc, waiting for instructions.

He reached out for the digital controls. This time he saw a wireframe representation of his hand grasping the stick. He moved the virtual stick right, and the drone banked away from the tower. The controls took some getting used to, but he was able to move the drone lower and get closer to the roof.

As he swooped down, he saw Mariko crouched in the open doorway. Bobu was stalking towards her, guns blazing. She ducked back but did not return fire. Was she out of ammo? If so, he had to get Bobu's attention, get him away from her.

He brought the drone down low and streaked over Bobu's head. He saw the monster look up and track the aircraft as it climbed back up into the sky. Caine struggled to turn his head and regain sight of Bobu, but all he could see were clouds.

Using the map, he circled back to top of the tower. Mariko was still crouched in the doorway, but Bobu was nowhere to be seen.

A harsh mechanical groan filled the air. Caine removed the visor and saw the window washing cart begin to ascend. The metal cables creaked and groaned as the winch sprung to life and pulled the cart back up into the housing.

The housing, damn it! The power controls must have been in the housing, he thought. The winch suddenly halted, then jerked back to life and lowered down. The cart was descending. Bobu was onboard.

He aimed at Caine and fired.

Caine ducked closer to the windows as the bullets ricocheted around him. He jogged backwards, running down the walkway, away from the descending cart. As he circled the building, he remembered the gap in the tube: it did not connect all the way around the tower. Soon it would end, and he would have nowhere left to go. Nowhere but down, at any rate.

He heard a loud mechanical hum behind him. Another gunshot rang out, striking the walkway inches from his feet. Bobu was moving the cart sideways along the track. He was herding Caine towards the edge of the walkway.

Caine dropped to his knees. He pressed his body against the curved glass of the observation deck, trying to make himself as small a target as possible. He winced as another shot struck the glass next to his head. Up above, he saw the tiny black dot of the drone, circling overhead. He slipped the visor back over his eyes.

Taking control of the drone, he dove for the tower, falling through the clouds like a meteor from the heavens. Another bullet struck the glass behind him, but he did not flinch. The hum of the cart grew louder. Soon, he knew, Bobu would not miss his shot.

The tower came back into the drone's view. Caine's body swayed as he struggled to process the flood of images. He banked around the tower, picking up speed. Another shot rang out. The bullet struck his arm. He cried out, clutching the wound with his control hand.

The motion sent the drone spiraling away from the tower. Caine saw the buildings below spinning, rushing up to meet him. The cart moved closer. Caine backed away another few steps. He knew he only had a few feet left behind him.

He grit his teeth and fought through the pain. Blood dripped from the bullet wound and mixed with the droplets of rain on the walkway.

He reached out again and gripped the virtual controls. The drone righted itself and reversed course, zooming back up through the clouds.

As he flew closer to the tower, he saw himself through the drone's camera. He was a tiny figure, crouched on a thin strip of metal, impossibly high above the city. The window washing cart was only twenty feet away. Bobu aimed his pistol.

Again Caine circled the drone around the tower while another shot struck the glass behind him. The window exploded into a spiderweb of cracks. Caine ignored the shards of falling glass and concentrated on controlling the drone.

As it approached his side of the tower, he saw himself from behind. And he saw Bobu, leaning out of the cart, aiming the pistol at his head. If Bobu took this shot, he would not miss.

Caine made one last adjustment. He swung the drone so close to the tower that its wings nearly skimmed the glass of the observation window. The roar of the jet engines filled the air.

Bobu looked up, and for a fraction of a second, his hideous face filled Caine's vision. The giant screamed with rage. His milky white eye stared at the drone's camera with dead, unseeing hatred.

Then the wing of the aircraft struck the cables. A horrendous metal shriek filled the air as the wingtip sheared through the steel wires. Bobu's body lurched in the cart. The impact jerked the metal frame away from the windows. The cart tumbled over as the cables snapped and whipped through the air. Then it plummeted towards the city below.

Caine caught a quick glimpse of Bobu's body plunging through space, as he fell from the overturned cart. Then his view filled with spinning buildings, looming closer and closer. He struggled to regain control of the stick, but the drone's wing was badly damaged. The craft spun through the air, flying closer and closer to the city skyline. If it struck one of the buildings, the explosives onboard would detonate.

Caine took a deep breath and reached out for the control stick one more time. Instead of fighting the spin, he eased the drone down into a dive. The view of the buildings was replaced by dark, rippling water.

Using the virtual controls, he increased thrust, pushing the drone down fast and hard. The water rushed towards him as the drone flew straight down in a nosedive. Caine ripped off the visor and watched the tiny impact as the drone struck the surface of the river.

A massive plume of water shot up into the air when the small aircraft exploded. For a moment, the white puff of vapor hung suspended in the atmosphere, like a cloud. Then it slowly dispersed into a fine mist and fell back down, mixing with the rain.

Caine dropped the visor and stood up. He wasn't sure if his legs were shaking or if the wind was still causing the tower to sway. He stepped though the broken window and walked onto the observation deck.

The wind howled as it gusted through the shattered window behind him. The maintenance door burst open, and Mariko limped towards him. He ran over to her, then stopped.

For a second, they simply stared at each other. Her lips parted, as if she were about to speak, but no words came out. Then, in a sudden burst of motion, she threw her arms around him in a tight embrace.

Caine was surprised, but he wrapped his arms around her in return. The shocking warmth of her body radiated through his own, melting the icy pain of his wounds, old and new. His limbs went soft, then numb, and for once, he simply gave way.

CHAPTER FORTY-THREE

Arinori Kusaka peered out the tinted window of the limousine as the vehicle snaked its way down the mountain road. He watched as they cruised past the tall, foliage-lined fences of the other country estates in the Gunma Prefecture. Then, beyond that, there was only the dark, twisting trees of the forest. On the other side of the road, a deep chasm fell off into a pitch-black valley.

The dry winds had warded off the rain dousing Tokyo, but a thick, damp mist crept down from the mountains. Only a few hours from the city, the area was beautiful and remote. He'd purchased his house here using a long chain of dummy corporations and aliases. The hidden, secret property was a perfect place to lay low. Now, under cover of darkness, it was time to make his way to the private airfield in Saitima.

He sipped from a glass tumbler of scotch. As they drove, he silently contemplated the forest outside the windows. The bottle of his beloved Karuizawa single malt was one of the few possessions he'd brought with him. But tonight, the exquisite drink brought him no joy. He tasted nothing. He felt only the sting of alcohol as it numbed his lips.

The top story in the morning news had praised the delegates of Japan, China, and the United States. They had braved the harsh weather and made the flight to the Senkaku Islands as planned. There, they shook hands and made empty promises of joint cooperation. Their speeches ensured a speedy, peaceful resolution to the territorial dispute, an outcome that would benefit both countries and their mutual allies.

Kusaka wiped his lips and sighed. As soon as he saw the report, he knew it was only a matter of time before the authorities tracked him down. So now he had to leave, scurry from his home like a common traitor. Not a hero. Not a savior of Japan or a herald of new era of strength and prosperity. Instead, he was a fugitive.

Fortunately, he was a wealthy man with near-limitless resources. Working with Bernatto had provided him with a mountain of untraceable cash. His company owned divisions and subsidiaries all over the world. Tonight, he would fly by private jet to his offices in Indonesia, a place where he could live like a king. A place where a private security force would ensure his safety. And a place that had no extradition treaties with the rest of the world.

He knew he could still influence the political landscape of Japan from afar. His money and connections had international reach, and he had acquired plenty of blackmail material over the years. It would take longer, but he could still achieve his aims. He could still save Japan from its relentless slide into mediocrity.

He took another sip of scotch, licking the droplets from his lips. It would not be easy. When the details of his failed plan came to light, there would be accusations. Political maneuvering. Many of his allies would move to distance themselves. His work with the CIA would brand him an American puppet. And other recriminations would follow. Criminal. Murderer. Traitor.

Pervert.

He shook his head and downed the remaining scotch in one long gulp. So be it ... he had survived worse. He would survive this. He would drag Japan kicking and screaming into a better future by sheer force of will. And one day, the people of his homeland would welcome him back with open arms.

He threw the empty tumbler on the floor of the limo and leaned back. The limousine slowed down as it rounded another curve in the mountain road. The huge vehicle jerked to an unexpected stop. A sharp tremor of fear ran through his body when he saw blinking lights through the front windshield. His heart rate slowed only when he realized the lights signaled construction, not the police.

"Why exactly are we stopping?" he asked his driver over the intercom.

"Looks like some construction ahead, sir. Just give me a minute. I'll have them clear the road."

The front door opened and slammed shut. His chauffeur walked through the fog, over to a pair of parked construction vehicles blocking the lanes. Some traffic cones and a few construction signs lined the road, but Kusaka didn't see any workers manning the vehicles. Probably on break. At this hour. No wonder the economy was sliding into depression.

Kusaka grabbed a clean tumbler from the limo bar and poured himself another glass of scotch. He was half-finished with it when he realized that he'd lost sight of his chauffeur. The man had been gone for several minutes and had not returned.

Cool mountain air rushed into the cabin as Kusaka powered down his window. He leaned out and surveyed the scene. The blinking construction lights lit up the fog, making large patches of mist glow orange.

"Mitsuo, where the hell are you? The jet isn't going to wait all night. Let's go!" Then Kusaka whirled around as he heard the passenger door open behind him.

"Stay where you are. Put your hands on your knees. Where I can see them." The cool voice betrayed no trace of emotion or anger. Kusaka did as he was told and found himself face to face with Thomas Caine. Caine held a small pistol with a long, narrow black silencer screwed onto the barrel.

Kusaka chuckled and smiled. "Well, well, so much for the CIA. I should have known Bernatto's dogs would screw things up. The man never gets his own hands dirty."

"You should have taken care of me yourself," Caine said.

Kusaka shrugged. "I take it my chauffeur isn't coming back?"

"Occupational hazard. He picked the wrong employer."

Kusaka eyed a leather-bound briefcase near his feet. "Is this about money? I can pay, you know. As much as you'd like."

Caine's lips curled into a sardonic smile. "I'm glad to hear that. Here." He removed a smartphone from his pocket and handed it to Kusaka.

The older man looked at the screen. A banking app filled the tiny screen. It was set up to authorize a large transfer of money from one of his corporate funds to an unnamed Swiss account. The sum was sizable, but to a man of Kusaka's wealth, it was nothing.

"That's it?" he asked. "Why didn't you just say so? Son, you should be working for me. I could pay you this every week."

"It's not for me, Kusaka-san. It's for Hitomi. And it's enough. Enough for her to live a normal, happy life. Small enough that no one will come looking for her. Now, please enter your account information and authorize the transaction."

"How do you even know she's alive?"

"I've had you under surveillance since this afternoon. I saw you load her into the trunk. I know you've drugged her. I know she's alive. Kusaka-san, please, don't waste my time. I told you before, I've dealt with men like you. Trust me when I say, eventually I will get what I want. The only question is how much pain you suffer first."

Kusaka looked Caine in the eye, and his joking demeanor dissolved. "Yes, you did say that. You also said that you've stared death in the face, Caine-san. I can see now that's true. When you look into the abyss, into the darkness like that ... it changes you. It changed my father. He was never whole after his war. So, what did you see, Caine-san?"

Caine cocked the pistol. "Why don't you tell me, Kusaka-san? What do you see right now?"

Kusaka stared at him another moment, then took a long, slow sip of his scotch. This time, he savored the flavor. It was exquisite. It tasted of wood, and earth, and soil. Of rain, and sun, and light. A woman's perfumed skin. Sweat and blood. It tasted of life, and everything he held dear. He swirled the liquid in his mouth, then swallowed. He thought of the darkness that awaited him.

"Tell her ... tell her I'm sorry," he said. His hands trembled as he entered some numbers into the phone and tossed it to Caine. He watched as the man checked the screen, then slid it back in his pocket.

"Do you want to know?" Kusaka asked. "Do you want to know why I—"

Caine's emerald eyes didn't blink as he pulled the trigger. A loud pop, like a champagne bottle being uncorked, filled the limo. A bright red hole decorated Kusaka's forehead. The old man gasped his last breath. He slumped forward, and his precious scotch sloshed across the seat. A tiny droplet of the amber liquid dripped down his finger and fell into nothingness.

Caine opened the trunk of the limo. The harsh glare of the trunk light illuminated a black body bag, stuffed between a few small suitcases. He unzipped the bag, revealing the face of Hitomi, angelic in her stillness.

Her eyes were closed, and her skin was deathly pale. For a moment, Caine worried that Kusaka had given her an overdose of whatever tranquilizer she was on. He pressed a finger to her neck and felt a faint pulse. He unzipped the bag further, only to discover she was naked.

He yanked out a suitcase and rummaged around until he found a large jacket. He wrapped it around her, lifted her from the bag, and set her down on the cold pavement. He gently slapped her cheek.

"Hitomi, wake up. Come on. It's me, Tom. You're safe now. Wake up."

Hitomi uttered a soft moan. She turned her head, and her breath became stronger. He lifted her to a sitting position. She trembled as the cold air washed over her. She pulled the coat tighter.

Caine brushed her hair back from her face. "Are you okay? *Dai joba desu ka?*"

She nodded and coughed. "*Hai. Dai jobo desu.*"

Her body shook as she struggled to stand, and Caine helped her to her feet. She looked over at the limo. The rear window was splattered with blood. "You ... you came back for me? Why?"

Caine contemplated her question, struggling to find words. Finally, he cleared his throat. "I came to Japan to find you," he said. "I couldn't leave until I did."

Her eyes cleared slightly as the haze of drugs wore off. She nodded. "I see. Thank you."

She watched in silence as Caine removed a gasoline can from the limo. Putting the vehicle in neutral, he rolled it to the edge of the road. He used a road flare to ignite the gasoline, tossed it in the car, then pushed it over the edge of the chasm.

The burning limo briefly illuminated the road as it teetered over the abyss. The fire drove away the shadows and bathed Caine and Hitomi in a warm, flickering light.

Then it plunged down into the darkness of the valley. Its burning glow disappeared from sight.

Caine watched for a few more minutes, then he turned and looked for Hitomi. She was wandering away from him, disappearing into the fog. "Hitomi!" he called after her. "Hey, wait! Where are you going?"

She didn't answer. All he could hear were his own words, echoing back to him through the empty night.

CHAPTER FORTY-FOUR

Isato Yoshizawa was buried in Yanaka Cemetery in the Taito ward of Tokyo, just north of Ueno. Caine had been to the cemetery before, in April, when the famous cherry trees exploded into bloom. They covered the grounds with electric pink blossoms, giving the cemetery road the nickname "Cherry Tree Alley." But now, in the fall, the gnarled trees were black and austere.

The funeral service was for family members only. In Isato's case, that meant a motley assortment of blood relatives, yakuza bosses, and other gang members affiliated with the Yoshizawa family. Caine was not invited, but Koichi met up with him afterwards at a small *shabu shabu* restaurant, in nearby Asakusa.

They sat cross-legged on floor cushions while a pot of broth boiled on the low table in front of them. They cooked mountains of local vegetables in the savory liquid and dipped paper-thin cuts of beef in a slice at a time. The thin, perfectly cooked meat absorbed the tangy sauce, and each bite burst with flavor.

Caine washed his food down with a cold Asahi beer while Koichi made small talk about the funeral.

"You wouldn't believe it," the old man said, after shoveling another helping of rice and vegetables into his mouth. "The row of cars must have been a hundred long. All American. Cadillacs, Lincolns, one guy even had an old El Camino. You know how much it costs to import those things? You're practically doubling the price!"

Caine nodded, slurping down some udon noodles. "Yoshizawa-san had a lot of friends."

Koichi shook his head. "Bah. Friends? Half the people there had threatened to kill him at one time or another. In the yakuza, your value isn't measured by the quality of your friends. It's the quality of your enemies that makes you a man."

After the meal, Koichi ordered another round of drinks. Caine took a sip of his beer, then stared at Koichi. The older man sucked in air through his teeth. "Go ahead. Ask. I know you've been avoiding the question."

"I thought it would be rude to be so direct."

Koichi smiled. "For a *gaijin*, your manners are definitely improving."

"All right. What's going to happen to Kenji?"

Koichi sighed. "It's a complicated matter. Kenji is neither yakuza nor civilian. He tried to walk a line between the two lives. Maybe in the end that saved him; I don't know. At any rate, the Yamaguchi-gumi council decided to let him live. They ordered him to leave Japan. He should be out of the country already. They gave him twenty-four hours. Then they reported the murder to the police and turned over the videotape evidence. In essence, they've banished him. They made it clear, if he ever comes back or interferes with yakuza business in any way, he'd better pray the police find him first."

Caine nodded. "Sounds like he got off pretty easy, all things considered."

Koichi cocked his head and gave Caine a strange look. "Do you think so? Maybe. Maybe not. It's a terrible thing to live like that. To lose your dreams and your reality in one stroke. Myself, I think I'd rather just die and get it over with."

"And the Yoshizawa clan? You guys still in business?"

Koichi shifted on his cushion. "Well, with Bobu gone, Tokyo Black is finished. I'm sure a few of his more fanatic followers will scurry off and try to regroup. But the yakuza wants nothing to do with them. The Yoshizawa clan will absorb the remains of the Shimizu organization. And, for the time being at least, I've been appointed chairman."

Caine toasted Koichi with his beer and took a sip. "I know it's not how you would have wanted it to happen, but congratulations anyway."

Koichi sipped his beer. "So, you heard from your friend? The one in Thailand?"

Caine knew that was as much as Koichi would divulge about matters concerning the Yoshizawa family. He took the hint and allowed the change of subject.

"Yeah, Rebecca. She finally got through to me. She's all right. Well, she's alive anyway. The doctors in Thailand said she was hurt pretty badly in the explosion, but she managed to escape. And she took out one of Bernatto's hired killers in the process so I guess she did okay."

Koichi nodded. "Sounds like a woman I wouldn't want to piss off."

Caine laughed. "Well, too late for that. We have some history there."

"You have history here, too. Will you be staying in Japan?"

Caine shook his head. "The Japanese and American governments both want me out of the country for a while, for obvious reasons."

Koichi nodded. "Well, there's always next time. Soon you'll come back and liven up an old man's life again, eh?"

Caine sipped his beer in silence. He stared at the knots and whorls of the wood table. The slab of oak was probably older than he was.

"Maybe I should have stayed away," he said. "I can't help but feel like somehow I'm responsible for what happened. To Kenji, to Isato ... hell, even Rebecca. It's as if ... somehow, I'm tainted. Everything I touch, everyone I care about ... when I'm around, they get hurt."

Koichi shrugged. "You left things unfinished before. You had to come back to tie up loose ends. And what if you had stayed away? What would have changed? Kusaka would have succeeded; innocent people would have died. Nothing would have changed for Kenji or Isato. They made their choices; they chose their fate. Just as we all do."

Caine nodded thoughtfully. "Maybe I never should have come here in the first place. Maybe things would have been better if I never got involved in this family."

"Oh, you think so? If Kenji had died that night, I would have given up more than my finger. Protecting the oyabun and his family was my responsibility. If I had failed and Kenji had died due to my negligence, the price would have been my life—a price I would have gladly paid."

Koichi took a long sip of beer and sighed. "I'll tell you something else. Maybe he didn't know how to show it, but Isato loved Kenji. If he could have somehow seen the future, if he knew that letting Kenji die that night would have stopped all of this from happening.... Well, I don't know much, but I knew that old gangster well. Better than my own father. And I tell you, he would not have traded a second of the time you gave him. Time to see Kenji grow up, go to school, become a man. No matter how things turned out, Isato would not have given up those years for anything, in this world or the next."

They were silent for a moment. Caine listened to the clacking of chopsticks and plates. The soft bubbling of the boiling pots filled the restaurant. The sounds were soothing, and he felt the melancholy fog begin to lift from his mind.

"Hey, what about that lady cop?" Koichi asked. "What was her name?"

"Mariko." Caine checked his watch. "Actually, I should get going. I'm meeting her for dinner later tonight."

Koichi insisted on paying the bill and tossed some yen from his wallet on the table. The two men stood and shook hands. As they walked out of the restaurant, Koichi slapped him on the back.

"You know, you think too much, Caine-san. All this talk of the past, the future, destiny ... what is all that about? Me, I'm just an old gangster. The word 'yakuza' comes from a losing hand of cards. That's what we are, the losers, the outcasts of polite society. So what do I know?

"Well, I'll tell you. The past and the future belong to the gods—or spirits, science, whatever you choose to believe in. You and me, we're just men. And all a man has is this moment in time, right now, staring us in the face. True, it's not much. Just one fraction of a second after another. But it's enough. At any moment, you could change your life. But then again, at any moment, the ride might be over, and then you have to pay the price for your ticket."

Caine caught a cab outside and looked back at Koichi as he drove off. The old man leaned on his cane and waved. Then he turned and walked down the street, flanked on either side by black, gnarled trees.

The night was clear, and the jeweled lights of Shinjuku were a dazzling sight. The glittering carpet of stars spread across the inky black velvet of the dark city streets. Caine knew there were alleys of death and ugliness hidden between the points of light. But still, he could not begrudge the view from the towering windows of the New York Bar, perched at the top of the Park Hyatt Tokyo.

"Quite a view, isn't it?" Mariko's voice was relaxed. Soothing.

Caine turned away from the window and gazed at her across the candlelit table. "Well, it's not as impressive as the view I got at Skytree tower." Even as he joked, he felt his stomach tremble as he recalled the dizzying sight of the city beneath his dangling feet.

Mariko laughed. The flickering candle reflected in her dark eyes, highlighting their newfound warmth and openness. The cold intensity of her stare seemed to have melted away. Her smiles looked natural, genuine.

Caine knew that, like him, Mariko had been touched by darkness. And when darkness had left its mark on you, moments of brightness could be brief and short-lived. He hoped Mariko's would last. He liked seeing her smile. It chased away some of his own dark thoughts about the last few days.

Her white silk cocktail dress wrapped around her like a kimono. The dip-dyed fabric faded to a dark black where the hem ended above her knees. A thin black band of black fabric cinched the dress closed at her waist. Caine thought it suited her. Sleek and modern, but somehow traditional at the same time.

Her hair fell in dark silken waves around her face, and she wore no jewelry. Caine realized that he was staring and smiled. He had to admit, she was even more beautiful than the spectacular view out the window.

"So I assume you'll be back on duty again soon?" Caine asked.

She sipped her wine and shook her head. "I don't know. We'll see. The Security Branch has convened a special anti-corruption task force. The director, Taro, and many others, they'll all face charges. After I testify before the committee, they said they would revisit the matter of my suspension."

"Revisit the matter? Your boss was a dirty cop. You saved the city!"

She nodded. "Yes, but it's not that simple. I disobeyed my superiors. I broke the law. I detained and even killed with no legal authority. I may lose my badge when this is all over as well."

Caine shook his head. "You did what you had to do. You were the only one willing to do your duty. Everyone was against you, even the people you were supposed to be able to count on. It just doesn't seem right."

"Caine-san," Mariko said, her voice quiet and thoughtful, "duty always has a price. Anything of value does. I had a duty to the Security Branch, but I also had a duty to my family. To my mother and sister. Now, that duty has been fulfilled. I am free. I know they can rest easy. If this is the price...."

Caine nodded. "It's a price you're happy to pay. I think I understand. And, for God's sake, please call me Tom."

She smiled again. "Tell me about the girl, Hitomi. What happened to her?"

"Well, to be honest, I don't exactly know. Rebecca, my handler, said she would arrange for the girl to get a visa and passport. I know she left Japan, but I don't know where she went. She didn't say goodbye, not that I blame her. I'm sure she wants to start over, put all this behind her. Thanks to Kusaka, she has enough money to start a life anywhere she chooses."

Mariko shuddered, and Caine regretted bringing up Kusaka's name. But then the song changed, and the music seemed to brighten the mood.

"So this is it," she said. "I can't believe it's over. You know, right now, at this moment, I honestly don't care what happens to my job at the Security Branch. I've given them enough of my life. I feel like that night we met in that bar, that was another person, another life. Mariko Smith ... she's gone now. I'm a different person."

They stopped talking as the waiter cleared away their dishes and refilled their wine glasses. A piano played soft, quiet jazz, as Caine leaned back in his chair. He took a sip of his dark red cabernet. Like the food, it was exquisite. Perfect.

"So this is where you wanted me to take you?" Caine asked. "You know, it's funny. I checked into this hotel the first night I got to Japan. I haven't spent a second here since."

Mariko was quiet for a second. She sipped her wine, then looked up at Caine. Her dark eyes were like liquid onyx in the warm glow of the candlelight.

"No, Tom, I took you here because I thought you would like it, but this is not where I wanted you to take me. I want to go back to that love hotel in Shinjuku. I haven't thought about going to a place like that in years. Now, tonight ... after all this, I can't think about anything else."

Caine touched her arm. "Mariko, you should know, I have to leave Japan tomorrow."

She grabbed his hand and stood up. "I know. So we should stop wasting time."

Their sex was all appetite and hunger. They were two souls, lost in the darkness, clawing for a taste of the light. The flickering neon signs outside bathed them in a pink glow as their bodies writhed and rolled on the enormous circular bed of the love hotel.

When it was over, they collapsed, glowing with sweat and exertion. Mariko rested her head on Caine's chest, and he felt the tickling caress of her long, dark hair running down his arm. His eyes grew heavy, Mariko's rhythmic breathing a lullaby. Soon they were asleep, clinging to each other as if to ward off the nightmares of the past.

Later into the night, the rain that had doused Tokyo earlier returned, and Caine woke to the distant sound of thunder. Raindrops pelted the window, and Mariko moaned softly as the sound pulled her from sleep.

"You know," Caine said softly, "I had a perfectly good suite at the Hyatt."

Mariko giggled. "This is better. For us, somehow this feels right."

"Whatever you say." Caine kissed her and slid his body on top of hers.

Mariko looked up into his eyes. "First promise me one thing. Tomorrow, when you leave, do not wake me. Do not say goodbye. I feel ... new somehow. Reborn. I do not want to start this life with goodbyes."

"No goodbyes," Caine agreed.

He entered her again but slowly this time. Their appetites

fulfilled, they focused on prolonging their brief taste of pleasure. Then they slept until dawn.

In the morning, true to his word, Caine quietly dressed and left the love hotel. He shut the door quietly and did not look back at Mariko.

There was no goodbye.

He walked out into the grey dawn and into the puddle-covered streets of Kabukicho. It was early, and the rain still poured down from the clouds overhead. The streets were empty. Caine walked alone past the bars and the batting cages and massage parlors, and all the other pleasures the district had to offer.

Soon he found himself walking under the Kabukicho gate. Its red lights blinked eternally, even at this hour, like a lighthouse beckoning to the lost and the damned. Caine paused just under the arch. He let the rain wash over him, let the thoughts and memories of the last few days settle. Some drifted away, while others were etched permanently in his mind.

It wasn't a long pause. Just a brief moment in time. A fraction of a second.

Then he stepped forward and passed through the gate.

CHAPTER FORTY-FIVE

Caine was woken from a restful, dreamless sleep by the chirp of his cell phone. Sitting up in bed, he yawned and rubbed the sleep from his eyes. He felt the gentle rocking motion of the waves as his new boat bobbed up and down in the bay.

Warm sunlight streamed in from the side porthole. It bathed his sleeping quarters in the warm, peaceful glow of morning. Soon the scorching hot Pattaya sun would begin to raise the temperature, but for now the air in the cabin was comfortable. A fresh sea breeze blew down from above deck. It smelled of salt and brine from the water outside.

Caine crawled out of bed and looked around the tiny cabin. He dropped to the floor and did a series of push-ups and sit-ups, his morning ritual. Then, when his body was dripping with sweat and his muscles begged for mercy, he stopped. He walked over to the small drafting table he had set up in the corner. Picking up his phone, he saw a waiting text message.

He did not recognize the number, but the sender's avatar was familiar. It was an anime character with neon green hair and huge, luminous green eyes. Masuka Ongaku.

He knew immediately that the message must have been from Hitomi.

It was a picture. A girl's feet, lying on a beach. In the distance, hazy and out of focus, Caine could make out aqua blue waves crashing on the shore. Her toenails were painted neon green.

Caine smiled. He didn't know what the picture meant or where Hitomi was. But she was out there, somewhere, on a beach, taking pictures of her toes. And that thought made him happy.

A voice called out from above deck. "Boss, looks like you got some company!"

It was Apinya, a local boy he had hired as a deckhand. Together, the two ran the boat as a charter. They took businessmen on fishing trips or the occasional sightseeing excursion to the stunning rock formations of Khao Phing Kan.

Something in the boy's tone told him his visitors weren't looking for a charter boat. He slipped his new Beretta Storm pistol into his waistband and made sure his shirt covered the bulge. "Okay, coming up."

He climbed the ladder and stepped onto the deck. The wood was already hot and burned the soles of his feet. Apinya, as always, wore a pair of denim cutoffs and no shirt. He pointed to the long pier that led from the shore to their boat's berth.

A woman in a wheelchair was moving down the pier, past the colorful fishing boats and shaved ice shacks. Men in cargo pants and t-shirts flanked her on either side. Their bulging muscles and wary stance screamed military. *Bodyguards*, Caine thought, *but who are they guarding?*

As the woman pushed herself closer, Caine caught a glimpse of copper red hair glowing in the sun. He leapt down from the boat and jogged over to her.

"Rebecca!"

The men tensed, but Rebecca turned and gave them a look. They took a few steps back and kept their eyes on Caine as she pushed the wheelchair over to him.

"Tom. You look good. Different somehow."

She was wearing a white linen blouse and khaki shorts. Caine looked at her legs. They were covered with stitches, scars, and burn marks. The wounds were healing, but they looked like they had been severe.

"I didn't know about the chair. I knew you were hurt, but I thought—"

She shook her head. "According to my doctors, I'm lucky to even be alive. The damage may not be permanent. They don't know yet. So we'll just have to wait and see."

"Rebecca, I'm sorry."

"Hey, if nothing else, I'm getting a hell of an upper body workout."

Caine paused for a moment. The wind picked up and blew at her fiery hair.

"Listen, the last time I saw you, at the prison ... I said things. Things I didn't—"

Rebecca cut him off. "Let's leave our mistakes in the past, Tom. We've both made our share, and I didn't come here to talk about that."

Caine nodded. "All right. So what brings you to Thailand?"

Rebecca pulled a manila folder from her Hermes bag. "Believe it or not, work. You're looking at the new Director of HUMINT."

Caine smiled. "They gave you Bernatto's old job."

"It was the least they could do, don't you think? They're cleaning house, and Japan was just the tip of the iceberg. God knows how many off-book ops and unsanctioned hit teams Bernatto was running. Someone's got to clean up the mess and get the department back on track."

"I can't think of a better person for the job," Caine said.

"Tom, I want you to come back. I don't know everything that happened, but I do know you were right about Bernatto. I can clear your record. You can come home. You can make a difference."

Caine thought for a moment "I can work with you, Rebecca, but not for the agency. I can't place my trust in a bunch of suits sitting behind desks. I can't make decisions about life or death based on someone else's morality. Not anymore. I'm strictly freelance now. I choose the missions. I choose the targets. And I choose when to say no. That's my offer. Take it or leave it."

Rebecca held the folder out to him. "Freelance, it is. Can you give me a quote for this target? Assuming you'll take the job."

Caine flipped open the folder. Stapled to the top of a thick dossier was a black-and-white photograph. It was blurry, grainy. Probably a video still pulled from a security camera. It showed a man in a black overcoat, walking out of what looked like a bank. There were burn marks on his face. He wore thick, wire frame glasses.

It was Allan Bernatto.

Caine's green eyes squinted in the harsh sun as he stared at the picture. His mouth twisted into a snarl.

"I'll take it. And this one's on the house."

THANK YOU!

Thank you for reading Tokyo Black. If you enjoyed this novel, would you please consider leaving an honest review for it at Amazon? Reviews are critical for helping independent authors bring their books to the attention of readers who might enjoy them. I would truly appreciate it, and it can be as short as you like.

If you would like to learn more about me and my books, please visit my website, andrewwarrenbooks.com, or my Facebook page.

Thank you very much.

AAW

THOMAS CAINE
will
RETURN!

Please Join my Readers Group!

You might get a chance to read the next Thomas Caine thriller for free! You'll also get access to special sales, contests, and new release info...

Please visit
AndrewWarrenbooks.com
for more details.
Thank you.

ALSO BY ANDREW WARREN

DEVIL'S DUE
A Thomas Caine Novella

TOKYO BLACK
A Thomas Caine Thriller

RED PHOENIX
A Thomas Caine Thriller

ABOUT THE AUTHOR

Andrew Warren was born in New Jersey, and studied film, English, and psychology at the University of Miami. He has over a decade of experience in the television and motion picture industry, where he has worked as a post production supervisor, story producer, and writer. He currently lives in Southern California.

Andrew loves to hear from his readers! Please feel free to contact him here:

www.andrewwarrenbooks.com
andrew@andrewwarrenbooks.com

Printed in Great Britain
by Amazon